Martial Book XIII: The Xenia

MARTIAL
BOOK XIII

THE XENIA

Text with introduction
and commentary by
T.J. Leary

Bloomsbury Academic
An imprint of Bloomsbury Publishing Plc

B L O O M S B U R Y

LONDON · OXFORD · NEW YORK · NEW DELHI · SYDNEY

Bloomsbury Academic
An imprint of Bloomsbury Publishing Plc

50 Bedford Square
London
WC1B 3DP
UK

1385 Broadway
New York
NY 10018
USA

www.bloomsbury.com

**BLOOMSBURY and the Diana logo are trademarks of
Bloomsbury Publishing Plc**

First published in 2001 by Gerald Duckworth & Co. Ltd.
Paperback edition first published 2016 by Bloomsbury Academic

Editorial material and arrangement © T. J. Leary 2001

M. Valerius Martialis: Epigrammata, ed. David R. Shackleton Bailey, Leipzig 1990
© K. G. Saur Verlag, Munchen and Leipzig

The translation of Martial, Book XIII, from pages 173-225 in *Martial: Epigrams*,
vol. III, Loeb Classical Library Volume 480, translated by D. R. Shackleton
Bailey, is used by permission of Harvard University Press. Copyright
© 1993 by the President and Fellows of Harvard College. The Loeb
Classical Library ® is a registered trademark of the President
and Fellows of Harvard College

British Library Cataloguing-in-Publication Data
A catalogue record for this book is available from the British Library.

ISBN: HB: 978-0-71563-124-9
PB: 978-1-35000-529-7

Library of Congress Cataloging-in-Publication Data
A catalog record for this book is available from the Library of Congress.

Typeset by T. J. Leary and Ray Davies

Contents

Preface and acknowledgements

Book 13 has received due attention from editors of Martial's collected work, but there has been no commentary since that of Friedländer. Friedländer was dealing with Martial's whole corpus, however, and his notes were therefore necessarily superficial. The notes accompanying Izaac's Budé translation and the two Loeb editions are no fuller, being constrained by the format of these series. The above aside, there is a short survey of Book 13 in Sullivan's general book on Martial, and the work has attracted the attention of several articles; but there remains much still to be said. This edition and commentary, intended as a companion to my commentary on Book 14, hopes to make up for past neglect and to provide a starting point for future endeavours. As will be obvious to anyone making a comparison, the translations which accompany the commentary are heavily indebted to Shackleton Bailey's Loeb, poems 12 and 119 being reproduced exactly.

Although many people have helped and encouraged me while I was working on this project, it is impossible to thank everyone here. Nevertheless, I cannot fail to mention my parents' continued interest in my undertakings and Brenda Bell's unstinting support. I am very grateful to the members of my Department for their hard work and ready assistance over a period when the teaching profession has been subjected to many changes and much uncertainty. I must also thank Professor K.M. Coleman and Mr Peter Howell, both of whom have read my typescript in full, and Professor Michael Winterbottom, who looked over a number of notes and pages. I have made considerable demands on these three scholars over the years, and whatever there is of merit in this edition is deeply indebted to their careful scrutiny and unselfish advice. Whatever faults there are must of course be attributed to me. Finally, I must record my thanks to Duckworth, and especially Deborah Blake and Ray Davies, for taking on a book of this nature.

*

Acknowledgement is made to the following publishers of some of my earlier work on Martial:

The Classical Association (Oxford University Press), for permission to use

Preface and acknowledgements

material published in my article 'Martial's Christmas Winelist', *Greece and Rome* 46 (1999), 34-41.

The Franz Steiner Verlag, Postfach 10 10 61, D-70009, Stuttgart, Germany, for permission to use material published in my chapter 'Martial's Early Saturnalian Verse' in Farouk Grewing (Hg.) *Toto Notus in Orbe: Perspektiven der Martial-Interpretation* (Palingenesia 65), Stuttgart 1998.

London, September 2001   T.J.L.

Bibliography

To save space in the commentary, full bibliographical details of standard reference works and works cited more than once are given here. For further bibliographies, see R. Helm, *Lustrum* 1 (1956), 299 ff., G.W.M. Harrison, *Lustrum* 18 (1975) 300 ff., M. Schanz and C. Hosius, *Geschichte der römischen Literatur bis zum Gesetzgebungswerk des Kaisers Justinian*,[4] Munich 1935, vol. II.548, Sullivan 328 ff., Grewing (ed.) 357 ff. and the commentaries on Martial listed below. Works published after 1999 have by and large not been consulted.

(A) Texts, translations and commentaries which have been referred to or consulted

F.G. Schneidewin (Leipzig 1867) (Teubner).

L. Friedländer (Leipzig 1886; text with commentary).

W. Gilbert (Leipzig 1901) (Teubner).

W.M. Lindsay (Oxford 1903; 2nd edn 1929) (*OCT*).

J.D. Duff (London 1905; in J.P. Postgate, *Corpus Poetarum Latinorum*).

E. Post, *Selected Epigrams of Martial*, Boston 1908, repr. Oklahoma 1967.

W.C.A. Ker (New York-London 1919; revised 1968) (Loeb).

W. Heraeus (Leipzig 1925; revised I. Borovskij 1976 and 1982) (Teubner).

C. Giarratano (Turin 1950).

H.J. Izaac (Paris 1961) (Budé).

M. Citroni, *M. Valerii Martialis Epigrammaton liber primus*, Florence 1975.

Peter Howell, *A Commentary on Book One of the Epigrams of Martial*, London 1980.

N.M. Kay, *Martial Book XI: a Commentary*, London 1985.

Michael N.R. Bowie, *Martial Book XII: a Commentary* (unpublished Oxford D.Phil. dissertation, 1988).

D.R. Shackleton Bailey (Stuttgart 1990) (Teubner).

D.R. Shackleton Bailey (Cambridge Mass.-London 1993) (Loeb).

Peter Howell, *Martial: the Epigrams Book V*, Warminster 1995.

T.J. Leary, *Martial Book XIV: the Apophoreta*, London 1996.

Farouk Grewing, *Martial Buch VI: ein Kommentar*, Göttingen 1997.

Christer Henriksén, *Martial Book IX: a Commentary*, vol. I Uppsala 1998, vol. II Uppsala 1999.

Bibliography

(B) Other works and abbreviations

(Commentaries on Classical authors are referred to in the text merely by
the name of the work or author and that of the commentator, and are not
included here. For ancient sources, the abbreviations of the *OLD* and of
L-S-J have generally been adopted. Periodical titles are abbreviated as in
L'Année philologique.)

Adams: J.N. Adams, *The Latin Sexual Vocabulary*, London 1982, 2nd
  impression 1987.
AL: *Anthologia Latina* 1.1 ed. D.R. Shackleton Bailey, Stuttgart 1982.
André *Alimentation*: J. André, *L'Alimentation et la cuisine à Rome*, Paris
  1961, 2nd edn 1981.
André *Oiseaux*: J. André, *Les noms d'oiseaux en Latin*, Paris 1967.
Balsdon *LL*: J.P.V.D. Balsdon, *Life and Leisure in Ancient Rome*, London-
  Sydney-Toronto 1969, revised 1974.
Mrs Beeton, *All About Cookery*, new edn. (n.d.), London-Melbourne.
Blanchard: Paul Blanchard, *Blue Guide: Southern Italy*,[6] London-New
  York 1989 (3rd impression).
Blümner *Priv.*: H. Blümner, *Die römischen Privataltertümer*, Munich
  1911.
Carcopino: Jérôme Carcopino, *Daily Life in Ancient Rome* transl. E.O.
  Lorimer, Harmondsworth (Penguin) 1941, repr. 1962.
CGL: *Corpus Glossariorum Latinorum* ed. G. Goetz, Leipzig 1888-1923.
CHCL: *The Cambridge History of Classical Literature* vol. I, edd. P.E.
  Easterling and B.M.W. Knox, Cambridge 1985; vol. II, edd. E.J. Kenney
  and W.V. Clausen, Cambridge 1982.
Ciarallo and De Carolis: Annamaria Ciarallo and Ernesto De Carolis edd.,
  Pompeii: Life in a Roman Town, Milan 1999.
CIL: *Corpus Inscriptionum Latinarum*, Berlin 1863-.
Citroni: Mario Citroni, 'Marziale e la letteratura per i Saturnali', *ICS* 14
  (1989), 201-26.
D'Arcy Thompson *Birds*: D'Arcy W. Thompson, *A Glossary of Greek Birds*,
  London-Oxford 1936.
D'Arcy Thompson *Fishes*: D'Arcy W. Thompson, *A Glossary of Greek
  Fishes*, London-Oxford 1947.
Drachmann: A.G. Drachmann, *Ancient Oil Mills and Presses*, Copenhagen
  1932.
D-S: C. Daremberg and E. Saglio, *Dictionnaire des antiquités grecques et
  romaines d'après les textes et les monuments*, Paris 1877-1919.
Ernout-Meillet: A. Ernout and A. Meillet, *Dictionnaire Etymologique de la
  Langue Latine. Histoire des Mots*,[3] Paris 1951.
Forbes: R.J. Forbes, *Studies in Ancient Technology*,[2] Leiden 1964-72.
Friedländer *Roman Life*: L. Friedländer *Roman Life and Manners under
  the Early Empire* – authorised transl. of 7th, enlarged and revised edn

of the *Sittengeschichte Roms*, J.H.Freese, L.A. Magnus and A.B. Gough, London 1907-13, reissued 1965.

GLK: *Grammatici Latini* ed. H. Keil, Leipzig 1857-80.

Gowers: Emily Gowers, *The Loaded Table*, Oxford 1993.

Grewing (ed.): Farouk Grewing ed., *Toto notus in orbe: Perspektiven der Martial-Interpretation*, Stuttgart 1998.

Grewing (1999a): Farouk Grewing, '*Mundus Inversus*: Fiktion und Wirklichkeit in Martials Büchern XIII und XIV', *Prometheus* 25 (1999), 259-81.

Grewing (1999b): Farouk Grewing, *Gnomon* 71 (1999), 594-9 (review of Leary's edition of Martial 14)

Griffin: Jasper Griffin, *Latin Poets and Roman Life*, London 1985.

Hilgers: W. Hilgers, *Lateinische Gefässnamen*, Düsseldorf 1969.

Housman *Class. Pap.*: J. Diggle and F.R.D. Goodyear edd., *The Classical Papers of A.E. Housman*, Cambridge 1972.

Howell: Peter Howell, *CR* 46 (1996), 36-8 (review of Shackleton Bailey's Loeb).

ILS: H. Dessau, *Inscriptiones Latinae Selectae*, Berlin 1892-1916.

Jennison: G. Jennison, *Animals for Show and Pleasure in Ancient Rome*, Manchester 1937.

Jones: Brian W. Jones, *The Emperor Domitian*, London-New York 1993.

Keller: Otto Keller, *Die antike Tierwelt* vols I-II, Leipzig 1909-13.

Kl.P.: Konrat Ziegler and Walther Sontheimer edd., *Der kleine Pauly: Lexikon der Antike in fünf Bänden*, Munich 1979.

Kühner-Stegmann: R. Kühner, *Ausführliche Grammatik der lateinischen Sprache* revised C. Stegmann, vol. I Hannover 1912, vol. II Hannover 1914.

Lausberg: Marion Lausberg, *Das Einzeldistichon: Studien zum antiken Epigramm*, Munich 1982.

Lindsay *Anc. Ed.*: W.M. Lindsay, *The Ancient Editions of Martial*, Oxford 1903.

Lindsay *Orth.*: W.M. Lindsay, 'The Orthography of Martial's Epigrams', *JPh* 29 (1903), 24-60.

L-H-Sz: *Lateinische Grammatik* vol. I, Manu Leumann, *Lateinische Laut- und Formenlehre*, Munich 1977; vol. II, J.B. Hofmann, *Lateinische Syntax und Stilistik* revised A. Szantyr, Munich 1965.

L-S: C.T. Lewis and C. Short, *A Latin Dictionary*, Oxford 1879.

L-S-J: H.G. Liddell and R. Scott edd., revised H. Stuart Jones and R. McKenzie, *A Greek-English Lexicon* (9th edn with revised supplement), Oxford 1996.

Marquardt *Prl.*: J. Marquardt, *Das Privatleben der Römer* revised A. Mau, Leipzig 1886.

Marquardt *Stv.*: J. Marquardt, *Römische Staatsverwaltung*, Leipzig 1881-5.

Miller: J. Innes Miller, *The Spice Trade of the Roman Empire*, Oxford 1969.

Bibliography

Moritz: L.A. Moritz, *Grain Mills and Flour in Classical Antiquity*, Oxford 1958.

Müller: L. Müller, *De Re Metrica*,[2] St Petersburg-Leipzig 1894.

N-H: R.G.M. Nisbet and Margaret Hubbard, *A Commentary on Horace Odes: Book 1*, Oxford 1970; *Book 2*, Oxford 1978.

Neue-Wagener: Friedrich Neue, *Formenlehre der lateinischen Sprache* vols I-IV revised C. Wagener, Leipzig 1802-1905.

OCD[3]: Simon Hornblower and Antony Spawforth edd.: *The Oxford Classical Dictionary*,[3] Oxford 1996.

OLD: P.G.W. Glare ed., *The Oxford Latin Dictionary*, Oxford 1968-82.

Otto: A. Otto, *Die Sprichwörter und sprichwörtlichen Redensarten der Römer*, Leipzig 1890.

Paoli: Ugo Enrico Paoli, *Rome: its People, Life and Customs* transl. R.D. Macnaughten, London 1963.

Platner-Ashby: S.B. Platner and T. Ashby, *Topographical Dictionary of Ancient Rome*, Oxford 1929.

Platnauer: Maurice Platnauer, *Latin Elegiac Verse*, Cambridge 1951.

Pollard: J. Pollard, *Birds in Greek Life and Myth*, London 1977.

Pompeii AD 79: John Ward-Perkins and Amanda Claridge, *Pompeii AD 79*, Exhibition Catalogue, London 1976.

Probst: O. Probst, 'Zu Martial III.58.12 ff.', *Philologus* 68 (1909), 319-20.

Raven: D.S. Raven, *Latin Metre*, London 1965.

RE: *Real-Encyclopädie der classischen Altertumswissenschaft*, Stuttgart 1893-.

Rediscovering Pompeii: Luisa Franchi dell' Orto and Antonio Varone edd., *Rediscovering Pompeii*, Exhibition Catalogue, Rome 1992.

Richardson: L. Richardson jr., *A New Topographical Dictionary of Ancient Rome*, Baltimore-London 1992.

Saller: R.P. Saller, 'Martial on Patronage and Literature', *CQ* 33 (1983), 246-57.

Scherf: Johannes Scherf, 'Zur Composition von Martials Gedichtbüchern 1-12' in Grewing (ed.), 118-38.

Schmid: W. Schmid, 'Ein *Xenion* des Martial und seine spätantike Verballhornung', in M. Renard and R. Schilling, *Hommages à J. Bayet*, Brussels 1964, 668-71.

Scott: Kenneth Scott, *The Imperial Cult under the Flavians*, Stuttgart-Berlin 1936.

Sebesta: Judith Lynn Sebesta and Larissa Bonfante edd., *The World of Roman Costume*, Madison Wi. 1994.

Seltman: Charles Seltman, *Wine in the Ancient World*, London 1957.

Siedschlag: Edgar Siedschlag, *Zur Form von Martials Epigrammen*, Berlin 1977.

Sullivan: J.P. Sullivan, *Martial: the Unexpected Classic: a literary and historical study*, Cambridge 1991.

ThLL: *Thesaurus Linguae Latinae*, Leipzig 1900-.

Bibliography

Toynbee: J.M.C. Toynbee, *Animals in Roman Life and Art*, London 1973.

White: P. White, '*Amicitia* and the Profession of Poetry', *JRS* 68 (1978), 74-92.

Woodcock: E.C. Woodcock, *A New Latin Syntax*, London 1959, repr. 1960.

Younger: W.A. Younger, *Gods, Men and Wine*, London 1966.

Introduction

(i) The title of Book 13

That Martial gave numbers to Books 1-12 of his epigrams can be taken as certain;[1] but the numbers of Books 13 and 14 are editorial. In the case of Book 14, MS evidence for its super- and subscripts (see Friedländer 17) makes it quite plain that its intended title was *Apophoreta*. That *Xenia* is the correct title of Book 13 is again indicated by MS evidence (Friedländer ibid.), but is also clearly spelled out by 13.3.1: 'in hoc gracili Xeniorum ... libello'. Nonetheless the numbers 13 and 14 are often convenient to use.

Both books were written for the Saturnalia (on which see (ii) 'The Roman Saturnalia' below),[2] recalling the dinner parties by which the festival was marked,[3] and deal with the presents by which it was characterised. It is from these presents that the books' names derive.

It was long the custom at dinner parties, wedding feasts, public sacrifices and the like to give left-over food to those attending 'to be carried away'.[4] Hence originated the word *apophoreta*.[5] As time went by, however, in addition to food, dinner party guests were allowed 'to carry away' other things associated with dinner: cutlery and crockery, furniture and even the slaves who had waited at table or been responsible for providing the entertainment. Eventually they were given presents which had no connection with dinners at all, and the term *apophoreta* came to include the wide range of gifts to be found in Mart. 14. It would not, therefore, have been an appropriate title in Martial's day for a book dealing almost exclusively with *apophoreta* of food.

As observation of the word's application by others will show, Martial's choice of *Xenia* as the title of Book 13 was happily made. Indeed, so natural does it appear that the word's rarity elsewhere in Latin is cause for surprise,[6] and it will be suggested below that Martial displays a degree of originality in adopting it. But before addressing other Latin usages, brief attention should be given the word in Greek.

One thinks at once of the ξεινήια or guest gifts which characterise the heroic code of hospitality in Homer. These gifts were given by a host to departing guests as material symbols of the friendship bond between them, and it is possible that, in choosing his title, Martial intended to recall this bond in the context of Roman *amicitia*, the role of which in gift-giving at the Saturnalia is discussed below (see (ii) 'The Roman Saturnalia', section D below). But although the provision of a meal for the departing guest appears to have been a typical element of heroic hospital-

1

ity rites (see Steve Reece, *The Stranger's Welcome: Oral Theory and the Aesthetics of the Homeric Hospitality Scene*, Ann Arbor 1993, 37), parting gifts tended to be objects of value rather than food: precious metals, arms and armour, household utensils, items of clothing (Reece ibid. 35-6). Exceptions do occur, however: Odysseus receives the wine with which he inebriates the Cyclops as a parting gift from Maron, the priest of Apollo (*Od.* 9.201 ff.):

> ὁ δέ μοι πόρεν ἀγλαὰ δῶρα·
> χρυσοῦ μέν μοι δῶκ' εὐεργέος ἑπτὰ τάλαντα,
> δῶκε δέ μοι κρητῆρα πανάργυρον, αὐτὰρ ἔπειτα
> οἶνον ἐν ἀμφιφορεῦσι δυώδεκα πᾶσιν ἀφύσσας
> ἡδὺν ἀκηράσιον, θεῖον ποτόν·

Although the word ξεινήιον does not actually appear here, mention of talents of gold and a pure silver mixing bowl justifies taking the wine as a gift of the same kind.

As well as signifying gifts in Homer, however, ξεινήιον can also be used of hospitable entertainment (e.g. at *Il.* 18.408, where Hephaistos receives Thetis). This double usage, of hospitality and gifts, is preserved by ξένια in later Greek, as is shown, e.g., in inscriptions: see D-S V.1008-9 s.v. *xénia* [Maurice Brillant]. It is often used, especially in the formulation ἐπὶ ξένια, of the reception and entertainment of strangers – who were regularly envoys or ambassadors; but survives too, albeit very rarely in Attica, of presents. These presents were not necessarily parting gifts, nor were they necessarily food (D-S loc. cit. 1008 n.14 cites examples of money), but whereas food is an exceptional gift in Homer, in the Classical period food gifts came to be regular. Thus, to leave inscriptions, when the word is used in Xenophon of gifts sent by peace-loving inhabitants to the Ten Thousand as it passes through their territory, and the nature of the gifts is specified, it is always food (note Xen. *An.* 6.1.15: 4000 bushels of barley meal and 1500 jars of wine).[7]

There are too many instances of the word ξενία for a comprehensive survey of Greek usage here. It is enough for current purposes to identify connections with friendly relations, gifts and food. In classical Latin, however, the word *xenia* survives elsewhere in only three authors. A complete survey is therefore both possible and necessary. Of limited relevance here is the word's application to gifts and fees in return for advocacy (Pliny *Ep.* 5.13.8; cf. *dig.* 1.16.6.3), save that all gifts in the Roman world were made to some extent in the context of *amicitia*. Of greater importance, however, is Pliny *Ep.* 6.31.14, where it is used of gifts to guests (more accurately, members of the emperor's *consilium*): 'summo die abeuntibus ... xenia sunt missa'. Note too Vitr. 6.7.4 on the reception of and provision for house guests: 'nam cum fuerunt Graeci delicatiores et fortuna opulentiores, hospitibus advenientibus instruebant triclinia, cu-

bicula, cum penu cellas: primoque die ad cenam invitabant, postero mitte-
bant pullos, ova, holera, poma, reliquasque res agrestes. ideo pictores ea
quae mittebantur hospitibus picturis imitantes xenia appellaverunt.' The
xenia at Pliny *Ep.* 6.31.14 are not necessarily food, for all that the words
quoted follow a description of entertainment at the emperor's table; but
note *abeuntibus*, given that Martial's *xenia* are *apophoreta*. As for the
xenia in Vitruvius, notable is that these are (pictures of) items of food,
although this food constitutes hospitable entertainment rather than gifts,
parting or otherwise. For *xenia*, or rather its diminutive, used specifically
of food which is also given as a present, one must, however, look to the later
Apuleius, whom Martial may of course have influenced (*Met.* 2.11.3):
'mittit mihi Byrrhena xeniola porcum opimum et quinque gallinulas et
vini cadum in aetate pretiosi'.

As is clear from the above, aspects of the Greek usage of ξενία can
therefore be paralleled by Latin testimony in contexts of friendship (or at
any rate hospitality and mutual dependence), departure and food. Nevertheless it is Martial alone, in extant Latin literature, who exploits the
word's connotations with any comprehensiveness, and it is he alone who
uses it specifically in the context of the Saturnalia. In consequence, while
it is clear that he was working within a received tradition, it seems also
that he has made the word his own.

Notes

1. See e.g. Mart. 5.2.5-6, which draws a contrast between Books 4 and 5, 6.1.1
'sextus mittitur hic tibi libellus', 10.2.1 'decimi ... libelli'. Note too Mart. 3.1.3
where, although he does not in fact assign specific numbers, Martial nevertheless
invites comparison between Book 3 and its predecessor.

2. Mart. 13 is less obviously Saturnalian than 14, especially if 13.1-2 are imports
from elsewhere in Martial's *corpus* (see 13.1-2 n. below). Nonetheless, note the
following themes (discussed more fully ad loc. or in the introduction below):
drunkenness (13.1.4), mid-winter (13.1.4, 16.1), dicing (13.1.5 ff.), verse composition (13.1.4 *sales*, 7-8), gifts (13.3.5; cf. 48.1-2 n.).

3. Regarding Book 14, note 1.1 *synthesibus* and 1.6 *convivae*. For the arrangement of poems in Book 13 to reflect the courses of a Roman banquet, see (iii) 'The
order of the epigrams' below.

4. Homer *Od.* 10.217 refers to masters bringing tidbits home from dinners for
their dogs, and the swineherd Eumaios speaks of being given food to take away
(φέρεσθαι) by Penelope (*Od.* 15.378-9).

5. For a fuller discussion of this term, see A. Stuiber in *JAC* 3 (1960), 155-9, s.v.
apophoreton.

6. Cf. the surprising rarity of the word *apophoreta* in Greek: L-S-J cites only
Athen. 6.229C, which refers to tableware given to guests by Cleopatra.

7. The nature of the *xenia* e.g. at Xen. *An.* 5.5.2, 25 is not specified.

(ii) The Roman Saturnalia[1]

(A) Origins

According to Varro (*L.* 6.22), 'Saturnalia dicta ab Saturno, quod eo die feriae eius'. Little is known, however, about the early worship of Saturn in Italy or, indeed, his introduction. Nevertheless, the god's function seems to have been agricultural: the Saturnalia features in Numa's calendar (17 December) between the festivals of the *Consualia* (in honour of Consus, god of the corn bin) and *Opalia* (in honour of Ops, a personification of abundance); the name Saturn was popularly derived from *satus* (Varro *L.* 5.64); and the god was commonly represented in literature as bearing a *falx* (see Mayor at Juv. 13.39). Further, given that devotees sacrificed to Saturn in Greek fashion, i.e. with bared heads (Festus 325M), he may have been a Greek import. Certainly the Romans themselves identified him with the Greek Kronos (see Fordyce at Verg. *A.* 7.47 ff. and cf. Section C below) who, fleeing Zeus' vengeance, took refuge in and civilised Italy (Verg. *A.* 8.319 ff.):

> primus ab aetherio venit Saturnus Olympo
> arma Iovis fugiens et regnis exsul ademptis.
> is genus indocile ac dispersum montibus altis
> composuit legesque dedit, Latiumque vocari
> maluit, his quoniam latuisset tutus in oris.

Whatever the truth behind Saturn's introduction to Italy, however, it was undoubtedly early since he had a Capitoline temple before Rome's foundation: Macr. 1.7.24, Dionys. H. 1.34.4, Festus 322M.

A temple to Saturn was, according to one tradition, subsequently dedicated by Tullus Hostilius or, according to another tradition, begun by Tarquinius Superbus (Macr. 1.8.1) but, depending on the version, dedicated by the dictator T. Larcius in 253 BC (Varro ap. Macr. loc. cit.), or Aulus Sempronius and M. Minucius, consuls in 257 BC (Livy 2.21.1 'aedes Saturno dedicata, Saturnalia institutus festus dies', Dionys. H. 6.1.4), or Postumus Cominius, consul in 261 BC and, by senatorial vote, in 253 BC. Ruins of an even later temple, built by L. Munatius Plancus in 42 BC, are still visible on the *clivus Capitolinus*. For full discussion, see Platner-Ashby 463 ff., Richardson 343.

The Saturnalian celebrations of historical times could well date from the consultation of the Sibylline books in 217 BC following the disaster at Trasimene in the Second Punic War: 'postremo Decembri iam mense ad aedem Saturni Romae immolatum est, lectisterniumque imperatum – et eum lectum senatores straverunt – et convivium publicum, ac per urbem Saturnalia diem ac noctem clamata, populusque eum diem festum habere ac servare in perpetuum iussus' (Livy 22.1.19).

(B) Celebration

The Saturnalia was initially confined to a single day (Macr. 1.10.2). Thus it remained for religious purposes: Festus 325M *dies*. In later years, however, popular celebrations were extended.

So far as is known, the Saturnalia in Republican times lasted three days (17-19 Dec.): Macr. 1.10.23,[2] and the extra days were dated 'secundis Saturnalibus' and 'tertiis Saturnalibus' (18-19 Dec.: Cic. *Att.* 13.52.1).

By the early Empire, the Saturnalia was the main holiday of the year (Balsdon *LL* 124), and the number of celebratory days increased. Thanks to Augustus, the law-courts adjourned for at least three days (Macr. 1.10.4). Caligula extended the holidays to five (Dio Cass. 59.6.4, Suet. *Calig.* 17.2; cf. Mart. 4.88.2, 14.79.2, 142.1), and seven-day celebrations are sometimes mentioned (Mart. 14.72.2, Lucian *Sat.* 2, Macr. 1.10.2), the extra two days being devoted possibly to the festival's commercial aspects: see below on *sigillaria* in section D.

Official celebration took the form of a *sacrificium publicum* (δημοτελεῖς ... ἑορτάς τε καὶ θυσίας: Dionys. H. 6.1.4) and a *convivium publicum* before the temple of Saturn, at which senators abandoned the toga for the *synthesis* (Marquardt *Stv.* III.587; cf. Mart. 14.1.1) and from which the people departed crying 'Io Saturnalia' (Marquardt ibid.). Starting wars and punishing criminals at this time was considered sinful (Macr. 1.10.1).

Private celebration, at any rate by school-masters and children, was facilitated by school holidays (Pliny *Ep.* 8.7.1, Mart. 5.84). People bathed in the morning to save time later (Tert. *Apol.* 42.4). A pig was sacrificed (cf. Hor. *Carm.* 3.17.14 ff. 'cras Genium mero/ curabis et porco bimestri/ cum famulis operum solutis'; see Marquardt *Stv.* III.587) and pork was traditional fare: cf. Mart. 14.71.1 'iste tibi faciet bona Saturnalia porcus'; dinners were given at which presents could be distributed or exchanged: see section D and (iii) 'The order of the epigrams' below, and various forms of entertainment and amusement prevailed: see section C below.

Very similar to the Saturnalia was the January kalends a few days later, when the new year was celebrated and the new consuls were inducted. This festival too was characterised by gambling, drinking, over-eating and laughter. Presents were exchanged, schools were adjourned and again slaves were accorded a measure of licence (see e.g. Libanius *Or.* 9: 1.393 ff. Foerster).

(C) Licence

The most noticeable characteristic of the Roman Saturnalia was the licence it allowed,[3] the festival being popularly perceived, like the Kronia, as an attempted recreation of the Golden Age, a time of freedom and happiness for all under the rule of the kind and just Saturn/Kronos. In fact the traditional seasonal freedoms could well have originated from the *lectisternium* decreed by the Sibylline priests in 217 BC (see section A above, D-S IV(2).1081 s.v. *Saturnalia* [J-A Hild]).

In sartorial acknowledgement of this licence, in addition to the *synthesis* with which the toga was exchanged (see section B above), men adopted the *pilleum*, a cap which usually indicated a slave's newly acquired freedom (see Kay at Mart. 11.6.4).

During the Saturnalia, slaves acquired partial parity with and even superiority over their masters, being exempt from punishment.[4]

Festivities were helped by general drunkenness (Mart. 14.1.9, 11.6.1, 15.5, Stat. *Silv.* 1.6.5, 95 f.), and gambling, usually forbidden by the aediles, was allowed (Mart. 4.14.7-9, 5.84, 14.1.3 'nec timet aedilem moto spectare fritillo'). Obscene jokes abounded: Adams 7.

Presiding over the festivities was a Saturnalian king, appointed by dicing or lot (Tac. *Ann.* 13.15). His command was law, whether to dance naked, sing, suffer a dunking in icy water or lift up a flute girl (Lucian *Sat.* 4; cf. Arrian *Epict.* 1.25.8). While the origins of the Saturnalian king may have been quite sinister,[5] in Classical times he was no more than a lord of misrule.

The general mood of the season is well summarised by Lucian, who has his Saturnalian law-giver, Kronosolon, legislate (*Sat.* 13) μηδένα μηδὲν μήτε ἀγοραῖον μήτε ἴδιον πράττειν ἐντὸς τῆς ἑορτῆς ἢ ὅσα ἐς παιδιὰν καὶ τρυφὴν καὶ θυμηδίαν· ὀψοποιοὶ μόνοι καὶ πεμματουργοὶ ἐνεργοὶ ἔστωσαν. κτλ. At the end of the festival the normal order was restored.

(D) Lotteries and gifts

Also characteristic of the Saturnalia and of fundamental importance to Martial's *Xenia* and *Apophoreta* was the giving of presents. As has already been remarked in passing ((i) above), gift-giving in the Roman world is inseparable from the conventions of *amicitia*, a relationship whose precise nature has been much discussed but can here be considered only briefly. The traditional view, that *amici* were either wealthy patrons or dependent clients, is still largely acceptable, although debate has continued over the precise nature of *amicitia* where poets are concerned. The view of Peter White, that the relationship between poets and their powerful friends was no different from that between other *amici*, has proved very influential; but his arguments that there was no distinct form of literary patronage and that poets were in any case for the most part financially self-sufficient have nonetheless been challenged.[6] Whichever view one accepts, however, it remains undeniable that many of the gifts mentioned in Martial's work are too small to constitute any significant form of financial support, and the context within which these small gifts are made needs to be established.

In 8.71 Martial states (lines 3-4) that the value of presents given at the Saturnalia should remain constant from year to year or increase, and complains that instead the value of Postumianus' has dwindled; and in 12.81 he complains that Umber gave more expensive presents before he became rich than afterwards. From such poems and other evidence[7] it would seem that donors were expected to give consistently and according to their means. Further, it has recently been convincingly argued that the bond uniting *amici* can be explained in terms of modern social exchange theory.[8] The argument goes that, although not bound by a legal contract, the recipient of even a small gift, favour or service is under a moral obligation to reciprocate; he is a social debtor until he does, and he risks indignation, resentment and social ostracism if he does not. A keen awareness of the comparative value of gifts and services is a natural consequence of such a relationship, and infringements of gift-giving conventions were therefore instantly recognised. At the same time, however, in keeping with the peculiar character of the Saturnalia, the usual obligation to reciprocate gifts was open to inversion. An example is supplied by Stat. *Silv.* 4.9, where the aristocratic Plotius Grypus is presented as having deliberately contravened what is expected of him by sending Statius a worthless book in return for the luxury edition he received. Similarly in Catul. 14, a poem on which Statius draws, Calvus is portrayed as having inverted normal expectation by sending Catullus, his friend and fellow neoteric, a book which is unspeakably bad, and Catullus promises to reciprocate in kind. Of course, in both these poems jocular humour is to the fore.

The humour relating to gift-giving in Mart. 13 is in part comparable. Martial plays on the traditional poverty of the poet in that, while it was common for verses to accompany gifts,[9] he jokingly suggests at 13.3.5-6 that a poor man like himself might use the couplets of Book 13 instead of gifts;[10] but he also betrays an amused awareness of the eager acquisitiveness of the recipient who has an eye to extra advantage. As noted earlier, the institution of *amicitia* helped promote a keen regard for the value of gifts and services. Of course, if one could benefit disproportionately from the exchange of gifts, so much the better: cf. the famous passage in Homer (*Iliad* 6.119 ff., noting especially lines 234-6) where Diomedes exchanges bronze armour for Glaucon's gold. In Book 13 Martial includes several epigrams in which the value of the gifts described is evident and in which, with a certain wryness, the materialistic or profit-conscious interests of their recipients are assumed, observed, mocked, undercut or frustrated: cf. e.g. at 9.2, 76.*le.*, 105.*le.*, 111.2, 117.2, 122.*le.* Also see on 113.1 *Opimi*.

*

The oldest established gifts traditionally given at the Saturnalia were small statuettes called *sigillaria* and candles or *cerei*.[11] Candles originally symbolised the return of the sun after mid-winter and are a common feature of mid-winter festivals. *Sigillaria* served as dolls,[12] or, representing divinities, were placed in household shrines (see *RE* IIA.2278.52

ff. s.v. *sigillum* [Hug]). *Sigillaria* could be bought in a special market, apparently also called the *sigillaria*[13] and held first in the colonnade of the Argonauts, and later in that of Trajan's baths.

The *sigillaria* which survive today are mostly earthenware and sometimes bronze; but gold, silver, ivory, lead, marble and other stone, wood and gypsum were also used. *Sigillaria* might also sometimes have been edible (cf. possibly Mart. 14.69 Leary *Priapus siligineus*). Human sacrifice has been associated by some with the Saturnalia (in connection with the Saturnalian king, thought to have been slaughtered, in the early days of the festival's existence, after a period of unrestrained licence),[14] but this is probably not to be accepted[15] and suggestions that wax *sigilla* were available as substitutes for sacrificial victims in later times (cf. Macr. 1.11.48) have been contested.[16]

The official Saturnalia in Domitian's time probably lasted five days, although reference is sometimes made to a seven-day holiday (see section B above). According to Praetextatus in Macrobius, the additional days arose thanks to the sale of *sigillaria* (1.10.24; cf. 1.11.50). It seems that these extra two days might have been called *sigillaria* as well: Aus. *Ecl.* 16.32 Green 'sacra sigillorum nomine dicta colunt'.

At the Saturnalian markets it would appear that one could also buy gifts other than statuettes: *dig.* 32.102.1 'lances ... quas de sigillaribus emi'; cf. Ovid *Ars* 1.407 f., Coleman at Stat. *Silv.* 4.9.23-45. Money was given to children or people of inferior status to make purchases, a fact which underpins Tiberius' insulting rebuttal of Claudius at Suet. *Claud.* 5; cf. SHA *Caracalla* 1.8 where *gratia* probably refers to money.

Whether during the Saturnalia or not, gifts could be distributed in various ways. For example, they could be sent, as is testified by Stat. *Silv.* 4.9 or Catul. 14. Otherwise they might be distributed in a dinner-party lottery, as is apparently the case with the gifts described in Book 13: cf. Mart. 13.5.2 'cum tibi sorte datur' and see ad loc. Of course, since it is impossible in a lottery for the normal conventions regarding the value of gifts to be observed, it was a form of gift distribution particularly well suited to the reversals of the Saturnalia.

In the context of Books 13 and 14, the dinner party lottery best compared is that at Petr. 56.7[17] '... cum pittacia in scypho circumferri coeperunt, puerque super hoc positus officium apophoreta recitavit'. Here the *pittacia* are riddling in that they bear legends which refer to punning substitutes for the gifts actually given. The *lemmata* in Book 13 are not puns, but their comparability with such legends is clear, and although not in themselves riddling, they often help explain what a riddle-like epigram is about.[18] Other such dinner-time lotteries occur at Suet. *Aug.* 75 (note 'titulis obscuris et ambiguis') and SHA *Elagabalus* 22.1.

Dinner parties aside, gifts or tokens entitling the recipient to gifts could also be distributed at shows; see Mart. 8.78.7 ff., Stat. *Silv.* 1.6.9 ff., 28 ff., *Dom.* 4.5.[19]

Notes

1. For an earlier version of what follows, and for the Saturnalia's contribution to the modern Christmas, see my introduction to the *Apophoreta*, 1-8.

2. Contrast Catul. 14.14-15, however.

3. Cf. Sen. *Ep.* 18.1 'December est mensis cum maxime civitas sudet. ius luxuriae publicae datum est', Lucian *Sat.* 5.

4. For the licence allowed slaves, see Acc. ap. Macr. 1.7.37, Macr. 1.10.22, 1.11.1, 1.12.7, Athen. 14.639B, Dio Cass. 60.19.3, Lucian *Sat.* 5, Hor. *Serm.* 2.7.4 f. 'age, libertate Decembri ... utere', Mart. 14.79.

The partial exchange of rôles by slave and master is mentioned at Sen. *Ep.* 47.14, Macr. 1.24.22 f. Not all masters entered into the spirit of things: the Younger Pliny withdrew to a secluded part of his villa so as not to be disturbed by servile revelry (*Ep.* 2.17.24).

For the exemption of slaves from punishment, cf. Mart. 14.79; see *RE* IIA.201-211 s.v. *Saturnalia* [Nilsson]. Note also Macr. 1.7.26.

5. See section D and n.14 below.

6. See White 74-92; also his *Promised Verse: Poets in the Society of Augustan Rome*, Cambridge Mass. 1993, esp. 29 and 34. Contrast e.g. Saller 246-57.

7. E.g. Lucian *Sat.* 14-16 and the much quoted letter of Fronto to Appian (van den Hout (Teubner 1988) 244-8): see e.g. White 87.

8. See Art. L. Spisak, 'Gift-giving in Martial', Grewing (ed.) 249; cf. Sullivan 13 f.

9. Cf. e.g. Mart. 7.46. Lucian states that gifts sent by a messenger should be itemised on a sort of delivery slip so that the bearers might not be open to suspicion of helping themselves *en route* (*Sat.* 15). The origin of poems accompanying gifts might lie partly in such delivery slips.

10. Cf. my note on Mart. 14.1.6. For a variation on the theme, cf. Mart. 5.18. Sullivan suggests (92) that the use of poems instead of gifts might originate with Martial's contemporary Julius Leonidas of Alexandria.

11. For *sigillaria*, cf. Sen. *Ep.* 12.3, Macr. 1.11.49, SHA *Caracalla* 1.8, *Hadrian* 17.3 'saturnalicia et sigillaricia frequenter amicis inopinantibus misit, et ipse ab his libenter accepit et alia invicem dedit'. Note also Mart. 14.170-82 and see Marquardt *Stv.* III.587 f.

As for *cerei*, note Mart. 14.39-44 (lighting equipment); cf. Macr. 1.7.33, 1.11.49.

12. For *sigillaria* as children's playthings, cf. Macr. 1.11.1, Sen. *Ep.* 12.3; see *RE* IIA.2279.5 ff. s.v. *sigillum* [Hug], Marquardt *Prl.* 641, Balsdon *LL* 91. Like Christmas, Saturnalian celebrations bore children very much in mind: see at 13.99 below.

13. Suet. *Nero* 28.2, Juv. 6.154 Schol. *Sigillaria* was also the name of a street: Gel. 2.3.5, 5.4.1.

14. See Sir James Frazer, *The Golden Bough: a Survey in Magic and Religion*,[3] London 1925-30, II.310 ff., citing F. Cumont, 'Les Actes de S. Dasius', *Analecta Bollandiana* 16 (1897), 5-16, in referring to the human sacrifice apparently conducted at the Saturnalia by Roman soldiers serving on the Danube.

15. See now the discussion of Stefan Weinstock, 'Saturnalien und Neujahrsfest in den Märtyreracten', in *Mullus: Festschrift Theodor Klauser*, edd. Alfred Stuiber and Alfred Hermann, *JAC Ergänzungsband* I, Münster 1964, 391-400, which recalls the possible influence of Babylonian/eastern ritual on the martyrdom of Dasius, and note W. Warde Fowler, *The Religious Experience of the Roman People*, London 1922, 107: 'There is ... not a trace of human sacrifice at Rome so long as the *ius divinum* was the supreme religious law of the state.'

16. Chr. Augustus Lobeck, *Aglaophamus* II, Königsberg 1829, 1081.

17. Which was probably not at the Saturnalia: Smith at Petr. 58.2.

18. See further at 13.11 below (introductory note).

19. On such *sparsiones*, see Howell on Mart. 1.11 (introductory section), Friedländer *Roman Life* II.15, Hugh Nibley, *CJ* 40 (1944-5), 515-43.

(iii) **The order of epigrams in the** *Xenia*

Reference has already been made to some of the entertainments that characterised Saturnalian festivities (see (ii) sections C and D), but little has been said about the dinner in the course of which such entertainments would have been held. Attempts to chart accurately the progress of the Roman *cena* are unfortunately confounded by the fact that, although there survive many works of literature[1] in which it is featured, these accounts are often imprecise and at times even conflicting. Indeed, according to Gowers, 7, 'no detailed, straightforward description survives of a normal Roman meal'. To complicate matters further, the Saturnalia sanctioned changes in normal eating patterns (Gowers 27). Consequently, while Martial's *Xenia* gives a great deal of information regarding food which might have been consumed at a Roman Saturnalian dinner, and while the epigrams in the book are carefully arranged according to food-type, thus calling to mind the courses of a Roman banquet, due caution should be exercised when drawing conclusions or making inferences as to actual practice, given also that the theme of the book (witness the title) is presents which happen to be food, rather than the other way round.[2]

Not surprisingly, the work which has been done on the ordering of Martial's poems has mostly concentrated on Books 1-12.[3] In addressing the subject, scholars often quote Mart. 7.85.3-4 'facile est epigrammata belle/ scribere, sed librum scribere difficile est', and now generally accept that Martial paid close attention to the beginnings and endings of his books.[4] It has been observed that they typically open with a dedication of some kind,[5] and even when not dedicated to the emperor directly it is notable that the books generally contain early poems which mention, address or flatter him.[6] Further, regularly within the compass of a domi-nant theme, the poems of each book are both held together, by such architectural devices as thematic cycles and pairing, and varied, e.g. according to subject matter and its treatment, poem length and metre.[7] Given the peculiar nature of Books 13-14 (see (v) 'Martial's poetic purpose' below), it is not possible for Martial to observe all of the principles of ordering which have just been outlined. In particular, he could not vary the length of his poems.[8] Nevertheless it is clear that Book 13 accords well with his general practice.

The arrangement of poems in Book 13 has already been discussed by Sullivan (12-13), but some refinement is possible (cf. my piece in Grewing (ed.), 39-40, much of which the following reiterates.) After some introduc-tory material,[9] the following main groupings are discernible: poems 6-60 deal with the *gustatio* or *hors d'oeuvres*; 61-78 deal with fowl; 79-91 deal

10

with sea-food; 92-100 deal with game; and 106-25, reflecting the *comissatio*, are concerned with wine. These main groupings are bound together by a number of loose chiastic devices: poem 5, dealing with pepper, corresponds with poems 101-5, describing seasoners and sweeteners (on which, see further below). Meanwhile poem 4, dealing with incense for divine offering (see *le*. n.) and flattering the emperor as ruler on earth and future ruler in heaven, corresponds with poems 126 (about unguent; cf. 101) and 127, on which see further ad loc. This poem refers most obviously to the rose garlands worn by guests, but contains also a flattering dedication of the poems in the book to the emperor: like those assembled by Philip and Meleager, they too form an integrated garland, and just as nature cedes its roses to Domitian in winter, so Martial surrenders to him his assembled poems. Within the main groupings of epigrams, there are in addition several sub-groupings. Thus, in poems 6-60 (the *gustatio*), we find leguminous or cereal-based substances (poems 6-12), salad or vegetables (13-14, 16-21),[10] fruit (22-9) and cheeses (30-3). Occasionally poems are arranged further, whether within these generic groups (see at 13.22.*le*. below) or not. Thus some epigrams are paired (35-6: both refer to Picene products; 38-9: note *haedus* in both epigrams; 54-5: note *petaso*). Otherwise, subject matter can be alternated: note 48 and 50, dealing with mushrooms and truffles respectively while 49 and 51 describe small edible birds. Nevertheless Martial was too much of an artist to allow over-regimentation to spoil the *varietas* of his work. Thus he continues with (larger) birds after 51, but not mushrooms.

Martial's care in the ordering of epigrams is particularly noticeable in poems 92-100, describing game. Poem 92 describes the hare as 'inter quadripedes prima mattea' and it is therefore appropriately placed first in the group.[11] Poems 93-6 see an alternation of fierce animals (boar, 93; oryx, 95) with docile ones (deer, 94; tame stag, 96), a graduated contrast being made in 94 between the passive deer, the (untamed) stag and the fierce boar. Finally, in poems 97-100, if one accepts Lindsay's undoubtedly correct transposition of Schneidewin's 98-9, we find the wild ass and its foal framing the loosely corresponding *caprea* and *dorcas*, while Lindsay's 99 and 100 form a pair since they both make reference to togas.[12]

In poems 101-5, which help mark the transition between food and wine (106-25), Martial deals first with olive oil (used for unguent or as a sauce) and then pairs types of fish sauce (102-3) and honey (104-5), in each pair describing a superior or more highly valued variety first. When talking of wine, he appears to treat mainly fine wines first and then lesser vintages – thus reflecting the practice at dinner parties of keeping inferior wine until late enough in the evening for quality not to matter, the guests having by this stage drunk enough to dull their palates.

Notes

1. Albeit of the lower genres: Gowers 22, Griffin 82-3.

2. Although Martial's interest is chiefly in presents, it might nonetheless be suggested, given its subject matter and arrangement, that he saw Book 13 as a cheap means (cf. 13.3) of having his readers (or 'guests') to 'dinner' (cf. Gowers 41-2). Such a 'meal' would certainly have the attraction of being more durable than the real thing and would conform with Grewing's suggestion (Grewing (1999a) 281) that by reading Martial's Saturnalian books one could reactivate the festival at will and whatever the time of year.

3. See e.g. Scherf 118-38, who gives a brief but convenient survey of some of the work done by others on this aspect of Martial's work: 122-4.

4. Garthwaite in Grewing (ed.), 157, Niklas Holzberg, *Martial*, Heidelberg 1988, 38.

5. Sullivan 217, Holzberg ibid.

6. A good example is Book 2, dedicated to Martial's friend Decianus, which flatters Domitian in poem 2.

7. See e.g. Kay's discussion of the ordering of poems in Book 11 (5-6) and Henriksén, 15 ff., on Book 9.

8. In Books 1-12, Martial tends to avoid the juxtaposition of couplets: Scherf 135.

9. Poem 3. For poems 1-2, see 13.1-2 n. below.

10. For poem 15, see *le.* n.

11. See 13.92.*le.*, 2 nn. below.

12. On the significance of these togas, see ad locc.

(iv) **The date of the *Xenia***

Friedländer's chronology for Martial's life and works, set out in his edition, 50 ff., has become canonical, although slight modification is at times possible. The *Xenia* and *Apophoreta* came after the *de Spectaculis*, which can be dated from Titus' inauguration of the Flavian amphitheatre in 80. Friedländer assigns them to the years 84/5, although he is probably wrong to suggest that both were intended for the same year: see below. The other books appeared afterwards, at regular intervals.

Given the careful arrangement in which the poems of Martial's *Xenia* and *Apophoreta* appear,[1] it is safe to assume that these books first saw publication in their entirety in the format in which they now survive. This makes it valid to date the publication of the whole collections by reference to individual poems within them, for all that these individual poems might conceivably have been circulated earlier.

A *terminus post quem* can be drawn from Mart. 13.4 *tus*:

> serus ut aetheriae Germanicus imperet aulae
> utque diu terris, da pia tura Iovi.

This poem cannot have been written before Domitian's assumption of the title 'Germanicus' to mark his success over the Chatti, and the collected *Xenia* must post-date it.

Using evidence from papyri, inscriptions and coins, T.V. Buttrey shows (*Documentary Evidence for the Chronology of the Flavian Titulature*, Meisenham am Glan 1980, 52 ff.) that Domitian assumed the title 'Germanicus' in 83, that he had not yet done so on 9 June (*CIL* XVI.29) but that, on the evidence of an Alexandrian coin (Dattari 618), he had by 28 August.[2] Martial's *Xenia* must have been completed after that.[3]

Given the *Xenia*'s Saturnalian context, a December publication date would have been appropriate. That Martial had the *Xenia* ready in time for publication in December 83 is possible; but otherwise it will have appeared in December 84.

Martial's *Xenia* do not yield a *terminus ante quem*. For this, one needs to look to his *Apophoreta*. They too must have been published in their final form after Domitian's adoption of the title 'Germanicus' (Mart. 14.170), and they must also have been published before the Dacian Wars began in 86. Martial could not otherwise have included a poem like 14.34 *falx*, which celebrates peace:

> pax me certa ducis placidos curvavit in usus.
> agricolae nunc sum, militis ante fui.

While Martial may have published his collected *Xenia* in December 83, that he published the *Apophoreta* at the same time seems unlikely given the challenges posed by writing the books (see (v) 'Martial's poetic purpose' below). If the works were published together, Friedländer's date of 84/5 is far more realistic; but it is more likely that Citroni has hit upon the truth (*Maia* 40 (1988), 11-12) in thinking that the books' different concerns (food as opposed to Saturnalian gifts in general) suggest different years and that Martial was prompted to attempt the more ambitious *Apophoreta* following the earlier success of the *Xenia*. The *Xenia* should therefore be assigned probably to 83/4, the *Apophoreta* to 85.

Notes

1. For the *Xenia*, see (iii) above. In the *Apophoreta*, there are two introductory poems after which the epigrams are carefully arranged so as to describe, alternately, the gifts of rich and poor donors (cf. Mart. 14.1.5 'divitis alternas et pauperis accipe sortes'), and grouping or pairing of poems is also evident. See in detail my introduction to the *Apophoreta*, 13-21.

2. For further, comparable evidence, see ibid. 10.

3. Mart. 13.74, referring to Domitian's rebuilding of the Capitoline temple of Jupiter, must have been written after 82, this date for the temple being supplied by a coin from Asia (Ephesus?): H. Mattingly, *Coins of the Roman Empire in the British Museum* II, London 1930 repr. 1966, Domitian 251.

(v) Martial's poetic purpose[1]

The presents described in Mart. 13, like those in Book 14, are all such as could actually have been given to people. But had Martial intended these books primarily as directories to help the unimaginative when choosing presents, as has apparently been supposed by some (note Lindsay, *Anc. Ed.* 37, quoted at Mart. 13.3.7 below), one is prompted to ask why he went to such lengths in ordering the poems they contain.[2] An obvious answer is that he was producing not mere lists of presents, but works with literary claims. Worth noting is that he would have been in his mid to late forties when writing the books and they are therefore not juvenilia. Secondly, he does not disown them, as he does the books mentioned at Mart. 1.113.2, and which, significantly, have not survived. Finally, although he sometimes appears dismissive regarding the quality of his verse (13.3; cf. 13.2, 127, 14.1.7-8), such self-denigration is in keeping with the epigrammatic tradition and 'bad' or trivial verse was conventionally associated with the Saturnalia (see at Mart. 13.1.1-4, 4; cf. my note at Mart. 14.1.7-8). If Martial did indeed think that his work was literary, however, there is an important and pressing question still to be addressed. Given that they are made up almost exclusively of couplets, Books 13 and 14 differ greatly in appearance from the remainder of Martial's extant work, and they are not instantly identifiable with that of works by other poets.[3] On what grounds therefore could he have considered that a succession of such couplets describing Saturnalian presents might constitute a suitable backdrop for a literary undertaking?

Citroni comments (207 f.) that the *Xenia* and *Apophoreta* present themselves almost as a practical guide to the Saturnalia and Saturnalian presents, and he makes reference to the Saturnalian mock-didactic verse spoken of in Ovid *Tristia* 2 (note especially 491 'talia luduntur fumoso mense Decembri'), noting that that there are connections between the subjects of this verse and some of the objects described in Mart. 14. Also, he observes that a number of the *Xenia* and *Apophoreta* give instructions as to the use of the gifts they describe. In Book 13 he notes e.g. 5, 8, 17, 40 and 110. This preceptive practice, Siedschlag observes (11), is otherwise not encountered in the epigrams. Nevertheless, Martial has clearly not confined himself to the tradition of Saturnalian didactic,[4] and it is necessary in establishing the literary context of Books 13-14 to look beyond the influence of this type of poetry.

There are two literary genres or forms which seem especially worthy of consideration. The first of these is dedicatory epigram. Epigrams had been used in dedicatory contexts from earliest times[5] and Martial's use of epigram to describe the gifts of Books 13 and 14 was therefore both natural and apt. To begin with, the language of dedicatory epigram is often appropriate.[6] Further, just as the brevity of the couplet made it suitable for dedicatory inscriptions on stone, so its length is well suited to poems posing as gift tags. Finally, a parallel can be drawn between the contractual nature of Roman religion and dedicatory sacrifice ('do ut des', 'do ut accipiam') and the reciprocity which underpinned Roman gift-giving and *amicitia*: cf. Grewing (1999b) 595, (ii) section D above.

The reciprocal nature of *amicitia* provides a bridge between dedicatory epigram and the second, more important literary form, that of the poetic catalogue. The poetic list or catalogue pre-dates Homer, e.g. whose Achaean catalogue (*Il.* 2.494-759) seems to derive in large part from the oral poetry of an earlier eastern Greek/Boeotian tradition.[7] Nonetheless, the verse catalogue endured as a feature of written poetry of various types. There was by the Flavian period a well-established tradition of Saturnalian 'catalogue' poems, poems which listed presents, frequently in the course of making some joke or humorous social comment. These poems, set usually in the context of *amicitia*, would often focus on the value of Saturnalian gifts, and the extent to which those people described in the poems profited or lost in exchanging them. An excellent example of such a Saturnalian catalogue poem, and one which has already been used to illustrate the inversions of Saturnalian verse, can be found in Statius *Silv.* 4.9.[8] Saturnalian catalogue poems in Martial include 4.46, 88, 5.18, 7.53, 72. Mart. Books 13 and 14 are clearly part of this tradition, and Book 14, which alternates expensive gifts with cheap ones, reflects the concern of such poems with material value (cf. Mart. 14.1.5, quoted above: (iv) n.1); but instead of listing many objects in one, unified poem,[9] Martial describes each object separately in a unified book of poems.

While the Saturnalian catalogue has been given particular attention here, it is nonetheless worth observing briefly that the poetic catalogue was principally a feature of epic and didactic works. It would be surprising, therefore, if Mart. 13 and 14 did not occasionally recall the catalogues of these genres too. A usage reminiscent of epic is noted e.g. at Mart. 13.23.1 'quem Setia misit'. As for the didactic catalogue, which links neatly back to the recollections of didactic poetry already noted by Citroni, one might compare the section on wines at the end of Book 13 with the catalogue at Verg. *G.* 2.89-102.

The question remains of why a poet in a literate society should want to write catalogue poetry at all: any function catalogues might have originally had e.g. in aiding oral composition would in Martial's day have been completely irrelevant. The answer is at least partly that composing such works posed a considerable artistic challenge. Not only was the subject matter generally unpoetic, but, as Martial was all too aware in the case of Books 13 and 14,[10] the possibility that his readers might become bored or lose patience with long strings of couplets was very real. Therefore he had constantly to strive for variety and interest (cf. Lausberg 453). Just as he would have enjoyed the challenge of writing such works, however, so his readers would have taken pleasure in gauging the cleverness with which he proceeded and succeeded in his literary *tour de force*.

15

Some of the devices used by Martial to captivate his readers have already been seen, e.g. in his grouping, sub-grouping and alternating of epigrams according to subject matter (see (iii) above). Others will emerge in the course of the commentary. His diversity aside, Martial's rich and characteristic humour, coupled often with literary allusion, is especially important. Although different in appearance from the rest of his work, the *Xenia* and *Apophoreta* are, it transpires, by no means unrepresentative of the poet.[11] Indeed, it has justly been remarked that his couplets are often pithier and more pointed than the longer epigrams of Books 1-12: Grewing (1999b) 260. Having written two books in the Saturnalian catalogue mould, however, it is nonetheless unlikely that he would have got away with a third and it is not surprising therefore that, having finished the *Apophoreta*, he turned to other forms of book composition.

Notes

1. Cf. my introduction to the *Apophoreta*, 21-23 and my piece in Grewing (ed.), 51 ff., although the ideas expressed below have been modified.

2. See (iii) and (iv) n.1 above.

3. While saying this, one should note with Lausberg (452) that the *de Spectaculis*, *Xenia* and *Apophoreta* are characteristic of the period in that they each deal with a single theme in contrast to the diversity of pre-Neronian books of epigrams.

4. Hence, e.g., he does not make extensive use of the traditional didactic vocabulary used by Ovid in his mock-didactic pieces. For this, see E.J. Kenney in *Ovidiana*, ed. N.I. Herescu, Paris 1958, 201-9. For Martial's usage, see at 13.5.2 *adde* below.

5. See P. Friedländer and H. Hoffheit, *Epigrammata. Greek Inscriptions in Verse from the Beginnings to the Persian Wars*, Berkeley-Los Angeles 1948. For later dedicatory epigrams, cf. *Anth.P.* 14.

6. Cf. Siedschlag 11, regarding Martial's use of *accipe* (in Book 13 note 9, 11, 45, 102) and, less often, of *sume* (in Book 13 note 12, 29). Other 'dedicatory' traces might perhaps be discernible in *mitto* and *aspice*: see at 13.3.5 and 58.1 below.

7. See e.g. G.S. Kirk, *Homer and the Oral Tradition*, Cambridge 1976, 38.

8. See (ii) section D above. Robert Colton argues that it shows a familiarity with Martial's work (*AC* 46 (1977) 544-56). Although Colton's parallels are not always convincing, such a familiarity is indeed likely; cf. Henriksén in Grewing (ed.), esp. 117, who suggests that the long-postulated ill-feeling between Martial and Statius arose when Statius invaded Martial's patch by writing short occasional verse. Statius' other Saturnalian poem, *Silv.* 1.6, contains a mini-catalogue of the food scattered at Domitian's Saturnalian show (lines 9 ff.).

9. See, however, at Mart. 13.48.1-2 below.

10. Note his suggestion, for all it is humorous, that one might like to leave poems out: Mart. 13.3.8; cf. 14.2.2-3.

11. Cf. J. Wight Duff, 'Varied Strains in Martial' in L.W. Jones (ed.), *Classical and Medieval Studies in Honour of E.K. Rand*, New York 1930, 91.

(vi) **Metre**

Statistics for Martial's choice of metre are given by Sullivan (227 n.22; cf. Bramble *CHCL* II.603). Of the 1556 epigrams surviving, 1235 are in elegiacs (79%), 238 in hendecasyllables (15%), 77 in choliambics (5%), and the remaining 1% is accounted for by hexameters and iambics. Of the 127 epigrams which today constitute Book 13 (but see 13.1-2 n. below), 125 are in elegiacs, there is one in choliambics and there is one in hendecasyllables.

The metrical notes which follow are not exhaustive, being intended merely as a convenience to those using the commentary. Detailed comment can be found in Friedländer, 26-50.

(A) Elegiacs

(1) Martial's hexameters generally compare well with the Augustan ideal, and in Book 13 one finds no examples of the extended polysyllabic line-endings to be found elsewhere (e.g. Mart. 14.128.1 *bardocuculli*, 215.1 *citharoedis*). Nor does one find any of the final monosyllables which the poet sometimes admits (e.g. 11.84.17 *cor*): in the case of 76.1 *idem est* and 92.1 *certum est*, *est* is prodelided and so does not count.

(2) In Martial's pentameters, however, the following peculiarities bear notice:

(a) Martial regularly breaks the 'rule' that the pentameter should end in a disyllable. In Book 13 he has, if not a disyllable, a quadrisyllable or its equivalent: note 21.2 *asparagis*, 42.2 *arboribus*; also 48.2 (where *difficilest* is effectively a quadrisyllable) and 3.8 'ad stomachum' and 43.2 'cum Libycis' (where the nouns and their prepositions form a unit).

(b) Martial admits a high percentage of spondaic pentameter openings (48 ex 135 = 35.5%). For Augustan figures, see Platnauer 37: the percentages of Ovid and Tibullus are less than half that of Martial.

(c) Martial allows an interchangeable pentameter half at 13.1.4; cf. 13.9.2. For Augustan avoidance of such lines, see Platnauer 14-15.

(B) Choliambics

Martial's use of choliambics in 13.61 follows the standard Roman practice after Catullus of allowing spondees in feet 1 and 3, but not in foot 5 (cf. Raven 62, who contrasts Greek and Varronian practice), and in that the caesura, after *sapores*, follows the fifth half-foot (cf. Sullivan 229).

The metre was associated with invective (Kay 203) but perhaps serves convenience and taste here, given both the quantities of *Ionicarum* and *attagenarum* and Martial's preference for choliambics over ordinary iambics.

(C) Hendecasyllables

In employing hendecasyllables for 13.81, Martial opens, as he always does, with a spondee, and his avoidance of elision is also characteristic: Raven 139, Sullivan 228-9. It is true that the metre can have Saturnalian associations (see Coleman's introduction to Stat. *Silv.* 4.9; cf. e.g. Catul. 14, Mart. 5.84), but had he been observing this connection here, he would have done so elsewhere in Book 13 too.[1] Instead, he selected the metre to reinforce his purpose in the poem, where the second line both corresponds with yet inverts the first: see 13.81.*le*. n. below.

Notes

1. Hendecasyllables could be employed for many different moods and types of poetry, as is indicated by Pliny, *Ep*. 4.14.3: 'his [sc. in hendecasyllabis] iocamur ludimus amamus dolemus querimur irascimur, describimus aliquid modo pressius modo elatius, atque ipsa varietate temptamus efficere, ut alia aliis quaedam fortasse omnibus placeant'.

(vii) The text

The text printed is substantially that of Shackleton Bailey's Teubner, the only difference of note being Gilbert's undoubtedly correct conjecture *Latiis* at 13.118.2 (cf. below); but close attention has been paid to other editions. Given the quality of these (cf. Kay 1 on Lindsay's *OCT* apparatus, citing Housman, *Class. Pap.* 1098), an independent collation of the MSS has not been thought necessary.

Recent treatments of Martial's MS tradition are listed by M.D. Reeve in L.D. Reynolds (ed.), *Texts and Transmission*, Oxford 1983, 238 n.1. To these and that of Kay (1 ff.), add those of Shackleton Bailey (Teubner v ff.) and Grewing 51-5. What follows derives from such earlier textual assessments and attempts to give the minimum required for convenient reference, bearing in mind Reeve (op. cit. 243): 'A thorough study of the tradition, however rewarding, would hardly benefit editors'.

As was shown by Schneidewin, the surviving MSS fall into three families. The archetypes of these families are designated A^A, B^B, C^C in Lindsay's edition, but are referred to here, following Heraeus' lead, as α, β, γ. The α family, which is made up of anthologies, contains excerpts from *Sp*. and Books 1-12, but has Books 13-14 in full. Of its three component MSS, T and R are relevant to Book 13.[1] T is generally more complete than R (Reeve op. cit. 241).[2] With regard to the β and γ families, see generally Kay 2. In Book 13, the β MSS omit 38 epigrams and jumble the order at 54 and 92. In contrast the γ MSS neither omit nor misorder.

A number of early MSS survive which cannot be allocated to a family. Amongst those noted by Reeve (op. cit. 241) is Leipzig Rep. 1.4^0 74 (saec.

ix^2/$_4$, Orléans?) ff. 25^r-26^v, which contains one of the *Xenia* (= Mart. 13.94; see M. Haupt, *Opusc.* I, Leipzig 1875, 290).[3]

Of the MSS which make up each of the three families, not one differs significantly from its siblings in agreement with the MSS of another family (cf. Kay 2). This suggests that there was no contamination from the time when the family archetypes were written to the 12th century, when contamination is apparent in France, notably between the MSS of the families α and γ.[4]

The date of these family archetypes cannot be precisely ascertained.[5] The β archetype appears to have been Italian, written in Beneventan minuscule in the 9th or 10th century; the γ archetype French, in Caroline minuscule in the 8th or 9th century. Of the α archetype, nothing can be said save that it probably originated in France. Nevertheless, it can be firmly inferred that not just one MS, as is all too often the case, but three survived the Dark Ages to spawn the three Martial archetypes.

Questions arise: did the three MSS which survived the Dark Ages stem independently and without contamination from a single source, and, if so, when was this source written?

All three families contain epigrams unique to them and all three families have unique good readings. This would suggest that the three pre-dark age MSS were indeed independent. Since divergence in error greatly outweighs instances of shared error between the three families, it seems too that contamination between these three MSS, albeit to some extent indicated,[6] was limited. That agreement in error does exist, however,[7] suggests a single exemplar.

The date of this exemplar is, however, subject to debate (cf. Grewing 54). Kay argues (3) that the general triviality of the shared errors suggests that it was an autograph.[8] But we know that non-authorial errors entered the text very early indeed (Martial refers at 2.8 and 7.11 to mistakes made by contemporary copyists), which with subsequent mistakes would have affected the tradition. Secondly, we know that the β tradition derives from Torquatus Gennadius' 'edition' of Martial in 401, and whatever the extent of his personal influence on the text, the family archetypes all contain unique readings suggestive of editorial activity which must by virtue of their uniqueness be pre-dark age.[9] Finally there is the editorial activity indicated by the suggestion, already noted, of pre-archetype contamination. Other scholars (e.g. Shackleton Bailey vii, Grewing 54) seem therefore to be right in arguing for an exemplar from late antiquity.

If the ultimate archetype of the three families were indeed an autograph, then, as has previously been argued, the editor who rejects the combined witness of two families against a third or the combined witness of all against conjecture, needs to be very sure of his ground.[10] If, however, the exemplar dates from late antiquity, the authority of MS unanimity is lessened; and although it is still the case that support for a reading by two families against the third deserves careful consideration, nevertheless

Shackleton Bailey's list (viii ff.) of instances where one family preserves the truth in the face of both the others is a salutary reminder against the use of rules of thumb in textual criticism. It is perhaps worth recalling here once more Gilbert's *Latiis* at 13.118.2 (*Tuscis*: codd), on which see ad loc.; cf. 13.2.2. Note also 13.109.2 where humanist emendation restores sense to a confused transmission, and cf. 13.44.2.

Sigla used in the commentary
Since the text which follows is not accompanied by an apparatus criticus, a formal and complete table of sigla does not seem necessary. The information given below is selected specifically to serve the convenience of those using the commentary. It is derived for the most part from Reeve, op. cit. 239-44, and then from the Teubners of Shackleton Bailey and Heraeus, from Lindsay's *OCT*, and from Citroni's edition of Book 1.

α : family archetype of TR.
β : family archetype of LPQf.
γ : family archetype of EXAVG.

A : Leiden, Voss. Lat. Oct. 56, saec. xi.
E : Edinburgh, Adv. 18.3.1, saec. ix^2.
f : Florence, Laur. 35.39, saec. xv^3/$_4$.
G : Wolfenbüttel, Gudianus Lat. 157, saec. xii.
L : Berlin Lat. 2^0 612, saec. xii.
M : marginalia Bongarsii, in a 1539 Paris edition in the public library at Berne, G.152.
P : Vatican, Pal. Lat. 1696, saec. xv.
Q : British Library, Arundel 136, saec. xv^2/$_3$.
R : Leiden, Voss. Lat. Q.86, *c*. 850.
ς : MSS and early printed editions containing humanist conjectures.
T : Paris Lat. 8071, saec. ix.
V : Vatican Lat. 3294, saec. ix^2/$_3$.
X : Paris. Lat. 8067, saec. ix^3/$_4$.

Notes

1. H has lost *Sp*. 1.1-18.4 (21.4 Sh.B) and everything after 1.4.2.
2. In Book 13, R has 6, 7, 8, 10, 13, 14, 24, 28, 30, 33, 38, 41, 46, 48, 52, 57, 58, 59, 62, 64, 65, 66, 67, 69, 70, 72, 73, 74, 75, 77, 86, 87, 90, 92, 96, 98, 99.1, 100, 122, 125, 127, i.e. 41 epigrams compared with T's 108. (T lacks 10, 12, 14, 25, 30, 35, 49, 57, 58, 59, 62, 64, 65, 66, 67, 69, 70, 73, 166.)
3. Cf. Munich Clm 6292 (saec. xi., Freising) ff. 118^r-119^v, which contains excerpts from Books 1-6 under the title 'Martialis e xeniorum' (see Reeve loc. cit.).
4. Reeve, op. cit., 241. Later contamination is discernible in Renaissance Italy, mainly between the β and γ MSS: Reeve, op. cit. 242.
5. For this paragraph and the two which follow, cf. Kay 2 ff.
6. See e.g. 65.2 n. below; note perhaps also 26.1 n., 99. *le*. n.

7. Kay lists agreement in error at 3 n. 9.

8. He nonetheless rightly and strongly rejects Schneidewin's suggestion that divergent readings which make equally good sense reflect author variants; cf. Grewing, 54 n.84, who quotes Shackleton Bailey, vii: 'trium recensionum lectiones varias ad poetam non redire ex ipsarum natura certo certius est'.

9. For possible editorial activity by α (represented by R), see e.g. 13.49.*le.*, 58.2 nn. below. For possible attempts at emendation in the β archetype, see e.g. at Mart. 13.28.2, 88.1, 109.2; note also the possible conjecture at 119.1. For editorial activity in the γ archetype, see e.g. at 13.23.1 *quem* below.

10. See my introduction to Book 14, loc. cit.; cf. W.M. Lindsay, *CR* 17 (1903), 49.

M. Val. Martialis
Xenia
[Liber XIII]

1

ne toga cordylis et paenula desit olivis
  aut inopem metuat sordida blatta famem,
perdite Niliacas, Musae, mea damna, papyros:
  postulat ecce novos ebria bruma sales.
non mea magnanimo depugnat tessera talo,   5
  senio nec nostrum cum cane quassat ebur:
haec mihi charta nuces, haec est mihi charta fritillus:
  alea nec damnum nec facit ista lucrum.

2

nasutus sis usque licet, sis denique nasus,
  quantum noluerit ferre rogatus Atlans,
et possis ipsum tu deridere Latinum:
  non potes in nugas dicere plura meas
ipse ego quam dixi. quid dentem dente iuvabit   5
  rodere? carne opus est, si satur esse velis.
ne perdas operam: qui se mirantur, in illos
  virus habe; nos haec novimus esse nihil.
non tamen hoc nimium nihil est, si candidus aure
  nec matutina si mihi fronte venis.   10

3

omnis in hoc gracili Xeniorum turba libello
  constabit nummis quattuor empta tibi.
quattuor est nimium? poterit constare duobus,
  et faciet lucrum bybliopola Tryphon.
haec licet hospitibus pro munere disticha mittas,   5
  si tibi tam rarus quam mihi nummus erit.
addita per titulos sua nomina rebus habebis:
  praetereas, si quid non facit ad stomachum.

4 *tus*

serus ut aetheriae Germanicus imperet aulae
utque diu terris, da pia tura Iovi.

5 *piper*

cerea quae patulo lucet ficedula lumbo,
    cum tibi sorte datur, si sapis, adde piper.

6 *alica*

nos alicam, poterit mulsum tibi mittere dives.
    si tibi noluerit mittere dives, emes.

7 *faba*

si spumet rubra conchis tibi pallida testa,
    lautorum cenis saepe negare potes.

8 *far*

imbue plebeias Clusinis pultibus ollas,
    ut satur in vacuis dulcia musta bibas.

9 *lens*

accipe Niliacam, Pelusia munera, lentem:
    vilior est alica, carior illa faba.

10 *simila*

nec dotes similae possis numerare nec usus,
    pistori totiens cum sit et apta coco.

11 *hordeum*

mulio quod non det tacituris, accipe, mulis.
    haec ego coponi, non tibi, dona dedi.

12 *frumentum*

tercentum Libyci modios de messe coloni
    sume, suburbanus ne moriatur ager.

13 *betae*

ut sapiant fatuae, fabrorum prandia, betae,
    o quam saepe petet vina piperque cocus!

14 *lactucae*

cludere quae cenas lactuca solebat avorum,
    dic mihi, cur nostras inchoat illa dapes?

Xenia [Liber XIII]

15 *ligna acapna*
si vicina tibi Nomento rura coluntur,
    ad villam moneo, rustice, ligna feras.

16 *rapa*
haec tibi brumali gaudentia frigore rapa
    quae damus, in caelo Romulus esse solet.

17 *fascis coliculi*
ne tibi pallentes moveant fastidia caules,
    nitrata viridis brassica fiat aqua.

18 *porri sectivi*
fila Tarentini graviter redolentia porri
    edisti quotiens, oscula clusa dato.

19 *porri capitati*
mittit praecipuos nemoralis Aricia porros:
    in niveo virides stipite cerne comas.

20 *napi*
hos Amiternus ager felicibus educat hortis:
    Nursinas poteris parcius esse pilas.

21 *asparagi*
mollis in aequorea quae crevit spina Ravenna
    non erit incultis gratior asparagis.

22 *uvae duracinae*
non habilis cyathis et inutilis uva Lyaeo,
    sed non potanti me tibi nectar ero.

23 *ficus Chiae*
Chia seni similis Baccho, quem Setia misit,
    ipsa merum secum portat et ipsa salem.

24 *Cydonea*
si tibi Cecropio saturata Cydonea melle
    ponentur, dicas 'haec melimela' licet.

25 *nuces pineae*
poma sumus Cybeles: procul hinc discede, viator,
    ne cadat in miserum nostra ruina caput.

26 *sorba*

sorba sumus, molles nimium tendentia ventres:
    aptius haec puero quam tibi poma dabis.

27 *petalium caryotarum*

aurea porrigitur Iani caryota Kalendis;
    sed tamen hoc munus pauperis esse solet.

28 *vas cottanorum*

haec tibi quae torta venerunt condita meta,
    si maiora forent cottana, ficus erat.

29 *vas Damascenorum*

pruna peregrinae carie rugosa senectae
    sume: solent duri solvere ventris onus.

30 *caseus Lunensis*

caseus Etruscae signatus imagine Lunae
    praestabit pueris prandia mille tuis.

31 *caseus Vestinus*

si sine carne voles ientacula sumere frugi,
    haec tibi Vestino de grege massa venit.

32 *caseus fumosus*

non quemcumque focum nec fumum caseus omnem,
    sed Velabrensem qui bibit, ille sapit.

33 *casei Trebulani*

Trebula nos genuit; commendat gratia duplex,
    sive levi flamma sive domamur aqua.

34 *bulbi*

cum sit anus coniunx et sint tibi mortua membra,
    nil aliud bulbis quam satur esse potes.

35 *Lucanicae*

filia Picenae venio Lucanica porcae:
    pultibus hinc niveis grata corona datur.

36 *cistella olivarum*

haec quae Picenis venit subducta trapetis
    inchoat atque eadem finit oliva dapes.

Xenia [Liber XIII]

37 *mala citrea*

aut Corcyraei sunt haec de frondibus horti,
   aut haec Massyli poma draconis erant.

38 *colustrum*

surripuit pastor quae nondum stantibus haedis
   de primo matrum lacte colustra damus.

39 *haedus*

lascivum pecus et viridi non utile Baccho
   det poenas; nocuit iam tener ille deo.

40 *ova*

candida si croceos circumfluit unda vitellos,
   Hesperius scombri temperet ova liquor.

41 *porcellus lactans*

lacte mero pastum pigrae mihi matris alumnum
   ponat, et Aetolo de sue dives edat.

42 *apyrina et tubures*

non tibi de Libycis tubures et apyrina ramis,
   de Nomentanis sed damus arboribus.

43 *idem*

lecta suburbanis mittuntur apyrina ramis
   et vernae tubures. quid tibi cum Libycis?

44 *sumen*

esse putes nondum sumen: sic ubere largo
   effluit et vivo lacte papilla tumet.

45 *pulli gallinacei*

si Libycae nobis volucres et Phasides essent,
   acciperes; at nunc accipe chortis aves.

46 *Persica praecocia*

vilia maternis fueramus Persica ramis:
   nunc in adoptivis Persica cara sumus.

47 *panes Picentini*

Picentina Ceres niveo sic nectare crescit
   ut levis accepta spongea turget aqua.

48 *boleti*

argentum atque aurum facile est laenamque togamque
  mittere; boletos mittere difficile est.

49 *ficedulae*

cum me ficus alat, cum pascar dulcibus uvis,
  cur potius nomen non dedit uva mihi?

50 *terrae tubera*

rumpimus altricem tenero quae vertice terram
  tubera, boletis poma secunda sumus.

51 *turdorum decuria*

texta rosis fortasse tibi vel divite nardo,
  at mihi de turdis facta corona placet.

52 *anates*

tota quidem ponatur anas, sed pectore tantum
  et cervice sapit: cetera redde coco.

53 *turtures*

cum pinguis mihi turtur erit, lactuca valebis;
  et cocleas tibi habe. perdere nolo famem.

54 *perna*

Cerretana mihi fiat vel missa licebit
  de Menapis: lauti de petasone vorent.

55 *petaso*

musteus est: propera, caros nec differ amicos.
  nam mihi cum vetulo sit petasone nihil.

56 *volva*

te fortasse magis capiat de virgine porca,
  me materna gravi de sue volva capit.

57 *colocasia*

Niliacum ridebis holus lanasque sequaces,
  improba cum morsu fila manuque trahes.

58 *iecur anserinum*

aspice quam tumeat magno iecur ansere maius!
  miratus dices: "hoc, rogo, crevit ubi?"

59 *glires*

tota mihi dormitur hiems et pinguior illo
  tempore sum quo me nil nisi somnus alit.

60 *cuniculi*

gaudet in effossis habitare cuniculus antris.
  monstravit tacitas hostibus ille vias.

61 *attagenae*

inter sapores fertur alitum primus
Ionicarum gustus attagenarum.

62 *gallinae altiles*

pascitur et dulci facilis gallina farina,
  pascitur et tenebris. ingeniosa gula est.

63 *capones*

ne nimis exhausto macresceret inguine gallus,
  amisit testes. nunc mihi Gallus erit.

64 *idem*

succumbit sterili frustra gallina marito.
  hunc matris Cybeles esse decebat avem.

65 *perdices*

ponitur Ausoniis avis haec rarissima mensis:
  hanc in piscina ludere saepe soles.

66 *columbini*

ne violes teneras periuro dente columbas,
  tradita si Cnidiae sunt tibi sacra deae.

67 *palumbi*

inguina torquati tardant hebetantque palumbi:
  non edat hanc volucrem qui cupit esse salax.

68 *galbuli*

galbina decipitur calamis et retibus ales,
  turget adhuc viridi cum rudis uva mero.

69 *cattae*

Pannonicas nobis numquam dedit Umbria cattas:
  mavult haec domino mittere dona Pudens.

M. Val. Martialis

70 *pavones*
miraris, quotiens gemmantis explicat alas,
et potes hunc saevo tradere, dure, coco?

71 *phoenicopteri*
dat mihi pinna rubens nomen, sed lingua gulosis
nostra sapit. quid si garrula lingua foret?

72 *Phasianae*
Argoa primum sum transportata carina.
ante mihi notum nil nisi Phasis erat.

73 *Numidicae*
ansere Romano quamvis satur Hannibal esset,
ipse suas numquam barbarus edit aves.

74 *anseres*
haec servavit avis Tarpei templa Tonantis.
miraris? nondum fecerat illa deus.

75 *grues*
turbabis versus nec littera tota volabit,
unam perdideris si Palamedis avem.

76 *rusticulae*
rustica sim an perdix quid refert, si sapor idem est?
carior est perdix. sic sapit illa magis.

77 *cycni*
dulcia defecta modulatur carmina lingua
cantator cycnus funeris ipse sui.

78 *porphyriones*
nomen habet magni volucris tam parva gigantis?
et nomen prasini Porphyrionis habet.

79 *mulli vivi*
spirat in advecto sed iam piger aequore mullus
languescit. vivum da mare, fortis erit.

80 *murenae*
quae natat in Siculo grandis murena profundo,
non valet exustam mergere sole cutem.

Xenia [Liber XIII]

81 rhombi
quamvis lata gerat patella rhombum,
rhombus latior est tamen patella.

82 ostrea
ebria Baiano veni modo concha Lucrino:
nobile nunc sitio luxuriosa garum.

83 squillae
caeruleus nos Liris amat, quem silva Maricae
protegit: hinc squillae maxima turba sumus.

84 scarus
hic scarus, aequoreis qui venit adesus ab undis,
visceribus bonus est, cetera vile sapit.

85 coracinus
princeps Niliaci raperis, coracine, macelli:
Pellaeae prior est gloria nulla gulae.

86 echini
iste licet digitos testudine pungat acuta,
cortice deposita mollis echinus erit.

87 murices
sanguine bis nostro tinctas, ingrate, lacernas
induis, et non est hoc satis: esca sumus.

88 gobii
in Venetis sint lauta licet convivia terris,
principium cenae gobius esse solet.

89 lupus
laneus Euganei lupus excipit ora Timavi,
aequoreo dulces cum sale pastus aquas.

90 aurata
non omnis laudes pretiumque aurata meretur,
sed cui solus erit concha Lucrina cibus.

91 acipensis
ad Palatinas acipensem mittite mensas:
ambrosias ornent munera rara dapes.

92 *lepores*

inter aves turdus, si quid me iudice certum est,
inter quadripedes mattea prima lepus.

93 *aper*

qui Diomedeis metuendus saetiger agris
    Aetola cecidit cuspide, talis erat.

94 *dammae*

dente timetur aper, defendunt cornua cervum:
    imbelles dammae quid nisi praeda sumus?

95 *oryx*

matutinarum non ultima praeda ferarum,
    saevus oryx constat quot mihi morte canum!

96 *cervus*

hic erat ille tuo domitus, Cyparisse, capistro,
    an magis iste tuus, Silvia, cervus erat?

97 *lalisio*

dum tener est onager solaque lalisio matre
    pascitur, hoc infans sed breve nomen habet.

98(99) *caprea*

pendentem summa capream de rupe videbis,
    casuram speres. decipit illa canes.

99(98) *dorcas*

delicium parvo donabis dorcada nato:
    iactatis solet hanc mittere turba togis.

100 *onager*

pulcher adest onager. mitti venatio debet
    dentis Erythraei: iam removete sinus.

101 *oleum Venafrum*

hoc tibi Campani sudavit baca Venafri:
    unguentum quotiens sumis, et istud oles.

102 *garum sociorum*

expirantis adhuc scombri de sanguine primo
    accipe fastosum, munera cara, garum.

Xenia [Liber XIII]

103 *amphora muriae*
Antipolitani, fateor, sum filia thynni:
  essem si scombri, non tibi missa forem.

104 *mel Atticum*
hoc tibi Thesei populatrix misit Hymetti
  Pallados a silvis nobile nectar apis.

105 *favi Siculi*
cum dederis Siculos mediae de collibus Hyblae,
  Cecropios dicas tu licet esse favos.

106 *passum*
Gnosia Minoae genuit vindemia Cretae
  hoc tibi, quod mulsum pauperis esse solet.

107 *picatum*
haec de vitifera venisse picata Vienna
  ne dubites, misit Romulus ipse mihi.

108 *mulsum*
Attica nectareum turbatis mella Falernum.
  misceri decet hoc a Ganymede merum.

109 *Albanum*
hoc de Caesareis mitis vindemia cellis
  misit, Iuleo quae sibi monte placet.

110 *Surrentinum*
Surrentina bibis? nec murrina picta nec aurum
  sume: dabunt calices haec tibi vina suos.

111 *Falernum*
de Sinuessanis venerunt Massica prelis:
  condita quo quaeris consule? nullus erat.

112 *Setinum*
pendula Pomptinos quae spectat Setia campos
  exigua vetulos misit ab urbe cados.

113 *Fundanum*
haec Fundana tulit felix autumnus Opimi.
  expressit mustum consul et ipse bibit.

114 *Trifolinum*

non sum de primo, fateor, Trifolina Lyaeo,
inter vina tamen septima vitis ero.

115 *Caecubum*

Caecuba Fundanis generosa cocuntur Amyclis,
vitis et in media nata palude viret.

116 *Signinum*

potabis liquidum Signina morantia ventrem?
ne nimium sistas, sit tibi parca sitis.

117 *Mamertinum*

amphora Nestorea tibi Mamertina senecta
si detur, quodvis nomen habere potest.

118 *Tarraconense*

Tarraco, Campano tantum cessura Lyaeo,
haec genuit Latiis aemula vina cadis.

119 *Nomentanum*

Nomentana meum tibi dat vindemia Bacchum:
si te Quintus amat, commodiora bibes.

120 *Spoletinum*

de Spoletinis quae sunt cariosa lagonis
malueris quam si musta Falerna bibas.

121 *Paelignum*

Marsica Paeligni mittunt turbata coloni:
non tu, libertus sed bibat illa tuus.

122 *acetum*

amphora Niliaci non sit tibi vilis aceti:
esset cum vini, vilior illa fuit.

123 *Massilitanum*

cum tua centenos expunget sportula civis,
fumea Massiliae ponere vina potes.

124 *Caeretanum*

Caeretana Nepos ponat, Setina putabis.
non ponit turbae, cum tribus illa bibit.

Xenia [Liber XIII]

125 *Tarentinum*
nobilis et lanis et felix vitibus Aulon
    det pretiosa tibi vellera, vina mihi.

126 *unguentum*
unguentum heredi numquam nec vina relinquas.
    ille habeat nummos, haec tibi tota dato.

127 *coronae roseae*
dat festinatas, Caesar, tibi bruma coronas:
    quondam veris erat, nunc tua facta rosa est.

Commentary

13.1-2: Alan Ker argues, at times rather cryptically but probably correctly, that these two poems are imports, properly belonging elsewhere in M's corpus (*CQ* 44 (1950), 23-4):

(a) They have nothing to do with *xenia*, whereas poem 3 is explicitly (line 1) an introductory poem to the work.

(b) There are structural problems with Mart. 13.1, which appears to comprise two fragments: the first four lines are 'about his old poems', which are to be discarded for new ones (so Ker; but see 13.1.1-4 n. below: the poems meant are not in fact old, but deliberately bad); and the second four explain why M is not interested in traditional gaming, his gaming being poetry.

Ker might additionally have observed that 'alea nec damnum nec facit ista lucrum', line 8, contradicts 'perdite Niliacas, Musae, mea damna, papyros', line 3. The word *perdite* and the similarity of sentiment between lines 5-8 and Mart. 14.1.12 ' "lude" inquis "nucibus": perdere nolo nucibus' (where M rejects nuts for light verse) might account for the insertion of these fragments at the beginning of Book 13.

(c) In the MS Q, the advertisement which announces the beginning of each new book duly appears at the end of Book 12, but then 'appears between 13.3 and 4 as well'. That this second advertisement appears after poem 3 rather than poem 2 is difficult to explain but is probably of no account. This is because Q clearly appreciated fully that poem 3 belonged to the *Xenia*: leaving aside the explicit nature of line 1, Q divides poem 3 into three sections, each with a *lemma*, the last of which is 'Ad lectorem de Xeniis'. Ker is therefore probably justified in deducing from Q's two advertisements that poems 1 and 2 have crept in from elsewhere.

(d) Finally, Ker refers to the title-headings (i.e. *lemmata*) in Books 13-14. (Regarding these, see Mart. 13.3.7 below.) MS agreement on these is not always unanimous, but discrepancies are few. In contrast, the headings preserved for Mart. 13.1-2 differ widely from MS to MS. Ker suggests that this derives from scribal invention in the absence of an archetypal precedent, and that this lack of precedent questions the original presence of the poems at all.

13.1

So that the tunny fry should not lack a toga and olives a cloak, or the foul bookworm fear the hunger of penury, waste, o Muses, papyrus from the Nile (the loss is mine): look, the drunken winter demands new jests. [5] My die does not fight it out with the great-hearted knucklebone, nor does the six shake my ivory with the one. This papyrus is my nuts; this papyrus is my dice-box. Such gambling makes neither loss nor gain.

1-4: passing allusion has already been made to an association between poetry and the Saturnalia and Saturnalian gifts (Intro. (v); cf. (ii) section D above). In keeping with the freedoms of the season (Intro. (ii) section C), this Saturnalian poetry was by tradition light: cf. Mart. 11.6.3-4 'versu ludere non laborioso/ permittis' and 11.15; and it was often jocular in tone (cf. Intro. (ii) section D above, Coleman's introductory note to Stat. *Silv.* 4.9 and note *sales* in line 4). It was also commonly, and as here, of professed poor quality: although these lines are probably imports from elsewhere in M's corpus, they are nonetheless clearly Saturnalian and refer to the composition of bad poetry. This is indicated by 'ebria bruma', line 4 (see below), and by the reference to tunny fry, olives and worms in lines 1-2: when it was not providing food for bookworms (see Coleman at Stat. *Silv.* 4.9.10), worthless poetry was traditionally consigned to wrapping olives or used for cooking fish (Coleman at Stat. *Silv.* 4.9.11-13; cf. Mart. 3.2.4).

Of course it is unlikely that M really thought his Saturnalian poetry was bad. For his self-denigration, see Intro. (v) above.

1 toga ... **et paenula**: cf. Mart. 3.2.5 'turis piperisve ... cucullus' and 4.86.8 'nec scombris tunicas dabis molestas'. The *paenula* was a heavy cloak, well suited to cold or wet weather: see Sebesta 229 and my note at Mart. 14.127.*le*. It was used by those who worked out of doors and was favoured by soldiers, especially centurions. For the toga, see Lillian M. Wilson, *The Roman Toga*, Baltimore 1924, Sebesta 13-45 [Shelley Stone]. The different garments here afford *varietas*, but possibly also distinguish the different uses to which M's poetry might be put (i.e. cooking fish or wrapping olives).

With *et*, cf. *aut*, 2. One would expect *neve/neu* in prose. For the poets' greater freedom, see L-H-Sz II.500, Woodcock §128iii.

cordylis: cf. Mart. 3.2.3-4 'ne nigram cito raptus in culinam/ cordylas madida tegas papyro'. The *cordyla*, here humorously personified, is a tunny fry according to Pliny *Nat.* 9.47 'cordyla appellatur partus (thynnorum)'; but the fish must have reached a reasonable size before it could be eaten; cf. Mart. 11.52.7 'vetus ... tenui maior cordyla lacerto' where the paradoxical *vetus* is humorous.

2 inopem ... famem: cf. Drac. *Sat*. 285 'frigus inopsque fames', Cic. *Dom*. 11. See too *OLD* s.v. *inops* §1b: 'marked by penury', which compares e.g. Tac. *Ann*. 14.62 '[Anicetus] non inops exilium toleravit'. Since bookworms cannot feel (or fear: *metuat*) penury, the word's appearance here is humorously inappropriate. The personification of the worm continues that of the tunny.

sordida blatta: the word *blatta* (of uncertain etymology) was applied to a variety of creatures and often those harmful to books; cf. Mart. 14.37.2 'admittam tineas trucesque blattas' and 6.61.7 'quam multi (auctores) tineas pascunt blattasque diserti' where it is mentioned in conjunction with the *tinea*. For *sordidus* used of a creature characterised by dirt or neglect, see *OLD* s.v. *sordidus* §2; cf. Mart. 14.83.2.

3 perdite Niliacas, Musae, mea damna, papyros: for the so-called 'parenthetic apposition' exemplified by this line and 13.9.1 below, see J.B. Solodow, *'Raucae, tua cura, palumbes'*: Study of a Poetic Word Order', *HSCPh* 90 (1986), 129 ff. and especially 153: Solodow comments on this line that 'The position of the vocative *Musae* perhaps blunts the effect of the inserted apposition, in which *damna* is in apposition to *papyros*'; but see on *Musae* below.

Niliacas ... papyros: i.e. Egyptian (see L-S s.v. *Nilus* §II2; cf. Ovid *Ars* 3.318 'Niliacis carmina lusa modis', Mart. 14.150.2 'pectine Niliaco' and 13.9.1, 57.1, 85.1 and 122.1 below). For Egyptian papyrus, cf. Apul. *Met*. 1.1 'papyrum Aegyptiam' and see Pliny *Nat*. 13.71 ff., who describes the varying qualities of papyrus. The inference naturally drawn here from *perdite* ('waste'; cf. Mart. 6.64.23 'perdere chartas') and 'mea damna' is that this papyrus is too good for the poems written on it. That bad poetry was often written on good quality material appears to have been a commonplace: one thinks at once of Suffenus (Catul. 22).

Good or at any rate untouched papyrus was highly regarded (see Coleman at Stat. *Silv*. 4.9.7, citing Catul. 22.4 f.) At 14.10, M jokes that the gift of papyrus there described is the more valuable, since it comes devoid of poetic scribblings. That he is unrepentant here regarding the extravagant use of good papyrus for indifferent literature is perhaps conveyed by the emphatic position of *perdite*, reinforced by alliteration of the letter p; but whatever the case, he justifies the expenditure by reference in line 4 to the season.

Regarding papyrus generally, see L.D. Reynolds and N.G. Wilson, *Scribes and Scholars: a Guide to the Transmission of Greek and Latin Literature*,[3] Oxford 1991, 2 f., E.G. Turner, *Greek Papyri: an Introduction*, Oxford 1968, 3 f., Paoli 175 f.

Musae: although M is more than happy to bear the expense of wasted papyrus, he humorously transfers all blame for bad writing to the Muses (whom one would usually expect to improve a poet's quality rather than squander his writing material). The alliterative juxtaposition 'Musae, mea damna' reinforces his apportioning of liability.

4 ebria bruma: for the Saturnalia's mid-winter date, see Intro. (ii) section B above; cf. e.g. Mart. 14.72.1 'mediae … tempore brumae', 138.1 'tempore brumali' and 16.1, 127.1 below. As for the drunkenness which characterised it, in keeping with the licence of the festival, see Intro. (ii) section C above and my note at Mart. 14.1.9 'madidi … diebus'; cf. 13.2.10 'nec matutina … fronte'. Drunkenness is used to excuse the quality of Symphosius' Saturnalian riddles (*AL* 281 praef. 17) and Ausonius' *Griphus Ternarii Numeri* (XV praef. 32-3 Green).

5 non mea magnanimo depugnat tessera talo: dicing characterised the Saturnalia, when the normal restrictions on gaming were lifted: see Kay at Mart. 11.6.2, citing Ulp. *dig.* 11.5.2 f., Cic. *Phil.* 2.56, Hor. *Carm.* 3.24.58, and Intro. (ii) section C above. Lines 5-8, revealing M's preference nonetheless for verse composition, form a *recusatio* of sorts.

tessera: Roman dice were cubic, with each side bearing a number from one to six, although not necessarily in the same pattern as ours, with opposite numbers totalling seven. Games required three dice, and the highest throw was a triple six. The singular *tessera* here is poetic. *Tali* (knucklebones) were rectangular block shapes with rounded ends. Four *tali* were needed for a game and the highest throw saw all sides different. On dice and knucklebones, see further my notes at Mart. 14.14, 15, 16, where more details and biographical information are given.

A rivalry existed between (players of) the two games: note Mart. 14.15 *tesserae*: 'non sim talorum numero par tessera, dum sit/ maior quam talis alea saepe mihi'. Here the dice do not mind being outnumbered by the knucklebones (four to three), provided the stake for dice games was higher (as was apparently the case: cf. Mart. 4.66.15 with Shackleton Bailey's Loeb note). This rivalry was evidently taken seriously by some, although to M it was a matter of indifference. Hence his use of mocking hyperbole: *depugnat* suggests a battle hard fought (see L-S s.v. *depugno* §1, ThLL V(1).617.83 ff. s.v. *depugno* [Lambertz]), while the *tali* (the underdogs?) put up an heroic struggle: with *magnanimus*, cf. the Homeric μεγάθυμος, and see Austin at Verg. *A.* 1.260 'magnanimum Aenean'. The conflict is further heightened by the (admittedly metrically convenient) juxtaposition of the alliterative *tessera* and *talo* and the fifth foot diaeresis. (Note that the t alliteration is balanced by the m sounds in 'mea magnanimo'.)

talo βγ: **telo** T. *Telum* could have been used of a die, as Shackleton Bailey observes in the apparatus criticus to his Teubner edition; but the line would then lose the rivalry between dice and knucklebones, and would be much the weaker in consequence. For the dative used after *depugno*, cf. Sil. 10.474 'depugnet morti iuvenis'.

6 ebur can be used of anything made of ivory. Here it refers to a dice box; cf. the *fritillus* below (line 7). The dice box was intended to prevent cheating, and the inside was therefore rifled with a groove which caught the corners of the dice when shaken so that it was impossible for throws to be subject to anything but chance; cf. Mart. 14.16 quoted below. (The name *fritillus* is onomatopoeic, from the rattle of shaken dice.) Hence this dice box is shaken alike by the highest throw (*senio*) and the lowest (*canis*).

For dice boxes generally, see my note at Mart. 14.16. For ivory dice boxes, see Blümner *Priv*. 413 n.12.

7 charta: i.e. the papyrus on which M writes Saturnalian verse. For the meanings of *charta*, see Naphtali Lewis, *Papyrus in Classical Antiquity*, Oxford 1974, 70 ff. and n. 2: while many have taken the word to refer to a sheet of papyrus, the current state of the evidence suggests that it refers to a roll. There is certainly nothing to preclude this interpretation here.

nuces: dicing for nuts, especially by boys (cf. Mart. 5.84.1), was a common Saturnalian activity. These nuts were used as a substitute for money (cf. playing poker for matchsticks), and the activity was lightly viewed. Dicing for nuts is often offered in M as the direct equivalent of light or trivial literature, whether writing it (Mart. 14.1; note especially lines 7 and 12) or reading it: note Mart. 14.185 and 5.30.5 ff.:

> sed lege fumoso non aspernanda Decembri
> carmina, mittuntur quae tibi mense suo,
> commodius nisi forte tibi potiusque videtur
> Saturnalicias perdere, Varro, nuces.

8 alea is first of all a game of chance, but it is also applied to the act of engaging in one, or to gaming or gambling: *OLD* s.v. *alea* §1a. 'Alea ... ista' or 'such gambling' is here metaphorical for 'writing poetry'.

nec damnum nec facit ... lucrum: of course, dicing for worthless nuts would not bring loss or gain either. M's real reason for not dicing is simply that he does not want to.

nec damnum ... facit: for the contradiction by these words for line 3, and its implications, see at 13.1-2 above.

Facere is the regular word in financial contexts for making a profit ('lucrum facere'; see *OLD* s.v. *lucrum* §2a; cf. Mart. 13.3.4 below) or making a loss ('damnum facere'; see *OLD* s.v. *damnum* §1b). Cf. in this regard Cic.

Ver. 3.110 'necesse est aut damnum aut certe non magnum lucrum fecisse
decumanos'. Nevertheless, it may also have had a technical sense in dice
games: note Mart. 14.16 *turricula*: 'quae scit compositos manus improba
mittere talos,/ si per me misit, nil nisi vota facit'.

lucrum: writing poetry was, of course, notoriously unremunerative; cf.
Ovid *Ars* 3.411 (also 405 ff.), Tac. *Dial.* 9.1 f., Juv. 7 etc. (For M's poetic
poverty, see at Mart. 13.3.6 below.)

13.2

You may be as big-nosed as you please. You may indeed be all nose, a nose
so big that Atlas, if asked, would refuse to bear it, and you may be able to
mock Latinus himself: you cannot say more against my trifles [5] than I
have myself. What good is it to gnaw tooth with tooth? You need meat if
you want to be satisfied. Don't waste your effort. Those who admire
themselves, for them keep your venom. I know that these things are
nothing – yet this nothing is not altogether nothing, if you come to me with
a well-disposed ear and not a morning countenance.

1 nasutus means 'having a big nose' (L-S s.v. *nasutus* §I), but is also used
metaphorically of a person of discernment. See Coleman's edition of Stat.
Silv. 4, 221, citing Phaedr. 4.7.1 'tu qui nasute scripta destringis mea' and
Howell at Mart. 1.3.6. M's point is that no matter how discerning his
addressee is, he cannot be more critical of his work than M is himself.

With *licet*, cf. Mart. 5.60.1 'allatres licet usque', 'you may bark as much
as you like'.

sis denique nasus: comparable but different humour can be found at
Catul. 13.13-14 'quod tu cum olfacies, deos rogabis/ totum ut te faciant,
Fabulle, nasum'.

2 quantum noluerit ferre rogatus Atlans: further hyperbole, which
now takes a humorously mythological turn. You may be a nose bigger than
heaven, which is what the (Hesiodic) Titan Atlas usually supported: see
OCD[3] s.v. *Atlas* [R.L. Hunter], *Kl.P.* 1.712.35 f. s.v. *Atlas* [M. Leglay]. In
fact, if asked, Atlas would have refused to bear heaven too: according to
Ovid (*Met.* 4.639 ff.) Atlas denied an hospitable reception to Perseus, who
then used the Gorgon's head to punish him, turning him into a mountain
(which then supported the heavens). Elsewhere in the tradition, he agrees
to fetch the apples of the Hesperides if Hercules supported his load in the
meantime, and Hercules had to trick him into resuming the burden
afterwards: Pherecydes ap. Schol. Ap. Rhod. 4.1396. But M is less interested in mythological details than in expressing in ridiculous fashion the
idea of a very large nose.

Rogatus Atlans is in effect the protasis of a condition; cf. Woodcock §92c, citing in illustration of the participial usage, e.g., Cic. *de Or.* 3.179 'haec tantam habent vim, paulum ut immutata cohaerere non possint', 'These (arrangements) have such force that, (if) slightly changed, they could not hold together.'

noluerit vett., Shackleton Bailey: **noluerat** codd. M occasionally uses the pluperfect indicative for the pluperfect subjunctive, but only *metri causa* (cf. Heraeus at 10.35.18).

3 possis αβ: **posses** γ. The present subjunctive is needed after *sis*, line 1. *Potes*, line 4, might account for γ's corruption.

deridere Latinum: Latinus was a mime actor, prominent at the time and especially favoured by Domitian. For details, see *RE* XIIA.937.40 ff. s.v. *Latinus* [Gudemann], *Kl.P.* 3.513.7 ff. s.v. *Latinus* [P.L. Schmidt], Courtney at Juv. 1.35. Mart. 9.28.1-4 testifies to his skill:

> dulce decus scaenae, ludorum fama, Latinus
> ille ego sum, plausus deliciaeque tuae,
> qui spectatorem potui fecisse Catonem,
> solvere qui Curios Fabriciosque graves.

At Mart. 1.4.5, Latinus is himself described as a *derisor*, having apparently made a fool of the jealous husband in a mime. M's point here is that even if his addressee is so discerning as to be able to mock the great Latinus himself, he still cannot surpass M's own criticism of his work.

4 nugas ... meas: for *nugae* applied to poetic trifles or the lighter forms of verse, see Fordyce at Catul. 1.4. M calls his own (not necessarily Saturnalian) work *nugae* elsewhere, e.g., at 1.113.6, 4.10.4, 5.80.3. For the trivial nature of Saturnalian verse, see at 13.1.1-4.

5 ipse ego quam dixi: that M is his own fiercest critic is brought home emphatically by the initial position of *ipse* (after the final position of *meas* in the previous line) and the very strong caesura after *dixi*. (It is unusual to find the sense of the pentameter resolved in the hexameter, rather than vice versa.) The elision of *ipse*, in itself unremarkable at this point in the line, nonetheless possibly contributes to the emphasis here. To put M's self-criticism into perspective, however, cf. Intro. (v) above.

5-6 quid dentem dente iuvabit/ rodere?: what M means is 'get your teeth into some meat (*carne*, line 6).' Grinding one's teeth, i.e. criticising his insubstantial trivia, brings no satisfaction. The action of grinding teeth is effectively illustrated by the polyptoton, while the imagery of acquiring substantial food is continued by *satur*, line 6: see *OLD* s.v. *satur* §1.

M uses similar words at Mart. 6.64.31-2 in warning off a critic: '... vacua dentes in pelle fatiges/ et tacitam quaeras, quam possis rodere, carnem', with which cf. Mart. 5.28.7 'robiginosis cuncta dentibus rodit'.

7 ne perdas operam: for the idiom, see *OLD* s.v. *perdo* §6b.

qui se mirantur: like Suffenus: 'tam gaudet in se tamquam se ipse miratur' (Catul. 22.17).

8 virus habe: for this use of *virus*, see *OLD* s.v. *virus* §1d. *Habes* (γ) is weak after *ne perdas*, and so to be rejected. Stronger punctuation is desirable after *habe* than the comma of Shackleton Bailey and others, and the semi-colon of Friedländer, Duff and Ker is attractive.

9 nimium codd.: **nihilum** Heinsius. Reading *nimium* makes for a difficult transition from *haec* (8) to *hoc* (9). One has presumably to understand *hoc* to refer to *nihil* (8) and translate *nimium* as something like the Loeb's 'altogether'. Heinsius' conjecture in contrast allows easy transition from *haec* to *hoc*, but introduces a different strain on the Latin. He would presumably understand the line to be saying 'this nothing is not absolutely nothing'; but if so the adverb has to be supplied *ex nihilo*. Given the difficulties of both readings, it seems safest to follow the MSS.

candidus aure: cf. Mart. 7.99.5 'lector candidus', Ovid *Trist.* 1.11.35 'his debes ignoscere, candide lector'; see *ThLL* III.244.67 ff. s.v. *candidus* [Goetz]. Note also Mart. 12. *praef.* 24 'de nugis nostris iudices candore seposito'.

10 nec matutina ... fronte: a morning countenance was sober and serious, the morning being the time of day reserved for business, law and finance: Balsdon *LL* 24. The litotes here stresses that it was the mood of the evening (in fact of dinner time) to which M's poems were suited. Cf. Mart. 10.20.18-21:

> haec hora est tua, cum furit Lyaeus,
> cum regnat rosa, cum madent capilli:
> tunc me vel rigidi legant Catones.

Cf. Mart. 4.8.7 ff. and see *ThLL* VIII.506.65 and 74 s.v. *matutinus* [Brandt].

mihi refers of course not actually to M but to his books; cf. Mart. 6.60(61).2 'me manus omnis habet', on which see Grewing in detail.

13.3

The whole collection of *Xenia* in this slim little book will cost you four sesterces when you buy it. Is four too much? It could cost two and the bookseller Tryphon will make a profit. [5] You can send these couplets to guests instead of a gift if sesterces are as scarce with you as they are with me. You will find their names attached to items by means of headings: if anything is not to your taste, you can pass it by.

1 omnis ... turba: for *turba* of a multitude of inanimate things, see L-S s.v. *turba* §B13, *OLD* s.v. *turba* §2c; cf. Gel. 9.15.9 'incipit ... verborum ... volumina vocumque turbas fundere'.

gracili ... libello: applied to unassuming books, *gracilis* appears again at Mart. 8.24.1-2 'si quid forte petam timido gracilique libello,/ improba non fuerit si mea charta, dato'. It is used also of poets of the lower genres and their unambitious themes: see *OLD* s.v. *gracilis* §4a; cf. L-S s.v. *gracilis* §B.

M's *Xenia* is not a long book, and *libellus* is possibly therefore a physically appropriate diminutive. As at Mart. 8.24.2, however, the word also reinforces the self-effacing *gracilis*; cf. Catul. 1.8-9 'quare habe tibi quidquid hoc libelli/ qualecumque'; see E.T. Sage, *TAPhA* 50 (1919), 168, and Coleman on Stat. *Silv.* 4.9.9 'praeter me', who observes that the term *libellus* in Martial can be a synonym for *liber*, but always with deprecatory or apologetic overtones. Such self-effacement is not to be taken at full face value, however: see Intro. (v) above.

Xeniorum: see Intro. (i) above.

2 nummis quattuor: Kenney notes (*CHCL* II.27): '... such information as exists about [sc. book] prices is both scanty and conflicting'. Nevertheless, one might observe that the deluxe edition of Mart. 1 referred to at 1.117.17 cost 5 denarii (20 sesterces) and, although we do not know its length, the materials alone for the luxury volume spoken of at Stat. *Silv.* 4.9.9 cost 10 asses (2.5 sesterces). Given that Book 1 is roughly twice as long as 13, the initial asking price for M's *Xenia* of 4 sesterces is probably not unusually high. While M's question as to whether even this might be too much could be humorous self-effacement (cf. 1.117.18 ' "tanti non es" '), his observation that it might still be sold profitably for two (lines 3-4) indicates nonetheless that booksellers did not do at all badly out of their authors; cf. at 'bibliopola Tryphon', line 4 below.

Nummis is ablative of price with *consto*; cf. L-H-Sz II.129.

empta: on participial phrases used as substitutes for substantival clauses, see Woodcock §95, L-H-Sz II.393 f.; cf. Mart. 14.1.2 'pillea sumpta'.

4 faciet lucrum: see at Mart. 13.1.8.

faciet βγ: **faciat** T. Lindsay, Ker and Giarratano print *faciat*; but the better supported *faciet* is preferable, since it establishes Tryphon's profit as certain.

bibliopola Tryphon: Tryphon is also known from Quintilian's *Institutio Oratoria*, the publication of which he had impatiently called for (*Inst.* 1 *praef.* 1). M mentions him again at 4.72. Other booksellers who stocked M's work were called Secundus (1.2.7; see Citroni's detailed note), Q. Valerianus Pollius (1.113.5) and Atrectus (1.117.13).

While the existence of a book trade at Rome is undeniable, we have very little idea of its extent and operations: see Kenney *CHCL* II.15-22 and especially 20 ff. Nevertheless, it is doubtful that M would have received any of the 2-4 sesterces paid to Tryphon for a copy of the *Xenia*. He might, however, have received a one-off fee on providing the bookseller with an exemplar from which copies for sale could be made: the provision of such exemplars can be inferred from Isid. *Orig.* 6.14.1. Compare Sherwin White on Pliny *Ep.* 1.2.5 *editione* and see perhaps Suet. *Gram.* 8, although this account contains many puzzles (see Kastner ad loc.).

bibliopola: although it appears in Aristotle fr. 140 (Rose) and several times in Greek comedy of the 5th-4th centuries BC (see e.g. R. Kassel and C. Austin, *Poetae Comici Graecae* VII, Berlin and New York 1989, 66 and 743: Nicophon 10.4 and Theopompus 79), this word is not testified in Latin before Augustus. It survives also at *CIL* VI.9218 and in Pliny, *Ep.* 1.2.6 and 9.11.2, where he is surprised to hear of *bibliopolae* in Lugdunum.

5ff.: β begins a new poem at line 5, and it is easy to understand why, given that the epigram falls into two distinct halves (cf. γ's beginning a new epigram at Mart. 14.2.3 and see my note ad loc.). Harder to explain is how β came to omit line 8.

5 haec ... disticha: cf. Mart. 14.2.2 'versibus explicitum est omne duobus opus'. Like *Xeniorum* (line 1) and the mention of *lemmata* (line 7), these words clearly establish Mart. 13.3 as belonging to the work that follows. Contrast Poems 1-2, which are probable imports (see 13.1-2 n. above).

hospitibus ... mittas: *mittas* is common of sending poems and presents: note Stat. *Silv.* 4.9.1-2 'libellum/ misisti mihi', Catul. 14.12 ff.; see *OLD* s.v. *mitto* §17b. Although the word appears to conflict with *hospitibus* and the scenario of a dinner-table lottery (see Intro. (ii) section D above, noting Mart. 13.5.2 'cum tibi sorte datur'), its usage here is not unparalleled in Book 13: note e.g. 6.1-2, 48.2, 69.2, 103.2; cf. 14.126.2, 132.1-2. Given the similarities between the *Xenia* and *Apophoreta* and dedicatory epigram (see Intro. (v) above), it is worth recalling that *mitto* is common of giving (sacrificial) gifts to the gods: *ThLL* VIII.1179.6 ff. s.v. *mitto* [Fleischer].

pro munere: see Intro. (ii) section D and n. 10 above.

6 si tibi tam rarus quam mihi nummus erit: cf. the shortage of money envisaged in line 3. Although M's direct literary earnings were likely to have been small (see at 'nummis quattuor' and 'bibliopola Tryphon', lines 2 and 4 above; cf. Mart. 13.1.8 *lucrum* n. above), and his protestations of poverty are common (see Sullivan 26-8), he was nonetheless probably reasonably provided for, although he might not have had the financial security he would have liked. See Sullivan loc. cit., Saller, esp. 249.

7 addita per titulos sua nomina rebus habebis: like Mart. 14.2.3-4 'lemmata si quaeris cur sint ascripta, docebo:/ ut, si malueris, lemmata sola legas', this line suggests that in M's day *lemmata* were not normally attached by poets to their epigrams. See Kay at Mart. 11.42.2 both for this point and on *lemmata* generally. Lindsay, *Anc. Ed.* 37, writes: '... use of title headings was a necessity, in order that a donor might find without difficulty the couplet which would suit the present he thought of giving.' This was no doubt partly true, but M's *Xenia* were of course more than just a compilation of mottoes for gifts: see Intro. (v) above. M's own explanation for the *lemmata*'s presence is joking, that they are to enable the reader to skip poems if he wants to; cf. Mart. 1 *praef.* 12 ff. 'si quis tamen tam ambitiose tristis est ut apud illum in nulla pagina latine loqui fas sit, potest epistula vel potius titulo contentus esse', and the joke at Mart. 14.2.3-4 (see further my introductory note to Mart. 14.2, and my note at line 3). For comparison between *lemmata* and the *pittacia* of dinner-table lotteries, see Intro. (ii) section D above.

titulos: given M's novel use of *lemmata*, it is not surprising that his use of *titulus* here as the heading of an individual poem lacks exact parallels. For its use of a book title, cf. in addition to Mart. 1 *praef.* 12 ff. quoted above, Quint. *Inst.* 2.14.4 'cum M. Tullius etiam in ipsis librorum ... titulis Graeco nomine utatur'.

rebus: i.e. the things described by the poems that follow.

8 praetereas, si quid non facit ad stomachum: cf. Mart. 10.45:

> si quid lene mei dicunt et dulce libelli,
>   si quid honorificum pagina blanda sonat,
> hoc tu pingue putas et costam rodere mavis,
>   ilia Laurentis cum tibi demus apri.
> Vaticana bibas, si delectaris aceto:
>   non facit ad stomachum nostra lagona tuum.

47

Given the contents of Book 13, M's use here of 'non facit ad stomachum' has a humorous double meaning. For the idiom, cf. also Cic. *Fam.* 7.1.2 'ludi ... non tui stomachi', Pliny *Ep.* 1.24.3 'Tranquilli mei stomachum multa sollicitant, vicinitas urbis, opportunitas viae, mediocritas villae, modus ruris, qui ...'; see *OLD* s.v. *stomachus* §3a, L-S s.v. *stomachus* §III.1. Regarding the polysyllabic line-ending here introduced by *stomachum*, see Intro. (vi) above.

praetereas: see *OLD* s.v. *praetereo* §5b for this usage; cf. Pliny *Ep.* 8.21.4 'ego nihil praetereo atque etiam non praeterire me dico. lego enim omnia ut omnia emendem.'

13.4 Incense

That Germanicus rule the heavenly palace late in time, and long rule the earth, offer pious incense to Jupiter.

le. tus: incense was widely used in worshipping the gods and was offered by the Greeks prior to symposia: see Sara Lilja, *The Treatment of Odours in the Poetry of Antiquity*, Helsinki 1972, 50-1. Sullivan, 12, thinks that the incense here is for offering to the Lares; cf. Juv. 9.137, 12.89; but this is contradicted by 'da ... Iovi', line 2, on which see further below. For offerings to the gods at the beginning of the *cena*, cf. [Quint.] *Decl.* 310.10 'et adisti mensam, ad quam cum venire coepimus deos invocamus'; see *Kl.P.* 1.1104.24-5 s.v. *Cena* [W.H. Groß].

Incense is cited as a Saturnalian gift again at Mart. 4.46.7, 7.72 and Luc. *Sat.* 16. It also appears as a (love) gift at Pl. *Truc.* 540. For incense in general, see Pliny *Nat.* 12.51 ff., *Kl.P.* 5.1354.54 ff. s.v *Weihrauch* [C.J. Classen]. Also Miller 103-4.

1 serus: cf. *diu*, line 2. On the 'serus in caelum redeas' motif, see in great detail N-H at Hor. *Carm.* 1.2.45, who note that the topic must have belonged to conventional panegyric and presumably went back to Hellenistic ruler cult. Regarding Domitian, they cite the following instances: Sil. 3.626 f., Stat. *Silv.* 4.2.22, *Theb.* 1.30 f., Mart. 8.39.5; cf. also 5.65.16. Full treatment can be found in Kenneth Scott, *The Imperial Cult under the Flavians*, Stuttgart-Berlin 1936, ch. 12.

M's flattery of Domitian has drawn modern criticism, given especially his later flattery of Nerva and Trajan; but he lived in difficult times (see Ker xiv, Ronald Martin, *Tacitus*, London 1981, ch. 2) and Domitian's reign, although it was unpopular to some, was, in any case, not without real administrative and military achievements (Sullivan 127). Also, M's subscription to the encomiastic tradition made it natural for him to begin books by flattering the most powerful man in the patronal hierarchy and, indeed, the fact that his praise is confined here to just a couplet is remarkably innovative and even daring: panegyric was usually lengthy.

aetheriae(-eae) … aulae β: **-rii … aulae** T: **-ria(-rea) … aula** γ. *Aetherius*, used substantivally as a name for Jupiter, is attested (Ampelius 9.1); but it is rare and in any case reference to Jupiter in the hexameter would undermine the centrality of *Germanicus* and pre-empt *Iovi* in line 2. It would also weaken the poem's contrast between heaven and earth (*terris*, line 2). T's reading can therefore be rejected. So too can γ's since the dative is required after *impero*. For the phrase 'aetheria aula', note Sen. *Thy.* 1078-9 'aetheriae potens/ dominator aulae'. For the concept of a heavenly palace, cf. Stat. *Silv.* 1.1.106 'caeli … aula'.

Germanicus: Domitian took this title to mark his defeat of the Chatti; cf. Intro. (iv) above. On the Chattan war, see Jones 128-131; also my notes at Mart. 14.34.1 'pax certa … ducis' and 170.1-2.

imperet: while Domitian at present rules the earth (cf. Stat. *Silv.* 4.2.14 'regnator terrarum'), the inference from 'da … Iovi' is that he does so with Jupiter's blessing, and possibly even on Jupiter's behalf: for Domitian as Jupiter's vice gerent, see Coleman at Stat. *Silv.* 4.3.128 f.: 'hunc habet beatis/ pro se Iuppiter imperare terris' and cf. N-H's very detailed note at Hor. *Carm.* 1.12.50 'orto Saturno'. In assuming, however, that Domitian will eventually rule heaven, the poem suggests that Jupiter intends at some stage to abdicate in his favour: Domitian's qualities as ruler are acknowledged as equal by the supreme authority. For M's equation of Domitian with Jupiter, see Sullivan 142 and my note at Mart. 14.1.2 'nostrum Iovem'.

2 da pia tura Iovi: for offerings of incense to Jupiter, cf. e.g. Cato *Agr.* 134.1, Juv. 12.89, 13.113 ff. For this use of *pius*, describing sacred objects or ritual offerings, cf. Tib. 2.2.3 'pia tura', Ovid *Ep.* 21.7, Mart. 8.8.3; see *OLD* s.v. *pius* §2b. *Do* is regular of such offerings: *OLD* s.v. *do* §1b.

13.5 Pepper

When a wax-coloured beccafico which shines with ample loins is given to you by lot, if you are wise, add pepper.

le. piper: see generally Kay at Mart. 11.18.9. Pepper came mostly from India (Miller 80 ff.) and is dealt with by Pliny at *Nat.* 12.26. It was used from early on in medical treatments, being employed in quantity as a condiment first under the Empire: *Kl.P.* 4.681.8 ff. s.v. *Pfeffer* [K. Ziegler]. Thereafter it was widely used in cooking: see Apicius *passim* and *RE* XIX.1424.37 ff. s.v. *Pfeffer* [Steier]. Domitian built 'horrea piperataria' at

Rome in 92: Platner Ashby 262 f., Richardson 194. When Trajan built his market place, he included shops for spices, from which, in mediaeval times, came the name Via Biberatica (cf. *piper*). Because of its high price (cf. Mart. 7.27.7), fake pepper was made using juniper berries. Pepper is elsewhere cited as a Saturnalian gift at Mart. 4.46.7; cf. perhaps 10.57. It is given in return for advocacy by a grateful client at Pers. 3.75.

1 cerea ... ficedula: regarding this bird, its name and its identity, see also at Mart. 13.49 *ficedulae*. Shackleton Bailey's rendition 'beccafico' is both sociologically apt, since the beccafico is a small bird eaten in Italy today, and etymologically appropriate (the name comes from *beccare*, peck, and *fico*, fig); but whereas the *beccafico* is a sort of warbler the *ficedula* is a kind of fly-catcher. It features in three of Apicius' recipes, each time with pepper (4.132, 141, 8.380 Budé); cf. Petr. 33.8, quoted at Mart. 13.49.*le*.
    Cereus ('pale yellow') is used at Mart. 3.58.19 of a turtle-dove. Ausonius applies it in his *Epistulae* to the thrushes given as a gift to Hesperius: 27.1.2 Green.

patulo lucet ... lumbo: with *patulo*, cf. Petr. 33.8 'pinguissimam ficedulam'. The word is several times used describing parts of the body (see *ThLL* X(1).795.9 ff. s.v. *patulus* [Bruun], *OLD* s.v. *patulus* §2d), and at Gel. 7(6).6.12 it describes the wings of birds watched by augurs; but its use here of a *ficedula*'s loins is apparently unique. In contrast, *lumbus* is commonly used of edible bird and animal loins (*ThLL* VII(2).1809.26 ff. s.v. *lumbus* [Salvadore], *OLD* s.v. *lumbus* §1c).
    Lucet refers here to the bird's colour (cf. *cereus*): *ThLL* VII(2).1694.39 ff. s.v. *luceo* [B], *OLD* s.v. *luceo* §2b.

2 sorte: **forte** ς, but the conjecture is clearly unfounded. For Saturnalian dinner-table lotteries, see Intro. (ii) section D above; cf. e.g. Mart. 14.1.5 'alternas ... sortes', 40.1 'sors dedit', 144.1 'sorte datur', 170.1.

si sapis: 'if you have any sense': see *OLD* s.v. *sapio* §6c. Given the food context, it is worth recalling, however, such punning passages as Cic. *Fin.* 2.24 'ut, cui cor sapiat ei non sapiat palatus': for *sapio* meaning 'to have taste', see *OLD* s.v. *sapio* §5.

adde: *addo* is commonly used thus, of ingredients etc. added to food. See e.g. *OLD* s.v. *addo* §3b. Its use in didactic contexts is especially marked; cf. Cato *Agr.* 75 'ovum unum addito et una permisceto bene' (in a recipe for *libum*), and its appearance in the *Xenia* is one of the ways in which the poem recalls the Saturnalian tradition of mock-didactic poetry: see Intro. (v) above; cf. the mock-didactic Ovid *Med.* 88 'et modicum e murris pinguibus adde cubum'.

13.6 Wheat gruel

I can send you wheat gruel; a rich man will be able to send you mead. If
the rich man won't, buy some!

This poem begins a series, ending with poem 12, on cereals or cereal
products and legumes (alternated in poems 6-9), both of which appear to
have made suitable gifts and *hors d'oeuvres*. For the association of such
foods with the ancient festivals of Rome, including the Saturnalia, see
Gowers 59. Although they are simple, they would still have featured in a
lavish *cena*: while new courses were introduced over the years, old ones
were not replaced and the *cena* therefore 'contains traces of the history of
Roman eating habits' (Gowers 17).

le. & 1 alica αβ: **halica** γ. For the orthography (cf. Mart. 13.9.2 *alica* Tβ:
halica γ), see Lindsay *Orth.* 46; cf. ἄλιξ and the pun at Mart. 12.81:

> brumae diebus feriisque Saturni
> mittebat Umber aliculam mihi pauper;
> nunc mittit alicam: factus est enim dives.

Alica was roughly ground wheat grain, to be identified with χόνδρος
(Moritz 148), or, as here, a sort of gruel made from it: for its preparation,
see André *Alimentation* 58-9. Cato, *Agr.* 85, gives the grain form as an
ingredient for *puls*, for which see Mart. 13.8.*le*. n. In general, see *Kl.P.*
1.1154.24 ff. s.v. *Chondros* [F. Kudlien]. It appears at Pliny *Ep.* 1.15.2 in
what seems to be a list of *gustatio* dishes: 'paratae erant lactucae singulae,
cochleae ternae, ova bina, halica cum mulso et nive ... olivae betacei
cucurbitae bulbi, alia mille non minus lauta'. Note that there too it is
paired with *mulsum*; cf. Sen. *Ep.* 122.16. (*Mulsum* was in fact the customary drink at the *gustatio*, or *promulsis* as the course was sometimes called:
see Smith at Petr. 34.1, Younger 192, 199, Marquardt *Prl.* 323. On the
drink in general, see 13.108.*le*. n. below.) This epigram therefore describes
the complement of its more expensive partner. Mart. 13.106 *passum*
describes in contrast a cheap substitute for *mulsum*.

That the grain form of *alica* was also given at the Saturnalia is indicated
by Stat. *Silv.* 4.9.31. Like the gruel, it was a lowly present.

1 poterit mulsum tibi mittere dives: cf. Mart. 14.153 *semicinctium*: 'det
tunicam locuples: ego te praecingere possum./ essem si locuples, munus
utrumque darem', 132 *pilleum*: 'si possem, totas cuperem misisse lacernas:/ nunc tantum capiti munera mitto tuo'. In contrast here the donor is
humorously unrepentant as to his gift's small worth, contrasting himself
strongly with the rich man by placing *nos* and *dives* at opposite ends of the
line. Other gifts specifically identified with the poor man in Mart. 13 are

e.g. 27 *petalium caryotarum* (note *pauperis*, line 2) and the *passum*, already mentioned, of 106; cf. also on 45 *pulli gallinacei* below.

On *mittere*, see at 13.3.5 above.

2 si noluerit mittere dives echoes the hexameter, in so doing delaying and thus heightening the effect of the closing *emes*. For the technique of build-up and closing effect, see Siedschlag 39 ff. M appears to relish the thought that the recipient of his small gift might, paradoxically, end up out of pocket as a result of his generosity.

emes α: **emis** β: **eme** γ. When the apodosis of a conditional clause contains an instruction, this can be conveyed by an imperative ('redargue me, si mentior': Cic. *Clu.* 62) and so *eme* is not impossible; but αβ's agreement on the final *s* makes *emes* probable. (*Emis* may just be a by-form of *emes*; cf. Lindsay's apparatus.) For the future indicative used thus, see Kühner-Stegmann I.144.

13.7 Beans

If pale beans foam in your red pot, you can often turn down the dinners of the luxurious.

le. faba: if correctly identified as *Vicia faba* L., the *faba* was a form of broad bean: see Mynors at Verg. *G.* 1.215 *fabis*. Although the plural form appears in Virgil and is in fact not uncommon (Mynors loc. cit.), the word was cited by grammarians (e.g. Varro *L.* 9.38) as one used only in the singular. The collective singular here, according with the other *lemmata* in poems 6-12, is sustained in line 1 by *conchis*. For the collective singular of *conchis*, cf. Juv. 3.293 'cuius conche tumes'.

For bean recipes, see Apic. 3.96, 5.190-2, 194-5 Budé. Beans were a traditional dish of the poor and lowly (cf. Juv. 3.293), as such being part of the main course at Mart. 10.48.16 and possibly 5.78.10. Otherwise they were served or eaten by the miserly; cf. Juv. 14.131, Mart. 7.78. For their inferior status, see too André *Alimentation* 36, Blümner *Priv.* 165. It accords with the philosophy behind the epigram here, that enough is as good as a feast. (Not dissimilar are the sentiments reflected by Hor. *Carm.* 1.31. Note especially lines 15-16 'me pascunt olivae,/ me cichorea levesque malvae' and see N-H ad loc.)

Beans are characterised as a cheap Saturnalian gift at Mart. 4.46.6; cf. 7.53.5, 10.14(15).5.

1 spumet: the action of foaming is usually transferred in Latin poetry from the contents to the pot; cf. Verg. *Ecl.* 5.67 'pocula bina novo spumantia lacte', *A.* 1.739 'spumantem pateram'; see *OLD* s.v. *spumo* §1. Here, however, M attributes it with stricter accuracy to the beans. For foaming beans, cf. Apic. 5.194 Budé 'pisam sive fabam coques. cum despumaverit, mittis porrum, coriandrum et flores malvarum', 5.191 'ubi despumaverit', 192 'despumatam'.

rubra ... testa: red (i.e. unglazed) earthenware signals low cost or humble station: cf. (with my notes) Mart. 14.114.1 'rubicundam ... testam', 106.1 'ruber urceus'. This accords with the fact that beans are simple fare. For *testa* in humble contexts, cf. also Tib. 2.3.47-8 'at mihi laeta trahant Samiae convivia testae/ fictaque Cumana lubrica terra rota' (describing modest ambitions).

By enclosing 'conchis ... pallida', 'rubra ... testa' contains the beans on the page as well as over the fire.

conchis ... pallida: *conchis* perhaps derives from κόγχος, although the latter is used not of beans but of a kind of soup made from lentils in their pods: Athen. 159F; cf. Apicius' 'concicla cum faba' (5.195 Budé).

Pallida contrasts with *rubra*. Red and white contrasts are common in poetry, albeit usually in more elevated contexts and genres (notorious is Lavinia's blush: Verg. *A*. 12.64 ff.). M's use of the contrast specifically in a lowly context is therefore probably a piece of deliberate inversion.

With *pallida*, cf. Mart. 5.78.10 'pallens faba', Ovid *Med*. 69-70: 'nec tu pallentes dubita torrere lupinos/ et simul inflantes corpora frige fabas'.

2 lautorum cenis saepe negare potes: inferior though the entertainment of lesser guests at the dinners of their patrons might prove (cf. at 13.41.*le*. below), clients could be driven, whether by hunger (the situation on which this poem's reversal is founded) or fear of the indignity of dining at home, to expend great effort on procuring invitations: cf. Mart. 2.14, 18 and 11.24 (and see Kay at line 15, who comments that it is difficult to say to what extent literary convention reflects real life). In saying that someone with enough, however basic it is, is able not only occasionally but often to turn down the dinners even of gourmets, M is, of course, not necessarily saying that this person would do so (cf. 2.69.3 'ipse quoque ad cenam gaudebat Apicius ire') but merely that he could. For one who can and does turn down dinners, at any rate initially (and who lives to regret his eventual succumbing), cf. the auctioneer Vulteius Mena at Hor. *Epist*. 1.7.55-64.

lautorum: for the adjective used substantivally thus, cf. 13.54.2 below, 7.48.4 'has vobis epulas habete, lauti', Pliny *Nat*. 18.108 'cocos tum panem lautioribus coquere solitos'; see *ThLL* VII(2).1054.34 ff. s.v. *lautus* [Beikircher].

saepe codd.: **nempe** Heinsius. The unanimously transmitted *saepe* is central to the poem's point, that self-sufficiency brings freedom and choice. *Nempe*, however, allows a hint of uncertainty which is uncalled for.

negare: *nego* is often used of declining dinner invitations. See *OLD* s.v. *nego* §3b; cf. Pl. *St.* 182 'nulli negare soleo, siqui' me essum vocat', Juv. 14.134, Mart. 2.69.8.

13.8 Groats

Steep common jars with porridge from Clusium so that, when you have eaten your fill, you can drink sweet new wine from the empties.

Like 13.6 *alica*, with which it corresponds in the alternation of cereals and legumes in poems 6-9, this epigram combines reference to a cereal and a drink.

le. far: originally used of crushed emmer, this word came to be used of coarse flour: see Coleman, citing Moritz 221, at Stat. *Silv.* 4.9.31 (where *far* is again a Saturnalian gift; cf. Mart. 4.46.6 and perhaps 10.15(14).5).

Like *alica* (Mart. 13.6), *far* was used to make *puls* (cf. line 2), the traditional form of Roman porridge eaten before the invention of baking (Pliny *Nat.* 18.83-4; see Moritz 149 f., Blümner *Priv.* 160 n.3, 162, André *Alimentation* 60, *Kl.P.* 4.1242.47 ff. s.v. *Puls* [W.H. Groß].) It was a simple dish (Pers. 6.40. Juv. 11.58; cf. the *alica*, *faba* and *lens* of the surrounding epigrams.) Apicius gives recipes at 5.179-82 Budé. It seems often to have been served with sausages: see at Mart. 13.35.2. This epigram is taken by the Loeb editors, ad loc., as suggesting that *puls* was thought to ripen new wine; but their notes possibly oversimplify: see on line 2 below.

Clusium was one of the oldest and most important towns in Etruria: *Kl.P.* 1.1233.39 ff. s.v. *Clusium* [G. Radke]. For the *far* that it yielded, cf. Pliny *Nat.* 18.66 'in transpadana Italia scio vicenas quinas libras farris modios pendere, circa Clusium et senas'.

1 imbue: cf. Quint. *Inst.* 1.1.5 'sapor quo nova (vasa) imbuas'.

plebeias ... ollas: for *plebeius*, see *OLD* s.v. *plebeius* §2b. With *olla* (which replaced the earlier form *aula*: Festus 23M), cf. Juv. 14.171 'fumabant pultibus ollae', Varro *Men.* 190; see *ThLL* II.1453.31 ff. s.v. *aula* [Münscher]. Regarding the vessel, found in every kitchen and made usually of earthenware or bronze, see Blümner *Priv.* 154-5, Hilgers 40. Again (cf. 13.7.1 n.), M's word-order here has the foodstuff contained by the pot.

2 in vacuis: *in* where one would expect *ex* is common in the context of drinking: see *ThLL* VII(1).774.36 ff. s.v. *in* [Bulhart], *OLD* s.v. *in* §24f and my note at Mart. 14.93.2; cf. 14.110.1. But although the *olla* appears, in the form *aula*, as a drinking vessel at Pl. *Mil.* 852 ff., it is more normally used for cooking and M may actually have in mind here boiling must down in it to make a syrup; cf. Mynors at Verg. *G.* 1.295 'dulcis musti ... decoquit umorem'. In other words, the quality of the syrup was thought to be enhanced if the *olla* had previously been used for *puls*, and it is therefore in this sense that *puls* was thought to 'ripen' new wine.

Vacuis gives contrast to *imbue* while also countering *satur*.

13.9 Lentils

Receive from the Nile lentils, a present from Pelusium. They're cheaper than wheat, dearer than beans.

le. lens: the lentil was a commonly farmed legume (see *RE* suppl. VIII.263.38 ff. s.v. *Linse* [H. Gossen]), which was consumed mainly by the lower classes. Thus Aristophanes *Plutus* 1004 has Chremylus say ἔπειτα πλουτῶν οὐκεθ' ἥδεται φακῇ.

Growing lentils was especially associated with Egypt: hence *Niliacam* and *Pelusia*, line 1; cf., with Mynors ad loc., Verg. *G.* 1.228 'Pelusiacae ... lentis': Pelusium was situated at the N.E. corner of the Nile delta, but like *Niliacam* (see at Mart. 13.1.3) here stands for the whole of Egypt. Mynors compares Jerome *in Ezech.* 30.15 'poeta Pelusiacam appellat lentem, non quo ibi genus hoc leguminis gignatur vel maxime, sed quod e Thebaide et omni Aegypto per rivum Nili illuc plurimum deferatur'. For Egyptian lentils, see further M. Schnebel, *Die Landwirtschaft im hellenistichen Ägypten*, Munich 1925, 191-3.

The word *lens* does not often survive in the plural (although see Varro *L.* 9.34) and the singular here accords with the other *lemmata* in poems 6-12. The word is singular also in line 1, where the appositional *munera* owes its plural to metrical convenience.

Apicius gives recipes for cooking lentils at 5.183-5 Budé.

1 accipe Niliacam, Pelusia munera, lentem: cf. Mart. 14.89.1 'accipe felices, Atlantica munera, silvas' and see my note on *munus* ad loc.: thus used, the word occurs less often with an adjective than with the genitive of a proper noun to express its origin (e.g. Sil. 14.663-4 'munera Rubri ... ponti' = pearls), although note also Verg. *G.* 3.527 'Massica ... munera'.

For the phenomenon of parenthetic apposition illustrated by both this line and Mart. 14.89.1, see at 13.1.3 above. By delaying *lentem* here, M allows for its easier comparison with *alica* and *faba* in line 2.

On *accipe*, see Intro. (v) and n. 6 above.

2 vilior est alica, carior illa faba: in their different ways, poems 6 and 7 establish that neither (the gruel made from) *alica* nor the *faba* is expensive. Given this, there is little meaning in an assessment of the relative cost of lentils. Metrically interchangeable pentameter halves (see Intro. (vi) above) help convey the ridiculous nature of the line's assertion, which pokes fun at the materialism with which Saturnalian gifts were often viewed; cf. Intro. (ii) section D above.

For the orthography of *alica*, see Mart. 13.6.*le*. and 1 n.

13.10 Flour

You could not count either the properties or the uses of flour since it comes in handy so often to the baker and the cook.

le. simila Rγ: **simula** β. It is difficult to decide between between *simila* and *simula* here; cf *similam* γ: *simulae* Rβ in line 1. Heraeus notes, however, that *simula* appears to have been the vulgar form, and although this need not have prevented M from using it, it is perhaps best avoided. (Shackleton Bailey attributes to γ the reading *simulam* in line 1, but this appears to be a misprint.)

The substance denoted by *simila* (cf. German *Semmel* and Italian *semolina*) seems to have been finely ground wheat flour. (L-S s.v. *simila* gives as the word's root *si*, i.e. 'to sift', comparing the Greek ἱμαλιά.) This flour was more commonly called *similago* (Moritz 173); cf. Cato *Agr.* 75 'farinae siligineae libram aut, si voles tenerius esse, selibram similaginis … indito'. Despite the epigram's talk of multiple properties or uses, *simila* appears in just two of Apicius' recipes: 5.180 Budé, for porridge, and 7.301 Budé, for a sort of confectionary. *Similago* does not appear in Apicius at all.

1 nec dotes ... possis numerare nec usus: cf. Columella 2.11.6 (of beans) 'inter ceteras dotes, hanc quoque enumerat'. For *dos* thus, see also L-S s.v. *dos* §II. For *numerare* meaning 'to enumerate', see *OLD* s.v. *numero* §5a. It is picked up here by *totiens*, line 2.

For γ's corruption of 'dotes ... possis' via *potes* to 'poteris ... poteris', see Heraeus' apparatus.

2 pistori γ: **pistoris** β: **pistorum** R. *Aptus* needs the dative (see *OLD* s.v. *aptus* §8c, L-S s.v. *apo* §IIIA) and so *pistori*, balanced at the line-end by *coco*, is inescapable. The positioning of these two words helps emphasise the flour's versatility.

In M's day, a well-established commercial baking industry would have taken care of ordinary, everyday demand (see Balsdon *LL* 19); but given his multiple uses for flour, this *pistor* is possibly a specialist confectioner; cf. the *pistor dulciarius* at Mart. 14.222: 'mille tibi dulces operum manus ista figuras/ extruet: huic uni parca laborat apis' and the *pistor* at Petr. 60.4.

Our knowledge of Roman pastry-work is lamentably thin, but a start is provided by J. Solomon, 'Tracta: a versatile Roman pastry', *Hermes* 106 (1978), 539-56.

13.11 Barley

Receive something which your muleteer will not give to the mules (who won't tell). I have given this as a gift not to you but to the inn-keeper.

i.e. the muleteer steals the barley to sell to the inn-keeper, while feeding the mules something cheaper, confident of their inability to report him. Sir Horace Walpole's Gothic Castle at Strawberry Hill extended and modified greatly a cottage built in 1698 by the Earl of Bradford's coachman and known locally as Chopp'd Straw Hall because he paid for it through similar fraudulence (J. Mordaunt Crook, *Country Life*, 7 June 1973).

This epigram is a sort of 'riddle', to which the *lemma* supplies the 'answer'. For similar 'riddling' epigrams or epigrams receiving clarification or explanation by the *lemma*, cf. e.g. 13.20, 54, 59, 65, 71, 72, 73, 75, 93, 103, 104, 106, 108, 109 below. Such poems accord with the practice of distributing Saturnalian gifts by means of a lottery (see Intro. (ii) section D above).

le. hordeum: a bowl of barley survives from Pompeii: *Rediscovering Pompeii* 83. Being suitable for human consumption and indeed a staple cereal in Antiquity (Mynors at Verg. *G.* 1.210), it was not the cheapest fodder: the poor man's mule ate hay, unless he was robbed even of that, as at Mart. 14.162 *faenum*: 'fraudata tumeat fragilis tibi culcita mula'. Nevertheless it was so little regarded that disgraced legionaries were made to eat it rather than wheat as part of their punishment: Suet. *Aug.* 24.2 'cohortes si quae cessissent loco, decimatas hordeo pavit', Livy 27.13.9. Thus it accords with the other, low-class foodstuffs described in poems 6-12, and it is perhaps not surprising that it features in none of Apicius' recipes. For its use in feeding both humans and animals, see *RE* VII.1282.62 ff. s.v. *Gerste* [Orth].

Although usage of *hordea* in the singular was considered barbaric by Quintilian (*Inst.* 1.5.16), it appears *metri causa* in Virgil (see Coleman at *Ecl.* 5.36), who also uses it to denote individual 'grains of barley'. Here *hordeum* accords with the singular *lemmata* of the surrounding epigrams.

1 mulio: muleteers were usually slaves, as is the case here: *tibi*, line 2, refers to the actual recipient of the gift, although it is his *mulio* who gets to handle it. Their status was low (cf. Sen. *Ep.* 47.15 'erras, si existimas me quosdam quasi sordidioris operae reiecturum, ut puta illum mulionem et illum bubulcum') and they were generally treated with contempt (note Juv. 8.148 'mulio consul' with Courtney; cf. Blümner *Priv.* 465 and n. 18.) At Suet. *Vesp.* 22.2 ff., a muleteer takes bribes to delay the emperor so that a litigant can put his case, and M's representation of the *mulio* here accords with this sort of corruption.

Mulio at the beginning of the line is balanced by *mulis* at the end. On M's practice of 'framing' lines with etymologically connected words, see Grewing (ed.) 334. In contrast to the *mulio*, some mules were highly valued (Mart. 3.62.5-6, Pl. *As.* 490-1), the mule being a favourite animal for light carriages (Courtney at Juv. 7.181) and suitable, in miniature breeds, as a pet: note Mart. 14.197 *mulae pumilae* with my notes ad loc. In general, see *Kl.P.* 2.370.17 ff. s.v. *Esel* [Richter].

non det βγ: **non dam** T. Lindsay (cf. Izaac) wonders whether T's reading corrupts *non das*; but although this may be so the matter is academic since *das* makes poor sense: the *mulio* cannot be the recipient in the poem, except as an agent coming between the *copo* and the poem's addressee, without there being a seeming contradiction between *accipe* and 'non tibi ... dedi' (line 2). (On *accipe*, see Intro. (v) and n. 6 above.)

2 haec ... dona: *dona* (acc. of respect/direct object?) conflicts with the singular *lemma*. Such numerical differences between poem and *lemma*, found also in Book 14 (see my note at Mart. 14.21.*le.*), are common in Book 13 and can be ordered as follows.

Sometimes after singular *lemmata* plurals are used for metrical convenience. This is the case here. Other metrically convenient plurals are to be found in 13.17, 38, 107, 110, 113, 115, 116. Cf. also 13.9.1 'Pelusia munera' above.

Sometimes after a plural *lemma* singulars are used which may be metrically convenient, but which can be classified further as 'generalising' in that they refer not to the actual gift in question but, e.g., to the group or species to which it belongs or the function or reputation which the foodstuff described typically fulfilled or enjoyed. Examples appear in 13.14, 18, 23, 27, 36, 52, 53, 60, 62, 63-4, 65, 68, 70, 74, 77, 78, 79, 80, 81, 86, 92.

Finally, although metrical convenience may be a factor, several poems contain poetic devices such as personification which call for singulars and which account for a further category of numerical differences between *lemma* and poem. Examples are provided by poems 13.22, 35, 71, 76, 82. Also 13.49, 59, 72.

coponi: the inn-keeper at Hor. *Serm.* 1.1.29 is described as *perfidus*, in accordance with the reputation of his profession (see T. Kleberg, *Hôtels, Restaurants et Cabarets dans L'Antiquité Romaine,* Uppsala 1957, 6, Lionel Casson, *Travel in the Ancient World,* London 1974, 204). Inn-keepers were notorious e.g. for putting too much water in the wine: see Howell at Mart. 1.56; contrast the humorous Mart. 3.57.1-2, describing a *copo* of Ravenna (where water was scarce) who sold *merum* as *mixtum*.

Otherwise, they were known for using their hostelries as a cover for brothels (Casson ibid.; cf. Smith at Petr. 61.6) and for robbing or killing their guests (Casson ibid. 204-5, Smith at Petr. 62.12). This *copo* was doubtless not alone in receiving stolen goods.

dedi Tγ: **dabo** β. Shackleton Bailey thinks *dabo* is possibly right; but *dedi* goes better after *accipe*, line 1, at which point title to the gift (if not actual possession) will have changed hands, and carries an air of finality which accords better with the reputation of the muleteer: the barley is as good as stolen already.

13.12 Corn

Take three hundred pecks from the harvest of the Libyan farmer, lest your land near the city die.

le. frumentum: corn was a staple food and played a significant part in the politics of Rome, given the extent to which popular contentment and even (especially under the Republic) civil order depended on an adequate food supply: see Peter Garnsey, *Famine and Food Supply in the Graeco-Roman World*, Cambridge 1988, 206 ff., 240-3. Domitian's notorious vine edict of 91 was perhaps intended to insure against the dangers posed by shortages: see B. Levick, *Latomus* 41 (1982), 68-9. For the careful regulation of corn supplies and prices, see *Kl.P.* 2.622.39 ff. s.v. *Frumentum* [G. Schrot].

When dealing with this poem, Friedländer suggests ad loc. that the corn it refers to might be for sowing in the erroneous belief that non-indigenous seed lessened soil exhaustion; but his preferred explanation, offered also by the Loeb editors, is along the lines that an occasional grain import of the size specified here would allow the farmer to let his land lie fallow every so often. Of these explanations, the latter is certainly the more likely.

Although translated 'peck' above, the *modius* is more meaningfully converted today into litres. (The weight of grain can vary according to strain and quality, which may be why measures of capacity are traditional.) Richard Duncan Jones, *The Economy of the Roman Empire*,[2] Cambridge 1982, 371, puts the Italic *modius* at 8.62 litres. Varro, *R.* 1.44.1, specifies a sowing ratio of 5 *modii* per *iugerum* (c. 0.25 km²); cf. Columella 2.9.1, Pliny *Nat.* 18.198. If the imported corn of this poem was intended for sowing, this would suggest a sowing area measuring 60 *iugera* (c. 15 km²); but this seems rather large for a 'suburbanus ager'. Consider that Columella gives as the maximum yield for cereals in Italy a fourfold increase, although he makes it clear that he is talking about days gone by rather than his own: 3.3.4. A holding of 60 *iugera* would therefore yield a maximum of 1200 *modii*. Columella, 2.12.7, gives a staffing ratio of 8 slaves per 200 *iugera* of arable land, that is 1 per 25. An estate of 60 *iugera* could therefore be worked easily by 3 slaves. Cato allowed his unchained field slaves 4 to 4.5 *modii* of corn per month (Cato *Agr.* 56; cf. Duncan Jones, op. cit. 146, for comparable figures from other sources). A yield of 1200 *modii* would more than adequately support three slaves (144-62 *modii per annum*) and leave ample for sowing or funding the purchase of more seed for sowing, livestock (1 ox per 50 *iugera*: Columella 2.12.7) and the master. For all it would have been minute in comparison, e.g., with the latifundia which destroyed Italy (Pliny *Nat.* 18.35), a holding of 60 *iugera* would therefore be a fairly comfortably viable concern, and would thus not accord with the poor productivity traditionally claimed for suburban estates and would deny the poem its humour (see below).

If the imported corn is to allow fallowing, however, then a much smaller estate is indicated. Columella recommends fallowing land in alternate years (2.9.4, 15, 10.7, 12.7-10; cf. Pliny *Nat.* 18.187, Varro *R.* 1.44.2-3), but he has in mind farms big enough for field rotation. Since the pentameter implies that the whole 'suburbanus ager' will die without the Libyan grain, clearly this is not a possibility here. Rather, it seems reasonable to take the 300 *modii* of line 1 to equal the entire farm's annual yield. This gives M's *ager* a size of some 15 *iugera* (c. 3.8 km²), i.e. quarter of the size of the earlier estate, but nonetheless still amply big enough for a smallholding that, while not unproductive, is principally a country retreat rather than a commercial concern (cf. Mart. 6.43 with Shackleton Bailey's Loeb note on line 4).

Shackleton Bailey observes (Teubner apparatus; cf. his Loeb note) that 300 *modii* seems a great deal for a Saturnalian gift and it is certainly out of proportion to the other gifts described in Book 13; but large gifts were not entirely unknown: e.g. Mart. 14.122 *anuli* (see my note ad loc.) implies a gift of money equal to or meeting that still needed for the Equestrian *census*; and in any case, in the light of the figures above, 300 *modii* is not as much as it might initially seem: given that 75 would be needed for the next year's sowing and the estate's owner would have to feed himself, his household (probably including at least two slaves: one to attend to the estate and one to his personal needs) and his livestock, there would be little to spare. The joke of the poem is, in fact, that it would take so *little* to save the farm from over-cultivation, the commonly proclaimed small-ness and poor productivity of suburban estates being a regular source of humour: see Izaac's Budé note on Mart. 11.18, 13.119.*le.* n. below; cf. e.g. Mart. 3.47, Quint. *Inst.* 8.6.73 (Cic. fr. 4 Courtney).

1 Libyci ... de messe coloni: by Libya is meant North Africa. For *Libycus* thus used, cf. also Mart. 13.45.1, 14.91.2 and see *OLD* s.v. *Libycus* §1a. For African corn, cf. e.g. Mart. 6.86.5 'Libycas messis' (with Grewing), Ovid *Med.* 53 'hordea quae Libyci ratibus misere coloni', Hor. *Carm.* 1.1.10; see G.E. Rickman, *The Corn Supply of Ancient Rome*, Oxford 1980, 108 ff., Courtney at Juv. 8.117 (with further bibliography).

Coloni could be farmers (*OLD* s.v. *colonus* §1) as they are principally here, but could also be inhabitants of or settlers in a Roman colony (*OLD* s.v. *colonus* §4a). It is possibly worth remembering that the area around Carthage was colonised by the Gracchi, Caesar and Augustus, and that the city was refounded as Colonia Iulia Carthago (see *Kl.P* 3.138.4 ff. s.v. *Karthago* [G. Schrot]).

2 sume approximates to *accipe*: cf. Intro. (v) and n. 6 above.

suburbanus ... **ager**: cf. Stat. *Silv.* 4.4.7 'suburbanis ... hortis'. The most popular areas for suburban estates were Tibur, Tusculum, Praeneste, Lanuvium and Nomentum. Ideally, they were about 15 miles from Rome. Not all were small and unassuming, of course: see Balsdon *LL* 196 ff., A.G. McKay, *Houses, Villas and Palaces in the Roman World*, 1975, 108 ff. Note too the profitable Nomentan estate owned by the Younger Seneca (see Pliny *Nat.* 14.48-52). It has often been supposed that M's own Nomentan estate was originally part of this land and was left to him by Seneca (see e.g. Sullivan 4, Howell at Mart. 1.105); but if so it is surprising that he never mentions his benefactor: see M. Kleijwegt, 'A question of patronage: Seneca and Martial', *Acta Classica* 42 (1999), 115.

moriatur: used of land, *morior* appears rare, although cf. Stat. *Theb.* 5.528 'moritur ... ad sibila (sc. serpentis) campus'. Of plants, however, it appears regularly: *ThLL* VIII.1494.21 ff. s.v. *morior* [Lumpe].

13.13 Beet

So that tasteless beet, the lunch of workmen, has flavour, o how often will the cook seek wine and pepper!

With this poem begins a series on salads and vegetables ending with Mart. 13.21.

le. betae: cf. Petr. 56.8, in the punning list of *apophoreta* there: ' "muraena et littera": murem cum rana alligata fascemque betae <accepit>'. Apicius gives several recipes involving beet. Note especially 4.175 Budé 'gustum versatile', which contains small white beets and, amongst other things, wine and pepper. For serving suggestions, see also Pliny *Nat.* 19.132. As is suggested by 'fabrorum prandia', line 1 (see ad loc.), it was a lowly dish: note Blümner *Priv.* 167; cf. Pers. 3.114 'plebeia ... beta'. Beet is also mentioned, in what seems to be a list of *gustatio* dishes, at Pliny *Ep.* 1.15.2: see Mart. 13.6.*le.* n. It is several times cited as a laxative: note e.g. Mart. 3.47.9 'pigroque ventri non inutiles betas', Pliny *Nat.* 20.71, and the relevance to this poem of these laxative properties is illuminated at Mart. 13.14.2 below.

1 fatuus meaning 'insipid' or 'tasteless' is found in classical Latin only in M; cf. Mart. 7.25.7 'dato fatuas ... mariscas', 10.37.9 'et fatuam ... cenare pelorida'; see *ThLL* VI(1).372.33 ff. s.v. *fatuus* [Hofmann]. Its meaning can be deduced from 'ut sapiant' and from the cook's frequent recourse to the seasoning effect of wine and pepper ('o quam saepe', line 2).

fabrorum prandia: *prandium* can be used generally of meals (cf. Mart. 4.49.3-4) but is usually applied specifically to the mid-day meal. This meal was never large (Carcopino 287), and a *prandium* qualified as here is likely to be extremely ordinary (cf. Mart. 14.81.1 'mendica ... prandia' with my note ad loc., Pers. 5.18 'plebeia ... prandia'): although a *faber* might be highly skilled (as was perhaps the 'faber argentarius' at *CIL* VI.9392) or specialised, like the 'faber oculariarius' (sic: *CIL* VI.9042), who may have made silver eyes for statues, many would have been just workmen or builders: see *OLD* s.v. *faber* §1c, L-S s.v. *faber* § 1B.

2 o quam saepe: exclamations are common in the epigrammatists: Siedschlag 102 n. 5. With M's usage here, cf. 14.119.2 'o quotiens ...' and 6.58.3 'o quam paene ...', at which Grewing gives discussion. The collocation 'o quam' and adverb occurs again at 7.31.7 (*diligenter*).

13.14 Lettuce

The lettuce which used to end our ancestors' dinners, tell me, why does it begin our feasts?

le. lactucae: the plural (contrast the generalising *lactuca* in line 1) agrees with *betae*, Mart. 13.13.*le*. For numerical differences between *lemma* and poem, see Mart. 13.11.2 n. above. Like beet, lettuce was credited with medical properties, again being regarded as a laxative: see on line 2 below, where see also for its use as an appetiser. In general, see *Kl.P.* 3.440.57 ff. s.v. *Lactuca* [K. Ziegler].

1 cludere ... cenas: for lettuce ending a meal, cf. *Mor.* 74 'grataque nobilium requies lactuca ciborum': the change in practice of which M speaks must have been post-Augustan. *Cludo* used to indicate the completion or ending of an activity survives elsewhere at Sen. *Tro.* 139 and Stat. *Theb.* 2.306-7 'regales epulas ... clusere dies'. Its meaning here is plainly established by the contrasting *inchoat*, line 2.

At Petr. 66.1 the word *cena* is used of a considerable feast, but it is not normally suggestive of such. *Daps*, on the other hand (line 2), has elevated associations (see *ThLL* VI.36.41 ff. s.v. *daps* [Gudeman], Coleman at Stat. *Silv.* 4.9.51-2 'aut cum me dape iuveris opima,/ expectes similis et ipse dapes'). M is contrasting present and past not only with regard to when lettuce was served but also with regard to the lavishness of the dinners at which it was served.

avorum: *avus* is a grandfather (*OLD* s.v. *avus* §2) or, as here, an ancestor (*OLD* s.v. *avus* §1). The word commonly suggests, again as here, the old-fashioned values and upright morality thought to characterise the past: see *ThLL* II.1611.73 ff. s.v. *avus* [Ihm]. With the genitive usage *avorum*, contrast the possessive adjective *nostras* in line 2.

2 cur nostras inchoat illa dapes?: M asks similar questions at 13.49 below and 14.121 *coclearia*: 'sum cocleis habilis sed nec minus utilis ovis./ numquid scis, potius cur cocleare vocer?'; cf. Siedschlag 83 n.7. The humour of these two epigrams rests on there being no logical answer to their questions. Here, however, while M's question humorously suggests by its choice of words (*cena/daps, avus*) that the eating of lettuce at the beginning of a meal is a definitive symptom of contemporary moral turpitude, a definite answer to it can nonetheless be attempted. At Hor. *Serm.* 2.4.59-60 'non lactuca innatat acri/ post vinum stomacho', we learn that lettuce and wine do not mix. Since most drinking at Roman dinners was done at the end (cf. Intro. (iii) above), it would make sense therefore to eat lettuce at the beginning. Indeed, lettuce appears to have been acknowledged as an appetiser: cf. Pliny *Nat.* 19.127 'stomacho fastidium auferunt cibique adpetentiam faciunt', Mart. 10.48.11, Pliny *Ep.* 1.15.2 (quoted at Mart. 13.6.*le.* n.), Columella 10.179. In this context, note also Mart. 11.52.5 'prima tibi dabitur ventri lactuca movendo/ utilis', remembering the laxative properties, already identified, of beet (Mart. 13.13). The topic of bowel action was of great interest to the Romans (see Kay 182-3), and M mentions astringents (cf. 13.26 and 116) and laxatives several times (note also 3.89.1, again referring to lettuce, and 13.29 below). The appearance of laxatives at the beginning of a meal or menu is especially common. Note also Mart. 10.48.7-8 'exoneratas ventrem mihi vilica malvas attulit'. It could be that they were intended to loosen one's bowels in the belief that this would aid digestion of the courses to come, a variation perhaps of 'vomunt ut edant': note Trimalchio's account of the arrangements he has made for guests needing to retire, and their amusement, not realising themselves 'in medio [lautitiarum], quod aiunt, clivo laborare' (Petr. 47.8).

inchoat RQ: **inchoet** βγ. *Inchoat* is universally favoured by editors, but as Heraeus notes (at Mart. 3.95.3 'cur hoc expectas (Tγ: -tes β) a me, rogo ... dicas'), choosing between indicative and subjunctive is very difficult. Is one dealing with a direct or indirect question? In addition to 3.95.3, note Mart. 3.88.2 'dicite, dissimiles sunt (γ: sint β) magis an similes?', 5.55.1 'dic mihi, quem portas (β: -es γ), volucrum regina?'. If, as Howell suggests (at Mart. 1.20.1 and 5.55.1), *dic* recalls the εἰπέ of Greek epigram, it is possible that M is reflecting the Greek graphic form.

13.15 Smokeless wood

If you farm land near Nomentum, I advise you, Countryman, to take wood
to your farmhouse.

1e. ligna acapna γ: **ligna actua** T: **ligna** (om. **acapna**) β. For *ligna
acapna*, see *ThLL* I.248.65 ff. s.v. *acapnus* [Diehl], to which Heraeus adds
Cass. Fel. 192.8 and Steph. *Thes.* s.v. ἄκαπνος. The correctness of γ's
reading seems firmly established, but there has been puzzlement over the
precise significance of *acapna* (unparalleled in this context, but possibly a
technical term: Howell 38) and the presence here of firewood, amidst salad
and vegetable dishes, is anyway difficult to explain.

Shackleton Bailey is probably correct in maintaining (in Appendix A of
his Loeb) that there is no reason for taking *villam*, line 2, to refer to M's
own villa at Nomentum (for which, cf. Mart. 13.12.2 n. above and at 119
Nomentanum below). Instead, he follows the view that the epigram is a
piece of neighbourly advice: 'Get your wood under cover, so that it will be
dry and smoke-free'. As regards the giving of advice, he is again probably
right; but as to the nature of the advice he is possibly mistaken. If keeping
wood dry is in question it seems natural to assume from the poem that
Nomentum was notoriously wet. Yet M tells us on two occasions that it
was dry (12.57.1; cf. 9.18.3-4 'sed de valle brevi quas det sitientibus hortis/
curva laborantes antlia tollit aquas'); and if Pala is correct to identify the
town as modern Casali (Corrado Pala, *Nomentum. Forma Italiae Regio* I,
vol. XII, Rome 1976, 12), rather than the nearby Mentana, as has become
traditional, then the large number of wells, cisterns and conduits found
there (ibid. 15) might corroborate what M says. (Pala himself, be it said,
draws no conclusions from the evidence, some of which is possibly conflicting). Shackleton Bailey tries to resolve any difficulty by saying (loc. cit.)
that 'dry as it might be, at least in summer, there would be some rain'; but
this attempt does not carry much conviction. It seems to me instead that
the wetness or otherwise of Nomentum is irrelevant to the poem. Rather,
I suggest that it is Nomentum's well-established country setting that is
important, since it is in the country that one found open hearths. (For the
topos, see D.West, *Reading Horace*, Edinburgh 1967, 4 f.) M's advice to his
neighbour is not to store firewood out of the rain, but to take pre-treated
and therefore smokeless wood with him from Rome when he visits his
estate. Howell 38 quotes Forbes VI.32, referring to the fuel used in
braziers indoors: 'wood was not smokeless unless specially pretreated and
selected'. Firewood could be made smokeless artificially by soaking it in
water, or in the lees of oil, and then drying it (Cato 130; cf. Pliny *Nat.* 15.4).
In choosing Nomentum as his typical rural setting here, M is more likely
to have been influenced by its general reputation and by metrical concerns
than by his personal associations with the place; but that he owned an

estate there himself nonetheless adds a self-conscious element to the ironic humour present in line 2: see at *rustice* below.

1 rura: for *rus* referring in particular to a land-holding or estate, see *OLD* s.v. *rus* §2, L-S s.v. *rus*. As for the plural, far more frequent in poetry than the singular, cf. Verg. *G.* 2.413-14 'laudato ingentia rura,/ exiguum colito' with Mynors and see Austin at *A.* 4.527.

2 moneo ... feras: for *moneo* thus, without *ut*, cf. Livy 33.35.9, Sen. *Ep.* 120.6; see L-H-Sz II.530.

rustice: a *figura etymologica* of sorts, with 'rura coluntur'. The *rusticus* was a country dweller, as opposed to someone who lived in a town. M's use of the word here is ironic since his addressee is not a real countryman who can take care of himself using the resources he has to hand but a city dweller who is seeking brief rural respite, who does not seriously cultivate his land (for the poor productivity of suburban estates, see 13.12.*le.* n. above), and who needs to take ready made accessories and conveniences with him when leaving town.

13.16 Turnips

These turnips which I give you, rejoicing in the winter cold, Romulus is accustomed to eat in heaven.

le. rapa: the turnip (*rapum, -i*, n./*rapa, -ae*, f.) or *brassica rapa* was a simple food (cf. Columella 2.10.22; see *Kl.P.* 4.1464.49 ff. s.v. *Rübe* [K. Ziegler], Blümner *Priv.* 167), and the donor therefore appears here to be specially commending his gift by mentioning its association with Romulus. (For gifts rendered valuable by their association with famous personalities, see my note at Mart. 14.98.*le.*) His recommendation is probably not without ironic and subversive humour, however. The notion that the deified Romulus preserved his simple tastes even in heaven originated possibly with the satirical Lucilius, to whom Bücheler and others ascribe the half-line at Sen. *Apoc.* 9.5. There Hercules recommends that Claudius be admitted to heaven since it is in the interests of the State that there should be someone 'qui cum Romulo possit "ferventia rapa vorare" '. Skutsch shows, with reference to Martial (cf. line 2 below) and Seneca, to Pompeian graffiti (*CIL* IV.3135, 7353, 8568, 8995) and to Enn. *Ann.* 110 Sk. 'Romulus in caelo cum dis genitalibus aevom/ degit', that the first part of this line was almost certainly 'Romulus in caelo': see his edition and, with greater clarity, *Studia Enniana*, London 1963, 111.

Apicius gives directions regarding the preservation of turnips (1.25 Budé) and recipes for cooking them (3.100-1 Budé). Turnips also feature in a sauce for crane or duck (6.214 Budé) and a fish recipe (exc. 7 Budé).

1 brumali gaudentia frigore rapa: turnips are a cold-season crop and December harvests are by no means impossible in southern Europe. For the Saturnalia's mid-winter date, see at 13.1.4 above.

gaudentia: cf. Pliny *Nat*. 18.131 '[napi] gaudent ... frigidis', Columella 3.2.15 '[vites Amineae] pingui ... arvo maxime gaudeant', 5.6.16 'parum gaudet ulmus in corpus nuda'; see *ThLL* VI(2).1708.22 ff. s.v. *gaudeo* [Hey].

13.17 A bundle of cabbage stalks

So that pale cabbage stalks do not disgust you, let the cabbage become green with water mixed with nitrate.

le. fascis coliculi γ: **fascis coli** T: **fasces coliculorum** β. T's reading supports γ's generic singular, the difference arising through haplography. The plural reading of β (cf. Mart. 13.38.*le.* 'fasces calamorum') was perhaps influenced by the metrically convenient 'pallentes ... caules', line 1. (For numerical differences between *lemma* and poem, see 13.11.2 n. above.)

The *coliculus* was either a small cabbage, or a cabbage stalk (a sort of broccoli?). That we have a bundle here suggests the latter. (For bundles, cf. Prop. 4.2.44 'iunco brassica vincta levi'.) *Fascis* survives surprisingly seldom of such bundles, being otherwise confined to Petr. 56.8 'fascem ... betae'. Cabbage was a staple Roman foodstuff (*RE* XI.1037.6 ff. s.v. *Kohl* [Orth]) and a traditional food of the poor: see Courtney at Juv. 1.134 'caulis miseris atque ignis emendus'. This is not to say, however, that it was shunned by the better off: it is, after all, an appetiser here rather than a main course. Apicius gives several recipes, either for *coliculi* alone (Apic. 3.88-92 Budé), or used in other dishes (see the Budé index).

M seems to have used the spelling *coliculus* for the diminutive: note Mart.12.25.4, 14.101.2 and 5.78.7 'coliculus virens' (where the *coliculus* is again part of the *gustatio*; cf. possibly also Hor. *Serm*. 1.4.15 ff.); but when not using the diminutive, he favoured *caulis*, as here (line 1). Lindsay makes no comment in *Orth*.

1 pallentes ... caules: cf. Juv. 5.87 'pallidus ... caulis', Automedon *Anth.P*. 11.325.2 (= Gow-Page *GP* 1550) κράμβης μήλινον ἀσπάραγον ('yellow shoot of cabbage'). Cabbage tends to become pale in the process of boiling, but this could be prevented or rectified ('viridis brassica fiat', line 2) by adding nitron to the water, nitron being a compound of potassium and sodium – like saltpetre; cf. Pliny *Nat*. 19.143 'nitron in coquendo etiam viriditatem custodit'; see Marquardt *Prl*. 342, *RE* XI.959.13 ff. s.v. *Kochkunst* [Orth].

moveant fastidia: cf. Ovid *Pont*. 1.10.7 'positae ... movent fastidia mensae'. For *fastidium* of distaste felt for food, cf. also Pliny *Nat*. 19.127, quoted at Mart. 13.14.2 above and see L-S s.v. *fastidium* §3, *OLD* s.v. *fastidium* §1, *ThLL* VI(1).316.8 ff. s.v. *fastidium* [Ammann]; for *moveo* thus, see further *OLD* s.v. *moveo* §16a, *ThLL* VIII.1545.58 ff. s.v. *moveo* [Wieland].

13.18 Cut leeks

Whenever you have eaten the strong-smelling shoots of Tarentine leek, give tight-lipped kisses.

le. porri sectivi: there were two types of leek (*porrus/-m*, *-i*, m., n.), *porrum sectivum / sectile / tonsile* and *porrum capitatum* (cf. Mart. 13.19 below). Hence Mart. 3.47.8 'utrumque porrum'. The *porrum capitatum* was allowed to grow so that a leafy head appeared at the top of the stalk – as with our leeks; cf. Priap. 51.16 'crescens ... in suum caput porrum'. In contrast, *porrum sectivum* was sown thickly and the young blades were cut and eaten like asparagus; cf. Columella 11.3.30 'porrum si sectivum facere velis, densius satum praeceperunt priores relinqui'.

Although Nero is said to have eaten *porrum sectivum* (in an attempt to improve his voice: Pliny *Nat.* 19.108), it was traditionally a poor man's dish; cf. *Moretum* 83-4 'secti ... famem domat area porri'. Hence the rich thug in Juv. 3 pretends that he can smell 'sectile porrum' (line 293) on his poor victim's breath; cf. 'graviter redolentia', line 1 below, and Mart. 5.78.5 'gravesque porri'.

While the variety of leek at Mart. 5.78.5 is not identified, *porrum sectivum* is served as a *gustatio* also at Mart. 10.48.9 'tonsile porrum' and 11.52.6 'porris fila resecta suis'. It occurs also, albeit not specifically as a *gustatio*, at Juv. 14.33 'filaque sectivi ... porri'. In general, see André *Alimentation* 27, 199 (used as seasoning). Apicius gives several recipes for or involving leeks (3.93-6 Budé), but none specifically for or involving *porrum sectivum*.

Columella, 8.11.14, also speaks of leeks from Tarentum, a town in southern Italy (Táranto) whose leeks appear from this poem to have been particularly strong, and from where one might otherwise obtain e.g. wool (Pl. *Truc.* 649) and pears (Cels. 4.26.5). This epigram begins a series of four where the gifts' origins are identified.

1 fila: cf. Mart. 11.52.6 and Juv. 14.33, both quoted above. For other instances of the word used of plants and the like, see *ThLL* VI(1).762.41 ff. s.v. *filum* [Lackenbacher].

porri: for the generalising singular, see 13.11.2 n. above.

2 oscula clusa dato: regarding the greeting kiss see Kay's introduction to Mart. 11.98, a poem complaining about a persistent *basiator*. Such kissing was known albeit relatively scarce in the late Republic, but became so popular in the 1st century that Tiberius passed an edict to stop it (Suet. *Tib.* 34.2), possibly to reduce the spreading of a common contemporary fungoid mouth disease. M has several epigrams on nuisance kissers. In addition to 11.98, note 2.10, 12, 21-3 (a cycle regarding a certain Postumus), 7.59 (on someone who gives cold kisses in mid-winter), and 12.59, especially lines 4-10, which catalogue people one would rather not be kissed by (at line 9, Nisbet suggests *illinc*: see Bowie's thesis):

> te vicinia tota, te pilosus
> hircoso premit osculo colonus;
> hinc instat tibi textor, inde fullo,
> hinc sutor modo pelle basiata,
> hinc menti dominus periculosi,
> †hinc† dexiocholus, inde lippus,
> fellatorque recensque cunnilingus.

In the present epigram, M is not attacking the greeting (or indeed any) kiss, however, but merely enjoins those doing the kissing to have regard for what they have been eating beforehand.

13.19 Headed leeks

Well-wooded Aricia sends outstanding leeks: note the green leaves on the snow-white stem.

le. porri capitati: for the 'porrum capitatum', see at Mart. 13.18.*le.* above. Aricia, line 1, was in Latium. On the quality of its leeks, note Pliny *Nat.* 19.110 'laudatissimum [sc. porrum] Aegypto, mox Ostiae atqu Ariciae'. Leeks aside, it was famous for its grove sacred to Diana, for which see Fordyce at Verg. *A.* 7.763. Hence *nemoralis*, line 1; but see further below. In general, see *Kl.P.* 1.546.41 ff. s.v. *Aricia* [G. Radke].

1 mittit Tγ: **mittis** β. Where the active voice of *mitto* is elsewhere used in Mart. 13 and 14 and its subject is a place (13.23.1, 112.2, 14.51.1, 70.2 Leary, 152.1; cf. 13.69.1 *dedit*, 14.38.1 and 150.2 *dat*), the place is not apostrophised. That and majority MS support guarantees *mittit* here. Regarding the usage of the word both in relation to exports and otherwise, see at 13.23.1 n. below.

praecipuos: for the meaning 'outstanding', see *OLD* s.v. *praecipuus* §2a, L-S s.v. *praecipuus* §II. The quality of these leeks is stressed by their size (note *stipite*, line 2, on which see ad loc.) and the emphasis given to their colouring (note the juxtaposition of *niveo* and *virides*).

nemoralis: cf. Ovid *Fast*. 6.59 'nemoralis Aricia', Lucan 6.75, *A.L.* 304.1, Cato *Orig.* 2.21 Jordan 'in nemore Aricino'. Note also Mart. 9.64.3 *nemorosa*.

2 stipite: *stips* is more appropriate to tree trunks and the like (*OLD* s.v. *stipes* §1) than insubstantial leek stalks. Thus it expands here on *praecipuos*, line 1; but it also adds an unexpected dimension to *nemoralis* in hinting that the grove of Aricia is a grove not of trees but leeks!

cerne comas: for *coma* of the awn of plants, see *OLD* s.v. *coma* §3b, *ThLL* III.1752.75 ff. s.v. *coma* [Leissner]. Helped by the c alliteration, *cerne* directs the reader pointedly to the distinguishing feature of the *porrum capitatum*. *Comas* is further emphasised by its position at the end of the line. On *verba videndi* in M, see generally at 13.58.1 below.

13.20 French turnips

The land of Amiternum brings these forth in fertile gardens. You can eat more sparingly the balls of Nursia.

le. napi: in his Loeb note, Ker identifies the *napus* as the French turnip (*Brassica napus* L). According to Pliny the difference between the *rapa* (see Mart. 13.16) and *napus* is artificial, depending on where or how one plants the seed, which is the same for both. See *Nat.* 18.129; cf. Columella 2.10.23: the *rapa* likes moisture; the *napus* prefers good drainage and light soil. The *napus* grows long and carrot-like, while the *rapa* is round (hence *pilas*, line 2). The *napus* was prepared for eating in the same way as the *rapa*: see Apic. 3.100-1 Budé, and being, like the *rapa*, a cold-season crop (Pliny *Nat.* 18.131) would also have been readily available at the Saturnalia.

Amiternum was a Sabine town famed for the prime quality of its *napi*: cf. Pliny *Nat.* 18.130. The best *rapae* came, however, from Nursia, some 30 km to the north of Amiternum: Pliny loc. cit.; with 'in Nursino agro' there, contrast 'Amiternus ager', line 1. This epigram turns on the rival merits of the two places' produce.

1 hos Tγ: om. β: **nos** ς. Heraeus compares Mart. 14.12.1 'hos (Tβγ: nos R) nisi de flava loculos implere moneta/ non decet', where the emphatic and better testified *hos* is clearly preferable. *Nos* is not impossible here, but *hos* is well attested and unobjectionable. Although the rivalry between Nursian and Amiternan produce was doubtless well known, the *lemma* nonetheless clarifies what it is to which *hos* refers. For the *lemma*'s explanatory function, see the introductory n. to 13.11 above.

felicibus ... hortis: *felix* survives thus used with *hortus* only here in classical Latin, but its meaning 'fertile' is common enough: *ThLL* VI(1).436.15 ff. s.v. *felix* [Ammann].

Hortus is commonly used of the fruit or vegetable garden: see *ThLL* VI(3).3015.58 ff. [Ehlers]. For details, see K.D. White, *Roman Farming*, London 1970, 246 f.; cf. Priap. 51.2, 15 (quoted below), 24, Prop. 4.2.41 ff., and see *OLD* s.v. *hortus* §1a. The plural form used here is admittedly metrically convenient (with *felicibus*) but is probably also a 'real' plural, i.e. it indicates more gardens than one: usually the plural form is used to designate not many vegetable gardens but a single pleasure garden (cf. Howell at Mart. 5.62.1.)

educat: cf. Priap. 51.15 'betas ... quantas hortus educat nullus' and see *OLD* s.v. *educo*² §1c.

2 Nursinas poteris parcius esse pilas: i.e. thanks to Amiternum you do not have to eat them at all. For *parcius* thus, cf. *OLD* s.v. *parce* §2. The strong p alliteration in this line is probably fortuitous. Although entirely different in subject and meaning, Mart. 14.26.2 'captivis poteris cultior esse comis' is comparable in form and arrangement. The expression 'Nursina pila' is unparalleled, but note *rotunda* of the *rapa* at Pliny *Nat.* 19.75 (contrast 'latiora ... et concava' of the *napus*).

13.21 Asparagus

The tender stalk which grew in coastal Ravenna will not be more welcome than wild asparagus.

le. asparagi: Ravenna, line 1, was an important sea-port in Cispadine Gaul: see *Kl.P.* 4.1342.40 ff. s.v. *Ravenna* [G. Radke]. Hence it is *aequorea* here (line 1). It produced asparagus remarkable for its size and weight (Pliny *Nat.* 19.54). Nevertheless, wild asparagus (*corruda*: Pliny loc. cit.) was commonly considered better than asparagus which was cultivated (cf. Pliny *Nat.* 19.146, Athen. 2.62E). In being superior not only to cultivated asparagus in general but to the tender produce of Ravenna (*mollis*, line 1) this epigram's wild asparagus is therefore doubly commendable.

For asparagus generally, see André *Alimentation* 23. Apicius gives recipes for asparagus *patinae* at 4.132-3 Budé and one for boiled asparagus at 3.72 Budé. Asparagus features as part of the *gustatio* also at Macr. 3.13.12: 'ante cenam ... turdum asparagus subtus'.

1 mollis ... spina: *mollis* occurs again of asparagus at Lucil. 945 'asparagi molles'. As for *spina* (here a generalising singular), cf. Columella 11.3.46 'cum spinam fecerit (asparagus)', Pliny *Nat.* 21.91 'ergo quaedam herbarum spinosae sunt, quaedam sine spinis ... in totum spina est asparagus'.

aequorea: cf. Mart. 10.58.1 'Anxuris aequorei', Ovid *Met*. 15.752 'aequoreos Britannos'. The word's usage of places near or connected with the sea survives only in poetry.

2 asparagis: on M's polysyllabic pentameter endings, see Intro. (vi) above.

13.22 Hard grapes

I am a grape unfit for wine ladles and useless to Lyaeus, but I shall be nectar to you if you don't drink me.

le. uvae duracinae: this poem begins a well-integrated section on fruit which ends with poem 29. The first two of these poems (22-3) are linked by reference to wine or Bacchus, poems 23 and 24 describe gifts which take their designations from places, 24 and 25 allude to a mythical or divine personage (other than Bacchus), 25 and 26 are linked by *poma*, and the remaining three (27-9) deal with produce from Syria or the East, 28 and 29 being linked by *vas* and all three having a genitive plural in the *lemma*. Laxative properties are identified in 29, contrasting with the astringent *sorba* of 26.

The grapes described by this poem were for eating, not vinting. Augustus speaks of his having some while on a drive: 'dum lectica ex regia domum redeo, panis unciam cum paucis acinis uvae duracinae comedi' (quoted at Suet. *Aug*. 76.2). Regarding them, see too Pliny *Nat*. 14.14 'vina non alibi tristiora, sed uva non alibi gratior callo, unde possit invenisse nomen durus acinus'. (On the formation *duracinus*, see L-H-Sz I.397.). A wall painting from Pompeii shows a glass bowl containing table grapes: *Pompeii* AD 79 256; cf. also 257. Mart. 5.78 has grapes as part of the 'secunda mensa'; cf. Hor. *Serm*. 2.4.71 ff., but serving grapes so late in the meal is characterised there as an innovation. Albeit preserved rather than fresh, grapes are listed as Saturnalian gifts also at Stat. *Silv*. 4.9.42.

Duracinus is used of other fruit at Pliny *Nat*. 15.39 (peaches) and 15.103 (cherries).

1: this line constitutes a hendiadys since *non habilis* equals *inutilis* while *cyathis* is paralleled by *Lyaeo*. The singular adjectives, with *uva* and the personifying *ero* (line 2), are poetic (one would not give as a present a single grape) and humorous: see at line 2 below. For other such numerical differences between poem and *lemma*, see at Mart. 13.11.2.

For the *cyathus*, a ladle used to transfer wine from the mixing bowl to cups, see N-H at Hor. *Carm*. 1.29.8, citing D-S I(2).1675 ff. s.v. *cyathus* [E. Pottier]. Also Courtney at Juv. 13.44.

Lyaeus refers here not so much to Bacchus himself as to the wine he represents. See N-H at Hor. *Carm.* 1.7.22 for the usage, and also the name's origins in the word λύειν (i.e. from care); cf. Hor. *Epod.* 9.37 f. 'curam metumque ... dulci Lyaeo solvere'. (Further examples of the metonymy at *OLD* s.v. *Lyaeus* §1b.) Mynors notes at Verg. *G.* 2.228-9 that the name Lyaeus appears in literary, but not in cult contexts. It is thought possibly to have appeared first in the mid 3rd century BC, in Leonidas of Tarentum (*Anth. P.* 6.154): see A.S.F. Gow and D.L. Page, *Hellenistic Epigrams* II, Cambridge 1965, 394.

2 nectar: the personified grape in this epigram has a sense of humour and paradox: it will be like the divine drink, i.e. very palatable, but only to one who does not drink it: 'non potanti'. For M's use of personification in the context of the Saturnalian *mundus inversus*, cf. 13.71.*le.* below.

13.23 Chian figs

A Chian fig is like old wine which Setia has sent. It carries with it wine unmixed and with it it carries salt.

le. ficus Chiae: a bowl of figs survives from Pompeii: *Rediscovering Pompeii* 84; cf. *Pompeii AD 79* 254, a wall painting showing two figs on a window ledge, and 256. Note also the very fine wall painting of figs in the triclinium of the villa at Oplontis (see *The Villa of Oplontis*, Naples (Casa Editrice ditta Vincenzo Carcavallo; ISBN 88-7666-193-X), 43). Figs seem commonly to have been given at the Saturnalia. In addition to the references at Mart. 13.28 (dealing specifically with *cottana*), cf. 4.46.10, 7.53.8 and Stat. *Silv.* 4.9.26, and see Gowers 59. Domitian appears to have distributed figs at his Saturnalian show: Stat. *Silv.* 1.6.15, although the line is corrupt: 'et quod percoquit †aebosia† caunos' (Courtney's *OCT*).

For Chian figs, cf. also Varro *R.* 1.41.6, Columella 10.414. They were especially noted for being pungent and tangy (cf. Mart. 7.25.8, quoted at 13.24.*le.* n. below, and note *salem*, line 2), and this appears to be the basis of their comparison with Setine wine here. (On this wine, see also at 13.112.*le.* below.) Setine was certainly a strong wine (cf. *merum*, line 2, of the figs) and was therefore usually tempered and cooled by snow: cf. Mart. 14.103.1 'Setinos, moneo, nostra nive frange trientes', 6.86.1, 9.2.5. That it was pungent and tangy as well seems a fair assumption.

Figs aside, Chios was also famous for wine: see *Kl.P.* 1.1148.18 ff. s.v. *Chios* [E. Meyer]; cf. Pl. *Curc.* 1.1.79, Hor. *Epod.* 9.34 'Chia vina'. This wine was of good quality and was often paired with Falernian (cf. Hor. *Sat.* 2.3.115, Tib. 2.1.28); but unlike Chian figs, and therefore unlike Setine, it seems to have been mild and smooth: at any rate this would explain why it was sometimes also blended with Falernian (cf. Hor. *Serm.* 1.10.24). The reader of this epigram is possibly intended to bear this difference at the back of his mind.

1 seni ... Baccho: like *Lyaeus* in Mart. 13.22.1, *Bacchus* is here used metonymically of wine. Other examples are cited at *OLD* s.v. *Bacchus* §2b, L-S s.v. *Bacchus* §1B3; cf. Mart. 13.119.1 below.

For the adjectival use of *senex*, see L-S s.v. *senex* §1a, *OLD* s.v. *senex* §2, Howell at Mart. 5.18.3; cf. 11.36.6 'senem ... cadum' in the context of old Falernian.

quem Setia misit: *mitto* is frequently used, often with a personified place name, of exports: cf. e.g. Verg. *G.* 1.57 'India mittit ebur' with Mynors. In Mart. 13, note also 19.1 above, 112.2, 121.1 below, and see at 104.1 and 109.2. In poem 43 the usage is inverted to describe home-grown produce. In addition, however, *mitto* also features in the vocabulary of epic catalogue (see Harrison at Verg. *A.* 10.172, 351 'tris quos ... patria Ismara mittit', 780 'missa ab Argis'), and this is of relevance here given the place of Mart. 13 in the tradition of catalogue literature: see Intro. (v) above.

quem Tβ: **quam** γ. The antecedent of *quem* is Bacchus, not the substantival *Chia*, as γ clearly thought in emending. Editorial activity by γ scribes is also evident in the *lemma*: not appreciating that *ficus* is there fourth declension, γ assumed that it was singular to agree with the singulars in the poem and so emended *Chiae* to *Chia*. Here, however, the singulars are generalising: one would not give a single fig; cf. 13.22.1 n. above.

13.24 Quinces

If quinces soaked in Cecropian honey are set before you, you can say '*These are honey apples*'.

le. Cydonea: sc. *Mala*. The word *malum* was regularly used with a qualifying adjective to designate fruit other than the apple and the adjective then came naturally to be used substantively on its own, as here: *Cydonea* were quinces, named after a city on the north coast of Crete and otherwise known as *cotonia/-ea*: see Pliny *Nat.* 15.37, Macr. 7.6.13 (On the form *cotonia/-ea*, which is probably cognate with but not derived from Κυδώνια, see Ernout-Meillet s.v. *cotoneus*.) For the regularity with which fruits are known by their locality, see Coleman at Stat. *Silv.* 4.9.26 'Thebaicaeve Caricaeve'.

The point of this epigram rests in a bilingual pun. *Melimela* (i.e. μελίμηλα, from μέλι and μῆλον) were normally apples of a naturally very sweet variety; cf. Varro *R.* 1.59.1 'mala ... quae antea mustea vocabant, nunc melimela appellant', Pliny *Nat.* 15.5.1 'mustea ... quae nunc melimela dicuntur a sapore melleo'. According to this poem, however, *real* 'honey apples' are not apples at all, but honeyed quinces, i.e. a different sort of *mala*. It is somewhat ironic that, as Howell notes at Mart. 1.43.4, untreated quinces are in fact bitter. Interestingly too, M implies elsewhere that he found *melimela* insipid: 7.25.7-8 'infanti melimela dato fatuasque mariscas:/ nam mihi, quae novit pungere, Chia sapit'.

Steeping quinces in honey (cf. *saturata*, line 1) as a means of preserving them accords with Apic. 1.20 Budé: 'ut mala Cidonia diu serventur: eligis mala sine vitio cum ramulis et foliis et condes in vas et suffundes mel et defritum et diu servabis'; cf. Pliny *Nat.* 15.60 '(cotonea) incoqui melle'. Preserved or at any rate dried fruit seems commonly to have been given at the Saturnalia (cf. crystallised fruit at Christmas): see Coleman at Stat. *Silv.* 4.9.27-8, Mart. 13.28.*le*. n. and 29 below.

1 Cecropio … melle: i.e. Attic honey, after Cecrops, mythical king and archetypal ancestor of Athens; cf. 13.105.2 'Cecropios … favos' below and see *OCD*[3] s.v. *Cecrops* [E. Kearns]. For Attic honey, see at Mart. 13.104.*le.* below. *Cecropio* affords with *Cydonea* an alliterative contrast of origins.

2 licet βγ: **placent** α Isid. *Orig.* 17.7.5. Most editors follow α and Isidore, but *licet* better suits a poem which does not deal with true honey apples. Shackleton Bailey (Teubner apparatus) compares Mart. 13.105.2 'dicas … licet'. M's practice of quoting words imputed to his addressee is documented by Siedschlag, 24. It is in keeping with epigrammatic tradition and can be seen again in Book 13 at 58.2.

13.25 Pine cones

We are the fruits of Cybele. Go away from here, traveller, in case our shower comes down on your unfortunate head.

le. nuces pineae: *nux* was used of the pine cone, *nucleus* of the nuts it contains; cf. Columella 12.5.2 'exemptis nucleis ipsas nuces pineas vacuas … incendunt', Pliny *Nat.* 15.35. It would, however, have been the *nuclei* that were eaten, although it seems from Varro *Men.* 581 (*nuclei* to accompany onion) and Apicius *passim* that they were used as complements or ingredients rather than being eaten on their own, as were the much larger almonds and walnuts. Nuts seem traditionally to have been part of the *mensa secunda* (note *Nux* 71) rather than the *gustatio*, although it is possible that these pine nuts were intended more as play things (see at Mart. 13.1.7 above) than as food. Pontic nuts were distributed at Domitian's Saturnalian show: Stat. *Silv.* 1.6.12.

1 poma sumus Cybeles: the cult of Cybele, the great Anatolian mother goddess, was one of the first from the east to be introduced to Rome (see Fordyce's introduction to Catul. 63). Cybele was associated at Rome principally with vegetation and agricultural production. Versions of the story regarding Attis, her beloved, differ, but according to Ovid, having sworn an oath of fidelity which he then broke, he castrated himself under a pine tree and died (*Fast.* 4.223 ff.), or he was metamorphosed into a pine tree (*Met.* 10.104). Whatever the version, however, because of him the pine tree became sacred to Cybele (cf. Phaedr. 3.17.4 'myrtus Veneri placuit ... pinus Cybebae') and was used to symbolise Attis during his spring festival.

For further details regarding Cybele and the Attis cult/story, see *Kl.P.* 1.725.46 ff. s.v. *Attis* [H. von Geisau], *OCD*[3] s.v. *Cybele* [F.R. Walton, J. Scheid]. The followers of Cybele were much maligned, and this epigram accords with popular prejudice (see below).

Pomum can be used of any fruit or produce (at Mart. 13.50.2 it is employed of truffles). The justification of its application to pine cones was nonetheless questionable, and underpins the anecdote at Macr. 2.6.1: after spectators were forbidden by edict from throwing anything but *poma* into the arena (the idea being that missiles should be soft), someone asked the jurist and wit Cascellius if the pine cone qualified. He replied that it did – if it was thrown at Vatinius, the author of a recent show, whose complaints at having been stoned had prompted the legislation.

procul hinc discede: death or injury from falling objects is a common literary topic, while narrow escapes were also seen as occasions for versification: see the examples and comments of N-H, 202, at Hor. *Carm.* 2.13. Mart. 1.12 and 82 celebrate the lucky escape of M. Aquilius Regulus from a falling portico. Damage by falling pine cones is not foremost in the canon of dangers typically encountered by the Roman *viator*, but it no doubt occasionally happened. Rather than giving a serious warning here, however, M is making a mockery of Cybele worship by recalling the conventional ritual cry of priests before a sacrifice or the like (cf. Verg. *A.* 6.258 'procul, o procul este' with Austin): he achieves humour by addressing παρὰ προσδοκίαν not *profani* but travellers, and by insuring not against defilement but a rather ridiculous source of injury.

2 ruina suggests not the dropping of a few pine cones but a shower, like the falling of hail at Lucr. 6.156-7: 'ruina/ grandinis ... sonitum dat'. It is almost as if the pine cones are actually threatening to pelt anyone who passes by.

13.26 Service berries

We are service berries, which tighten over-loose bowels. It is better that you give this fruit to your boy than yourself.

le. sorba: berries of the service tree (*Sorbus domestica* L) were noted for their astringent qualities: cf. Priap. 51.10 'sorbumve ventres lubricos moraturum', Pliny *Nat.* 23.141 '(sc. sistunt alvum) sorba sicca'. (M describes another astringent at 13.116 below. Contrast the laxatives at Mart. 13.13 and 14, as well as 29.) This epigram humorously advises a master not to eat the berries himself (which, although recommended by Columella (5.10.19), might interfere with the digestion of his meal: see at Mart. 13.14.2); but, for reasons explained below, he is to give them to his catamite instead. Not only was it customary to fill one's napkin at dinner with food to take home to one's *puer* or slave (note Petr. 60.7, 66.4), but it was traditional to pass on unwanted Saturnalian gifts. These gifts were handed over not only by masters to slaves (cf. Mart. 14.70 Leary *Copta Rhodiaca*), but by patrons to clients (cf. Mart. 5.19.11 ff. and possibly 13.121) and by acquaintances to one another (Mart. 7.53.1 f.; also possibly 13.107 and 6.75.4).

Apicius gives a recipe for 'patina de sorbis calida et frigida' (4.160 Budé). As well as being eaten (they ripen in October), the berries could be made into some sort of liquor (see Mynors at Verg. *G.* 3.380, citing Pliny *Nat.* 14.103 (*vinum*) and Pallad. 2.15.5). Although the precise nature of this drink is uncertain, cf. Richard Mabey, *Flora Britannica*, London 1996, 206, who refers to the possibility that an alcoholic drink was made from the berries of the Chequer tree (*Sorbus torminalis* L): hence the many Chequers Inns in Kent. He suspects that the drink 'was a ratafia, like sloe-gin and cherry brandy'.

1 sorba sumus corresponds to 'poma sumus', 13.25.1. *Poma* in this poem comes in line 2.

molles ... tendentia ventres: for *venter* of bowels, see *OLD* s.v. *venter* §3; cf. Larg. 200 'ea quae ventrem molliunt, tamquam lac', 13.116.1 below. *Mollis* is regular of loose bowels. Largus aside, cf. Cels. 3.12.6 'cibus ... qui mollem alvum praestet'. In advocating the use of laxatives, Mart. 3.89.1 'mollibus utere malvis' may reflect some consciousness of this sense.

tendentia R: **durantia** β: **dican-** vel **ditan-** γ. R's *lectio difficilior* is surely right. *Tendentia* or 'tautening' (Shackleton Bailey's translation; cf. *OLD* s.v. *tendo* §5a) contrasts here with *molles*, the same words being used in contrast at Ovid *Ep.* 4.92 (of a bow): 'si numquam cesses tendere, mollis erit'. Heraeus suspects β's reading of being a gloss, and refers to Mart. 13.29.2 'duri ... ventris'. He attributes γ's reading to a corruption of β (β ⇒ duantia ⇒ γ), comparing Mart. 1.66.8, where γ has *duo* for *duro*.

2 puero: i.e. *cinaedo*, as Gilbert and others note (see *OLD* s.v. *puer* §3 for this meaning). M's point is that boys with leaky bowels are unpleasant to bugger; cf. Mart. 11.88 with Kay. That buggery might have caused the incontinence in the first place is a possibility, if the sphincter were ruptured; but this would probably not have been common. (My thanks to Dr J.A. Leary.)

Given that Mart. 13 was written for the Saturnalia, and given the licence this festival allowed (see Intro. (ii) section C above), the number of rude poems contained by the book is surprisingly low (also 65 and 71). In contrast, compare the proportion of obscene poems in Books 1-12, put by Ker as a quarter (Loeb xiii) and even then not considered by him to be high. (Counter to Ker's views are those of Lord Macaulay, who judged M 'as great a beast as Aristophanes': *The Life and Letters of Lord Macaulay* II, London 1876, 448 ff.)

13.27 Dates in foil (?)

The golden date is offered on the Kalends of Janus; and yet this is usually the gift of a poor man.

1e. petalium caryotarum: *caryotae* were dates from Syria (Varro *R.* 2.1.27) or Egypt (Petr. 40.3). They were distributed at Domitian's Saturnalian show (Stat. *Silv.* 1.6.20), although such distributions were probably also known throughout the year: see Kay at Mart. 11.31.10 'et notas caryotidas theatris'. That they were cheap but customary gifts at the January Kalends is confirmed by Mart. 8.33.11-12 quoted below. (For the January Kalends, which was celebrated in much the same way as the Saturnalia, see Intro. (ii) section B above.) Pliny, *Ep.* 1.7.6, cites them in conjunction with figs (cf. Mart. 13.28) and mushrooms (cf. Mart. 13.48). Their juice was abundant and the wine made from it was strong: Pliny *Nat.* 13.44.

petalium γ: **petadium** β: **petavivum** T: **palathion** Salmasius. Of the three MS readings, only γ's means anything at all, and its sense is difficult. Hence Salmasius' conjecture: a παλάθη was a kind of cake made of fruit (Hdt. 4.23, Athen. 11.500D) and an example of the diminutive παλάθιον is attested at Polem. *Hist.* 88 Preller (= Athen. 11.478D). Salmasius was followed by Schneidewin, Friedländer and Gilbert. The MSS all agree on *peta-*, however. Such unanimity is admittedly no guarantee of correctness: note e.g. the case of Mart. 13.118.2 *Latiis* Gilbert: *tuscis* codd., where Gilbert is clearly right (see ad loc.); but MS agreement still deserves serious consideration: see Intro. (vii) above. Consequently *palathion* cannot be accepted unreservedly, and there is reason also to hesitate over *pentadium* (cf. *Anth. P.* 6.190.3 πεντάδα τὴν σταφυλῆς εὐρώγεα), which was suggested only to be discarded by Heraeus. Attention must therefore revert to the difficult *petalium*, which has been printed by editors since Lindsay (cf. *CR* 17 (1903) 48) and must be compared with πέταλον, used either of a leaf or of a very thin sheet of metal, and *petalum*, glossed at Isid. *Orig.* 29.21 as 'aurea lamina'. Shackleton Bailey (cf. Ker) appears to follow the 'leaf' meaning in very tentatively translating 'stem'; but an alternative possibility (cf. *OLD* s.v. *petalium*), given Mart. 8.33.11-12 'hoc linitur sputo Iani caryota Kalendis,/ quam fert cum parco sordidus asse cliens', might be that these dates are covered by or wrapped in metal foil. Roman craftsmen were skilled in the manufacture of foil (see R.J. Forbes, *Studies in Ancient Technology* VIII, revised edn. Leiden 1971, 185-6), and it can be inferred from the rest of Mart. 8.33 that *sputum* in line 11 is used in contemptuous reference to very thin metal: the poem deplores by means of a catalogue of hyperbolic comparisons the thinness of a bowl given as a present by a certain Paulus; cf. *OLD* s.v. *sputum* §1. Also, understanding *petalium* here as referring to foil packaging stands in easy relationship to the *vasa* of Mart. 13.28-9 and *cistella* of 36.

1 aurea ... caryota and the other singulars in the poem are generalising: no matter what one's circumstances (cf. line 2), one is unlikely to give just a single fig – although one might find ways of giving a present that amounted to one; cf. the joke of Mart. 13.28 below (line 2 n.) For other such numerical differences between poem and *lemma*, see 13.11.2 n. above.

aurea: the colour of these dates makes possible the paradox that something 'golden' should be the customary gift of a poor man. (For other gifts specifically identified as poor man's, see at 13.6.1 above.)

13.28 Jar of Syrian figs

These Syrians, which have come to you stored in a turned cone, if they were larger, would be fig.

le. vas cottanorum: *cottana* were small figs from Syria: cf. Pliny *Nat.* 13.51 'Syria ... peculiares habet arbores ... in ficorum autem [genere] caricas, et minore eius generis, quae cottana vocant'; see *RE* VI.2122.12 ff. s.v. *Feige* [Olck]. They were common exports (Juv. 3.83 'advectus Romam quo pruna et cottana vento') and, like the prunes with which they were often paired (cf. Mart. 13.29), were popular if modest Saturnalian gifts: cf. Mart. 4.88.6 'nec quae [sc. testa] cottana parva gerit', 7.53.7 and see Coleman at Stat. *Silv.* 4.9.27-8. Compare also the figs at Mart. 13.23. Like dates (cf. Mart. 13.27), figs were also associated with the January Kalends: Ovid *Fasti* 1.185 ff.

For *vas*, see *OLD* s.v. *vas* §1a. The kind of container meant is clarified by 'torta ... meta', line 1. *Meta* testifies to its conical shape (*OLD* s.v. *meta* §1), while *torta* indicates that it was earthenware, thrown on a potter's wheel; cf. *testa* at Mart. 4.88.6 and Stat. *Silv.* 4.9.43 'Cumano patinas vel orbe tortas'. Mart. 5.18.3 'acuta ... testa' describes a similar container (used for damsons; cf. 13.29 below). While some conical jars were perhaps specifically manufactured for figs, it seems that the base of a fractured *cadus* was also commonly used: see Coleman at Stat. *Silv.* 4.9.27-8 on *turbo*. Given *condita*, line 1, see too her note (ibid.) on *condere*, usual for 'to store': being imports to Rome, these figs were preserved rather than fresh; cf. 13.24.*le*. n. above.

2 ficus erat: *ficus* is used generically here; cf. Mart. 7.53.8 'et Libycae fici pondere testa gravis'. M jokes that these *cottana* are too small to count as real 'fig'.

erat αγ; **erant** β. The reading of αγ is numerically incongruent with *haec*, *venerunt* and *forent*, and Duff accordingly comments that *erant* is possibly correct; but it is more likely that *erat* is attracted to the generic singular *ficus* and that β preserves an attempt to emend the original. (Friedländer is probably wrong to compare the numerical incongruity of Mart. 14.19(18).1 'alea parva nuces ... videtur (videntur P)': although I comment there that *nuces* operates grammatically as a singular, I would have done better to refer with Heraeus to Mart. 4.66.16 'alea sed parcae sola fuere nuces', observing that P was possibly right.)

For the use of the indicative in the apodosis of unreal conditions, see L-H-Sz II.328.

13.29 Jar of damsons

Take plums wrinkled through the decay of foreign old age: they tend to loosen the load of constipated bowels.

le. vas Damascenorum T: **-arum** βγ. As Heraeus explains, βγ preserve a late spelling. Damsons or Damascus prunes are listed as cheap Saturnalian gifts at Stat. *Silv.* 4.9.26 'Thebaicaeve Caricaeve'; cf. Mart. 5.18.3 'acuta senibus testa cum Damascenis' and 7.53.7 'cum canis ... prunis'. It was common to attribute their wrinkled appearance to old age and *senectae*, line 1, compares with *senibus* and *canis* in the passages just cited. While Pliny *Nat.* 15.43 'in peregrinis arboribus dicta sunt Damascena' goes on to say that damsons grown in Italy are 'nec umquam in rugas siccata, quoniam soles sui desunt', *peregrinae*, line 1, confirms that M's damsons were imports.

A bowl of prunes survives from Pompeii: *Rediscovering Pompeii* 82; cf. *Pompeii AD 79*, a wall painting depicting a container of what might be prunes. Syrian prunes appear as an appetiser at Petr. 13.11. Note too that prunes are an ingredient of Apicius' 'gustum versatile' (4.125 Budé). (Apicius' other recipes involving prunes are mainly for sauces and seasonings, although he gives directions for storing prunes at Exc. 6 Budé.) The laxative properties of prunes mentioned in the present poem seem not to be attested elsewhere in Latin, although they are perhaps better attested today than those of the laxatives M describes elsewhere. For these laxatives and their inclusion in the *gustatio*, see at Mart. 13.14.2.

On the use here of *vas*, see 13.28.*le.* n. above.

1 pruna peregrinae carie rugosa senectae: *senecta* survives elsewhere in context of fruit and trees e.g. at Pliny *Nat.* 16.117 ff., where it appears several times (as does *senesco*). *Caries* survives here only with regard to shrivelled fruit (*OLD* s.v. *caries* §1d), although its connotations of drying out (cf. *ThLL* III.456.3 ff. s.v. *caries* [Elsberger]) are appropriate, and it is used elsewhere too in the context of extreme old age: cf. e.g. Priap. 57.1 (of an old woman, likened to a crow). *Rugosus vel sim.* is equally applicable to old people and fruit; aside from *rugas* in Pliny *Nat.* 15.43, quoted above, cf. Ovid *Fast.* 1.185 *rugosa*, describing a fig.

2 sume is similar to *accipe*: cf. Intro. (v) and n. 6 above; but it is also common of taking medicinal preparations and food (*OLD* s.v. *sumo* §3). A similar ambiguity occurs at Mart. 14.207.1, where *sumere* can refer to both accepting a gift and putting on clothing.

duri ... ventris: see at Mart. 13.26.1 for *venter* of the bowels. With *durus*, cf. Hor. *Serm.* 2.4.27 'dura ... alvus'. The usage is (not surprisingly) confined to medical works and the lower genres: *ThLL* VI.2305.18 ff. s.v. *durus* [Bannier].

solvere ... onus: excrement and undigested food are often signified by *onus*: *OLD* s.v. *onus* §1c; cf. Mart. 1.37.1 'ventris onus misero, nec te pudet, excipis auro' (which is apparently imitated at *SHA Elagabalus* 32.2: Howell 187). In Greek (3rd century AD), note τὰ φερόμενα (Philum. ap. Aët. 9.12: see L-S-J s.v. φέρω). As for *solvere* of loosening the bowels, see *OLD* s.v. *solvo* §10 and L-S s.v. *solvo* §IIA3.

13.30 Cheese from Luna

A cheese stamped with the impression of Etruscan Luna will afford your slaves a thousand lunches.

le. caseus Lunensis: Luna was an important port (Sil. 8.482, Enn. *Op. Inc.* 1 Sk. = Pers. 6.9, Pliny *Nat.* 3.50), which was situated in northern Etruria, near modern Carrara. Its cheeses were remarkable for their size: cf. Pliny *Nat.* 11.241 'Luniensem magnitudine conspicuum, quippe et ad singula milia pondo premitur'. Hence the cheese in this epigram can feed a thousand times its recipient's slaves (*pueris*, line 2; γ's *puero* would weaken the hyperbole). Cheeses were apparently common gifts at the Saturnalia: cf. Stat. *Silv.* 4.9.36, Mart. 4.46.11. This poem begins a series of four, each from a different region. Cheese is mentioned elsewhere as part of the *gustatio* at Mart. 11.52.10. For general information, e.g. regarding its production, see *Kl.P.* 3.44.37 ff. s.v. *Käse* [L.A. Moritz], Blümner *Priv.* 190 ff., *RE* X.1489.45 ff. s.v. *Käse* [Kroll], André *Alimentation* 152 ff. See too Mynors at Verg. *G.* 3.400-403.

1 signatus imagine: Shackleton Bailey (Loeb note) is surely correct in suspecting that cheeses from Luna were stamped with a crescent-shaped mark; cf. the rose motif adopted for the reverse of coins from Rhodes. *Imago* survives in Plautus of the imprint left by a signet ring (*Ps.* 56 'expressam in cera ex anulo suam imaginem', 1202), while *signatus* is usual of something marked with a stamp: see L-S s.v. *signo* §B2a, *OLD* s.v. *signo* §6; cf. Ovid *Met.* 15.169 'ut ... novis facilis signatur cera figuris'.

2 praesto, thus used of food, seems surprisingly rare; cf., however, Pliny *Nat.* 18.16 'T. Seius ... assibus populo frumentum praestitit', 21.82; see *OLD* s.v. *praesto* §8a. The strong p alliteration of the pentameter, to which *praestabit* contributes, appears to have no particular significance.

pueris here refers to slaves, who were not necessarily children: see *OLD* s.v. *puer* §5a, N-H at Hor. *Carm.* 1.38.1 *puer*; cf. the usages of 'boy' collected s.v. in Jean Branford, *A Dictionary of South African English*,³ Cape Town 1987. It was standard practice to take food home from dinners for one's slaves, and to pass on Saturnalian gifts: see 13.26.*le.* n. above.

prandium: for this meal, see at Mart. 13.13.2. That it was not substantial is of no importance here given the large number of meals envisaged.

13.31 Vestine cheese

If you want to take moderate, meatless breakfasts, this hunk comes to you from a Vestine flock.

le. and 2: **caseus Vestinus** β: **testinus** γ: **Lunensis** T. *Lunensis* comes from Mart. 13.30.*le.* and so needs no further consideration. The Vestini (cf. β, of which γ is an obvious corruption) lived in central Italy, between the Apennines and the Adriatic. They were farmers (Juv. 14.179 ff.) and hunters (Sil. 8.515-16). In general, see *Kl.P.* 5.1229.56 ff. s.v. *Vestini* [G. Radke]. For Vestine cheese, cf. Apic. 4.126 Budé 'adicies ... caseum Vestinum', Pliny *Nat.* 11.241 'proximum autem urbi Vestinum [caseum] eumque e caedicio campo laudatissimum'. (The Pliny MSS offer both *aestinum* (F¹) and *Vescinum* (TD²), a reading which prompted Furlanetto to conjecture *Vescinus* here; but *aestinum* lends support to βγ's reading in -*est*- while *Vescinum* is rejected by editors of Pliny: see D. Detlefsen, *Hermes* 40 (1905) 578 referring to Livy 10.21.8 and Mommsen in *CIL* X, 463; cf. Mayhoff's apparatus.)

1 ientacula: on the Roman breakfast, see Marquardt *Prl*. 265, Carcopino 287. It was usually a very moderate meal (cf. *frugi*), eaten mostly by children and the elderly. Pliny describes his uncle as having '[cibum] levem et facilem' (*Ep*. 3.5.10), and many would have made do with no more than a drink of water. A breakfast including meat (note *carne* here) would have been very unusual, and indicative of such gluttony as that for which e.g. the emperor Vitellius was known (Suet. *Vit*. 13.1). For a breakfast of (bread and) cheese, see Apul. *Met*. 1.18.

In describing breakfast, this epigram accords with Mart. 13.30, which deals with lunch (*prandium*); cf. Festus 250M 'prandicula antiqui dicebant quae nunc ientacula'.

sumere: for *sumo* of taking food, see Mart. 13.29.2 n. above. It is unlikely here to mean *accipere*.

frugi Tβ: **frugis** γ. The reading of γ is inappropriate to cheese (hardly a fruit or crop) and easily discarded. The indeclinable adjective *frugi* is used of a meal also at Pliny *Ep*. 3.1.4 'cena non minus nitida quam frugi', and Juv. 3.167 'frugi cenula'.

2 haec ... massa: T's *missa* (sc. *ientacula*) is impossible, given the singular *venit*. *Massa*, which introduces a new element, is used of cheese also e.g. at Ovid *Met*. 8.666 'lactis massa coacti' and Mart. 8.64.9 'massa ... lactis alligati'.

grex can be used of a wide variety of animals but, left unqualified, is most commonly applied to sheep: *OLD* s.v. *grex* §1b. In writing of Apennine cheeses, Pliny says expressly that cheese from Liguria came mostly from the milk of sheep (*Nat*. 11.241). Since he refers to Vestine cheese in the same passage (see above), and then immediately continues with the apparently contrasting 'et caprarum gregibus sua laus est', it is possible to infer that sheeps' milk rather than goats' was used for Vestine too.

13.32 Smoked cheese

The cheese which has imbibed not just any hearth and not every smoke but Velabran, that cheese has flavour.

le. caseus fumosus: cf. Athen. 3.113C ὅμοιον τῷ φουμῶσῳ τυρῷ. This cheese alone of the four in the series is not identified by region in the *lemma*; but note *Velabrensem*, line 2. The Velabrum was an area of low-lying ground between the N.W. slope of the Palatine and the Capitol and was known as a centre for trade in wine, food and oil: see Kay at Mart. 11.52.10 'et Velabrensi massa coacta foco', who cites Pl. *Capt*. 489, Hor.

Serm. 2.3.229, *CIL* 6.9716 f., 33933 and Platner Ashby 549-50. See also Richardson 406.

Smoking cheese was evidently a common practice (and is continued today: *RE* X.1492.33 s.v. *Käse* [Kroll]), but Velabran was clearly considered the best of its kind. Kay suggests (loc. cit.) that it could well be Velabran to which Pliny refers at *Nat.* 11.241 'et caprarum gregibus sua laus est, in recenti maxime augente gratiam fumo, qualis in ipsa urbe conficitur cunctis praeferendis'.

1: for the scansion of this line, see 13.112.1 n. below.

2 bibere is used of smoke also at Hor. *Carm.* 3.8.11 'amphorae fumum bibere instituere' (for smoking wine, see Mart. 13.123.*le.* n.); cf. *ThLL* II.1967.75 ff. s.v. *bibo* [Münscher], which cites similar uses of *bibere*, e.g. of colours (Pliny *Nat.* 31.123, 34.98) and of sun-bathers soaking up the sun: Juv. 11.203.

13.33 Cheeses from Trebula

Trebula gave us birth. A double attraction commends us, whether we are softened by a gentle flame or steeped in water.

le. casei Trebulani: there were several towns called Trebula: see *Kl.P.* 5.936.23 ff. s.v. *Trebula* [G. Radke]; cf. Howell at Mart. 5.71.1. Ker (Loeb note) locates this Trebula in Sabine country, but Shackleton Bailey (Loeb note; cf. *OLD* s.v. *Trebulanus*) puts it further from Rome, on the border of Samnium and Campania. Wherever it was, however, its cheese was apparently good to eat, whether toasted or moistened with water – although no details survive regarding how exactly this toasted or moistened cheese was served or eaten. Nevertheless, whereas Mart. 13.30-1 are linked by references to lunch and breakfast, poems 32-3 both refer to taste.

Of the four cheese epigrams, only this one has a plural *lemma*. Given that M himself was not bothered by numerical differences between *lemma* and poem (see Mart. 13.11.2 n.) but appears to have maintained numerical consistency in the *lemmata* of grouped epigrams (see e.g. 13.9 and 14 *lee.* nn. above), it is possible that some (early?) scribe, influenced by *nos* and *domamur*, emended the original.

1 Trebula nos genuit: this statement of the cheese's provenance is reminiscent, perhaps intentionally, of Virgil's epitaph: 'Mantua me genuit'; but the grandeur of the words serves in any case to enhance its status.

commendat gratia duplex: Heraeus compares *AL* 353.10 Riese (= *AL* 38.10 ShB) and Ven. Fort. 2.16.113. *Gratia* is used of service berries at Columella 5.10.19.

2 domamur: the word is used at Ovid *Met.* 8.650 of boiling pork: 'partem ... sectam ... domat ferventibus undis'. Note also e.g. Pliny *Nat.* 20.5 'pastillos ... igni lento in aceto domet' and see *ThLL* V(1).1946.32 ff. s.v. *domo* [Bannier]. Both soaking and heating would have a softening effect.

The combination of fire and water is common: both are elements; both had ritual and purificatory associations: *OCD*[3] s.v. *Water* [J.H. Croon, A.J.S. Spawforth]; both were regarded as prime necessities of life ('Aqua et igni interdicere' therefore came to mean 'to outlaw', while 'aqua et igni accipere' meant 'to greet', especially a newly wed bride: see *OLD* s.v. *aqua* §5h); and both could be agents of destruction: note e.g. Livy 26.29.4 'obrui Aetnae ignibus aut mergi freto satius illi insulae esse'. If M intended any particular resonances when mentioning fire and water here, *domamur* would, of course, suggest the last (note also that in Persia water was demanded with earth as a token of submission: cf. e.g. Hdt 5.18); but he probably intended no more than to describe actual practice in preparing Trebulan cheeses.

13.34 Onions

Since your wife is an old woman and your parts have expired, you can be satisfied with nothing other than onions.

le. bulbi were a type of onion, here probably *Muscari comosum* Mill.: André *Alimentation* 20-1, Henderson at Ovid *Rem.* 797; cf. *RE* III.669.63 ff. s.v. βολβός [Olck]. They appear to have been common Saturnalian gifts (cf. Mart. 4.46.11, Stat. *Silv.* 4.9.29-30), and they were regularly part of the *gustatio*: note Apic. 4.175-6 Budé, and cf. Pliny *Ep.* 1.15.2 quoted above (Mart. 13.6.*le.* n.). (For onion recipes generally, see Apic. 7.305-9 Budé.) Their supposed aphrodisiac qualities are often cited (cf. Mart. 3.75.3 'bulbi ... salaces', Ovid *Ars* 2.422, Petr. 130.7, Columella 10.105-6) and underpin this poem. (On the anaphrodisiac qualities for which onions were also noted, see Gowers 296-7.)

1 cum sit anus coniunx: *anus* is regularly used of a woman too old or unattractive for sex and is used thus of a wife again at Mart. 14.147.2 'si te congelat uxor anus'. In the lower genres, it is often abusive; cf. N-H at Hor. *Carm.* 1.25.9.

mortua membra: cf. Ovid *Am.* 3.7.65 'nostra ... iacuere velut praemortua membra'. Whereas at Mart. 14.147 the husband is put off by his wife's age, *et* with *mortua* hints that this is not wholly the case here: his impotence too may be due to age.

Membrum is usually, but not always, applied to the male sex organ (Adams 46). Given *iacuere*, the plural form *membra* in the Ovid passage just cited must be poetic and the word must refer to the penis; but *membra* is sometimes used instead of the testicles (Adams 69, citing Tib. 1.4.70 'et secet ad Phrygios vilia membra modos'), and its doing so here would allow a play on the shape of the onions.

Although this is a mildly rude poem, it is nonetheless by no means an exercise in Saturnalian obscenity, and the word *membrum* is not an offensive one (cf. Adams 224). For the surprising lack of obscenity in M's *Xenia*, see at Mart. 13.26.2 n. above.

2 satur: given the situation outlined in line 1, all the addressee can do is resort to onions in the hope that they will cure him; but whatever the case, they will at least fill his stomach. The poem plays on two meanings of *satur*, which can have the sense both of satisfied hunger (*OLD* s.v. *satur* §1) and sexual gratification; cf. the similar ambiguity at Mart. 14.69.1 'si vis esse satur' and note the sexual sense of *satis facio* (Adams 197).

13.35 Lucanian sausages

Daughter of a Picene sow, I come, a Lucanian sausage. From this is given a welcome crown to snow-white porridge.

le. Lucanicae: the *Lucanica* was a regional variety of sausage which originated from the area immediately south of the Bay of Naples (for the Lucani, see *Kl.P.* 3.744.29 ff. s.v. *Lucani* [G. Radke]), but which spread thanks initially to the army (Varro *L.* 5.111.1). These *Lucanicae* are from Picenum, which was in central Italy on the Adriatic coast and which also produced pears (Pliny *Nat.* 15.55), apples (see Courtney at Juv. 11.74), a type of bread (see at Mart. 13.47) and olives (see at Mart. 13.36.*le.* below: poems 35 and 36 form a pair).

According to Apicius, 2.61 Budé, the Lucanian sausage was made with pork (cf. *porcae*, line 1), and it was flavoured with pepper, cumin, savory, rue, parsley and bay leaves. Pork was traditional at the Saturnalia (see Intro. (ii) section B above), and Lucanian sausages appear to have been a common present: cf. Mart. 4.46.8, Stat. *Silv.* 4.9.35. Since sausage meat was of inferior quality, it is not surprising to find these sausages referred to in lists of paltry gifts; note also the cheap *botellus* at Mart. 14.72. That sausage was a usual part of the *gustatio* is confirmed by Mart. 5.78: note προπίνειν, line 3, and line 9, quoted below.

1 filia Picenae venio Lucanica porcae: the offspring of a sow is a piglet, not a sausage, and one does not normally think of sausages (or even piglets) as daughters. Given also the meagre nature of the average sausage, the grandiloquence of this interlocking and alliterative line is totally inappropriate and its effect is therefore comic. Clearly we are dealing here with a sausage endowed with a self-mocking sense of humour. For similar personifying uses of *filia*, see N-H at Hor. *Carm*. 1.14.12 'silvae filia nobilis'; cf. Mart. 14.90.1 'silvae filia Maurae', 13.103.1 below.

Metrical concerns aside, had M written *venimus* (and *filiae*) to agree with the plural *lemma*, he would have diluted the force of the personification (for numerical differences between *lemma* and poem, see 13.11.2 n. above). With *venio*, cf. 13.82.1 *veni* below.

2 pultibus ... niveis grata corona datur: cf. Mart. 5.78.9 'et pultem niveam premens botellus'. Given the lowly status of sausage (and of the porridge-like *puls*: see at Mart. 13.8.*le*.), M's choice of *corona* is probably not without humour. *ThLL* classifies M's usage with other miscellaneous examples of things that form a circle (IV.987.68 ff. s.v. *corona* [Gudeman]), and if this is correct it seems most likely that the sausage was a long one and extended around the edge of the plate, surrounding and containing the viscous *puls*. In this case, *premo* at Mart. 5.78.9 must carry the sense of confining or shutting in (*OLD* s.v. *premo* §28).

hinc: i.e. from the act of coming (*venio*, line 1).

13.36 A small box of olives

This olive, which has come, taken from the Picene mills, both begins and ends our feasts.

le. cistella olivarum: the olive was eaten both as part of the *gustatio* (Marquardt *Prl*. 215 n.13; cf. Petr. 31.9, Pliny *Ep*. 1.15.2, quoted at 13.6.*le*. above) and as dessert (Marquardt *Prl*. 318; cf. Mart. 5.78.20). Hence the pentameter here.

On Picenum, from where these olives come (*Picenis*, line 1), see at Mart. 13.35.*le*. A small box of Picene olives is cited as a Saturnalian gift also at Mart. 4.46.12-13 'Piceno quoque venit a cliente/ parcae cistula non capax olivae'; cf. 4.88.7 and 7.53.5, where the olives come in containers of wicker work. Mart. 4.46.13 describes inferior produce, but good quality Picene olives were valued by diners, especially for their size: Pliny *Nat*. 15.16, cited by Howell at Mart. 1.43.8. The area still produces olives today: Kay at Mart. 11.52.11.

Kay notes (ibid.) that olives for eating were generally picked before they were fully ripe, in September. Those designated for oil were not harvested until November/December, i.e. the season of the Saturnalia (cf. Columella 12.52.1, Verg. *G*. 3.519 'venit hiems: teritur Sicyonia baca trapetis'). The olives in this poem may have been intended originally for oil extraction ('Picenis ... trapetis', line 1), but have been diverted after harvesting to the table (see below on *subducta*). Like those at Mart. 11.52.11 'quae ... senserunt ... frigus'; cf. 7.31.4, they too might have felt the winter frosts and, being therefore spoiled for eating, would be well qualified to partner the lowly sausages at Mart. 13.35.

For olives in general, see *Kl.P.* 4.243.22 ff. s.vv. *Öl, Ölbaum* [W.H.Groß]. A bowl of olives survives from Pompeii: *Rediscovering Pompeii* 81.

1 haec: the single olive here generalises. For numerical differences between *lemma* and poem, see 13.11.2 n. above.

subducta trapetis: *subducere* can indicate theft (see *OLD* s.v. *subduco* §6a), which may well be relevant here. The *trapetum*, for which the olive was intended, was not a press (*pace* the Loebs) but a stone mill, which was designed to grind olives into a paste prior to pressing. An example survives from Pompeii: *Rediscovering Pompeii* 1. See further *Kl.P.* 5.926.37 ff. s.v. *Trapetum* [W.H. Groß], Forbes III.103, Drachmann 7 ff. and fig. 1.

2 inchoat atque ... finit oliva dapes: cf. Mart. 13.14.1-2, noting *inchoat* and *dapes* there too. Given the quality and possible history of the olives of this poem, M's use of the elevated *daps* (see at Mart. 13.14.1 'cludere ... cenas') is not without irony.

13.37 Citrons

These fruits are either from the leafy branches of the Corcyraean garden, or they were the Massylian dragon's.

le. mala citrea: cf. Largus 158 'mala citrea', Pliny *Nat.* 15.47, 17.64, 23.105 and the 1st-2nd century grammarian Cloatius Verus cited at Macr. 2.15. The citron tree (*Citrus medica* Risso), which originated in the north of India, has fruit larger, less acid and thicker skinned than our lemon (*Citrus limonum* Risso). It was commonly thought to have medicinal properties and was admired – or not (Pliny *Nat.* 13.103) – for its scent. For further details, see André *Alimentation* 78-9, 78 n. 67.

The citrons described here are of the very finest quality and must therefore have come, the poem asserts, from either the garden of Alcinoos (on which see further below), or from that of the Hesperides, two mythical gardens to which M refers elsewhere when disparaging the produce of his own estate (10.94.1-2): 'non mea Massylus servat pomaria serpens,/ regius Alcinoi nec mihi servit ager'. M's use in illustrating the citrons' outstanding quality of alternatives which occupy the whole poem recalls the format found in Greek epigrams praising either artists or their work: see Siedschlag 81; cf. also on 13.96 below.

Apicius gives several recipes for or involving the citron fruit or its leaves: see the Budé index.

1 aut Corcyraei sunt haec de frondibus horti: Corcyra (today Corfu) was identified with Homer's Phaeacian Scherie from early on: see *Kl.P.* 3.306.25 ff. s.v. *Korkyra* [E. Meyers]; cf. Thuc. 1.25.4. In some accounts, Alcinoos, king of the Phaeacians, is grandson to the island's eponym (see *Kl.P.* 1.266.57 s.v. *Alkinoos* [H. von Geisau]), and he was worshipped there in historical times: Thuc. 3.70.4. Alcinoos was a byword for munificent hospitality (cf. e.g. Mart. 4.64.29) and the abundance of his orchard, described at *Od.* 7.112-21, became proverbial in Latin poetry. See Mynors at Verg. *G.* 2.87, who refers to Otto 53; cf. Prop. 1.14.24, Ovid *Am.* 1.10.56, Pliny *Nat.* 19.49, Mart. 8.68.1 'Corcyraei pomaria regis'. At Mart. 7.42.6 giving fruit to Alcinoos is the equivalent of carrying coals to Newcastle.

horti: see at 13.20.1 above.

2 aut haec Massyli poma draconis erant: cf. Mart. 10.94.1, quoted above. The Massyli were a people who lived on the N.W. coast of Africa (*Kl.P.* 3.1070.22 ff. s.v. *Massyli* [M. Leglay]), but the adjective *Massylus* was often used by the poets just to mean 'African' (*OLD* s.v. *Massylus*). The land of the Hesperides was variously located in Cyrenaica, at the pillars of Hercules near Mt Atlas and on an island off N. Africa's Atlantic coast: see *Kl.P.* 2.1117.59 ff. s.v. *Hesperiden* [H. von Geisau].

Erant with the possessive genitive indicating ownership parallels and varies the previous line's 'sunt ... de ...' with the ablative and a possessive genitive indicating provenance.

13.38 Beestings

We give beestings which the herdsman drew off from the first milk of their mothers while the kids were not yet standing.

le. colustrum: only here do beestings (the first issue of mothers' milk) appear as a Saturnalian gift or as part of the *gustatio*, although one can perhaps compare the cheeses of Mart. 13.30-3. They were considered harmful to lambs, and doubtless therefore also to kids; cf. Columella 7.3.17 'exiguum lactis emulgendum est, quod pastores colostrum vocant: ea nisi aliquatenus emittitur, nocet agno' (cited by Shackleton Bailey: *CPh* 73 (1978) 295). Note too Pliny *Nat.* 11.237 on *colustratio*, a disease of young asses caused by their mothers' first milk. Thus, while *subripere* can have connotations of stealthy or covert action or acquisition (cf. *OLD* s.v. *subripio* §2), the *pastor*'s motivation here in taking advantage of the kid's initial immobility would not have been governed by self interest. Instead, one should perhaps focus on the relevance to milking of the word's literal sense.

The origins of the word *colustrum* are doubtful. In addition to the variant spelling *-los-* (see Columella, cited above), the feminine form (*colustra -ae*) also survives. For M's usage here, note, however, in addition to the MSS, *GLK* 5.576.1 'colustrum generis neutri, ut Martialis [ut qui] colustrum luteum'. (Heraeus interprets *luteum* as an extra in the text used by the grammarian, and dismisses the possibility that 'ut qui colustrum luteum' is a fragment of some other, choliambic poem by M.)

1: on the scansion of this line, see at Mart. 13.112.1. For another delayed relative, see Mart. 13.50.1. Note also e.g. Mart. 14.110.1, 192.1, 112.1, and 211.2.

surripuit γ: **subripuit** α. (The poem is omitted by β.) Whereas Shackleton Bailey follows γ, most editors print *subripuit*, a spelling which is attested in every instance of the word in M (Lindsay *Orth.* 38); but the weight of evidence for one or the other is not compelling.

pastor is usually used of a shepherd, but can be applied to any herdsman: *OLD* s.v. *pastor* §1. Since newly born kids find their feet very quickly (they cannot suckle otherwise), this *pastor* has moved promptly.

2 de primo matrum lacte colustra damus: *damus* (last word of the poem) balances and contrasts with *surripuit* (first word). *Colustra* is tautologous after 'de primo ... lacte', but not obtrusively so. Its plural accords with *matrum* and *haedis*, line 1, and serves metrical convenience, but contrasts with the *lemma*. This is perhaps singular to agree with the *lemma* of Mart. 13.39, *haedus*, since poems 38 and 39 form a pair (cf. Intro. (iii) above). For M's indifference to numerical discrepancy between *lemma* and poem, see Mart. 13.11.2 n. above.

13.39 A kid

Let the animal, frolicsome and of no use to the green vine, pay the penalty: young though he be, he has already harmed the god.

le. haedus: damage to vines by goats was a common problem, and the subject of goats destroying vines and being sacrificed as punishment ('det poenas', line 2) became a regular literary theme; cf. Mart. 3.24.1-2 'vite nocens rosa stabat moriturus ad aras/ hircus, Bacche, tuis victima grata sacris' and see Mynors in detail at Verg. *G.* 2.380 ff. Contrast Mart. 8.50(51).12 'ipse tua pasci vite, Lyaee, velis' where the *caper* is so fine that, contrary to normal practice, Bacchus would actually encourage its crop destruction. Although the poem's subject is easily discernible from the literary tradition, the *lemma* here nonetheless clarifies further what it is. For other explanatory *lemmata*, see at 13.11 above.

The *haedus* does not feature elsewhere as a Saturnalian gift, but it is a birthday present at Mart. 10.87.17; cf. 3.58.37, where a country caller brings the 'vagientem matris hispidae fetum'. In surviving literature, it appears elsewhere not as part of the *gustatio*, but as a main course, albeit in modest dinners: Mart. 10.48.14, Hor. *Serm.* 2.2.120, Juv. 11.66 ff. 'haedulus et toto grege mollior, inscius herbae/ necdum ausus virgam humilis mordere salicti,/ qui plus lactis habet quam sanguinis'. If suitable for a modest main course, however, this gift would make a lavish appetiser. As such, it is to be seen as an expensive version of the beestings in Mart. 13.38 (note *haedus* in both epigrams). This pairing of cheap and expensive equivalents (cf. 13.54-5, 102-3 below; also 104-5) prefigures one of the principles behind the pairing of epigrams in Book 14, where the alternation of cheap and expensive gifts underpins the order of poems (see my introduction).

For kid recipes, many of which double for lamb, see Apic. 8.357-66 Budé.

1 lascivum pecus: *pecus* is often used of animals other than sheep, usually by the poets (*OLD* s.v. *pecus* §1c), but note Columella 1 proem. 'pecus caprile'.

Goats are often associated with lack of sexual inhibition (Coleman at Verg. *Ecl.* 2.64 'florentem cytisum sequitur lasciva capella') but, especially given *tener* in line 2, it is likely that the friskiness of this kid is due to youth; cf. Ovid *Met.* 13.791 'tenero lascivior haedo' (of Galatea) and see *OLD* s.v. *lascivus* §1.

et viridi non utile Baccho: as often, and as is made clear by *viridi*, Bacchus here refers metonymically to the vine. In contrast, *deo* (line 2) refers to the god himself.

With the litotes 'non utile', cf. *nocuit*, line 2. Goats were in fact notorious for attacking not just vines but any kind of vegetation: cf. Juv. 11.66 ff. and Verg. *Ecl.* 2.64 (both quoted above), and Verg. *G.* 4.10 (on the damage by goats to flowers visited by bees).

2 iam tener: so destructive is this kid that it did not need long to offend the god. For *tener* of youth, see *OLD* s.v. §2a; but given the present context of food, the word also suggests tenderness for eating (see *OLD* s.v. *tener* §3). Kids tasted better the younger they were: cf. Juv. 11.66 ff., quoted above, and this poem therefore both condemns and commends.

Instead of 'iam tener', T has 'sed tamen'; but explanation rather than an adversative is needed after 'det poenas'.

13.40 Eggs

If white liquid flows around yellow yolks, let the Hesperian sauce of the mackerel season the eggs.

le. ova: eggs were so well established as part of the *gustatio* that the phrase 'ab ovo ... ad mala' (Hor. *Serm.* 1.3.6-7) became proverbial of the passage of a meal from the first course to the last; see Porphyrio's explanation ad loc., André *Alimentation* 152-3; cf. Mart. 10.48.11, Varro *R.* 1.2.11 'ne illud quidem ovum vidimus, quod in cenali pompa solet esse primum' and Hor. *Serm.* 1.4.12 ff. (which gives details as to the best eggs to choose). Note too Mart. 5.78.5, 11.52.7 and 8, Pliny *Ep.* 1.15.2 (quoted at Mart. 13.6.*le.* n.) and Petr. 33.3 ff., where the eggs served at Trimalchio's *gustatio* turn out to be not what they seemed (see Smith ad loc.). Eggs seem also to have been standard albeit meagre Saturnalian gifts, being listed at Stat. *Silv.* 4.9.30; cf. *SHA Elagabalus* 22.1 where 'ova pullina' are distributed as a 'joker' in a dinner-table lottery.

The eggs described in this epigram are presumably fried. Apicius' brief recipe for fried eggs involves a wine sauce: 'ova frixa: oenogarata' (7.322 Budé). Contrast the *garum* used as seasoning in this poem. For other recipes for or using egg, see the Budé index.

1 candida si croceos circumfluit unda vitellos: the colour contrast between *candida* and *croceos* is reinforced by c alliteration. *Croceus* can be used of a wide range of yellow or saffron-coloured things (*OLD* s.v. *croceus* §2). *Candidus* is applied elsewhere (twice) to egg-white also at Pliny *Nat.* 29.40. *Unda* does not survive otherwise of egg-white, but is not unknown of liquids besides water (*OLD* s.v. *unda* §3) and it goes well with *circumfluit* in describing the flow of egg-white before, preserving its undulating outline, it hardens in the pan.

2 Hesperius scombri ... liquor: i.e. Spanish *garum*, for which see 13.102.*le.* n. below. Being of the highest quality, it lends sophistication here to the simple egg it is to season (for this use of *tempero*, see *OLD* s.v. *tempero* §6a). Pliny describes how *garum* was made at *Nat.* 31.93 (note his use of *liquor*): 'aliud etiamnum liquoris exquisiti genus, quod garum vocavere, intestinis piscium ceterisque quae abicienda essent sale maceratis, ut sit illa putrescentium sanies'.

On the use of the name Hesperia, signifying 'the western land', see N-H at Hor. *Carm.* 1.28.26 and 36.4. What was meant by it depended on one's standpoint, whether in Greece or Rome.

13.41 A sucking pig

Let a rich man place before me the nursling of a sluggish mother, fed on pure milk, and eat from the Aetolian hog.

le. porcellus lactans β (**-tens** γ): **porcellus** α (R in Shackleton Bailey's apparatus; but this appears to be a misprint). Although Servius distinguishes at Verg. *G.* 1.315 between *lactans* and *lactens*, the forms are in fact both admissible, as Citroni remarks at Mart. 1.43.7 'lactantes ... metas' (TXV: *lactentes* EG). Therefore, while editors favour β's reading here, γ's need not be wrong; cf. *ThLL* VII(2).848.25 ff. s.v. *lactans* [Heine].

Pork was a usual Saturnalian dish, as is noted above: Intro. (ii) section B. Mart. 14.71 *porcus*, which is cited there, describes a pig given as a Saturnalian present. In that poem, as here, reference is made also to boars (regarding which see at 13.93.*le.* below); but while Mart. 14.71 suggests that the pig it describes is as good as boar (which was usually regarded as superior: Mart. 8.22.1), this poem humorously adopts a different tack: the rich man is more than welcome to his boar if he serves his poor guest with the sucking pig he would rather have anyway. The poem has in mind the practice by some wealthy hosts (contrary to the egalitarian spirit of the Saturnalia) of grading the service given their guests according to their social rank (cf. Pliny *Ep.* 2.6, Juv. 5; see Smith at Petr. 31.2, Gowers 212-13 and compare the notes on 13.7.2 above, 48.*le.*, 121.2, 123.1 'tua ... sportula' below), but for once this custom is not criticised.

Sucking pig seems normally to have been a main course rather than an appetiser. Apicius gives recipes at 8.367-83 Budé, the last recipe being for an accompanying sauce. For further details, see André *Alimentation* 138. Petr. 40.4 describes as *apophoreta* not real sucking pigs, but pastry models: 'circa autem minores porcelli ex coptoplacentis facti, quasi uberibus imminerent, scrofam esse positam significabant. et hi quidem apophoreti fuerunt'. A *porcus* is a *xeniolum* at Apul. *Met.* 2.11.3, quoted in the Introduction (i) above.

1 lacte mero pastum: *merus* is usually used of wine, and this is the assumption underpinning its use of milk e.g. at Ovid *Fast.* 4.369 (the wine of the simple past) and Lucr. 1.260 (in the context of calves, unsteady on their feet). Here it stresses that the piglet is totally unweaned, indicating that, as with the *lalisio* at 13.97 below and the kid at Juv. 11.66 ff. (quoted at 13.39.*le.*), it is therefore all the more desirable.

pigrae ... matris alumnum: at Mart. 7.27.2 *piger* is used of a boar well fattened on acorns and therefore good for eating. Here, although it reflects the inertia of the sow, who is not eaten, her size serves to emphasise the piglet's suitability for the table, not least through the alliterative juxtaposition of *pastum* and *pigrae*.

Given 'lacte ... pastum', the root of *alumnus* is possibly worth recalling: see *OLD* s.v. *alo* §1a: 'to suckle, nurse, feed (offspring)'.

2 Aetolo de sue: cf. Mart. 13.93.2 'Aetole ... cuspide' and see 13.93.*le.* n. below. M refers here, of course, as there, not to the boar actually slain by Meleager, but one of equivalent size.

De indicates that, unlike Virro at Juv. 5.115-16, the rich man here is not served the whole 'Aetolian' boar himself (see *OLD* s.v. *de* §10), whereas apparently the poor man feeds on the whole piglet. This reversal of the expected coincides with the poem's atypical approval of different meals for different classes. (For boars served whole, see again 13.93.*le.* n. below.)

Mynors, unlike most earlier editors, takes *sus* at Verg. *G.* 3.255 'ipse ruit dentesque Sabellicus exacuit sus' just to mean 'swine', commenting that there is no evidence earlier than Ovid for *sus* equalling *aper*, since in passages like Lucr. 5.25 the sense is ironical: 'the famous Calydonian boar is to the true philosopher only a "bristly Arcadian pig" '; cf. Costa's note ad loc. on the jingle 'Arcadius sus'. As one of the instances where he thinks *sus* does equal *aper*, Mynors cites Mart. 11.18.18 'sus Calydonius'; but he is probably wrong to do so since M is here debunking the story (Kay notes ad loc. the jingle of *mus* and *sus*). Mynors' other example is Stat. *Theb.* 6.836, which can stand. In the present epigram *sus* is metrically convenient, while *aper* is not; but it is probably also debunking, according with the poor man's dismissal of the rich man's fare provided he has his sucking pig.

13.42 Seedless pomegranates and azaroles

We do not give you azaroles and seedless pomegranates from Libyan branches, but from Nomentan trees.

le. apyrina et tubures: these were exotic fruits, subsequently grown in Italy. Both this poem and the next (note 'quid tibi cum Libycis?', line 2) are concerned to promote local over imported produce; cf. perhaps the patriotic literature cited by Hollis at Ovid *Ars* 1.56 'haec [sc. Roma] habet ... quicquid in orbe fuit'.

Apyrina (cf. ἀπύρινα) were pomegranates which were sweet (Pliny *Nat.* 23.106) and seedless (Columella *Arb.* 23.1), or whose seeds were small (Sen. *Ep.* 85). They came originally from Africa and more particularly Carthage: Columella 12.42.1, Pliny *Nat.* 13.112. Hence 'de Libycis ... ramis' in line 1, q.v. ad loc. They are not mentioned elsewhere as presents, or as part of the *gustatio*, although pomegranate seeds are eaten as such at Petr. 31.11.

Pomegranates, albeit not necessarily *apyrina*, are depicted in two still lifes from Pompeii: *Pompeii AD 79* 255-6.

As for *tubures* (Tγ: -beres β, likewise at Mart. 13.43.2), see Heraeus at Mart. 13.43, who adds to his references in *Woch. kl. Philol.*, (1907) 212, Pallad. 3.25.32 and Macr. 3.19.2 (where he suggests *tubur* for *Tibur*). See too V. Lundström, *Eranos* 7 (1907), 76. There is uncertainty as to what in fact the fruit was. Ker (Loeb note) identifies it as probably being the jujube (*Zizyphus vulgaris* Lmk), but this seems to be ruled out by Pliny *Nat.* 15.47, who speaks of *zizypha* (he uses the word's neuter form) and *tubures* as being separate. (Pliny, incidentally, mentions Syrian *tubures* as well as the African variety.) The *OLD* holds that it was probably the azarole or oriental medlar.

According to Suetonius (*Dom.* 16.1) *tubures* were given as a present to Domitian on the day before his assassination: 'pridie quam periret, cum oblatos tubures servari iussisset in crastinum, adiecit "si modo uti licuerit".'

1 de Libycis ... apyrina ramis: cf. Mart. 13.43.1 (where the same line-ending is used, although there in considered contrast, of Italian pomegranates) and note the balancing 'de Nomentanis ... arboribus', line 2. For *Libycus* meaning 'North African', see at Mart. 13.12.1. For its poetic use of Carthage, see *OLD* s.v. *Libycus* §2.

2 de Nomentanis ... arboribus: cf. Mart. 10.94.3-4 'Nomentana ... arbore'. For Nomentan and other suburban estates (note 'suburbanis ... ramis', Mart. 13.43.1 below), see at Mart. 13.12.*le.* and 2 above. While it would be natural to take this poem to refer to gifts from M's own estate, his promotion of its produce here would then conflict with his practice elsewhere, which is jokingly to belittle it: see at 13.119.*le.* below. (That the poem is intended to be ironically self-effacing is intrinsically unlikely: again cf. 13.43.) It is possible therefore that M chose Nomentum to contrast with Libya not so much because he had an estate there (although personal knowledge of the place would doubtless have influenced him in part), but because it was a (metrically) convenient local agricultural area; cf. the possibility that, personal links notwithstanding, he chose Nomentum at 13.15 above (see the note on the *lemma*) because it was convenient as a representative country setting.

On the polysyllabic line-ending, see Intro. (vi) above.

13.43 The same

Picked from suburban branches, seedless pomegranates are sent, and home-grown azaroles. What do you want with Libyan?

le. idem: regarding *apyrina*, *tubures*, their exotic origin and the concern of this poem and the last to promote local produce, see at Mart. 13.42 *le.* n. above. Also relevant to this poem are the comments on *Libycis* (line 1) and 'de Nomentanis ... arboribus' (line 2).

Although the subject and sentiments of both poems are the same, repetitiveness is avoided through variation of expression; cf. Mart. 13.63-4, poems also on the same subject, in which the same wordplay is exploited in different ways. While it is understandable that an artist might be attracted to producing variations on a theme, it is not clear why M should have chosen for his variations in Book 13 the subjects in particular of poems 42 and 63. One wonders therefore whether, when he wrote these duplicate poems, he originally intended both to survive in the final collection, or whether he was experimenting and had planned eventually to keep just one of each.

1 lecta: *lego* is the usual verb for picking fruit: *ThLL* VII(2).1124.50 ff. s.v. *lego* [v. Kamptz]; but the participle can also have the sense 'choice' (*OLD* s.v. *lectus* §2), and although it is generally applied in this sense to things other than fruit (*ThLL* loc. cit. 1133.27 ff.), it is perhaps at work in the background here.

mittuntur: on *mitto*, see at 13.23.1 above. The point of the present poem is that the produce it describes is *not* sent from Libya.

2: regarding the polysyllabic pentameter ending introduced by *Libycis*, see Intro. (vi) above.

vernae: M uses the word similarly e.g. at 10.30.21 (of home-grown *lupi*). Cf. also Mart. 3.1.6 'debet enim Gallum vincere verna liber' (i.e. one written at Rome).

13.44 A sow's udder

You would think it not yet an udder: the pap flows with such abundance, swelling with living milk.

le. sumen: the sow's udder was a favourite delicacy: see Courtney at Juv. 11.138, André *Alimentation* 138. Apicius gives recipes both for dishes of which the udder was an ingredient (4.141-2 Budé) and for the udder cooked alone (7.258-9 Budé). It would appear from Pers. 1.53 that it was served piping hot: 'calidum scis ponere sumen'.
   The *sumen* appears elsewhere as a (luxury) gift at Mart. 7.78.3, and Caecilianus steals 'mammas suminis' at Mart. 2.37.2 to take home as unofficial *apophoreta*. It is a main-course dish at 11.52.13 and Macr. 3.13.12, but features as part of the *gustatio* again at Mart. 10.48.12 'madidum thynni de sale sumen'. Although udders were rather exceptional pork dishes, it is relevant to recall that pigs were traditional Saturnalian fare: see Intro. (ii) section B above.

1 esse putes nondum sumen: i.e. you would think from the fact that it appears still to be lactating ('sic ... tumet', lines 1-2) that it is not the cooked dish but still part of the living animal. As Izaac suggests, the udder has presumably been filled again, after cooking, with milk. This sort of serving trick would have appealed to Roman diners; cf. the fish at Petr. 36.4, which appear to be swimming in the sauce.

Heraeus punctuates with a colon after *sumen*; cf. Giarratano and Gilbert. This is perhaps preferable to the semi-colon of Shackleton Bailey and others, signalling that what follows explains the poem's opening assertion.

2 effluit et ... tumet ς: **-uet et** β: **-uet** γ: **et fluit et** T. Given that the swelling *papilla* must already be flowing, β's future tense (caused by homoeoteleuton with *et*?) can be discarded at once, as can γ's comparable reading (which compounds haplography). T's present tense reading has therefore been accepted by most modern editors; but Shackleton Bailey is surely right, along with Schryver and Friedländer, to adopt the humanist emendation. While *fluo* can indeed be used of bodily liquids (*OLD* s.v. *fluo* §2b) and Celsus uses it several times of loose bowels (*OLD* s.v. *fluo* §5b), it is not generally used in 1st century Latin of the source which issues these liquids: see *ThLL* VI(1).970.53 ff. s.v. *fluo* [Bacherler]. In contrast *effluo* (*ec-* in T's exemplar?) can be used both of the liquid and of the container *vel sim.* which gives the liquid issue: see *ThLL* V(2).194.63 ff. s.v. *effluo* [Leumann], citing e.g. Petr. 71.11 'amphoras ... gypsatas, ne effluant vinum', Jahn at Pers. 3.20 'effluis amens': '*Effluere* autem sicut *manare* et similia non solum de liquore, qui fluit, sed etiam de re, quae fluere facit vel sinit ... ponitur', and Munro at Lucr. 6.971

There are fewer parallels to the use of *tumeo* here than one might expect, but cf. Calp. *Ecl.* 5.33 'tumidis spument tibi mulctra papillis'.

vivo lacte: like 'ubere largo' in line 1, this ablative usage is instrumental, but has also an adverbial function since it expands on *sic*. With *vivus*, cf. Luc. 6.554-6 'nec cessant a caede manus, si sanguine vivo/ est opus'.

papilla actually denotes the nipple or teat (L-S s.v. *papilla* §IIa), but is often employed of the whole breast or udder. It is used of animals less often in poetry than in prose.

13.45 Poultry chickens

If I had Libyan birds and pheasants, you would receive them; but as it is receive birds of the farmyard.

le. pulli gallinacei: *pullus* can be used of young animals in general, but applies specifically to young fowl (*OLD* s.v. *pullus* §1c). It appears with *gallinaceus* again at Pl. *Capt.* 849 'pullos gallinaceos', *Curc.* 450, Varro *R.* 3.9.10; cf. 'gallus gallinaceus' at Pl. *Aul.* 465.

Chickens are not indigenous to Italy, being imports from the east (André *Alimentation* 127); but they soon became assimilated and regarded as local produce. The chicken is therefore characterised as simple fare at Hor. *Serm.* 2.2.121, Juv. 11.71 and Petr. 46.2. In these instances, however, as at Mart. 10.48.17 and 11.52.14, it forms part of the main course. As part of the *gustatio*, in contrast, it would not necessarily be negligible, being presented as such in this poem only in comparison with the more exotic pheasants and guinea fowl (on which see below). The poem's assertion that the giver would give better gifts if he could nonetheless conforms to a standard pattern; cf. Mart. 14.132 and 153, quoted at 13.6.1 above.

Apul. *Met.* 2.11.3 (see Intro. (i) above) speaks of chickens as *xeniola*. At Mart. 2.37.5, Caecilianus steals a 'femur ... pulli' as an unofficial *apophoreton*. Apicius' numerous recipes for chicken can be found from the Budé index.

1 Libycae ... volucres et Phasides: references to the guinea fowl's African origins are standard in identifying the bird (on *Libycus*, see at Mart. 13.12.1). Note Varro *R.* 3.9.16, Pliny *Nat.* 10.74 and see the quotations below. The pheasant (*Phasianus colchicus*) owes its name to the River Phasis in Colchis, which flows into the Black Sea. See Coleman at Stat. *Silv.* 4.6.8 'Phasidis ales', who refers to D'Arcy Thompson *Birds* 298 ff. The introduction of these birds to the Graeco-Roman world lies behind Mart. 13.72 *Phasinae* and 73 *Numidicae*; but, although they could be found in M's day in a productive Roman farmyard (Mart. 3.58.15-16 'Numidicaeque guttatae/ et impiorum phasiana Colchorum'; cf. Pliny *Nat.* 10.132), the former being bred the same way as peafowl (Columella 8.12.1), they remained a rare and luxury food (D'Arcy Thompson *Birds* 299-300 gives references; see too André *Alimentation* 131-2, Pollard 93.) Hence Vitellius included 'Phasianarum ... cerebella' in a sumptuous dish dedicated to Minerva (Suet. *Vit.* 13.2). (Apicius gives a recipe for the 'pullus Numidicus' at 6.240 Budé.)

The two birds are regularly mentioned together. In addition to this poem, Mart. 3.58.15-16 and 13.72-3, cf. 3.77.4 'nec Libye mittit nec tibi Phasis aves', Petr. 93.2 'ales Phasiacis petita Colchis/ atque Afrae volucres placent palato,/ quod non sunt faciles', Juv. 11.139 'Scythicae volucres' and 142-3 'Afrae avis'. They were both distributed at Domitian's Saturnalian show: see Stat. *Silv.* 1.6.77-8.

2 at βγ: tu T. T's reading is very colourless. For the use of an adversative with *nunc* to mean 'as it is', see *OLD* s.v. *nunc* §11a, citing e.g. Verg. *A.* 4.3.340 ff. 'me si fata meis paterentur ducere vitam/ auspiciis ... Priami tecta alta manerent, ... sed nunc Italiam ... Lyciae iussere capessere sortes'; cf. the use of νῦν δέ in Greek (e.g. at Thuc. 3.113.6, 4.126.1).

accipe, after the caesura, balances and contrasts with *acciperes* at the beginning of the line. On the word here, see Intro. (v) and n. 6 above.

13.46 Apricot peaches

We had been peaches of small worth on our maternal branches. Now on adoptive ones we are peaches of price.

1e. persica praecocia β: **praecoqua** γ: **praecocta** T: **cocta** R: om. ς. Although it can be paralleled in early editions of Columella (e.g. at 12.37 'uvas praecoquas … legito'), the form of γ's *praecoqua* is not classical (see *ThLL* X(2).512.54 ff. s.v. *praecox* [Breimeier]). Also suspect is T's rare form *praecocta* (see *ThLL* X(2).509.52 ff. s.v. *praecoquo* [Korteweg]), which, with R's abbreviation, is a likely corruption of β's *praecocia*. While the meaning of *praecocia* here has been debated, the correctness of the reading is therefore generally accepted.

The poem describes peaches which are nothing special when grown from their own root stock, but became so (and therefore expensive) when grafted onto another. (For the general familiarity of Roman readers with the grafting process, see Mynors at Verg. *G.* 2.73-82.)

Shackleton Bailey (Loeb note), who follows *RE* 19(1).1025 [Steier] (note lines 25 ff.), takes *praecocia* to mean 'early'; cf. Pliny *Nat.* 15.40 'post autumnum maturescunt Asiatica, aestate praecocia', and suggests that the adoptive root stock is perhaps that of a superior (= later?) peach variety. (Steier compares Pallad. 2.15.2 'inseritur eadem persica in se'.)

In contrast, however, Friedländer, amongst others, thinks that the epigram concerns peaches (*Prunus persica*) grafted onto an apricot tree (*Prunus armenica*) or *praecox*: see *ThLL* X(2).513.63 ff. s.v. *praecox* [Breimeier]; cf. Dioscorides 1.115 τὰ δὲ μικρότερα καλούμενα δὲ ἀρμενιακά, ῥωμαϊστὶ δὲ βρεκόκκια (= πρεκόκκια: Galen 12.76, 6.593 Kühn). He cites Calp. *Ecl.* 2.42, concerning peaches grafted onto a plum (*Prunus domestica*). In favour of this idea is that it makes for a greater contrast between *maternis*, line 1, and *adoptivis*, line 2, and a hybrid fruit may well have commanded a higher price than fruit bred within a species. Also, although Steier observes, loc. cit., that grafting peaches onto apricots is mentioned by neither the *Geoponica* nor Palladius, arguments *ex silentio* are of limited worth, especially as both works bear witness to a considerable interest in cross-grafting and mention much more difficult, inter-family and generic grafts; cf. A.S.Pease, 'Notes on Ancient Grafting', *TAPhA* 64 (1933), 70.

1 vilia is emphatically placed, stressing the meanness of ungrafted peaches, and finds both contrast and balance in *cara* at the end of line 2. *Fueramus*, in the middle of the hexameter and echoed by *ramis* at the end, contrasts meanwhile with 'nunc … sumus' in the pentameter, where it is to *nunc* that the reader's attention is particularly drawn.

maternus, describing a fruit's natural root-stock, cannot be paralleled exactly (although see *OLD* s.v. *maternus* §4, and note perhaps Verg. *G.*

2.82 'non sua poma', remembering *matris*, line 19); but it is a natural word-choice, given the regularity with which *adoptivus* and similar words are used in the context of grafting. See the detailed note of Henderson at Ovid *Rem*. 195 'fac ramum ramus adoptet', who cites, in addition to Ovid *Ars* 2.652 and *Med*. 6, numerous instances from Columella and the Elder Pliny.

13.47 Picene loaves

Picene bread grows with its white nectar just as a light sponge swells when it has soaked up water.

le. panes Picentini: for the location of Picenum, and its other products, see Mart. 13.35.*le*. n. According to Pliny, *Nat*. 18.106, Picene bread was made of *alica* (for which see Mart. 13.6.*le*. n.). The *alica* was steeped for nine days, and then kneaded with raisin juice so as to look like (flat slabs of) pastry dough (*tracta*, for which see Solomon, cited at 13.10.2 above) and baked. Pliny adds 'neque est ex eo (pane) cibus nisi madefacto quod fit lacte maxime mulso'; cf. 'niveo ... nectare', line 1, and see the note ad loc. Regarding the bread, see additionally André *Alimentation* 70. At Macr. 3.13 it is a luxury main course. It features in the recipe for 'sala cattabia Apiciana' given at Apic. 4.126 Budé.

   The adjective *Picentinus* is not widely attested, but appears outside M and Apicius (loc. cit.) e.g. at Pliny *Nat*. 15.55 '(pira) Picentina' and Pomp. *Att*. 8.12c.2 'sine Picentinis cohortibus'.

1 Ceres: this metonymy for corn or bread is common: cf. Cic. *ND* 2.60 'fruges Cererem appellamus, vinum autem Liberum', Mart. 3.58.6, Verg. *A*. 1.701, Luc. 4.381 and see *OLD* s.v. *Ceres* §2b; cf. the use of *Lyaeus* at Mart. 13.22.1.

niveo ... nectare: i.e. honey mixed with milk. *Nectar* is applied to honey elsewhere e.g. at Verg. *G*. 4.164 and Mart. 13.104.2. *Niveus* is also used of milk e.g. at Verg. *Ecl*. 2.20 and Ovid *Met*. 13.829. The milk was presumably heated to help the honey dissolve; cf. Apicius' instructions in his recipes for various kinds of *dulcia*: 7.297 ff. Budé.

crescit: there survive no precise parallels of *crescere* as used here, but it was similarly applied in a wide range of contexts, e.g. of rivers swelling, towns growing and of the waxing moon. See *OLD* s.v. *cresco* §3a, *ThLL* IV.1178.58 ff. s.v. *cresco* [Burger].

2 ut ... spongea: sponges were very familiar domestic objects (see generally D-S IV(2).1442-3 s.v. *spongia* [Maurice Besnier]), and M's simile is one which would have met with instant understanding. Lucretius uses a sponge simile of eating and tasting at 4.617 ff.: 'principio sucum sentimus in ore, cibum cum/ mandendo exprimimus, ceu plenam spongiam aquai/ siquis forte manu premere ac siccare coepit'.

turget: contrast *tumet* at Mart. 14.144.2 (at which see my note). While the sponge there swells 'expresso ... imbre' (thus becoming *levis*), it does so here (being initially *levis*) through absorbing water ('accepta ... aqua'; for similar uses of *accipio*, see *OLD* s.v. *accipio* §11a).

13.48-51: on the ordering of these poems, see Intro. (iii) above; cf. the grouping of *tubera terrae*, *boleti* and *ficedulae* at Juv. 14.7-9. Birds (thrushes?) and mushrooms are displayed together in a still life panel from Herculaneum: *Pompeii* AD *79* 255.

13.48 Mushrooms

It is easy to send silver and gold and a cloak and a toga; to send mushrooms is hard.

1e. boleti: the *boletus* has generally been identified as the 'Agaricus Caesareus', and was a fungus regarded by the Romans as a great delicacy; cf. Mart. 3.45.6, 7.20.7, 12.48.1. Hence the *boletar* of Mart. 14.102 Leary is indignant at being used, despite its elevated name, for cabbage. For details and discussion of the growth, see Howell at Mart. 1.20.2, *RE* XX(2)1378.1 ff. s.v. *Pilze* [Steier], André *Alimentation* 43. It was often contrasted with more ordinary *fungi*, e.g. by poets commenting on the practice amongst certain hosts (see Mart. 13.41.*le*. n. above) of according inferior service to inferior guests. Mart. 1.20 aside, cf. 3.60.5 and Juv. 5.146-7. *Boleti* naturally made for a luxury present (cf. Mart. 7.78.3) and the point of this poem seems to be that they were difficult to send at the Saturnalia not, as Friedländer suggests (at Mart. 1.20.2), because they were out of season, but because (cf. Shackleton Bailey's Loeb note) it was preferable to keep them for one's self, parting instead with other expensive items (cf. 13.125.2 n. below and see the notes on line 1).

Boleti were a regular part of the *gustatio*: cf. Pliny *Nat.* 16.31 'boletos suillosque, gulae novissima inritamenta', Sen. *Ep.* 108.15, and several recipes can be found in Apicius (7.313-15 Budé).

1-2: the composition of this couplet is very skilful. The poem is a miniature which prefigures such compositions as Mart. 7.53, where again a catalogue of Saturnalian gifts is preface to a shrewd observation (lines 9 ff.):

> vix puto triginta nummorum tota fuisse
> munera, quae grandes octo tulere Syri.
> quanto commodius nullo mihi ferre labore
> argenti potuit pondera quinque puer!

(For Saturnalian catalogues, see Intro. (v) above.) The present catalogue
(of four gifts) occupies the hexameter, with which is contrasted the pentameter's single gift of *boleti*. Within the hexameter, there is a balance
between precious metals and clothing, and a contrast between the elided
'argentum atque aurum' and the internal rhyme of 'laenamque togamque'.
(The elision after *argentum* can be paralleled elsewhere in M only at 2.61.5
and 4.11.5: Birt in Friedländer, 35.) The use of '-que ... -que' after *atque*
affords further variation. In the pentameter, 'difficile est' is emphatically
placed, as is *boletos*, which is circumscribed by diaeresis and the caesura;
and *mittere* begins each half-line.

1 argentum: gifts of silver such as the Minerva described by Mart. 14.179
were clearly very expensive and it is not insignificant that Lucian has his
Saturnalian law-giver Kronosolon decree that the poor who give silver
should be punished: *Sat.* 16. Nevertheless, while M has an expensive gift
in mind in this epigram, silver gifts were by no means all ruinous: note e.g.
Mart. 4.88.3 and 8.71.

aurum: gold gifts could again range in value from the small to the very
weighty. In Mart. 14 they include a hair pin (14.24), a chased gold bowl
(14.95) and a Victory given to the emperor and celebrating his triumph
over the Chatti (14.170).

laenamque togamque: clothes were often given as presents: cf. Homer
Od. 8.392, 15.123 ff., Verg. *A.* 3.482 ff. For their distribution at the
Saturnalia, cf. Suet. *Aug.* 75, Mart. 14.124-58. Concerning the first garment cited here, there has been much debate, but it seems that it was a
warm, thick cloak (cf. Varro *L.* 5.133 'laena, quod de lana multa, duorum
... togarum instar'). For more details, see Lillian M. Wilson, *The Clothing
of the Ancient Romans*, Baltimore 1938, 112 ff., Sebesta 229 [Goldman]. It
appears as a Saturnalian present also at Mart. 14.138 where it is presented as a rich man's gift. On the toga, see at 13.1.1 'toga ... et paenula'
above. It seems also to have been a common Saturnalian gift. It features
in two of the *Apophoreta* (Mart. 14.124-5), again being cast as an expensive
present.

2: on the polysyllabic 'difficile est' at the pentameter-close, see Intro. (vi)
above.

Boletos mittere, βγ, is corrupted to 'b. nam mihi' (T) and 'b. haec tibi' (R).
Lindsay's explanation is plausible, that the corruptions originate in the
abbreviation of *mittere* to *mī*. On the use of *mittere* here, see 13.3.5 n.
above.

Commentary

13.49 Beccaficos

Although the fig nourishes me, why, since I feed on sweet grapes, did not the grape rather give me my name?

le. ficedulae βγ: **ficedula** R. Although R's singular agrees numerically with the personifying elements of the poem, this is not grounds for rejecting the better supported plural: as Heraeus notes (at Mart. 13.59 below) α often has singular *lemmata* where βγ have plurals, appearing (*pace* Borovskij at 13.72) sometimes to have introduced them deliberately for the sake of consistency between *lemma* and epigram; but for such numerical differences, see 13.11.2 n. above.

M's fondness for etymologising receives general discussion at 13.71.*le.* below. For this poem specifically, see Grewing (1999a) 266. In having the personified *ficedula* question here, with pedantic logic, why, since it also ate grapes, it had not been called an *uvedula* instead, this poem achieves humour similar to that at Mart. 14.121 *coclearia*:

> sum cocleis habilis sed nec minus utilis ovis.
> numquid scis, potius cur cocleare vocer?

In fact, as Aristotle knew (*HA* 8.592b.22), and despite the translation 'beccaficos' here (on which see at 13.5.1 'cerea ... ficedula' above), the bird did not eat figs or fruit at all. Instead, it is a type of fly-catcher, probably the *Muscicapa striata* Pall. or *Muscicapa atricapilla* L., although the exact identity is uncertain: *Kl.P.* 2.578.1 ff. *Fliegenfänger* [W. Richter]. *Cereus* at Mart. 13.5.1 might point to the former, which is a lightish brown. (On the possible applications of *cereus*, see J. André, *Études sur les termes de couleur dans la langue latine*, Paris 1949, 157.)

The *ficedula* must have been a common gift, but it is not specifically referred to elsewhere as such. (For bird gifts, see my note at Mart. 14.73-6 (describing pets); cf. 8.78.7 and 13.51 ff. below, and note also the section on fowl beginning with poem 61.) The *ficedula* appears, however, as part of the *gustatio* also at Petr. 33.8 (note *gustantibus*, 33.3): 'pinguissimam ficedulam inveni piperato vitello circumdatam', and twice at Macr. 3.13.12. For recipes (all involving pepper), see Mart. 13.5.1 'cerea ... ficedula' n. above. It was a luxury dish (Mayor on Juv. 14.9, Blümner *Priv.* 178) and, according to Favorinus (Gel. 15.8.2), was the only bird eaten whole by leading epicures. See further André *Alimentation* 123.

1 cum ... alat is concessive (cf. Shackleton Bailey's apparatus criticus) while *cum ... uvis* is causal. M achieves further *varietas* by following the third person active *alat* with the first person middle *pascar*. (For this use of *pasco* with the ablative, see *OLD* s.v. *pasco* §6a.)

On the scansion of this line, see Mart. 13.112.1 n. below.

13.50 Truffles

We truffles, who with tender head burst the earth which nourishes us, are produce second only to mushrooms.

le. terrae tubera: although ranked below *boleti*, truffles were nonetheless also luxury items: cf. Juv. 5.116 ff., 14.7-9 and see *RE* XX.1383.1 ff. s.v. *Pilze* [Steier]. For ways to prepare them, see Apic. 7.316-321 Budé. Apicius also provides a recipe for preserving truffles (1.27 Budé), but as André notes ad loc., they did not keep for long and those described here are therefore probably fresh. They would coincide well with the Saturnalia, being seasonable from November to March (*Mrs Beeton's Book of Household Management*, first published 1861, enlarged edn London 1982, repr. 1987, 597). For further information, e.g. regarding different varieties and growing conditions, see André *Alimentation* 45 and *RE* art. cit. 1381.6 ff.

1 rumpimus altricem tenero quae vertice terram/ tubera: this line conflicts with Pliny's description (*Nat.* 19.33) of the truffle as a natural marvel since it had no need of a root: 'undique terra circumdata nullisque fibris nixa ... nec utique extuberante loco, in quo gignuntur, aut rimas sentiente'. Note also Mrs Beeton's observations, op. cit. 598: 'The Truffle grows in clusters, some inches below the surface of the soil ... As there is nothing to indicate where they are, dogs have been trained to discriminate their scent, by which they are discovered'. It is possible that in writing this poem M mistakenly assumed that truffles came up like the mushrooms with which they are compared.

The line is very carefully arranged, as indeed is the whole of M's epigram. Coming first word in the poem, *rumpimus* is balanced by the only other verb, *sumus* (last word). Helped by its prominent position, it suggests also the use of some force and therefore points the paradoxical contrast between the truffles' softness ('tenero ... vertice') and their evident strength. Since *altricem* is separated from *terram* by 'tenero ... vertice', the effect of *rumpimus* is clearly illustrated: the earth is visibly split. At the same time, however, M admits a unifying interlocking patterning: 'altricem tenero ... vertice terram'. Meanwhile, by ending the hexameter with *terram* and beginning the pentameter with *tubera*, he echoes the *lemma*. Finally, he emphasises the relative status of *tubera* and *boleti* by juxtaposition in line 2.

Altrix survives surprisingly rarely of the earth as a nourisher specifically of plants: see the passages cited at *ThLL* 1.1770. 81 ff. s.v. *altrix* [v. Mess.]; cf. *OLD* s.v. *altrix* §2b.

Vertix is commonly used of the tops of plants (*OLD* s.v. *vertix* §3b). Failure to see that this plant-top must be an emerging growth rather than lofty foliage, and to appreciate the delayed relative (others at 13.38.1 n.

above), may have resulted in Tγ's *de* for β's *quae*; but an instrumental sense for 'tenero ... vertice' is clearly what is required.

13.51 Decade of thrushes

Perhaps a garland woven from roses or rich nard pleases you, but one made of thrushes pleases me.

le. turdorum decuria: thrushes were a choice dish (Mart. 3.77.1, Hor. *Ep.* 1.15.41) and appear as a common gift: cf. Hor. *Serm.* 2.5.10, Mart. 2.40.3 and 6.75.1. (For other bird gifts, see at 13.49 *le.* above.) Served with asparagus, they form part of the *gustatio* at Macr. 3.13.12 (quoted at Mart. 13.21.*le.*), but could also be served later in the meal: see at Mart. 13.92.1 below and cf. Petr. 69.6 (note *epidipnis*) where 'turdi ... siliginei' are served. Apicius offers several recipes in which *turdi* feature as ingredients, and has also a recipe for the birds stuffed (exc. 29 Budé). For further information, see André *Alimentation* 122, D'Arcy Thompson *Birds* 149.

It would appear that thrushes were commonly strung in a hoop and, although this poem (line 2) and Mart. 3.47.10 'illic coronam pinguibus gravem turdis' supply the only evidence (see *ThLL* IV.937.74-5 s.v. *corona* [Gudeman]), that this hoop was called a *corona*. M here takes advantage of this usage in expressing his humorously pragmatic preference for a hoop of thrushes, which he could eat, rather than the other *coronae*, or chaplets, which were associated with banquets. (Similarly pragmatic humour can be seen in Mart. 13.41, for which see the *le.* n.)

While *corona* as in 'hoop' lacks parallels outside M, *decuria*, as used here, appears in exactly the same way at *Ed. Diocl.* 4.27 'turdorum decuria 𐆠 sexaginta'; but no other parallels survive, and it is perhaps not surprising that the gloss 'sive corona' crept into the *lemma* in the β MSS. Given the agreement of M and Diocletian's edict, it seems that ten thrushes to a hoop might have been standard.

1 [corona] texta rosis ... vel divite nardo: for rose garlands, see at 13.127 *le.* n. below. References to nard usually have in mind the oil extracted from the plant (cf. e.g. Hor. *Carm.* 2.11.15 ff.); but a garland of nard is nevertheless mentioned, in a list of banquet luxuries, at Luc. 10.164: 'accipiunt nardo florente coronas'. For this use of *dives*, meaning in effect 'precious', see *OLD* s.v. *dives* §5, *ThLL* V(1).1591.26 ff. s.v. *dives* [Bauer].

2 corona placet: these concluding words make ultimate and unifying sense of the poem while at the same time, through being delayed, making more pointed the contrast between the hexameter's *tibi* and the pentameter's *mihi*.

13.52 Ducks

Let the duck indeed be served whole, but it is tasty only in the breast and neck. Return the rest to the cook.

le. anates: considerations of taste aside, tackling a whole duck as part of the *gustatio* would have challenged all but the most gluttonous of diners. It is therefore not surprising that the 'paludis aves' at Mart. 11.52.4 form part of the main course; cf. Macr. 3.13.12. For the sake of appearances, however, it was clearly considered best to serve the duck whole, even if one ate just some of it.

The National Archaeological Museum, Naples, contains a mosaic depicting a magnificent duck obviously intended for eating: see Michael Grant, *The Art and Life of Pompeii and Herculaneum*, Milan 1979, 70. For duck recipes, see Apic. 6.212-217 Budé. Although this poem is concerned with duck as food, the bird seems also to have been considered good for digestive ailments and features in consequence in several folklore remedies (see Smith at Petr. 56.3).

1 tota … anas: this generalising singular marks another instance of numerical difference between *lemma* and poem: see at Mart. 13.11.2.

pectore: cf. the remark of Mrs Beeton (584): 'the breast alone is considered by epicures worth eating'.

2 cervice: while *pectore* is easily understandable, *cervice* is less so. Presumably the nape of the bird's neck is meant (cf. *OLD* s.v. *cervix* §1) rather than the actual neck, which would furnish little meat, or even the wings: *cervix* is often used of the 'shoulders' of animals: *ThLL* III.949.13 ff. s.v. *cervix* [Probst].

13.53 Turtle doves

When I have a plump turtle dove, lettuce farewell, and keep your snails. I don't want to waste my appetite.

le. turtures: turtle doves were a luxury: cf. Mart. 3.60.7 'aureus immodicis turtur te clunibus implet', 7.20.15, and see André *Alimentation* 121. As such they are a lover's gift at Pl. *Bac.* 68; cf. Mart. 3.82.21, and were given by legacy hunters at Juv. 6.39. Apicius gives two recipes for cooking them: 6.220 and exc. 30 Budé. While the birds are not mentioned specifically as a *gustatio* elsewhere, they accord here with the earlier gifts of *ficedulae* (13.49), *turdi* (13.51) and *anates* (13.52) and are contrasted in the poem with snails and lettuce, less appealing appetisers in preference to which these *turtures* are eaten. Snails are a cheap Saturnalian gift at Mart.

4.46.11 (cf. the cheaper snail shells at Stat. *Silv*. 4.9.32-3, at which see Coleman for useful details regarding snails) and are listed, apparently as appetisers, at Pliny *Ep*. 1.15.2 (quoted at Mart. 13.6.*le*. above). For lettuce, see at 13.14 above.

1 cum pinguis mihi turtur erit: the β MSS have 'cum m. t. p.', thus losing the important emphasis placed on *pinguis* by Tγ: this turtle dove is doubly valuable for being good quality. For fattening turtle doves, see Columella 8.9, esp. 1-2. The *ficedula* served at Petr. 33.8 (quoted at Mart. 13.49.*le*.) is *pinguissima*.

Erit with *cum* here is a generalising-iterative future, of the type much favoured by Ovid, e.g. at *Ars* 2.529 'cum volet, accedes; cum te vitabit, abibis'. See L-H-Sz II.621-2 and R.P. Oliver, *CPh* 53 (1958) 105. M might not often receive turtle doves, but whenever he does, he spurns more ordinary fare.

The singular *turtur* is generalising. For such numerical differences between *lemma* and poem, see 13.11.2 n. above.

valebis: possibly influenced by *erit*, VX preserve *valebit*; but, as Heraeus observes, this third person usage is unparalleled. With (the more immediate and lively) *valebis*, he compares Mart. 6.78.5 (of a patient who dismisses his doctor for telling him not to drink) and 2.92.3:

> natorum mihi ius trium roganti
> musarum pretium dedit mearum
> solus qui poterat. valebis uxor.
> non debet domini perire munus.

2 et cocleas tibi habe: Courtney notes at Juv. 3.186 that 'tibi habe' 'is normally a brusque form of refusal "I don't want" '. Here, however, the brusqueness is tempered by humour. Whereas M earlier addresses the lettuce specifically, here he achieves *varietas* by addressing potential donors or hosts in general. In doing so he engineers via *tibi* a contrast with *mihi*, line 1.

perdere nolo famem: not 'I do not want to spoil my appetite' as Ker translates, since this would imply that the *turtur* is part of a later course which would be enjoyed less if the snails and lettuce had been eaten earlier. Rather, M is not going to *waste* his appetite on inferior appetisers when he could expend it on better. For *perdere* in this sense, see *OLD* s.v. *perdo* §6a.

13.54 Cured ham

Let me have a Cerretanian ham or one, it may be, sent from the Menapians; let the sumptuous devour ham which is fresh.

le. perna: Mart. 13.54 is a 'riddling' epigram, like those listed at 13.11.*le.*, in that the *lemma* clarifies what the epigram is about. The *lemma*'s explanatory function here is complemented, however, by the fact that this epigram and the next form a clearly recognisable pair describing respectively humble and more extravagant versions of the same gift (cf. Mart. 13.38-9 and 102-3; see 39.*le.* n. above): with 'lauti de petasone vorent', line 2, cf. Mart. 13.55.*le. petaso*.

Scholars have nonetheless disagreed as to what in fact the precise difference was between the *perna* and *petaso*. The most likely explanation seems that of Mayor at Juv. 7.119 'siccus petasunculus': firstly, the *perna* was a part of the *petaso* (cf. Athen. 14.657E: πετασῶνος μέρος ἑκάστῳ κεῖται, ἣν πέρναν καλοῦσιν, *Ed. Diocl.* 4.8, quoted below); secondly, and crucially, while the *petaso* was fresh (Mart. 13.55.1 'musteus est'), in contrast the *perna* was preserved, whether salted (cf. Cato *Agr.* 162 'pernas sallire sic oportet') or smoked: Hor. *Serm.* 2.2.117 'fumosae cum pede pernae'. Since Cerretanian and Menapian *pernae* were the best (cf. *Ed. Diocl.* 4.8 'per<n>ae optimae petasonis sive Menapicae vel Cerritanae'), M's point in this poem seems to be as follows: he would prefer to have his own, whole salted ham, and a high quality salted ham at that, rather than the alternative: a fresh and consequently expensive but perhaps inferior piece of meat devoured together by sumptuous and undiscriminating gluttons. (On *de*, line 2, see at 13.41.2 above. The sentiment of 13.41 is not dissimilar.)

André also refers to Athenaeus (at Apic. 292 Budé; cf. *Alimentation* 142 and n. 115), but he disagrees with the distinction between fresh and preserved. His reasons are that both *perna* and *petaso* are cooked with dried figs (see Apic. 290-2 Budé), which suggests to him that both were salted, as does the fact that both were imported from Gaul: Varro *R.* 2.4.10. Given the length of the journey, he argues that neither could have been imported fresh. But it does not follow, it seems to me, that ham cooked with figs must have been salted and, while his argument from Varro is certainly powerful, his conclusion that 'comme Athénée ... n'établit aucune distinction entre πετάσων et πέρνα, on peut penser que *perna* est le jambon au sens strict (patte arrière), tandis que *petaso* est l'épaule (patte avant), dite également jambon' appears unfounded and certainly makes no sense of Mart. 13.54-5. André derives the word *petaso* from the Greek πέτασος, a round hat with a wide brim, and thinks in terms of a large round cut of meat; but the *OLD* more credibly suspects a Gallic loan word.

A *perna* is listed as a humble Saturnalian gift at Stat. *Silv.* 4.9.34, while Pers. 3.75 (cf. Juv. 7.119 *petasunculus*) cites one as the gift of a grateful client in return for advocacy. Cured ham appears to feature as a *gustatio* at Naevius *Com.* 65 'aliquid prius opstrudamus, pernam, sumen, glandem'. It was, however, also suitable at the end of a meal, after the diners had been drinking: Hor. *Serm* 2.4.60, and regularly featured as a main course too; cf. Mart. 10.48.17. It should be remembered that pork was traditional Saturnalian fare: see Intro. (ii) section B above.

1 Cerretana T: **C(a)eretana** βγ. The former spelling is generally better attested: *ThLL Onomasticon* 349.6 ff. s.v. *Cerretani* [Reisch]; cf. *Ed. Diocl.* 4.8 cited above. The Cerretani lived in Hispania Tarraconensis, along the Pyrenees (Pliny *Nat.* 3.22). The area continues to produce ham today (see *Kl.P.* 1.1115.3-4 s.v. *Cerretani* [R. Grosse]), the most famous being *jambon de Bayonne*.

1-2 missa … de Menapis: the Menapii lived on the west bank of the Rhine, near its mouth. Although famed for its pork, the area produced numerous other things as well. See *Kl.P.* 3.1203.11 ff. s.v. *Menapii* [M. Leglay]. For the contraction of *Menapiis* here, see Neue-Wagener I. 189-90. For *mitto* used of exports (and for its use in catalogue literature), see Mart. 13.19.1 n. above.

2 lauti de petasone vorent: for *lautus* used substantivally, see at Mart. 13.7.2 *lautorum* above. It accords well with the gluttonous *vorent*.

13.55 Fresh ham

It's fresh. Hurry, and don't put off your dear friends, for I want nothing to do with an aged ham.

le. petaso: see generally 13.54.*le.* n. above. Like the *perna*, the *petaso* would probably not have been eaten only as a *gustatio*. Although more palatable and therefore valued more highly than the smoked or salted *perna*, this was only so long as the *petaso* was fresh, and it very quickly went bad (the reason, perhaps, why pork is not kosher); cf. the unappetising *petaso* at Mart. 3.77.6. Hence the urgency of *propera*, line 1.

1 musteus est: *musteus* can be used of a variety of foodstuffs (e.g. cheese, pepper), but survives elsewhere of meat possibly only at Varro *Men.* 12 '[recentes] musteos in carnario fluitare suspiciunt' (see *ThLL* VIII.1711.70-4 s.v. *musteus* [Oomes]). The adjective developed from the word *mustum*, for new wine (cf. 13.8.2 above), which in turn is a substantival usage of the earlier adjectival form *mustus*, which means much the same as *musteus*.

nec differ: for this use of *differo*, cf. *OLD* s.v. *differo* §4β, L-S s.v. *differo* §1B3β. Its force here with *nec* is 'actively encourage': the addressee is charged by the donor (who clearly plans to share the meal: *mihi*, line 2) to issue invitations as quickly as possible to their other friends. The use of *nec* to negate a second imperative is more common in verse than in prose, but finds parallels e.g. in Cicero's correspondence: note *Att.* 12.22.3 'habe tuum negotium nec ... existima', and see L-H-Sz II.340.

2 vetulo: when used of (Falernian) wine, *vetulus* is 'a familiar endearing diminutive' (Fordyce at Catul. 27.1); but its apparently unique application here to meat is perhaps more akin to M's use of the word elsewhere of an ageing and sexually disgusting *amica*; cf. 3.32.1-2, 76.1, 8.79.1. Such a correlation, if justified, is not without humour.

13.56 A womb

Perhaps a womb from a virgin pig might take your fancy more, but the maternal womb from a pregnant sow takes mine.

le. volva: on the spelling, cf. Lindsay *Orth.* 32-3: there is no way of telling whether M used *vu-*, *vo-* or both forms in writing such words as *volgus*, *volnus*, *volt* and *voltus*. The best course for editors is therefore probably to choose one and then remain with it. Like Lindsay, Shackleton Bailey has *volva* here, but he prints *vulva* in line 2 (and at 7.20.11, where the *volva* is one of the unofficial *apophoreta* stolen by Santra). In contrast, I follow Lindsay throughout.

Although pork was a standard Saturnalian dish (see Intro. (ii) section B above), some pork dishes were more common than others. Sow's womb was, at any rate in Diocletian's day, dearer than any other kind of meat (*Ed. Diocl.* 4.4) and had earlier attracted sumptuary legislation (Pliny *Nat.* 8.209). It is classed as a luxury at Pliny *Ep.* 1.15.3; cf. Hor. *Ep.* 1.15.41 and Macr. 3.13.12 – where it is a main course. That it appears in Mart. 13 as a *gustatio* is perhaps an indication of extreme luxuriousness. Extreme luxuriousness is certainly suggested by M's unhesitating and unashamed preference in line 2 for the very best type of womb: although sow's womb of any variety was a luxury (and all wombs were cooked in similar fashion: Apic. 7.252-5, 257 Budé), preference was given to the wombs of pigs which had conceived over those which had not. Accordingly, when a 'stericula (volva)' is served at Petr. 35.4 to represent Virgo in a food arrangement recalling the zodiac (cf. *virgine* in line 1), it is accorded muted acclaim: cf. Petr. 35.1 'ferculum est insecutum ... non pro expectatione magnum'. A further distinction was made between the wombs of sows which had miscarried (or had their pregnancies interrupted; cf. 'gravi de sue', line 2) and those which had come to term, the former being preferred: Pliny *Nat.* 11.210 '(volva) eiecta partu melior quam editu'.

1-2: the emphatically placed *me*, line 2, contrasts with *te*, similarly placed in line 1. *Capiat*, line 1, is countered by *capit*. 'De virgine porca' finds contrast and variation in 'materna ... volva'. For *virgo* thus used, cf. Mart. 6.47.5 'virgine porca' and Pliny *Nat.* 28.43 (again of food). *Gravis*, line 2, often means 'pregnant': *OLD* s.v. *gravis* §2b.

13.57 Egyptian bean

You will laugh at the Nile vegetable and its clinging threads when you pull at the troublesome fibres with teeth and hand.

le. colocasia: i.e. the *Arum colocasia* L or Egyptian bean (on *Niliacus*, line 1, see at 13.1.3 'Niliacas ... papyros' above). It was cultivated in Italy in the Elder Pliny's day (*Nat.* 21.87), and it was also found wild in Sicily: Coleman at Verg. *Ecl.* 4.20. It was valued for its edible roots. These, however, were very fibrous (Pliny ibid. 'caule ... araneoso in mandendo'), and the use of 'rotulas ... colocasiae' ('little wheels' or cross sections) which is prescribed at Apic. 6.216 Budé would no doubt therefore have made for easier eating. (For Apicius' other *colocasia* recipes, which essentially involve boiling, see the Budé index.)

This epigram can be interpreted in different ways. For instance it could be taken as a comment on the amusement caused by the *colocasia*'s uncut fibres (*lanas*, line 1, corresponding with *fila*, line 2), which, being *improba* (line 2), become stuck in a diner's teeth. Having become hopelessly entangled, all he can do is laugh (*ridebis*, line 1). The amusement to be derived from food which is difficult to eat decorously is well established: hence activities like apple bobbing at children's parties, and the challenge of eating the troublesome *colocasia* would accord well with the light-hearted entertainments which characterised Saturnalian celebrations. (For examples, see Intro. (ii) section C above.) An alternative is to gloss *ridebis* as 'defy': see Shackleton Bailey's tentative Loeb note. He presumably envisages a recipient to whom eating the Egyptian bean presents little difficulty; but there are unlikely to have been many recipients of such accomplishment, and there seems little point in a poem to flatter one of them. Therefore of the two the former explanation appears more probable.

1 lanas ... sequaces: *lana* as used here is unparalleled in surviving classical Latin; but note Coleman, *LCM* 19 (1994) 149 on the versatility of the word, and see *ThLL* VII(2).914.41-50 s.v. *lana* [Heine]: it is used of the insides of gourds and the like by Gregory of Tours and in the Latin Oribasius. With *sequaces*, cf. Pliny *Nat.* 14.11 of vines: 'vidique etiam totas villas et domos ambiri singularum palmitibus ac sequacibus loris', Sen. *Phaed.* 1087. It is picked up by *improba*, line 2.

2 improba ... fila: for *improba* with the sense of 'troublesome', see *ThLL* VII(1).693.46 ff. s.v. *improbus* [O. Prinz]. With *fila*, cf. Mart. 8.33.13 'lenta minus gracili crescunt colocasia filo' and see *OLD* s.v. *filum* §4c.

morsu ... manuque: cf. Juv. 14.297 'laeva morsuque tenebit'. M has arranged his words carefully so that the stuck *fila* are positioned between the teeth that hold them and the hand that pulls them. Alliteration reinforces the effect.

When not picked by hand, teeth were freed using toothpicks, for which see my note at Mart. 14.23.*le*.

trahes: for the meaning 'to (try to) pull out or away', see *OLD* s.v. *traho* §5a, which cites e.g. Verg. *A*. 11.816-17 'illa manu moriens telum trahit, ossa sed inter/ ferreus ad costas alto stat vulnere mucro'.

13.58 Goose liver

See how the liver swells greater than the great goose. In wonder you will say 'Where, I ask, did this grow?'

le. iecur anserinum: goose liver was a luxury: hence the point of Mart. 3.82.19, describing how the sumptuous Zoilus gives it to his dogs while serving inferior food to his guests; cf. *SHA Elagabalus* 21.

Geese bred for their livers were fattened on figs: Hor. *Serm*. 2.8.88 'et ficis pastum iecur anseris albae', and such liver was consequently called *ficatum*; cf. the Italian *figata* and the French *foie*. The birds would have been kept in dark cellars since this was believed to discourage exercise detrimental to fattening (Sen. *Ep*. 122.4, quoted at 13.62.*le*. below), and their livers grew very big (Pliny *Nat*. 10.52). Indeed, the joke of this poem rests on the huge size of the liver it describes: although the goose from which it came was big, paradoxically, the liver seems even bigger.

For the above and further references and information, see D'Arcy Thompson *Birds* 327, Courtney and Mayor at Juv. 5.114 'anseris ... magni iecur' and Coleman at Statius *Silv*. 4.6.9-10 'quis magis anser/ exta †ferat†'. See too Marquardt *Prl*. 431, Blümner *Priv*. 177 n. 8.

Goose liver is not referred to elsewhere as a *gustatio* and Apicius gives no recipes for it (although see the Budé index for other types of *iecur*). For geese as presents, note Ar. *Av*. 707. Half-eaten geese are sent by Cyrus to his friends so that they can taste them too: Xen. *An*. 1.9.10.

1 aspice is emphatically placed, stressing the importance of visual assessment in appreciating the poem's point; cf. Mart. 14.109.2. Further emphasis is achieved through the chiasmus, which juxtaposes for contrast *iecur* and *ansere* between the counter-balanced *magno* and *maius*.

On the use of introductory *verba videndi*, see Siedschlag 9. Such words were used by the Greek poets predominantly in the description of art-works. Later, however, there was greater freedom of application and indeed their use of artworks in Latin poetry is uncommon. Given the similarities of the *Xenia* and *Apophoreta* to dedicatory epigram (see Intro. (v) and n. 6 above), it is perhaps relevant to comment that such words are familiar from grave inscriptions. For a *verbum videndi* near the end of a poem, see 13.19.2 above.

2 'hoc, rogo, crevit ubi?': R's *mihi* is very weak compared with the humorous *ubi* (βγ), which, through being postponed to the end of the line, emphasises the wonder with which the liver's size is regarded. Lindsay suggests that *ubi* was corrupted to *tibi*, which R then tried to emend.

On the parenthetic *rogo*, see L-H-Sz II.472. As for the practice of quoting words imputed to the addressee, see on Mart. 13.24.2 above.

13.59 Dormice

The whole winter I sleep, and I am fatter at the season when nothing but sleep nourishes me.

le. glires (-ris LQ) βγ: **clis** R. R's singular ending accords with the personifying elements of the poem, but should be rejected in favour of the better attested plural: see 13.49.*le.* n. above.

This epigram is a sort of riddle, to which the *lemma* supplies the answer. See the introductory n. to 13.11 above, and cf. Ausonius *Technopaegnion* 13.9 Green quoted below. The paradox that the dormouse is fatter at the very time when it does not eat follows on from the 'size' paradox in 13.58, and here is emphasised by the prominent placing of 'illo/ tempore'. M's conjunction of paradox and personification in this poem recalls his conjunction of etymology and personification elsewhere, e.g. in 13.49 above. On his use of personification, see generally 13.71.*le.* n. below.

The edible dormouse (*Glis glis*) was regarded as a great delicacy (they still command a high price) and they were banned by the sumptuary laws of M. Scaurus (115 BC) and Claudius: Pliny *Nat.* 8.223, 36.4. They can grow to a length of some 20 cm (excluding the tail), and were artificially fattened on beech nuts (Pliny *Nat.* 16.18) in special pens or containers called *gliraria*: Varro *R.* 3.12.2, 3.15, Keller I 191. They were first stuffed and then baked: Apic. 8.397 Budé. Dormice are served as a *gustatio* at Petr. 31.10 'ponticuli etiam ferruminati sustinebant glires melle ac papavere sparsos', and are given as gifts (albeit not *apophoreta*) at Mart. 3.58.36 'somniculosos ille porrigit glires'.

1 tota mihi dormitur hiems et pinguior illo/ tempore sum quo ...: in fact dormice accumulate their fat in the autumn preparatory to hibernation and, contrary to 'me nil nisi somnus alit', line 2, wake occasionally during the winter to feed from stores laid down earlier; but had M known this, or acted on his knowledge, it would have destroyed the epigram's point. Similarly, the application of such knowledge would have destroyed the point of Ausonius *Ephem*. 1.5-6 Green 'dormiunt glires hiemem perennem,/ sed cibo parcunt' (where the sleepy Parmeno's over-indulgence the night before is contrasted with the sleepy dormouse's abstention from food), and likewise the riddle at *Technopaegnion* 13.9 Green 'dic, cessante cibo somno quis opimior est? glis'. M's positioning of *tota* here gives emphasis to the length of the dormouse's winter hibernation, while the impersonal passive *dormitur* helps convey the deepness of its sleep.

13.60 Rabbits

The rabbit rejoices in living in dug out caves. He has shown secret routes to enemies.

1e. cuniculi: as well as meaning 'rabbit', the term *cuniculus* was applied to the mines or tunnels used in siege operations (*OLD* s.v. *cuniculus* §2b). These tunnels, so the epigram alleges (line 2), were devised in imitation of rabbit warrens. (For etymologising in M, cf. 13.71.*1e*. n. below.) In fact, since tunnelling is an obvious means of attacking a fortified position or city, the name almost certainly came later, as would have *cunicularius*, the military term for a digger of mines or tunnels: Veg. *Mil*. 2.11.5, *Amm*. 24.4.22.

The word *cuniculus* appears to be an Iberian import: see Ernout-Meillet s.v. *cuniculus*. At any rate, rabbits were particularly associated with Spain: Catul. 37.18 'cuniculosae Celtiberiae fili' (of Egnatius); cf. Pliny *Nat*. 8.217. Given its military application, it is possible that, like many words, it was introduced to Latin by the army.

Wall paintings of rabbits intended for eating survive from Pompeii (*Pompeii AD 79* 255, 257), but unlike the hare (see on 13.92 *lepores* below) they are seldom mentioned as food in literature, whether Greek or Latin. Indeed in Athenaeus the rabbit is known only at second hand (9.400F, quoting Polybius 12.3.10). Further, there is just one reference to rabbit in Apicius (2.54 Budé), in which its meat ranks a lowly third, behind peacock and pheasant, as the main ingredient for *esicium*, a kind of forcemeat or mince dish apparently prescribed by doctors: see Izaac's notes ad loc. and cf. Apic. 2.53 Budé, describing *esicium simplex*: 'esiciola coques et sic ad ventrem solvendum dabis'. Despite the laxative qualities of other food-stuffs in the *Xenia* (see at 13.14.2 above), there is, however, nothing in the poem to suggest a medical motive for introducing *cuniculi* here. Instead, while indulging his liking for puns and etymology, it is possible also that M is betraying his Spanish origins in treating a source of food less favoured in Rome than his homeland.

1 in effossis ... antris: T's *offensis* might just possibly square with counter-attacked enemy siege works, but goes ill with 'gaudet ... habitare'. Since the whole point of the 'tacitas ... vias' in line 2 is that they are buried, the better attested *effossis* is clearly right.

Antrum appears not to survive elsewhere of a rabbit warren (or siege excavation), but its use here is natural enough.

cuniculus, after the plural *lemma*, is a generalising singular. Similar instances of numerical incongruity are cited at 13.11.2 above.

2 monstravit Tγ: **monstrabit** β. M's etymologising clearly requires the perfect tense. *Monstro* has the sense here both of showing the way (*vias*) and of teaching: cf. *OLD* s.v. *monstro* §§1a,2.

tacitas ... vias: see *OLD* s.v. *tacitus* §8, L-S s.v. *tacitus* §A2b; cf. the use of *occulte* (significantly juxtaposed with *cuniculis*) at Cic. *Agr.* 1.1: 'quae res aperte petebantur, ea nunc occulte cuniculis oppugnatur'. (Although the section before this quotation is lost, Cicero's concern seems to be with the suppression of a land-legacy by money-lenders and protection racketeers who find it financially profitable to keep a dependent usurper in power: cf. Jonkers ad loc.)

hostibus is most naturally taken here to refer to those laying siege; but the *cuniculus* could also be used by the besieged: cf. Caes. *Gal.* 3.21.3 where a besieged army of Aquitani uses *cuniculi* to undermine the siege works thrown up by their attackers.

13.61-78: these poems, which deal with fowl, make up the first group of poems describing main courses. Several of the birds here described were to be found in the farmyard of Faustinus (Mart. 3.58.12 ff.): see Probst 319-20.

13.61 Francolins

Of the flavours of fowl, the taste of Ionian francolins is reckoned to be foremost.

For M's choliambics, see Intro. (vi) above.

1e. attagenae have been variously identified, but were probably francolins or black partridges: see D'Arcy Thompson *Birds* 60-1, Pollard 61. According to Pliny *Nat.* 10.133, the bird had formerly been rare, but in his day they could be found in the Alps, Gaul and Spain, where M perhaps first encountered them. They were choice dishes, and the Ionian *attagen* was particularly admired; cf. Hor. *Epod.* 2.54 f., Ovid *Fasti* 6.175, Pliny

Nat. 10.133 'attagen maxime Ionius celeber'; see Dunbar at Ar. *Av.* 249, André *Alimentation* 122.

Apicius gives two recipes for *attagenae* (6.218 and 220 Budé), which were cooked in the same way as partridges and turtle doves. An *attagen* large enough for two is one of the unofficial *apophoreta* stolen by Caecilianus at Mart. 2.37.3.

1 fertur: the other recommendations in Book 13 all contain a personal note and it is therefore interesting that the *attagen* is given a third person endorsement here. M may have wanted to enhance the gift's value by suggesting it was above him.

primus: see on the use of *prima* at 13.92.2 n. below. The word has prominence at the end of the line, although its placing is doubtless partly metrical.

2 gustus picks up *sapor* in line 1. In using it to mean 'taste' (see *OLD* s.v. *gustus* §2) rather than to refer to the first course dishes described by the earlier poems (*gustus = gustatio*), M marks the beginning of a new section.

13.62 Fatted hens

The obliging hen is fed on both sweet grain and darkness. Ingenious is the palate!

le. gallinae altiles: this epigram on hens precedes two on capons. For general information about fowl, see D'Arcy Thompson *Birds* 33-44. The poem is linked to the next by the idea of plumpness: with *altiles* here (from *alo*), cf. 'ne ... macresceret' in 63.1; and it follows naturally on from the previous epigram's concern with taste: note *sapores* and *gustus* in poem 61 and cf. 'ingeniosa gula est', line 2 below.

The adjective *altilis* is commonly, but not exclusively applied to birds (note the snails at Pliny *Nat.* 9.174 and sacrificial cattle at Varro *R.* 2.1.20), and it can be used substantivally on its own to refer to fattened birds without danger of confusion: note e.g. Hor. *Ep.* 1.7.35, Juv. 5.168. It is used of the *gallina* also at Macr. *Sat.* 3.13.12 and Pliny *Nat.* 10.139. Note also Petr. 65.2, on which see below. At Petr. 69.8 we find 'anser altilis'.

Mayor collects details at Juv. 5.115 of methods by which table birds were artificially fattened. He quotes Varro *R.* 3.9.19-20 'eas includunt in locum tepidum et angustum et tenebricosum, quod motus earum et lux pinguitudini inimica, ... evulsis ex alis pinnis et e cauda farciunt turundis hordeacis, partim admixtis farina lolleacia aut semine lini ex aqua dulci'; cf. Sen. *Ep.* 122.4 (quoted by Mayor at Juv. 5.114): 'aves quae conviviis conparantur, ut immotae facile pinguescant, in obscuro continentur: ita sine ulla exercitatione iacentibus, tumor pigrum corpus invadit et super

Commentary

membra [s: superba umbra *vel. sim. codd.*] iners sagina succrescit'. Both of these passages mention the darkness cited by M in line 2 and Varro gives some idea as to what M might mean by 'dulci ... farina' (see line 1 n. below). Mayor records that the fattening process took 20-25 days.

Unlike the ordinary chicken (see 13.45.*le*. n. above), fattened hens were a great luxury, and that they were served at Petr. 65.2 as *matteae* (i.e. tid-bits served late in the meal) is an indication of just how vulgar Trimalchio is. (Mart. 13.92, on which see below, identifies the *turdus* as an ideal *mattea*.) The sumptuary laws of C. Fannius Strabo in 161 BC first attempted to ban fattened hens although these laws were inevitably circumvented: Pliny *Nat*. 10.139-40.

1 pascitur et ... facilis gallina: the hen is so obliging or stupid (there is an implied contrast between *facilis* and *ingeniosa*, line 2) that it eats everything put before it, including darkness(!): the prominent position of *pascitur* at the beginning of both hexameter and pentameter and the repetition of *et* carry great emphasis. The bird is therefore easily exploited by the ingenious *gula*.

dulci ... farina: at *R*. 3.9.20 'aut semine lini ex aqua dulci' Varro has apparently in mind a mixture of water and linseed, referred to at Larg. 187 as 'lini seminis farina'. *Aqua dulcis* can mean 'fresh water' as opposed to salt: see 13.89.2 n. below; but fresh water on its own seems improbable here. It is more likely that Varro has in mind a sort of hydromel (note that Pliny *Nat*. 10.52 speaks of fattening geese 'lacte mulso'), that to tempt the obliging hen all the more M's 'ingeniosa gula' uses grain soaked in hydromel here.

gallina: while this generalising singular conflicts with the plural *lemma*, the plural *lemma* agrees with the plural *lemmata* of the other poems on fowl. For numerical differences between *lemma* and poem, see 13.11.2 n. above.

2 tenebris: the effect of the syllepsis is perhaps comparable with that of the paradoxical 'nil nisi somnus alit' at 13.59.2 above. Battery hens today are in fact kept under lights rather than in darkness since, when it is dark, they go to sleep rather than eating or laying.

ingeniosa gula est: the throat was commonly regarded as the seat of taste: see *OLD* s.v. *gula* §2b; cf. Mart. 14.220.2 and see Grewing at 6.11.5-6 'tu Lucrina voras, me pascit aquosa peloris:/ non minus ingenua est et mihi, Marce, gula'. That man's taste could devise ways of subverting nature for its own enjoyment was a commonplace; cf. Mart. 14.117.2 'ingeniosa sitis', Petr. 119.33 ff. 'ingeniosa gula est. Siculo scarus aequore mersus/ ad mensam vivus perducitur etc.'

116

13.63 Capons

So that the cockerel does not grow too thin through draining his loins, he has lost his testicles. Now I will consider him – a cock!

le. capones: this poem and the next depend on an untranslatable pun. A *gallus* is a cockerel, whereas a *Gallus* is a eunuch. Since the cockerel in this poem has been castrated, it has changed from being a *gallus* to a *Gallus*. (There is a comparable joke at Mart. 11.74.2 'Baccara Gallus erit', on which see Kay.) According to Ovid, who follows the usual tradition, the name *Gallus* came originally from the Phrygian river of that name whose waters drove those who drank them into a frenzy during which they emasculated themselves. (See Bömer at *Fast.* 4.182, who also cites modern linguistic explanations.) The *Galli* who followed the earth-mother goddess Cybele, however (cf. 13.64.2 below), castrated themselves to emulate her youthful consort Attis, who had mutilated himself after having broken a vow of chastity (cf. Ovid *Fast.* 4.223 f.; a slightly different version at *Met.* 10.104 f.). These *Galli* travelled about begging and prophesying and attracted widespread censure and suspicion, castration being regarded with sufficient repugnance for Domitian to ban it by edict in about 85 (see C. Henriksén, 'Earinus: an imperial eunuch in the light of the poems of Martial and Statius', *Mnem.* 50 (1997), 284 n. 5). For general information regarding Cybele and her worship, see conveniently *OCD*[3] s.v. *Cybele* [F.R. Walton, J. Scheid]. For the hostility with which Galli were viewed, see my notes at Mart. 14.204.

The reason for castrating cockerels is given by Mrs Beeton, 288: 'The male fowl, the capon, and the female bird, the poularde, are both, by treatment while young, made incapable of generating, with the result that their size is increased and they both become fatter than ordinary fowls'; cf. Pliny *Nat.* 10.24 'facilius ita pinguescunt'. While mindful of this, M manages to add humour by recalling the belief that excessive sexual activity caused emaciation in humans; with 'ne nimis ... macresceret', line 1, cf. e.g. Catul. 89, noting *macer* in line 6.

Apicius gives a capon recipe at 6.250 Budé (note too that he includes cock testicles at 4.167 Budé in a recipe for a fricassee), and capons are the gift of a country caller at Mart. 3.58.38. A (damaged) wall painting from Pompeii shows a cockerel (*Pompeii* AD 79 256), although one cannot tell whether or not it has been castrated.

1 exhausto ... inguine: although exploiting sex for its humour, this epigram is hardly obscene since *inguen* is a common euphemism for *mentula* and appears in the full range of literature from epigram to epic and educated prose: see Adams 47-8. On the surprising lack of obscenity in Mart. 13, see at 26.2 above.

2 amisit testes: the singular verb, agreeing with *gallus*, is generalising (note too *macresceret*, line 1). On numerical discrepancies between *lemma* and poem, see 13.11.2 n. above.

Amittere is common of losing a body part: *OLD* s.v. *amittere* §8b. While the capon has lost his testicles, it appears possible that Cybele's *Galli* removed their penises as well: see Kay at Mart. 11.72.2, citing e.g. Mart. 2.45 and 9.2.13 f. On the word *testis*, see generally Adams 67. Although it 'never wholly lost its literal sense in the classical period' and it is often found used humorously in puns involving witnesses (cf. Mart. 7.62.6), it occurs too in sober prose (e.g. Pliny *Nat.* 11.263, Suet. *Nero* 28.1) and, like the use of *inguen* (see above), its use in this poem is inoffensive.

Varro (*R.* 3.9.3) and Columella (8.23) declare that 'castrated' cocks are deprived not in fact of their testicles but of their spurs. Depriving them of the ability to fight would also have resulted in their growing fat, but would have made the humour of M's poem impossible.

13.64 The same

The hen submits in vain to her sterile husband. He should have been the bird of Mother Cybele.

le. idem: on the capon, see at 13.63.*le.* n. above, at which see also for the earth-mother or 'Magna Mater' Cybele (line 2) and the *gallus/Gallus* pun on which these two poems turn. On the *idem* poem in Book 13, see 43.*le.* n. above.

1 succumbit sterili ... **marito**: *succumbo* introduces a humorous personification, which is sustained by *marito*: hens do not adopt the missionary position. For *maritus* and the like used in animal contexts, see N-H at Hor. *Carm.* 1.17.7. The word is suggestive of potency (cf. *OLD* s.v. *maritus* §2) and so is paradoxical after *sterili*. Regarding the generalising singular, cf. 13.63.2 n. above.

2 hunc R: hanc βγ. Although Gilbert prints *hanc*, his apparatus agrees with the unanimous preference of other editors for *hunc*. *Hunc* is clearly right after *maritus*. *Hanc* may have been introduced under influence of *gallina* or, as Heraeus suggests, that of e.g. 13.65.1, 67.2 and 74.1 below.

It was not unusual for goddesses to have particular birds associated with them. Thus Juno had her peacock (D'Arcy Thompson *Birds* 277) and Venus her dove (see at 13.66.2 'tradita ... deae' below). In this poem M jokingly suggests a suitable bird for Cybele.

13.65 Partridges

This bird is served very rarely at Ausonian tables. You are accustomed often to play it in the swimming pool.

le. perdices: the species of partridge described here is unknown, but that most commonly referred to is the red-legged *Perdix (Caccabis) graeca/saxatilis*: D'Arcy Thompson *Birds* 234. Another red-legged partridge, common in Spain and found also in Italy, was the *Perdix rufa*, possibly to be identified with the 'picta perdix' in the farmyard of Faustinus (Mart. 3.58.15): D'Arcy Thompson *Birds* 235; but there is considerable room for uncertainty: note e.g. G. Friedrich, *Philologus* 68 (109) 117, Probst 319-20.

A partridge is depicted in a still life from Pompeii: *Pompeii AD 79* 257; cf. 255, where the species of the bird is less certain. Apicius gives three recipes for partridge (6.218-20 Budé) and one for a sauce to accompany it (exc. 31 Budé).

1 Ausoniis ... mensis: the Ausones were early inhabitants of Campania, and *Ausonius* came therefore to mean 'Roman' or 'Italian'. It was used especially in grand, elevated or epic contexts (cf. Hor. *Carm.* 4.4.56, Verg. *A.* 3.378, 9.639, Mart. 12.5(2 + 6.1-6).3), and M has used it deliberately here to contrast with the pentameter's vulgarity (on which see below).

avis (aut γ) haec R: perdix β. *Aut* is an insignificant palaeographical corruption. *Perdix* was probably an explanatory gloss which became incorporated into the text. It spoils the poem, which is otherwise one of the 'riddling' epigrams to which the *lemma* supplies the 'answer'. See the introductory n. to 13.11 above.

Regarding the generalising singular *avis* (contrast the plural *lemma*), see 13.11.2 n. above.

rarissima βγ: carissima (kar-) R. Although knowledge of the partridge appears to have been fairly widespread, it was nonetheless expensive to eat (*Ed. Diocl.* 4.24) and so, it seems, was rarely served. The reading of βγ provides an important contrast with *saepe*, line 2. It is probable that R's reading was influenced by 13.76.2 'carior est perdix' below; cf. Schmid 668 n.2.

2 hanc in piscina ludere saepe soles: this is the reading of α, which is universally accepted by modern editors. As to what it means, however, there is disagreement. Some think that 'perdicem ludere' refers to a type of swimming activity; others that it has an obscene or sexual meaning.

Friedrich, art. cit., thinks that the line refers to the noise a swimmer makes when some water goes down the wrong way and that this is here compared to the sound a partridge makes on take-off when someone has flushed it. Not only does this explanation allow the epigram little force or impact, but it suggests that Romans were generally poor swimmers (which was probably not the case: Balsdon *LL* 221), and it hardly squares with *ludere*: drowning is never fun.

Izaac also wonders whether the phrase might refer to swimming, comparing such phrases as 'faire la planche' and 'le chien crevé', but this, like Friedrich's explanation, hardly makes for a pointed epigram. Far more satisfactory is the alternative suggestion he records, taken up by Shackleton Bailey, that *perdix* puns on πέρδεσθαι: while partridges served at table are very rare, farting in the swimming pool is not.

Still better perhaps is the explanation of Probst, 320 n.1, recalled by Schmid (668 n.3). Probst cites Isid. *Orig.* 12.7.63 'perdix de voce nomen habet, avis dolosa atque immunda. nam masculus in masculum insurgit, et obliviscitur sexum libido praeceps' (cf. Athen. 9.389C), and suggests that 'playing the *perdix*' is a reference to aquatic sex, and sodomy in particular. (For the sexual applications of *ludere*, see Adams 162.) This is jocularly insulting to the reader, it accords with the tenor of 13.26 above (for M's use of obscenity in the *Xenia* and generally, see on line 2 *puero*), and contrasts even more strongly than farting with the lofty *Ausonius* of the previous line. While eating partridge may have been rare, aquatic sex was not uncommon (see Kay at Mart. 11.21.11 'hanc in piscina dicor futuisse marina', who refers to A. Cameron, 'Sex in the Swimming Pool', *BICS* 20 (1973) 149-50; cf. Griffin ch. 5.)

Several scholars have tried to explain how β came to read 'hanc in lautorum condere saepe soles' and γ 'hanc in lautorum ma(n)dere saepe soles'. The MSS' agreement on *lautorum*, if it is indeed wrong, would suggest early contamination between β and γ, and this, combined with the assumption of other early editorial activity (cf. Intro. (vii) and n. 9 above), underpins the most detailed exposition, by Schmid, art. cit. Schmid argues that a β scribe did not understand *ludere* and could not grasp the relationship between the *perdix* and the *piscina*, which he took to be a breeding tank for gourmet fish rather than a swimming pool. Although discounting *piscina* because of its perceived association with fish, however, he did not reject the idea of breeding for gourmet consumption. Accordingly, he replaced *piscina* with *lautorum* and *ludere* with *condere*, understanding *saepe* as the ablative of the noun *saepes*. That *saepe* is in fact an adverb was then realised by a γ scribe, who tried to emend β. With *lautorum* he understood *mensis*, and he changed *condere* to *mandere*.

13.66 Doves

Never profane tender doves with treacherous tooth if the sacred rites of the goddess of Cnidus have been entrusted to you.

le. columbini βγ: **-in(a)e** R: **columbae** vel **-bi** ς. Given the feminine *columbas* in line 1, Lindsay, Ker and Duff follow R's *columbinae*; but this form does not occur elsewhere. Concern about gender also lies behind the humanist *columbae*; cf. the texts of Schneidewin, Friedländer and Gilbert. (The humanist *columbi* may have been influenced by 13.67 *palumbi*.) As Heraeus indicates, however, with *columbini* is to be understood *pulli*, and *pulli* makes no gender distinction. Heraeus refers to *ThLL* s.v. *columbinus* (i.e. III.1734.42-3 [Wulff]), which cites Varro *R.* 3.7.9 and Cicero *Fam.* 9.18.3. He is followed by Izaac, Giarratano and Shackleton Bailey.

The words used by the Greeks and Romans to refer to doves or pigeons were often applied very generally (D'Arcy Thompson *Birds* 227, 241), and it is not always possible to identify exactly a particular bird type. Given poems 53 and 67, it is, however, likely that the birds in this epigram are not turtle- or ring-doves.

For details on keeping doves and on dovecotes (cf. Mart. 3.58.18, 12.31.6), see D'Arcy Thompson *Birds* 243. Apicius gives recipes for dove sauce at 6.221-4 Budé: 'in palumbis, columbis'.

1 ne violes: for *ne* + present subjunctive in a general prohibition, see L-H-Sz II.337. Were the prohibition specific to a single occasion, the perfect subjunctive would have been used.

periuro dente Rβ: **perduro** γ. *Perdurus* is late and very rare: the *OLD* and L-S cite just Papin. *dig.* 48.3.2.1, where it means 'very harsh'. Shackleton Bailey suggests *praeduro* in his Teubner, but without conviction: 'num ... ?'. (His Loeb note is slightly more in favour: 'fort. ...'.) The idea of a hard tooth would contrast with *teneras*; but an adjective suggesting treachery would better suit *violes* and the humour of the poem as a whole: see below on line 2.

With the transferred use of *periuro*, cf. Stat. *Silv.* 4.6.77-8 'periuroque ense superbus/ Hannibal'.

2 tradita si Cnidiae sunt tibi sacra deae: Venus had three shrines at Cnidus in Caria, where there was also a celebrated statue of her: see N-H at Hor. *Carm.* 1.30.1 *Cnidi*. The dove was of course Venus' bird (see D'Arcy Thompson *Birds* 244-6), and, since they were known for their conjugal affection and chastity (D'Arcy Thompson *Birds* 241), doves were common lovers' gifts (Pollard 16; cf. 13.53.*le.* n. above, 67.*le.* n. below.) In maintaining that anyone who has been initiated into the sacred rites or mysteries of Love should avoid eating dove for fear of breaking faith (hence *periuro*, line 1), M's poem explores the ridiculous dilemma posed by a love symbol that is also a foodstuff.

tradita ... sacra: for the 'traditio sacrorum', cf. Apul. *Met.* 11.29. Note too Cic. *Tusc.* 1.29 'reminiscere, quoniam es initiatus, quae tradantur mys-

121

teriis', Quint. *Inst.* 5.13.60 'omnes fere qui legem dicendi quasi quaedam mysteria tradiderunt ...'.

si Cnidiae Shackleton Bailey: **si Gnidiae** Rγ: **sic nitidae** β. Most modern editors follow Rγ in printing *Gnidiae* rather than *Cnidiae*; but see Housman, *Class. Pap.* 1141 ff., followed by Shackleton Bailey: whatever the MS readings here, inscriptional evidence and metrical arguments from other texts indicate that *Cnidus* is the correct spelling. (In contrast, *Gnosia* at 13.106.1 below should be left alone since, although *Cnosus* was the usual form, the spelling *Gnosus* is 'as old as the reign of Augustus': Housman *Class Pap.* 1142.)

The β reading would seem to suggest a gift not of doves, but of initiation into divine rites in order to stop the recipient from eating doves. This is laughable; but it is possibly worth commenting that the reading represents an attempt to make sense of SICNIDIAE (not SIGNIDIAE) following an incorrect word division.

13.67 Ring-doves

Ring-doves slow and dull the loins: let him not eat this bird who wants to be ruttish.

le. palumbi β (**-bo** ut vid. L) γ: **palumbus** R. Lindsay suggests that R's reading is possibly correct; but a singular *lemma* here would conflict with the plural *lemmata* of the other poems on birds and fowl.

That this poem deals specifically with the ring-dove (*Columba palumbus*) is confirmed by *torquati* in line 1; cf. Prop. 4.5.65 'torquatae ... columbae'. Whereas the previous poem advises the lover not to eat doves for fear of committing sacrilege, this poem advises him to avoid them for fear of impotence. Given the reputation doves had for voluptuous kissing (cf. Mart. 11.104.9 with Kay, 12.65.8; see Otto 83) and their erotic associations (Pollard 144, referring to Artemid. 2.20), the alleged effect of eating them is surprising: in terms of *homophagia* one would expect the opposite: see E.R. Dodds, *The Greeks and the Irrational*, Berkeley and Los Angeles 1951, 277. Perhaps impotence is the punishment for sacrilege.

The anaphrodisiac qualities of the ring-dove are attested nowhere else, but the status of the *palumbus* as a luxury dish is established by Hor. *Serm.* 2.8.91 'vidimus ... poni ... sine clune palumbes'. See too D'Arcy Thompson *Birds* 301, who observes that the bird was a dainty, but could also be used as a diet for invalids. For the sauces with which it could be served, see 13.66.*le.* n. above. For fattening ring-doves, see Cato *Agr.* 90.

Ring-doves are (lovers') gifts at Theoc. 5.96 and 133. They are (stolen) *apophoreta* at Mart. 2.37.5.

1 inguina ... **tardant hebetantque**: on the word *inguen* for *mentula*, see
at 13.63.1 above. For similar uses of *hebeto*, see *ThLL* VI(3).2584.82 ff. s.v.
hebeto [Groth]. *Tardo* and *hebeto* are commonly used in conjunction: cf. e.g.
Cels. 2.1 'auster aures hebetat, sensus tardat', Pliny *Nat.* 7.76.

2 salax: *salio* is appropriate of animal sex (Adams 206) and, when applied
to men or gods, *salax* is pejorative or implies sexual excess: cf. Priap. 34.1
'deo salaci' and Mart. 11.25.1 (where it is transferred to the *mentula* of a
certain Linus). In this poem M is not seriously advising against dove
consumption so much as poking fun at would-be sexual athletes.

While *salax* is used here of people (who avoid anaphrodisiac food), the
adjective can also be transferred to food thought to promote virility: cf. e.g.
Mart. 3.75.3 'bulbique salaces', 10.48.2 'herba salax' (i.e. *eruca*), Ovid *Ars*
2.422, Priap. 51.21.

13.68 Yellow birds

The yellow bird is taken in with rods and nets when the young grape is
swelling with wine still green.

le. galbuli Tγ: **galbi** β. This bird was probably the golden oriole (χλωρίον):
Pollard 50, D'Arcy Thompson *Birds* 332, who notes that 'In Italy ... it
comes in early April [i.e. before the grapes are ripe; cf. line 2 below] and
leaves in late September'. Being out of season, the bird would have made
an expensive Saturnalian gift.

As D'Arcy Thompson observes (loc. cit.), the bird is known in Italian
dialect by many names; cf. W.M. Lindsay, *CPh* 13 (1918), 18. In support
here of Tγ's *galbuli*, it is tempting to cite Pliny *Nat.* 30.94: 'avis icterus
vocatur a colore ... hanc puto Latine vocari galgulum'; cf. 10.73 'quae cum
fetum eduxere abeunt, ut galguli, upupae'; but although it seems that
Pliny is thinking of the same bird, it is possible that the two words have
different derivations: see André *Oiseaux* 80. While noting that *galbeoli* is
preserved at Schol. Bern. Verg. *G.* 4.14, Heraeus suggests instead that β's
galbi might be correct. He cites *CGL* 5.502.9 *galvus*, 2.31.57 *galucis* and
Isid. 12.7.34 *gaulus*. Since certainty is impossible, however, it seems
wisest to follow the majority MS reading.

1 decipitur calamis et retibus: *decipere* here effectively means *capere*:
ThLL V(1).178.51 ff. s.v. *decipio* [Simbeck]; cf. [Sen.] *Oct.* 411-12 'calamo
levi/ decipere volucres', Ovid *Met.* 3.587-8 'linoque solebat et hamis/ decipere ... pisces', Columella 8.2.2 'per aucupem decipitur'. The verb's singular
subject is generalising; see 13.11.2 n. above.

Regarding the fowler's use of rods when hunting, see my notes at Mart.
14.216. Having lured his prey into a particular tree, whether by using
decoys or imitating bird calls, he would then ensnare it by stealthily

reaching up with an extendible reed smeared with bird-lime. The procedure is described e.g. at V.Fl. 6.260 ff. and Sil. 7.674 ff.

Kay reports at Mart. 11.21.5 that the net used for hunting birds 'was about 60 metres long and 1-2 metres high'. These nets are described by Varro at *R*. 3.5.14, and are comparable with those used by ornithologists today to catch small birds for ringing. They are stretched between trees in such a way as to be unobtrusive (cf. Ovid. *Rem*. 516 'quae nimis apparent retia, vitat avis') and sag sufficiently for the birds not to be damaged on contact.

On fowling generally, see Blümner *Priv*. 526 ff., Pollard 104 ff. and D-S V.693-4 s.v. *venatio* [Georges Lafaye].

2 turget: cf. Pliny *Nat*. 25.94 'quoniam tum maxime sucis herbae turgeant'; see *OLD* s.v. *turgeo* §1b.

viridis is common of unripe fruit (*OLD* s.v. *viridis* §3a), and its transferral here to the juice of an unripe grape is not unnatural; but its use in conjunction with *merum*, used normally of fully fermented and undiluted wine, is particularly telling: of course the juice is undiluted, but the fact that it is called green *merum* emphasises just how far off it is from being fermented too: this grape is very young indeed.

rudis survives here only of unripe fruit (*OLD* s.v. *rudis* §1b), although it commonly means 'young'.

13.69 Catta birds

Umbria has never given us Pannonian *catta* birds. Pudens prefers to send these gifts to his 'master'.

1e. cattae: given the context, *cattae* must here be birds. In addition, it may be noted that *catta* does not survive of a cat before the 4th century and that there is no tradition of eating cats: see Heraeus ad loc.

As to the nature of this *catta* bird, there is, however, great uncertainty. Friedländer ad loc. makes etymological comparisons with the Greek κωτιλάς (used of a sparrow) and with French and Prussian, but his idea of something like a jackdaw is by no means convincing. A more likely possibility is that the bird is a kind of francolin or grouse. This is suggested by Heraeus' references ad loc. to the Latin Oribasius, which uses *gantula/gattula* to reflect ἀτταγήν; cf. *ThLL* VI(2).1692.55-8 s.v. *gantula* [Leumann], André *Oiseaux* 50-1. Since *attagenae* are to be found at Mart. 13.61 above, André's suggestion of the hazel grouse (*Tetrastes bonasia*) is perhaps to be favoured here: note too that these birds are found today in Hungary and the former Yugoslavia, which would accord with *Pannonicas*, line 1.

While native to Pannonia, it seems that *catta* birds were bred in Italy by M's Umbrian friend Pudens (for whom see below). M's point in the poem seems to be to complain that Pudens sends him ordinary Umbrian produce while preserving his exotic Pannonian birds to give to his fancy boy (see below on the meaning of *dominus*); cf. 10.29, where M complains that the Saturnalian gifts Sextilianus used to send him he now sends to his mistress.

1-2: the pentameter closely corresponds to the hexameter, thus enhancing the contrast between the gifts Pudens gives and their recipients. 'Pannonicas ... cattas' corresponds with 'haec ... dona' as does *dedit* with *mittere* (cf. 13.3.5 'hospitibus ... mittas' n. above). *Umbria* is replaced by *Pudens*, and *nobis* is countered by *domino* as is *numquam* by *mavult*.

2 domino Rγ: **dominae** β. Of β's reading, Lindsay remarks 'fort. recte'. It is accepted by Friedländer and Heraeus (although, as Shackleton Bailey notes, Heraeus has -*no* in his apparatus). Friedländer argues that gifts of birds to a mistress would be natural enough (cf. Pollard 139 f. and 13.66.2, 53.*le.* nn. above), whereas they would be less naturally given by Pudens to the emperor – which is how he would interpret *domino*. But *dominus* could also be used of a catamite, Pudens was not averse to catamites (see below), and catamites often received birds: see G. Friedrich, *Hermes* 43 (1908) 635-6, referring to Petr. 85.5; cf. Ar. *Av.* 704-7 with Dunbar. In printing the better attested *domino*, along with most other modern editors, Shackleton Bailey refers in his Teubner apparatus to Schuster, *RhM* 75 (1926), 341-2 and his own note at Mart. 5.57.2. Although Howell interprets *dominus* there in the context of *resalutatio* rather than sex, Shackleton Bailey's case for *domino* here is nonetheless easily supported by his reference at 5.57.2 to 11.70.2 (at which, see Kay) and 12.66.8. Note too δεσπότης at Ach. Tat. 5.26.7.

Pudens: M's friend Aulus Pudens came from Sarsina in Umbria (Mart. 7.97). Regarding his interest in boys note, in addition to Mart. 8.63, 1.31 and 5.48: it is possible that the *dominus* referred to in the current poem is Encolpos. Since he had travelled widely on military service (cf. Mart. 6.58), Pudens may have imported his *catta* birds from Pannonia himself. For further details of the man and the much debated question of whether he achieved the primipilate, see Howell at 1.31 and 5.48.

13.70 Peacocks

Do you admire him whenever he displays his jewelled wings, and can you hand him over, harsh man, to the cruel cook?

Mart. 14.211 *caput vervecinum* bears some similarity:

mollia Phrixei secuisti colla mariti.
  hoc meruit tunicam qui tibi, saeve, dedit?

So too, perhaps, does Petr. 56.5 'et facinus indignum, aliquis ovillam est et tunicam habet'.

1e. pavones βγ: **pavo** R. For arguments against R's singular, see at 13.49.*le.* above. This poem's singulars are generalising.

Peacocks were much admired for the beauty of their tails. They were also eaten as delicacies. Whereas Hor. *Serm.* 2.2.23 ff. comments that the peacock's fine feathers do not guarantee fine taste, this poem remarks on the paradox that someone can admire their beauty and nonetheless destroy it in order to eat them. Thus it is that the addressee is *durus* in line 2 (for the meaning 'harsh', 'pitiless', see *OLD* s.v. *durus* §5a). The cook, meanwhile, is *saevus* because he carries out the pitiless master's desires in killing and cooking the bird once it has been handed over to him. For *trado* in a similar usage, cf. Pl. *Rud.* 857 'hunc ad carnuficem traderent'.

On the admiration with which the bird was regarded and for other details, see D'Arcy Thompson *Birds* 277-81 and Pollard 91 ff. For the peacock as food, see *RE* XIX.1417.50 ff. s.v. *Pfau* [Steier], André *Alimentation* 131-2. The first person to have served peacocks was said to be Hortensius the orator and contemporary of Cicero: Pliny *Nat.* 10.45, Varro *R.* 3.6.6, and the innovation seems to have been immediately successful: Cic. *Fam.* 9.20-2. The first to sell peacocks fattened for the table was M. Aufidius Larco: Pliny loc. cit. Mayor goes into great detail at Juv. 1.143 regarding the price of peacock (and peacock eggs) and its status as a delicacy. He also refers to works on how to breed and keep them.

Apicius gives no peacock recipes as such, but note 2.54 Budé 'esicia de pavo primum locum habent ita si fricta fuerint ut callum vincant'. At Suet. *Vit.* 13.2, 'pavonum cerebella' are part of a sumptuous dish dedicated by Vitellius to Minerva.

1 miraris, quotiens gemmantis explicat alas: although the poem makes no specific reference to the peacock and the *lemma* can therefore be regarded as explanatory (cf. the introductory n. at 13.11 above), this line refers to the bird in language used so often of the peacock that the epigram's riddle is not very taxing; cf. Ovid *Med.* 33 'laudatas homini volucris Iunonia pinnas/ explicat', Phaed. 3.18.8 'pictis ... plumis gemmeam caudam explicas', Pliny *Nat.* 10.43 'gemmantes laudatus exponit colores', Stat. *Silv.* 2.4.26, Ovid *Am.* 2.6.55 etc.

According to Ovid (*Met.* 1.722-3), the peacock acquired its jewelled tail when Juno transferred to her bird the hundred eyes of the dead Argus. The epithet 'jewelled' is appropriate given the tail's highly decorative general appearance; but it is worth recalling also that *gemma* (cf. *geminare*?) is used firstly not of jewels but of the buds or 'eyes' of vines and the like (see

ThLL VI(2).1753.60 ff. s.v. *gemma* [I. Kapp], Ernout-Meillet s.v. *gemma*). Thus *gemmans* is particularly appropriate to the tail's ringed patterning.

13.71 Flamingoes

The ruddy feather gives me my name, but my tongue has savour to gourmands. What if my tongue should talk?

1e. phoenicopteri: cf. the Greek φοινικόπτερος (Ar. *Av.* 273; cf. possibly Cratin. *Nem.* fr. 121 ὄρνιθα φοινικόπτερον), which means 'scarlet-feathered'. Hence the personified flamingo of this poem notes in line 1 that 'dat mihi pinna rubens nomen'; cf. Mart. 3.58.14, describing flamingoes in Faustinus' farmyard: 'nomenque debet quae rubentibus pinnis'. M was fond of such etymologising (although it must be remembered in the latter case that *phoenicopterus* is metrically difficult), and his practice looks back to a considerable poetic tradition: Grewing (ed.) 318. Other examples in the *Xenia* and *Apophoreta* in which the gifts themselves are allowed to speak are e.g. Mart. 14.43.1 'nomina candelae nobis antiqua dederunt' (in a poem about a *candelabrum*) and 202.2 'si mihi cauda foret, cercopithecus eram' (in a poem about a tailless Barbary ape). Note too 13.49 and 14.121, where the *ficedulae* and *coclearia* query the justification of their names, given that other names are etymologically equally possible; also the clear grasp of etymology by the *aphronitrum* at Mart. 14.58. Grewing sees the personification of these gifts and the learning with which they are endowed as reflecting the 'mundus inversus' or inversion of the natural order of things occasioned by the Saturnalia: Grewing (1999a) 261, 280.

Thanks to the flamingo's etymologising here, the poem falls into the riddle category, where the *lemma* supplies the answer; see the introductory n. to 13.11 above. On the numerical difference between the plural *lemma* and the first line's *mihi*, see 13.11.2 n. above. (The plural *nostra* does not count, being dictated by metrical considerations.)

The flamingo which M's poem features was probably the Greater Flamingo, *Phoenicopterus ruber roseus*. Unknown as food in Republican times, it later became a great delicacy. In general, see D'Arcy Thompson *Birds* 304-5; cf. Juv. 11.139. For eating flamingo brain, cf. *SHA Elagabalus* 20. As for tongues, note Sen. *Ep.* 110.12 and Suet. *Vit.* 13.2 (where they form part of the dish mentioned in 13.70.*1e.* n.) Although tongues feature in neither of the recipes extant in Apicius (6.232-3 Budé), Pliny, *Nat.* 10.133, asserts that 'phoenicopteri linguam praecipui saporis esse Apicius docuit'; cf. *sapit*, line 2.

The flamingo is one of the birds distributed at Domitian's Saturnalian show: Stat. *Silv.* 1.6.77. The others are pheasants and guineafowl; cf. Mart. 13.72-3 below.

1-2 sed lingua gulosis/ nostra sapit: it is possible that in addition to meaning 'name', *nomen*, line 1, carries also the sense of 'fame' or 'reputation' (see *OLD* s.v. *nomen* §11b). While the flamingo's name and fame derive, as far as most people are concerned, from its red feathers, however, the *gulosus* is interested only in the taste of its tongue; cf. the paradox in the previous poem that one could both admire the peacock and nevertheless destroy its beauty by cooking it. In the present poem, however, the interest of the *gulosus* is likely to be very short-lived 'si garrula lingua foret', line 2. As was explained by Housman (*Class. Pap.* 738), 'This is the old wearisome indecency, ever fresh and entertaining to Martial and his public: lingua, si garrula foret, narraret fortasse gulosorum ora manducantium impura esse.' The *gulosus*' liking for flamingo tongue would not survive his being identified by it as a *fellator*. (For the revulsion with which the *os impurum* was regarded, cf. e.g. Mart. 7.95.14-15, a poem which deals with people one would prefer not to be kissed by.) Regarding obscenity in Book 13 and in M generally, see on 13.26.2 *puero* above. Grewing alludes to the power the peacock has over the *gulosus* in being able to betray his sexual tastes as being another instance of Saturnalian inversion: Grewing (1999a) 270.

lingua: in addition to etymologising (see *le*. n. above) and the possible ambiguity of *nomen*, this poem indulges also in a good deal of sexual *double entendre* which operates on several levels. Thus, while red feathers account for the flamingo's name, the adjective *rubens* also has associations which carry over into the rest of the poem: a connection was made between the colour red and the Phoenicians (cf. Isid. 19.17.5, cited by Robert Maltby, *A Lexicon of Ancient Latin Etymologies*, Leeds 1991, 472), the Phoenicians were commonly ascribed a fondness for oral sex, and so there is a play on *phoenicopterus* and φοινικίζειν; cf. M.A.P. Greenwood, *CPh* 93 (1998), 246 n. 35. Furthermore, and in the context of such associations (cf. Grewing (1999a) 269-70), the word *lingua* calls to mind the penis-tongue ambivalence of such poems as Mart. 11.61 (see Kay's introductory note) and 3.81 where, in his sexual encounters with women, the eunuch Baeticus uses his tongue as a penis substitute. The flamingo's tongue has savour to the *gulosus*, but, the poem hints, so does the penis which it comes also to symbolise.

gulosis: the throat was recognised as the seat of taste (see at 13.62.2 above) or appetite (*OLD* s.v. *gula* §2a). The adjective *gulosus* is similarly ambiguous since it can mean both 'gourmet' and 'gourmand': see M.A.P. Greenwood, art. cit., 245 n. 34, citing *ThLL* VI(2).2358.5 ff. s.v. *gulosus* [G. Meyer]. M entertains the ambiguity here in conjunction with the ambivalence of *lingua* prior to the confirmation in line 2 that the *gulosus* is no gourmet but a gourmand whose gluttony includes a voracious appetite for

Commentary

fellation. The application of eating metaphors to sex and especially oral sex is, of course, well testified: see Adams 138-141.

Gulosus is used substantivally again in M e.g. at 7.20.22. It is used in the context of oral sex again at Mart. 11.61.13 where it describes the tongue of the cunt-licking Nanneius.

2 garrula: *garrulus* is usual of a bird which can speak: *OLD* s.v. *garrulus* §2a, but the word is also used of someone who betrays secrets: *OLD* s.v. *garrulus* §1c. The rather surreal concept of a tongue which can still talk after having been cut out and cooked builds on the fantasy of an articulate flamingo which can explain the origin of its name and which has power over humans. The concept of a talking penis, albeit a symbolic one, is even more surreal.

13.72 Pheasants

I was first brought across by the keel of Argo. Before that nothing but Phasis was known to me.

le. Phasianae β: **Phasiani** γ: **Phasianus** α. Both masculine and feminine forms of the adjective *Phasianus* are used substantivally of the pheasant (*Phasianus colchicus*). Here Heraeus follows β, Lindsay γ. In support of β, which is clearly right, Heraeus refers to the feminine *transportata*, line 1, and compares Mart. 3.58.16, where an 'impiorum Phasiana Colchorum' features in Faustinus' farmyard. He might also have cited 13.73.*le. Numidicae*: given the frequent pairing of the two birds (see at 13.45.1 above), it would have been surprising had M used different genders for the *lemmata* of consecutive poems describing them and referring to their introduction to the Graeco-Roman world. Although Shackleton Bailey has *Phasiani* in his Teubner, this is a misprint, as can be deduced from his apparatus; see too his Loeb, vol. 1, vii n.1. (It is unfortunate that in correcting *Phasiani*, his Loeb text admits a different misprint in *Phasinae*.) Regarding α's singular, see 13.49.*le.* n. above. That it is in numerical agreement with the personifying singulars of the poem is no support for it.

Regarding the pheasant's origins in Colchis and its luxury status as food, see at 13.45.1 above. Like the flamingo in the previous epigram, the pheasant in this poem is well aware of the origins of its name: hence its reference to the River Phasis in line 2. The etymologising in this poem links it with the 'riddling' epigrams, examples of which are cited in the introductory n. to 13.11 above and whose content is explained or clarified by the *lemma*.

1 Argoa primum sum transportata carina: the Argo was traditionally the first ship (cf. Catul. 64.11, Ovid *Am.* 2.11.1-2, Luc. 3.193 ff.), and this is perhaps celebrated here by the heavily spondaic hexameter's somewhat

129

stately progress and by *Argous*: lofty contexts are often marked by the adjectival form of a proper noun acting as a possessive: see Coleman at Stat. *Silv*. 4.6.42 *Argoos*, referring to E. Löfstedt, *Syntactica* I,[2] Lund 1942, 107 ff. The bird had not seen any water other than the Phasis before the appearance of the Argo although it takes some pride in being one of the first to be conveyed by sea afterwards. (There is some justification for the bird's claim to be an early export since the Greeks knew it by 425 BC: Dunbar at Ar. *Av*. 68.) Of course there is an element of humour in the idea of a winged bird having to wait for the invention of ships in order to travel.

For the different versions of the Argo's return journey (only one of which mentions the Phasis), see *Kl.P*. 1.538.36 ff. s.v. *Argonautai* [H. von Geisau].

argoa Τβγ: **argia** R. Although Isid. *Orig*. 12.7.49 transmits the reading *argiva* when quoting this epigram, the MS variant *argua* (B¹T) also survives, which gives added support to the already well-attested *argoa*.

13.73 Guinea fowl

Although Hannibal had a surfeit of Roman goose, the barbarian never ate his own birds.

le. Numidicae: regarding the guinea fowl (*Numida meleagris*), see at 13.45.1 above. Gilbert suggests that Hannibal did not eat guinea fowl because he lacked taste, but *barbarus*, line 2, finds contrast in *Romano*, line 1, and is therefore more likely here to suggest his foreignness (*OLD* s.v. *barbarus* §1) than to indicate his lack of civilisation. The point of the poem seems to rest on this, that guinea fowl was introduced to Italy only after the threat posed by Hannibal and Carthage was over (cf. Varro *R*. 3.9.18 'haec novissimae in triclinium ... introierunt'), and, given the time he spent campaigning against Rome, he was therefore unable to eat his native birds.

1 ansere Romano: while it is possible that Hannibal did indeed eat (a great deal of) goose in Italy, the qualification *Romanus* has a further, metaphorical dimension here in that it calls to mind the Capitoline geese and their part in saving the Temple of Jupiter from invasion by Gauls: see at 13.74 *le*. below, where see also for geese as food. That Hannibal had his fill of Roman goose is a humorous reference to the fact that, despite many years of trying, he was, like the Gauls, unable to capture the city.

2 ipse suas ... aves: that Hannibal's birds were guinea fowl is not made clear by the poem, which falls into the category of 'riddling' epigrams dependent on their *lemmata* for the 'solution'. See the introductory n. to

13.11 above. *Ipse* is not strictly necessary, but its juxtaposition with *suas* emphasises the epigram's point.

Numquam is not to be taken literally, being instead a hyperbolical reference to the fact that Hannibal spent few of his early years in Carthage: he was taken to Spain in 237 BC at the age of about ten, having already sworn never to be a friend of Rome, and did not return until 203, after he was defeated by Scipio at Zama. For details, see *OCD*[3] s.v. *Hannibal* [B.M. Caven], *Kl.P.* 2.935.21 ff. s.v. *Hannibal* [H. Volkmann].

13.74 Geese

This bird saved the temple of the Tarpeian Thunderer. Are you surprised? A god had not yet made it.

This poem appears twice in T, here and after 13.124, possibly through a confusion of the numbers LXXIV and CXXIV. It is structured in the same way as Mart. 11.38: 'mulio viginti venit modo milibus, Aule./ miraris pretium tam grave? surdus erat.' For M's use elsewhere of the sequence striking fact, question, explanation, see Siedschlag 26. Similar to M's use of *miraris* here is his use of *quaeris/requiris*: see Siedschlag ibid. and cf. 13.111 below.

le. anseres: although the permanence of the Capitol was a long-established literary device (cf. e.g. Hor. *Carm*. 3.30.8 f. 'crescam laude recens, dum Capitolium/ scandet cum tacita virgine pontifex', Verg. *A*. 9.447 f. 'dum domus Aeneae Capitoli immobile saxum/ accolet'), the security of this permanence was from time to time challenged. Most famously the Capitol was threatened by the Gauls who invaded it in 390 BC, on which occasion it was saved by the cackling of geese, which raised the alarm: see Livy 5.47. M's poem initially appears to comment on the unlikely source of the Temple of Jupiter's salvation on that occasion; but the concern of *miraris*, line 2, turns out to be with its past vulnerability in general. Once the divine Domitian (*deus*, line 2) had rebuilt it, however, after its recent destruction for the third time by fire, it was, M affirms, safe from all future threats.

Domitian's lavish restoration of the temple (see Richardson 223) was completed or at any rate dedicated in 82: see Intro. (iv) n.3 above, and was but one of the highlights of an extensive building programme: see at 13.91.1 'ad Palatinas ... mensas' below, Jones 79 ff. and his notes at Suet. *Dom*. 5 'plurima et amplissima opera incendio absumpta restituit, in quis et Capitolium, quod rursus arserat'. M flatters Domitian again through reference to the temple's reconstruction at 9.3.7-8, where he asks how Jupiter could repay the emperor for what he had done. (Regarding M's flattery of Domitian, see generally at 13.4.1 *serus* above.) It must have been with Domitian's rebuilding at least partly in mind that even general references were made after 82 to the temple's permanence, e.g. to parallel the permanence expected of the temple of the Flavian *gens* (Mart. 9.1.5 with Henriksén ad loc.), while further specific examples are supplied by Stat. *Silv.* 4.3.160-1 'donec ... renatae/ Tarpeius pater intonabit aulae' (to parallel the expected permanence of Domitian's reign) and Stat. *Silv.* 1.6.101-2, which remarks that the memory of Domitian's Saturnalian show will last 'dum ... terris,/ quod reddis, Capitolium manebit'.

Like the 'argutus anser' of Mart. 3.58.13, the geese which this poem envisages as a present would have been free range; contrast the geese kept for their livers, who would have been housed in batteries (see at 13.58.*le.* above, q.v. also for geese given as presents). On geese for eating, see D'Arcy Thompson *Birds* 326-7. Apicius gives two recipes, both of which involve boiling and sauce (6.229, 235 Budé).

1 haec avis is a generalising singular (contrast the plural *lemma*), for which see 13.11.2 n. above. The hexameter contains a sort of numerical metathesis: while in actual fact several birds saved a single temple, here one finds *avis* in the singular and *templa*, for metrical reasons, in the plural.

Tarpei βγ: **Tarpeia** α. If one adopts α's reading, one must scan *i* as a short vowel, which would be exceptional (cf. Müller 310), and so the majority MS testimony is vindicated. For discussion of M's use of the adjective *Tarpeius* (exclusively in connection with Jupiter), see Henriksén at Mart. 9.1.5.

2 miraris: cf. *Sp.* 28(25).2 'desine mirari' in a poem flattering Titus.

deus γ: **deos** αβ. It is possible that αβ understood *avis* with *illa* and had therefore to find an object; but the result is nonsense.

Although Octavian is called *deus* at Verg. *Ecl.* 1.6, this is probably just a bucolic gesture of gratitude and respect; cf. Calp. *Ecl.* 1.84, where the term is used in similar fashion of Nero. Reference to Domitian as *deus* is a rather more complex matter, however, given such passages as Pliny *Paneg.* 2.3 and Suet. *Dom.* 13.2 'pari arrogantia, cum procuratorum suorum nomine formalem dictaret epistulam, sic coepit: dominus et deus noster hoc fieri iubet.' It has recently been argued that those who spoke of the emperor while he lived as 'dominus et deus' did so for opportunistic reasons of their own rather than as a result of imperial prompting, while those who later attributed such praise to the emperor's insistence did so to support a rhetorical opposition between his behaviour and that of his successor Trajan whom they were praising through a binary comparison. See L. Thompson, '*Domitianus dominus*: a gloss on Statius *Silvae* 1.6.84', *AJPh* 105 (1984), 469-75, who begins by quoting lines 81 ff., arguing that they reflect Domitian's actual position:

tollunt innumeras ad astra voces
Saturnalia principis sonantes
et dulci dominum favore clamant:
hoc solum vetuit licere Caesar.

If Thompson is correct, M's flattery of the emperor as a god is therefore self-initiated, prompted not by imperial insistence but by the hope of imperial favour. Since Domitian is described in this poem as having restored Jupiter's temple, however, he cannot, as elsewhere, be equated directly with Jupiter himself; but equal powers can nonetheless be attributed to him: cf. 13.4.1 *imperet* n. above and note also Stat. *Silv.* 4.3.16 'qui reddit Capitolio Tonantem', which suggests that Domitian's authority was even greater than Jupiter's.

With the idea that the buildings of gods would endure, whereas those of men would crumble or fall, compare perhaps the scholia at Pindar *O*. 8.40 ff. on how the parts of the Trojan wall constructed by the Olympians Poseidon and Apollo were indestructible, but not the section built by the mortal Aeacus.

13.75 Cranes

You will disturb the lines and the letter will not fly complete if you waste one of Palamedes' birds.

le. grues explains 'Palamedis avem' in line 2 (for the explanatory function of *lemmata*, see the introductory n. to 13.11 above). Palamedes, the son of Nauplius of Euboea, was known for his inventiveness (see *Kl.P.* 4.418.32 ff. s.v. *Palamedes* [H. Gärtner]) and his cunning: it was he who detected Odysseus' pretended insanity when attempts were made to recruit him to fight at Troy: Hyg. *Fab.* 95.2. One of his most notable discoveries, although it was attributed to others as well (see Tac. *Ann.* 11.14), was the alphabet: he was said to have invented it, or at least certain letters, through observing the flight of cranes; cf. Aus. *Technopaegnion* 14.25 Green 'haec gruis effigies Palamedica porrigitur U'. M refers to the story again at 9.12(13).7, describing the name Earinus, in latinised form Vernus and represented by the letter V, 'quod pinna scribente grues ad sidera tollunt'.

On one level, Mart. 13.75 is saying that its addressee will throw into disarray (*OLD* s.v. *turbo* §4b) the lines of birds in formation (*OLD* s.v. *versus*[1] §3) and the whole letter of the alphabet (*OLD* s.v. *littera* §1), that is presumably again to say the letter V (or U), will fly through the air incomplete if just one crane is missing or lost (cf. *OLD* s.v. *perdo* §3), or even squandered (*OLD* s.v. *perdo* §6a). The full complement of cranes is needed for this letter to be formed, and by wasting a single bird of those given to him, the recipient stands to undo Palamedes' great work. Ironic humour is, of course, to the fore.

So far, so good; but there is more: in the context of the epigram, it is difficult not to suspect that *versus* is intended also to carry the sense of 'line of writing' (*OLD* s.v. *versus*[1] §4) or even 'line of poetry' (*OLD* s.v. *versus*[1] §5), and to note that *littera* can mean 'line of writing' too (*OLD* s.v. *littera* §4a) or possibly writing generally (see Shackleton Bailey's Loeb note). Presumably the point of the poem is then that if the recipient of the cranes here squanders just one of his gifts, he would not only disturb Palamedes' alphabet, but he would destroy M's poem: writing a poem is impossible without letters, and the word *versus* (amongst others in the epigram) is impossible without the letter V/U. This explanation would of course yield an unparalleled usage of *volabit*, but not an unfeasible one.

In commenting on the poem, Friedländer and Shackleton Bailey suggest that M had in mind when writing it Luc. 5.711 ff. (they refer in particular to 716):

> Strymona sic gelidum bruma pellente reliquunt
> poturae te, Nile, grues primoque volatu
> effingunt varias casu monstrante figuras;
> mox ubi percussit tensas Notus altior alas,
> confusos temere inmixtae glomerantur in orbes,
> et turbata perit dispersis littera pinnis.

This is possible.

Because of the crane's southern migration, it would have been an expensive dish in winter, which is the point behind 'hiberna ... grue' at Stat. *Silv.* 4.6.8 (see Coleman ad loc.). Wasting a Saturnalian gift of such birds was therefore all the more to be avoided. Cranes are a luxury dish also at Hor. *Serm.* 2.8.85-6 'pueri ... ferentes/ membra gruis sparsi sale multo non sine farre'; cf. Ovid *Fasti* 6.176. Apicius gives several recipes, all of which would also do for duck (6.212-17 Budé), although 213 contains a note specific to crane: 'gruem cum coquis, caput eius aqua quam non contingat' sed sit foris ab aqua. cum cocta fuerit, de savano calido involves gruem et caput eius trahe: cum nervis sequetur, ut pulpae vel ossa remaneant; cum nervis enim manducare non potest'.

For information regarding cranes, see further Mynors at Verg. *G.* 1.120. The birds were caught by means of nooses (Hor. *Epod.* 2.35), but were also bred in captivity: Varro *R.* 3.2.14.

13.76 Small woodcocks

Whether I am woodcock or partridge, what does it matter if the flavour is the same? Partridge is dearer. That's how it tastes better.

1e. rusticulae or woodcocks (*Scolopax rusticola*) were clearly a common dish although (and therefore?) no recipes survive. They are associated with *perdices* (lines 1 and 2) again at Pliny *Nat.* 10.111 'ambulant aliquae [sc. aves], ut cornices ... currunt [sc. aliae], ut perdices, rusticulae'. (On the *perdix*, see 13.65.*le.* n. above.) The noun *rusticula* survives of woodcocks in these two places alone, while the substantival use of *rusticus* is even less common, apparently surviving in line 1 alone. (Elsewhere the word is used to qualify *gallina*, as at Varro *R.* 3.9.16 'gallinae rusticae sunt in urbe rarae'; cf. Columella 8.2.1, 8.12.)

While the epigram's somewhat cynical observation that people base their evaluation of something on its price rather than its quality can here be set in the context of the attention to material value which characterised Roman giving and receiving (see Intro. (ii) section D above), the sentiment is nonetheless commonplace; cf. Hor. *Serm.* 2.2.23 ff., Juv. 11.16 'magis illa iuvant quae pluris emuntur' with Courtney and Mayor ad loc. With the epigram one should perhaps compare those in Mart. 14 in which cheap artefacts protest that they are nevertheless as efficient or effective as more expensive versions: note poems 62, 90, 104.

On the numerical difference between the *lemma* and the poem's personifying singular, see at Mart. 13.11.2 above.

1 sim an γ: **si mansi** T: **si maneat** β. The readings of T and β, which attempt to fill out the omission of *perdix*, make no sense: a woodcock cannot change species. The choice of γ's reading is therefore easy, even though the elision of a monosyllable other than in the first foot is exceptional: see Birt in Friedländer, vol. 1, 36 and n.2.

quid refert: i.e. it does not matter. For question words which equate to negatives, see Siedschlag 21, who cites in addition Mart. *Sp.* 3.1, 5.48.1, 7.24.2, and 10.4.2.

2 carior est perdix: Heinsius suggested *at* for *est*, but the unanimously transmitted *est* is perfectly sensible and the pentameter's opening words are clearer for containing an expressed verb.

Carior is balanced by *magis*.

sic γL: **si** TPQf. The latter reading was possibly influenced by *si sapor*, line 1.

13.77 Swans

With weakened tongue, the swan, which chants of its own death, modulates sweet songs.

le. cycni: the Greeks ate birds regardless of species (Pollard 104), and swans appear as food several times in Greek (D'Arcy Thompson *Birds* 180). In Latin, note also *AL* 190.93.

There were several things for which swans were famed (*Kl.P*. 5.42.15 ff. s.v. *Schwan* [W. Richter]): their long necks and white feathers, their wisdom, their aggression and, of relevance to this poem, that they sang before they died. For references to the phenomenon and full discussion, see W. Geoffrey Arnott, 'Swan songs', *GR* 24 (1977), 149-53. Despite the scepticism of some, both ancient and modern, that dying swans 'sing' is a fact. Arnott explains (152): 'The whooper [swan] ... has a remarkably shaped trachea, convoluted inside its breastbone; and when it dies, the final expiration of air from its collapsing lungs produces a "wailing, flute-like sound given out quite slowly" '. In her detailed analysis of the structure and organisation of the poem, Lausberg argues that it reflects the song's euphony and sweetness: 347 f.

1 defecta γ: **defacta** α: **deficiens** β. With γ's reading (of which α's is a palaeographical equivalent), cf. Ovid *Met*. 13.477-8 (describing the death of Polyxena): 'illa super terram defecto poplite labens/ pertulit intrepidos ad fata novissima vultus'. *Deficiens* makes for a weaker and less paradoxical juxtaposition with *dulcia*: if strength, albeit declining, still remains to the bird its song is less impressive.

2 cantator ... **funeris ipse sui**: on the generalising singulars (also in line 1), which contrast with the plural *lemma*, see at 13.11.2 above.

    Cantator is a rare word, surviving here only in classical Latin with the genitive thus and elsewhere only at Varro *L*. 8.57 and Gel. 16.19.2 'vetus ... et nobilis Arion cantator fidibus fuit'. The more usual *cantor* would have presented metrical difficulties.

13.78 Porphyrions

Does a bird so small have the name of a huge giant? It also has the name of Porphyrion of the Green.

le. porphyriones: Pliny describes these birds as having a long narrow neck, long red legs and a red beak (*Nat*. 10.129; cf. 11.201) and declares that superior specimens were to be had from the Balearic islands. As to the bird's identity, however, there is some uncertainty, although it is probably the purple gallinule (*Porphyrio caeruleus*): D'Arcy Thompson *Birds* 253. No recipes for the bird survive in Apicius, but the Septuagint's use of πορφυρίων to translate the mysterious *tinshemeth* at Lev. 11.18 (in a list of unkosher food) is further indication that the bird was eaten.

    The *porphyrio* is a (lover's) gift at Ar. *Av*. 707.

1 volucris ... **parva**: regarding the generalising singular, see at 13.11.2 above. The purple gallinule is not in fact a particularly small bird, measuring some 45 centimetres in length (18 inches); but *parva* is justifiable in relation to 'magni ... gigantis' (for opening contrasts in M's work, see Siedschlag 25 and 29 ff.). Porphyrion was one of the giants who made war on the gods; cf. Hor. *Carm.* 3.4.54, Claud. *Gigant.* 35, 115; see *Kl.P.* 4.1064.11-20 s.v. *Porphyrion* [H v. Geisau]. The point of the poem seems to be to express surprise in the hexameter that a relatively small bird and a giant should have the same name, and then to remark in the pentameter that the bird's name was nevertheless, and no less surprisingly, also that of a charioteer who, despite being called 'Purple', belonged to the Green faction. Nothing is known today of this Porphyrio(n) (contrast the fame of the Byzantine Porphyrius Callopas: see Alan Cameron, *Porphyrius the Charioteer*, Oxford 1972); but like modern turf jockeys charioteers would have been small (children even, like Crescens the Moor: Balsdon *LL* 322) and the humour of the poem would be much extended if he were renowned for *especially* diminutive size (cf. Juv. 8.32 'nanum ... Atlanta vocamus', Mart. 6.77.7, Prop. 4.8.41). On circus factions, see my notes at Mart. 14.131.1 and 55.1, where the likelihood is raised that M supported the Greens.

gigantis β: **cicadis** γ: om. T. Difficulties of number and case aside, large crickets clearly have no place here. Heraeus questions Gruter's question mark after *gigantis* (earlier editors had a comma), but the poem's point, as outlined above, is much weakened without it.

2 et nomen ... habet: for *nomen* with an appositional genitive, see *OLD* s.v. *nomen* §1a, citing Tac. *Hist.* 1.47 and Vell. 2.27.5. '[Sulla] Felicis nomen adsumpsit.'

Porphyrionis Tβ: **Purpurionis** γ. Lindsay considered γ's reading possibly correct (see e.g. Aug. Zimmermann, *Archiv für lateinische Lexikographie und Grammatik* 13 (1904), 478, who notes Lucius Furius Purpurio, the military tribune at Livy 27.2.10); but the better attested Greek spelling is hard to dismiss after the *lemma*.

prasini: sc. *factionis*; cf. Suet. *Nero* 22.1 'et quondam tractum prasini agitatorem ... querens'. Instead of *prasini*, Lipsius suggested *prasinus* (with *Purpureonis*), understanding the word with *auriga*: that a small bird should have the name of a giant called Porphyrion is no stranger than that a Green charioteer should be called 'Purple'; but his assertion that the poem's humour is lost in the transmitted text is unfounded and indeed by introducing an extra subject he may even have weakened it. (My thanks to Dr Norma Aubertin-Potter of the Codrington Library, Oxford, for a transcription of Lipsius' note, from his 1621 edition (Venice), 80-1.)

Regarding the double genitive (with *Porphyrionis*), see L-H-Sz II.65-6, D.R. Shackleton Bailey, *Propertiana*, Cambridge 1956, 223.

13.79-91: this section deals with sea food and fish, some of which (*rhombi, lupi, murenae* and *mulli*) could be found in the *piscina* of Apollinaris (Mart. 10.30).

13.79 Live mullets

The mullet breathes in the sea water brought with him, but languishes, already sluggish. Give him the living sea and he will be strong.

le. mulli vivi: the red mullet (D'Arcy Thompson *Fishes* 264 ff.) was a great delicacy under the empire (Blümner *Priv.* 182 and n.21), and large specimens of the fish in particular attracted high prices: see Mayor at Juv. 4.15 and Kay at Mart. 11.49(50).9. This epigram refers to the practice of bringing mullet to the table alive in glass vessels of sea water (for *aequore*, line 1, see *OLD* s.v. *aequor* §3b) so that diners could watch their colours change as they died from oxygen starvation: Pliny *Nat.* 9.66 'mullum expirantem versicolori quadam et numerosa varietate spectari proceres gulae narrant, rubentium squamarum multiplici mutatione pallescentem, utique si vitro spectetur inclusus', Sen. *Nat.* 3.17.2; cf. 18.1. The fish would then have been taken away and cooked. Apicius gives recipes for mullet e.g. at exc. 15 and 16 Budé, and recipes for sauces to use with mullet at 10.444-5 Budé. See too André *Alimentation* 100.

M's use of *vivi* here is not without irony, as the poem makes clear. There the mullet (the singular is generalising; see 13.11.2 n. above) is alive (note *spirat*, line 1), but the extent of its vitality is qualified by the contrasting *languescit* (line 2; note the corresponding position of the verbs at the beginning of both lines) and 'iam piger' (line 1). In fact the fish is only as 'alive' as the water in which it is swimming, and 'vivum da mare', line 2, suggests that the water is in fact 'dead'; for *vivus* of fresh or continuously flowing (and therefore oxygenated) water, see *OLD* s.v. *vivus* §6. Its application to sea water is slightly unusual, but fully justified here on literary grounds. (For *mare* meaning 'sea water' as opposed to 'sea', see *OLD* s.v. *mare* §5, L-S s.v. *mare* §IIA.)

The mullet appears as a valuable gift e.g. at Mart. 7.78.3 and Juv. 6.39 (where it is a present used by legacy hunters fishing for inheritances; cf. Mart. 2.40.4), and a half mullet is one of the unofficial *apophoreta* stolen by the dinner guest Caecilianus at Mart. 2.37.4 to take back to his boy.

1-2 spirat in advecto sed iam piger aequore mullus/ languescit: Schneidewin has commas after *advecto* and *piger*, a full stop after *mullus* and a question mark after *languescit*; but the commas are unnecessary and we have already been told that the fish is 'iam piger' and so there is no need to ask whether it is languishing. Friedländer, Gilbert, Heraeus, Lindsay and Izaac differ by having a semi-colon after *mullus* and a full stop after *languescit*; cf. Giarratano who has a comma after *mullus*. This, however, makes *languescit* sound repetitive after 'iam piger'. Heinsius' conjecture *languenti* dispenses with the apparent repetition but robs the poem of the strong contrast between *spirat* and *languescit* and greatly weakens the force of the adversative *sed*. As Housman's note reveals (*Class. Pap.* 738), the potential in 'iam piger' and *languescit* for superfluity or repetition can successfully be removed only by admitting no punctuation at all, besides a full stop after *languescit*. Housman is followed by Duff, Ker and Shackleton Bailey.

2 vivum da mare, fortis erit: for the construction, which is in effect conditional, see L-H-Sz II.657; cf. Mart. 3.35.2 'adde aquam, natabunt'. With the exception of Shackleton Bailey, all editors punctuate with a colon after *mare*, but for a conditional sentence this is unnecessarily and even disruptively strong. It is perhaps worth noting here too that while the very effective sense pause after *languescit* occurs in a position regularly observed by the Augustan elegists (Platnauer 26), a sense pause at the third foot diaeresis is somewhat rarer: although occurring at least a dozen times in Ovid, it is found nowhere in Tibullus and only once in Propertius.

Fortis erit gives balance and contrast to *languescit*.

13.80 Murries

The large murry that swims in the Sicilian deep has not the strength to submerge its sunscorched skin.

le. murenae were eels of a type particularly admired, especially those from Sicily. Regarding them, see Blümner *Priv.* 183 and Mayor at Juv. 5.99 'Virroni muraena datur, quae maxima venit/ gurgite de Siculo', who compares Macr. 3.15.7 'accersebantur autem murenae ad piscinas nostrae urbis ab usque freto Siculo, ... illic enim optimae a prodigis esse creduntur'; note too Varro *R.* 2.6.2, Pliny *Nat.* 9.169.

At Horace *Serm* 2.8.42 ff., where a *murena* is served with shrimps, Nasidienus describes the sauce which accompanies it, declaring that the flesh of the *murena* taken before spawning is better than that of one taken after. For other sauces to go with *murena*, boiled or roasted, see Apic. 10.449-54 Budé. A *murena* recipe is given at exc. 16 Budé. Two eels, obviously intended for eating, are depicted in a still life from Pompeii (*Pompeii AD 79* 255).

One of the punning *pittacia* at Petr. 56.9 reads 'muraena et littera'. Although the guest in fact received 'murem cum rana alligata fascemque betae', the appearance of *murenae* in Petronius as well as M suggests that they might have been common gifts. At Mart. 2.37.5 a 'latus murenae' is mentioned among the unofficial *apophoreta* stolen by Caecilianus.

On the generalising singulars in this poem, in contrast to the plural *lemma*, see 13.11.2 n. above.

1-2: Macrobius, ibid., goes on to describe the phenomenon upon which M's epigram centres: 'Graece πλωταί vocantur, Latine flutae, quod in summo supernatantes sole torrefactae curvare se posse et in aquam mergere desinunt atque ita faciles captu fiunt'. (Aristotle says much the same of turtles: *HA* 8.3.4; cf. Pliny *Nat.* 9.35.) The point of M's epigram might be to draw attention to the murry's size (*magnae*, which Q adds to the *lemma*, is doubtless drawn from *grandis*, line 1), the fact that despite it, it has not the strength (*non valet*, line 2) to submerge, and that although the water is deep ('in Siculo … profundo', line 1), ironically, this is of no help to the eel.

2 exustam … sole cutem: cf. Tib. 2.3.9 'nec quereror quod sol exureret artus', Cels. 1.3.10 'si quis … exustus in sole est, huic … perfundem … oleo corpus'. *ThLL* V(2).2126.35 ff. s.v. *exuro* [Schmeck] cites only these two parallels.

13.81 Turbot

However wide a dish bears the turbot, the turbot is nevertheless wider than the dish.

le. rhombi: the turbot, 'noblest of the flatfish' (D'Arcy Thompson *Fishes* 223), can grow extremely large, and the difficulty of finding a suitably sized dish for one provides the subject also of Juv. 4: note especially line 72 'sed derat pisci patinae mensura', at which Courtney cites Mrs Beeton: 'Turbot often grow to considerable size … It must be noted that if cooking a whole turbot, a turbot kettle (shaped) will be required'. Whereas Juvenal's lengthier treatment has the emperor's *consilium* summoned to discuss what to do, M here exploits the couplet's brevity to produce a neatly turned conceit: the poem is carefully written so that the two lines are corresponding, both being in the same metre (on M's choice of hendecasyllables here, see also Intro. (vi) above) and containing verbal parallels; yet the second line is also an inversion of the first. Thus *quamvis* is followed by *tamen* and *lata* by *latior* – albeit now applied not to the *patella* but to the fish. *Rhombus* at the beginning of the second line meanwhile helps emphasise the poem's point by following hard on *rhombum* at the end of line 1; and both *rhombum* and *rhombus* are positioned so as to balance and contrast with *patella*.

Regarding the turbot, see also Blümner *Priv.* 184 and Courtney at Juv. 4.39. As to its luxury status, note e.g. Mart. 3.45.5, Hor. *Serm.* 2.1.115-16 (where it is ranked with peacock) and 2.2.95-6: 'grandes rhombi patinaeque' bring scandal and ruin. According to Pliny, *Nat.* 9.169, the best turbot came from Ravenna.

1-2: the poem's singulars (contrast the *lemma*) are generalising; see 13.11.2 n. above.

1 lata … patella: on the *patella*, see Hilgers 239-41 and D-S IV(1).341 s.v. *patella* [E. Pottier]. The *patella Cumana* of Mart. 14.114 is of earthenware and would have been used in fairly ordinary contexts. Given the luxury status of the turbot, however, a much finer *patella* would be expected here. Hilgers cites examples of silver and gold: 240-1.

The use of *lata* with *patella* here suggests a colloquial weakening of the latter's diminutive sense; cf. Courtney at Juv. 10.82 'magna fornacula' and Smith at Petr. 63.5 'valde audaculum'. In preceding the noun it possibly carries some emphasis, which would mean that it is undercut all the more by *latior* in the following line.

gerat γ: **cerat** T: **regat** β. Tβ's readings are easy corruptions of γ's. Although *gero* does not survive elsewhere of a plate, it is used of a wine flagon at Apul. *Met.* 8.11, an earthenware jar of figs at Mart. 4.88.6 and a perfume jar at 7.94.1.

13.82 Oysters

Drunk with Baian Lucrine, I have just come, a shellfish. Now in my luxuriousness I thirst for famous *garum*.

le. ostrea must be n. pl. since one would not make a present of a single oyster. Oysters were a delicacy even in Mycenaean times (D'Arcy Thompson *Fishes* 191) and remained a luxury dish in the Roman period: D'Arcy Thompson ibid.; cf. e.g. Mart. 3.45.6 and 7.78.3. At Pliny *Ep.* 1.15.3 and Macr. 3.13.12 they are part of the *gustatio*, but, on the evidence of this poem, they could clearly be a main course as well; cf. the *echini* of 13.86 below. (It is perhaps worth noting incidentally that oysters and *echini* are often paired.). According to Pliny, *Nat.* 9.168, Sergius Orata was the first to farm oysters, at Baiae, by which he meant the Lucrine Lake: cf. 'Baiano … Lucrino', line 1. This lake, situated between Puteoli and Baiae, made an ideal oyster bed, being shallow and, thanks to the surrounding volcanic activity, warm (for the conditions suited to oysters, cf. Pliny *Nat.* 32.59). The oysters it produced acquired an outstanding reputation: cf. Sen. *Ep.* 78.23, Mart. 3.60.3, 6.11.5 and 12.48.4, where they are a legacy hunter's gift. For further gifts of oysters, see Green at Aus. *Epist.* 14.

On oysters in the ancient or Roman world, see further A.C. Andrews, *CJ* (1948) 299-303, Blümner *Priv.* 188-9 and Courtney at Juv. 4.140-2. For Lucrine oysters, see Mayor at Juv. 4.141 and K.M. Coleman, *CQ* 44 (1994) 554-6. Regarding the Lucrine Lake, see Mynors at Verg. *G.* 2.161-4.

Apicius gives recipes for several sauces other than the *garum* of line 2 which could be used with oysters (1.31-2, 9.413 Budé). On *garum*, see generally the notes at 13.102-3 below.

1 ebria Baiano ... **Lucrino**: Baiae had a reputation for drunkenness and debauchery; cf. Seneca's description of the place (*Ep*. 51.4): 'videre ebrios per litora errantes et commissationes navigantium'. By juxtaposing *ebria* and *Baiano* here, M playfully recalls this reputation while actually describing oysters 'steeped' or 'soaked' in the water of the Lucrine Lake. For this metaphorical use of *ebrius*, see *OLD* s.v. *ebrius* §3. The idea of drinking is continued by *sitio* in line 2.

veni modo βγ: **modo veni** T. Both readings are possible with no difference in meaning, although βγ's yields a lighter, more poetic line by avoiding the diaeresis admitted by T in the third as well as the fourth foot.

With *veni*, cf. *venio* at 13.35.1 above where again the personifying singular follows a plural *lemma*. (For numerical differences between *lemma* and poem, see 13.11.2 n. above.) *Modo* is picked up by *nunc* in the following line. (For other such combinations of *modo* and *nunc*, see *ThLL* VIII.1305.40 ff. s.v. *modus* [Pligersdorffer].) Oysters are in season from April to September, and so this Saturnalian oyster probably arrived in the recent rather than immediate past; but poetic licence here makes for a more graphic effect.

2 nobile ... **garum**: it is possible that M has particularly in mind Pompeian *garum* here. Not only was this renowned (Pliny *Nat*. 31.94; see T.J. Leary, *Acta Classica* 37 (1994) 112), amply meriting the adjective *nobilis* (for its meaning 'celebrated', see *OLD* s.v. *nobilis* §2b), but it would also have been geographically appropriate to the Lucrine oysters of the poem.

M admits further humour here by inviting a contrast between *nobile*, stressed by the alliterative *nunc*, and *ebria*, which is similarly placed at the beginning of line 1: as well as meaning 'celebrated', the adjective *nobilis* can suggest lofty and aristocratic values, qualities and exploits out of keeping with the Baian drunkenness recalled by the hexameter.

luxuriosa, which allows for additional contrast with the lofty connotations of *nobile*, has as its principal sense here 'marked by/displaying luxury' (*OLD* s.v. *luxuriosus* §3b), but can, at a secondary level, also mean 'given to self-indulgence' (*OLD* s.v. *luxuriosa* §3a). In confirming the luxury status of oysters, the principal meaning suggests that they have a right to expect to be served with a luxury sauce. The latter meaning, which is made possible by the personifying verbs, accords with the decadent associations of Baiae and the liking for *garum* found among extravagant or luxurious eaters.

Commentary

13.83 Prawns

Blue Liris, whom the wood of Marica shades, nurtures us. Prawns from there, we are a mighty throng.

le. squillae are served as a luxury dish at Juv. 5.80 ff., where Courtney suggests that bear-crab, lobster or crayfish are in question (cf. D'Arcy Thompson *Fishes* 104). Pliny presumably means something similar by *squillae* at *Ep.* 2.17.28: 'mare non sane pretiosis piscibus abundat, soleas tamen et squillas optimas egerit'. The term *squilla* could, however, be applied to a wide range of crustaceans (D'Arcy Thompson *Fishes* 104), and while D'Arcy Thompson thinks this poem describes fresh-water crayfish (ibid.), the smaller fresh-water prawn is also a possibility (cf. the Loeb's translation, adopted here) and perhaps accords better with the oysters of the previous epigram. If prawns are intended, sufficient are presumably meant (cf. 'maxima turba', line 2) to constitute a main course by themselves; but small *squillae* could also be used to embellish a principal dish (e.g. the *murena* at Hor. *Serm.* 2.8.42).

1 caeruleus ... Liris: the Liris is a river in Campania, near Minturnae, whose lower reaches are now called the Gargiliano; but the upper course is still called Liri. N-H have a detailed note at Hor. *Carm.* 1.31.7.

For *caeruleus* of rivers, see *ThLL* III.104.40 ff. s.v. *caeruleus* [Goetz]. Fordyce notes at Verg. *A.* 8.64 that the word is conventionally applied to river gods (cf. *ThLL* ibid. 83 ff.), which would accord with the river's personification here.

amat must here have as its principal meaning 'cares for' (for this sense, of divine nurture, see *OLD* s.v. *amo* §8a), since the poem's concern is with the source of the *squillae* rather than the river's feelings for them.

silva Maricae: the original functions or concerns of Marica are unclear (cf. *Kl.P.* 3.1025.52 ff. s.v. *Marica* [G. Radke]), and she was variously regarded as Venus, Diana and Circe. In Virgil she is the mother of the Latins: *A.* 7.47. What is certain is that she had a grove (Livy 27.37.2 'lucum Maricae') through which the Liris flowed; cf. Mart. 10.30.9, Hor. *Carm.* 3.17.7, Luc. 2.424 'et umbrosae Liris per regna Maricae'. It is to the shade cast by this grove that *protegit*, line 2, principally refers: cf. *OLD* s.v. *protego* §1a, which gives several examples featuring trees. *Protegit* might also carry the sense 'protect', however, in which case the 'silva Maricae' looks after the Liris which in turn looks after the *squillae*; cf. on *amat* above.

2 hinc T: **hic** β: **hunc** γ. The readings of βγ make little sense. For *hinc* referring to a person (or personification), cf. L-H-Sz II.209.

143

13.84 Parrot wrasse

This parrot wrasse, which has come eaten away by the sea waves, is good as regards its entrails, but for the rest it has a poor flavour.

1e. scarus: frequent off the coasts of Greece and Asia (Columella 8.16.9), this fish was in the time of Tiberius brought from the Carpathian Sea (off the Ionian coast) and planted by Optatus, the *praefectus classis*, in the sea between Ostia and Campania: Pliny *Nat.* 9.62. According to Ennius' *Hedyphagetica*, fr. 28.8 Courtney, the biggest and best specimens were caught off the coast of Pylos ('Nestoris ad patriam'). Ennius describes the fish (7) as 'cerebrum Iovis paene supremi' (see Courtney ad loc.) and its luxury status is also apparent from e.g. Hor. *Epod.* 2.50, *Serm.* 2.2.22 and Petr. 119.33-4 where, like the mullet of 13.79 above (see *1e.* n.), 'ad mensam vivus perducitur'. D'Arcy Thompson notes (*Fishes* 240) that 'It should be eaten trail and all, as Belon found was still the case in Crete (*de Aquatil.*, p. 239): "insipidus est scarus, nisi cum suis fecibus edatur" '; hence the point (see below) of M's poem. Note that it is the 'scarorum iocinera' that form an ingredient of the lavish dish dedicated by Vitellius to Minerva: Suet. *Vit.* 13.2.

Assuming that the text is correct (see Howell ad loc.), the *scarus* appears again in a Saturnalian context at Mart. 5.18.8, albeit in a metaphor rather than as a gift.

1 aequoreis ... adesus ab undis: cf. Mart. 10.51.8 'aequoreis ... aquis', Ovid *Ars* 1.528. In marine contexts, *adesus* is more usually applied metaphorically, e.g. to rocks; cf. Ovid *Ep.* 10.26 'scopulus raucis adesus aquis'; but M's use here plays on its literal meaning. The epigram asserts that only the innards are any good because the outside of the fish has already been eaten by the buffeting of the sea.

2: the pentameter halves are metrically identical save for the final syllables (cf. Intro. (vi) above for interchangeable pentameter halves) and this, combined with carefully ordered and corresponding wording in each half, emphasises the contrast between the fish's palatable organs (for this meaning, see *OLD* s.v. *viscus* §3a) and the rest of it.

13.85 Coracinus

Leader of the Nile market, coracinus, you are snapped up. No glory of the Pellaean palate is before you.

1e. coracinus: almost certainly the *Tilapia nilotica*: D'Arcy Thompson *Fishes* 124. The fish's Egyptian origins (cf. *Niliaci*, line 1) are confirmed by Pliny, *Nat.* 5.51; cf. 32.56 'coracini Nilo ... peculiares', who also attests to its paramountcy there (*Nat.* 9.68): 'alii alibi pisces principatum obtinent, coracinus in Aegypto ...'; cf. *princeps*, line 1.

There are a hundred or so different species of tilapia, widely distributed over sub-Saharan Africa and extending eastward from the Nile basin to Israel, Jordan and Syria. The fish is also found in the aquaria of fish-fanciers, whence escapees have come to colonise waters as distant even as Florida. The tilapia remains an important table fish in tropical countries.

1 princeps is similarly employed at Columella 3.8.5, of fine wine. See too *OLD* s.v. *princeps* §5b.

Niliaci ... macelli: for *Niliacus* meaning 'Egyptian', see at 13.1.3 'Niliacas ... papyros' above. The *macellum* was principally a fish or meat market, although other foodstuffs were also sold; cf. Ter. *Eun.* 255 'ad macellum ubi advenimus,/ concurrunt laeti mi obviam cuppedinarii omnes,/ cetarii lanii coqui fartores piscatores/ quibus et re salva et praedita profueram'; see D-S III(2).1457.1 ff. s.v. *macellum* [Henry Thédenat], *RE* XIV.129.26 ff. s.v. *macellum* [K. Schneider]. The fine *macellum* at Pozzuoli gives one a good impression of such places, especially when it is not flooded due to bradyseismos. So does the *macellum* off the forum at Pompeii. See too J.B. Ward Perkins, 'From Republic to Empire: reflections on the early architecture of the Roman West', *JRS* 60 (1970), 15-16. That M has any one *macellum* particularly in mind here is, however, unlikely.

raperis in the sense here used is natural enough although seemingly unparalleled in surviving classical Latin; but cf. Jerome *Ep.* 57.2 'ante hoc ferme biennium miserat Iohanni episcopo supra dictus papa Epiphanius litteras arguens eum in quibusdam dogmatibus et postea clementer ad paenitentiam provocans. harum exemplaria certatim Palestinae rapiebantur vel ob auctoris meritum vel ob elegantium scriptionis.'

2: the pentameter elaborates on the hexameter. It is carefully arranged so as to create tension between alliterative groupings (*Pellaeae* with *prior* and *gloria* with *gulae*) and grammatical agreement. There is further an alternation of adjectives and nouns which nevertheless allows the enclosing of one adjective-noun pair by the other.

Pellaeae ... gulae parallels 'Niliaci ... macelli', line 1; cf. *prior* which picks up *princeps*. The adjective *Pellaeus* comes from Pella, the capital of Macedonia and birth place of Alexander. It comes therefore to mean in the poets 'Alexandrian' (as perhaps here, given the sophistication for which the city was known), 'Ptolemaic' or 'Egyptian'. See Mynors at Verg. *G.* 4.287, *OLD* s.v. *Pellaeus* §2c. Its grandeur further reinforces *princeps*. For the throat as organ of taste, see at 13.62.2 above.

13.86 Sea urchins

Although the sea urchin pricks your fingers with its sharp shell, it will be soft once its cover is put aside.

le. echini: described by Ennius as *dulces* (fr. 28.11 Courtney), sea urchins were a great luxury: André *Alimentation* 104. At least five species are eaten in the Mediterranean, of which *Echinus (Paracrentosus) lividus* is the best and most common: D'Arcy Thompson *Fishes* 72. At Hor. *Serm.* 2.4.33, *echini*, from Misenum, are part of the *gustatio*; cf. Pliny *Ep.* 1.15.3, Macr. 3.13.2. It seems from this epigram, however, that they could also be served as a larger dish; cf. the oysters of 13.82 above. According to Pallad. 13.6, *echini* grew large in December, and they were thus ideal for consumption at the Saturnalia.

   Sold fresh rather than salted (as at *Ed. Diocl.* 5.9), *echini* came either with or without their shells: *Ed. Diocl.* 5.7-8. Recipes such as Apic. 9.415 Budé must have in mind shelled urchins since otherwise the accompanying sauce would not flavour them. Nevertheless it is clear from 'digitos ... pungat', line 1, that, unless eaten raw (which is possible), they could also be cooked unshelled; cf. the story at Athen. 3.91C-D of a Spartan at a dinner, who bit into a sea urchin, shell and all, in his ignorance and, although he cursed the φάγημα μιαρόν, added that he would not be beaten by it although he would not eat another.

   It is possible that this epigram sounds a mock philosophical note: perseverance brings its reward. Cf. perhaps Petr. 33.5 ff., esp. 7: 'ego [sc. Encolpius] paene proieci partem meam, nam videbatur mihi iam in pullum coisse'; but the apparently unappetising dish is not what it seems and the eggs turn out to contain *ficedulae*.

1: the succession of dental sounds in this line is possibly intended to help convey the idea of prickly hardness, in contrast with the urchin's soft interior (*mollis*, line 2).

iste: for the use of this word without particular or emphatic reference to the second person, see *OLD* s.v. *iste* A§4.

testudine ... acuta: *testudo* is usually used of a tortoise shell (cf. *cortex*, line 2, used of a tortoise shell e.g. at Phaedr. 2.6.12, Pliny *Nat.* 9.35); cf., however, its use in connection with the Crab at Man. 2.198 ff.: 'aspice ... testudine cancrum/ surgere'. It is of course not actually the shell that is sharp, but the spines on it.

pungo: the singular verb (contrast the plural *lemma*) is generalising. See further at 13.11.2 above. *Pungo* is elsewhere used e.g. of prickly hedgehog-type bristles (Pliny *Nat.* 8.221). The damage which sea urchin spines can inflict is extensive: they break off easily, they are very difficult to dig out, infection sets in rapidly and respiratory difficulty and muscular weakness sometimes ensue. Pliny recommends treatment with urine: *Nat.* 28.67, but very hot water (60° C) is today preferred! (See P.M. Leary, *Don't Die in the Bush*, Cape Town 1994, 105-6.)

2 cortice deposita α: **deposito** βγ. *Cortex* can be of either gender but survives more commonly in classical Latin as masculine than feminine (cf. *ThLL* IV.1068.11 ff. s.v. *cortex* [Probst]). As Heraeus observes, it is definitely feminine at Mart. 14.209.1. (For other feminine occurrences, see Neue-Wagener I.985-6.) Although M was not bound to consistency in his usage (Virgil makes *cortex* feminine at *Ecl.* 6.63 but masculine elsewhere), the feminine *deposita* is preferable here as *lectio difficilior*.

13.87 Murexes

Ungrateful fellow, you put on cloaks dyed with our blood twice, and this isn't enough: we are things to eat.

1e. murices: there are several species of these large snails, but the most important were *Murex brandaris, Murex trunculus* and *Purpura haemastoma*: D'Arcy Thompson *Fishes* 209. Although known principally for the purple dye extracted from them, they made also a luxury dish: cf. Hor. *Serm.* 2.4.32 with Muecke, Macr. 3.13.12 and Luc. *Cyn.* 11. See too D'Arcy Thompson loc. cit., André *Alimentation* 104, and note the *murex* shells amongst other foodstuffs in a Pompeian still-life: *Pompeii AD 79* 257. The *Murex brandaris* has remained a foodstuff in the Adriatic even in modern times: D'Arcy Thompson *Fishes* 210. Presumably the *murices* would have been prepared for eating along the lines suggested by Apicius when treating snails generally (Apic. 7.323-6 Budé).

  Since a minute quantity of purple dye was obtainable from each snail, it was extremely expensive. It is because of this expense that the addressee of this poem is called *ingratus* in line 1: someone who is not content with wearing valuable purple, but eats the *murex* as well is mean beyond measure. The words 'non est hoc satis', line 2, sound even more indignant if Heinsius' conjecture *bis* is adopted in line 1 instead of *de* (codd. and most editors): 'sanguine bis nostro tinctas' would refer not just to any purple but the magnificent and outstandingly costly Tyrian *dibapha*; cf. e.g. Ovid *Am.* 3.171 'nec quae bis Tyro murice lana rubet' and Hor. *Carm.* 2.16.35 'bis Afro murice tinctae' with N-H. Although Shackleton Bailey remarks in his Loeb note that *bis*, while attractive, is not necessary, there is further support for it in that *tingo* appears not to survive elsewhere with *de*.

  For an historical and technical account of the use of purple dye and further details regarding dye-producing snails, see conveniently Forbes IV.114 ff.

1 sanguine … nostro: cf. e.g. Mart. 14.154.1 'ebria Sidoniae … de sanguine conchae', Pliny *Nat.* 9.135 'laus ei summa in colore sanguinis concreti' and the dye/blood imagery suggested by the robe in Aeschylus *Ag.*: see Oliver Taplin, *The Stagecraft of Aeschylus: the Dramatic Use of Exits and Entrances in Greek Tragedy*, Oxford 1977, reissued 1989, 315.

lacernas: the *lacerna* was a cloak made initially of wool, although other fabrics were later used, and, while originally worn by soldiers, was later adopted also by civilians. It was not necessarily expensive: poor quality *lacernae* were often given by patrons to their clients (see Courtney at Juv. 9.28); but those dyed in purple could be extremely costly: cf. Mart. 8.10.1-2 'emit lacernas milibus decem Bassus/ Tyrias coloris optimi'. See further Sebesta 225 fig. 13.4, 229, Blümner *Priv.* 215, *RE* XII.327.52 ff. s.v. *lacerna* [Lange], D-S III(2).901 s.v. *lacerna* [H. Thédenat].

2 esca sumus: the *murices* seem resigned to being killed for their dye, but apparently (and humorously) regard being eaten as beneath them.

13.88 Gobies

In Venetian country, for all a banquet might be lavish, a goby is usually the high point of the dinner.

le. gobii: regarding these fish, see D'Arcy Thompson *Fishes* 137-9: they were small (Columella 8.17.14 *exiguus*), of the gudgeon type, cost very little (Juv. 11.37 contrasts them with *mulli*, Lucil. ap. Var. *L.* 7.47 with tunny), and were generally held in low esteem (cf. Diog. L. 2.67 and the ironic Athen. 7.309D). It would seem from this poem, however, that they were nonetheless conventionally accorded some status in Venetia (Veneto), where they were common in the lakes and lagoons (some species can live in all but fresh water: D'Arcy Thompson *Fishes* 138). The people north of the Po were known for having their own traditions, cultural life and ways of speech (see Fordyce *Catullus* x), and this individuality is possibly of some relevance here. Regarding the Veneti, see generally *Kl.P.* 5.1164.44 ff. s.v. *Veneti* [G. Ürögdi], *OCD*[3] s.v. *Veneti*[2] [E.T. Salmon, T.W. Potter].

1 lauta Tγ: **pauca** β. The latter reading, which makes poor sense in comparison with the better attested *lauta*, may preserve an attempted emendation of *lauca*.

2 principium cenae: Shackleton Bailey translates 'start of the meal'; cf. Ker's 'beginning of the dinner'; but if these gobies are an appetiser (the poem's singular is generalising), one would expect them in the section 13.6-60 above. Since there is no reason to suspect that the epigram has been displaced (indeed, the poem accords neatly with the next: see 13.89.1 n. below), *principium* must either be suspect or must carry some other meaning. There is nothing in the transmission to indicate textual corruption and so it must therefore be taken instead to refer to the importance accorded to the goby locally; cf. possibly *OLD* s.v. *principium* §7a and note also, with Smith's translation ad loc., 'summa cena' at Petr. 41.4: Roman diners would have been delighted by the frozen Black Sea gobies which reportedly came to life again in the pan (Athen. 8.331C, Pliny *Nat.* 9.177), and a similar trick might have rendered the fish a *pièce de résistance* in Venetia.

13.89 Sea bass

The woolly sea bass breasts the mouths of Euganean Timavus, having fed on fresh water with sea salt.

le. lupus: the sea bass was renowned for its aggression (cf. Ovid *Hal.* 23 'immitis et acer'), for which it is sometimes known as the sea wolf in English. It came into fashion with the epicures of Augustus' time: D'Arcy Thompson *Fishes* 141, those called *lanati/lanei* (cf. line 1) being most prized; cf. Pliny *Nat.* 9.61 'luporum laudatissimi qui appellantur lanati a candore mollitiaque carnis'. Although specially bred for the table (cf. Blümner *Priv.* 182 n.8, Mart. 10.30.21), it was also caught wild. That it frequents the sea near river mouths (Opp. *Hal.* 1.114) but is also found upstream prompted debate concerning where it was best taken: while those caught in the Tiber 'between the bridges' were especially admired by some (Pliny *Nat.* 9.169, Macr. 3.16.13), others thought that sea water bass were better than fresh: cf. Columella 8.16.4 'doctaque et erudita palata fastidire docuit fluvialem lupum'. Still others questioned whether in fact provenance made any difference: cf. Hor. *Serm.* 2.2.31 'unde datum sentis lupus hic Tiberinus an alto/ captus hiet'. M's epigram seems to be in keeping with this last view since, given the peculiar nature of the River Timavus (see below), it is impossible to decide whether its *lupi* are fresh or saltwater specimens.

Apicius gives just one *lupus* recipe: 4.159 Budé 'patina de pisce lupo'. A *lupus* is one of the unofficial *apophoreta* stolen from the dinner table by Caecilianus at Mart. 2.37.4 and is a legacy hunter's gift at 2.40.4. Phyllis extorts one as a lover's gift at Mart. 11.49(50).10.

1 Euganei ... ora Timavi: regarding the Euganei, see *Kl.P.* 2.412.59 ff. s.v. *Euganei* [G. Radke]; cf. Livy 1.1.3 'inter mare Alpesque incolebant'. They were associated with several cities in Venetia (thus this poem follows easily after the last: cf. 13.88.1 'in Venetis ... terris'), e.g. Verona, Altinum and Patavium (Mayor at Juv. 8.15). The River Timavus (now the Timavo) is identified with them also at Sidon. Apoll. *Carm.* 9.194 'Euganeus ... Timavus', Luc. 7.192 ff., Sil. 12.215 ff.

Concerning the River Timavo, which flows into the Gulf of Trieste, somewhat to the west of Aquileia, Coleman notes at Verg. *Ecl.* 8.6 that 'About 1½ kilometres inland, a number of underground streams (cf. *A* 1.245) emerge from high cliffs ... to form the *lacus Timavi* (Livy 41.1). Most [but not all] of the emergent streams appear to have been saline, whence the river was locally known as "the source and mother of the sea" (Strabo 5.214 citing Polybius).' The precise number of emergent streams is unclear (contrast the nine in Virgil, *A.* loc. cit., with M's seven: 4.25.5), but it is enough to know that there were several when explaining *ora* here. (For *os* of a river mouth, see *OLD* s.v. §5c.) That some of these outlets were fresh provides the basis for the paradoxical nature of line 2.

excipit: similar uses of *excipere* meaning 'to sustain the force of' can be found at Caes. *Gal.* 4.17.9 'sublicae ... agebantur qua ... vim fluminis exciperent' and Sen. *Ag.* 408a 'tumidum classis excepit mare'. See *OLD* s.v. *excipio* §11a.

2 aequoreo dulces cum sale pastus aquas: this line has been crafted in a careful interlocking arrangement of noun-adjective pairs in which *aequoreo* and *dulces* are juxtaposed for contrast and there is further contrast between *aequoreo* at the line's beginning, and the fresh water *aquas* at the end. *Varietas* is admitted by the (singular) ablatives with *cum* and the (plural) accusatives with *pastus*.

On *pastus* thus used, see Mynors at Verg. *G.* 3.143: 'With the animal as subject, the verb is passive in form and middle in sense ..., and can take ... a direct object'; cf. *G.* 3.314, 4.181. The word does not appear to survive anywhere else having as its subject a fish and being applied to water.

For *dulcis* of fresh water, see *OLD* s.v. *dulcis* §2a, citing e.g. Cato *Agr.* 112 'ex alto ... sumito mari ... quo aqua dulcis non perveniet'.

13.90 Gilthead

Not every gilthead deserves praise and high price, but the one whose sole food will be the Lucrine shellfish.

le. aurata: for the gilthead (*Sparus aurata*), so called because of the golden band between its eyes, cf. Pliny *Nat.* 32.43. Although a sea fish, it also frequents inshore waters or estuaries (see D'Arcy Thompson *Fishes* 293 and cf. the *lupus* of 13.89 above), and it was bred in *piscinae* (Columella 8.16.8). It is wholly carnivorous, and the nature of its teeth accords with a diet of shellfish: D'Arcy Thompson ibid. The fish is praised as sweet and tasty above all others at Athen. 328B. It is indeed possible that its flavour varied according to the shellfish upon which it fed; cf. the debate

referred to in context of the previous poem (13.89.*le.* n.) as to whether *lupi*
were best taken from the sea or rivers. Nevertheless, to assert that only
those fed on the 'concha Lucrina', i.e. oysters, were worth anything is to
insist on very high standards: Lucrine oysters were luxuries in their own
right: see at 13.82.*le.* above.

Apicius gives two recipes for sauces to accompany gilthead (10.462-3
Budé), and one for a gilthead *patina* (4.158 Budé).

1 omnis, referring to the fish, is countered by *solus*, line 2, referring to its
food.

aurata: when not applied substantivally to the gilthead, this adjective
was used of gilded objects, some of which were extremely costly. M is
playing on the uses of *aurata* by juxtaposing it here with *pretium*.

2 erit αγ: **erat** β. Both Shackleton Bailey ('aeque bonum') and Heraeus
('non male') concede that β's reading may be correct, but print the better
attested (and more difficult) *erit*.

13.91 Sturgeon

Send the sturgeon to Palatine tables. Let rare gifts enhance ambrosial
feasts.

le. acipensis βγ: **acipenses** T: **acipenser** ς. Regarding the sturgeon,
Acipenser sturio, see Blümner *Priv.* 181, D'Arcy Thompson *Fishes* 7-8. It
is an impressive fish which can grow to some four metres in length. For
metrical reasons the rare form *acipensis* is understandable in line 2 (see
Müller 477); but since the *lemma* is prose, Heraeus suggests that the
humanists' *acipenser* could be right here. Note the palaeographical close-
ness of *acipenser* and T's *acipenses* (T's plural is out of keeping with the α
MSS's apparent dislike of numerical differences between *le.* and poem: see
13.49.*le.* n. above), and compare the use of *rusticulae* (*le.*) and the (even)
rarer but metrically convenient *rustica* (line 1) in 13.76 above. Heraeus
nonetheless follows βγ in printing *acipensis*, which is not demonstrably
wrong.

There was a long-standing tradition of sending gifts of (large or valuable) fish to rulers: cf. Hdt. 3.42 and see Courtney 198, on Juv. 4, who
refers to Suet. *Tib.* 60 and Sen. *Ep.* 95.42. In a series of poems describing
gifts of fish, it would therefore have been surprising had M not addressed
one to the emperor, and his choice of a sturgeon as subject is also not
surprising. It is true that the fish had fallen out of fashion in Pliny's day
(*Nat.* 9.60), even though it was rare: 'cum sit rarus inventu'; but as this
epigram shows, its reputation had recovered by the time M wrote (cf.
André *Alimentation* 97), and its status as a royal fish has endured. Ker's

citation of English common law bears repetition (7 Coke's Reports 16A): 'whales and sturgeons are royal fish, and belong to the King by his prerogative'.

M's epigram goes further, however, than just dedicating a sturgeon to the emperor. He equates the emperor's feasts (signalled here by 'Palatinas ... mensas', line 1) with those of Jupiter (note 'ambrosias ... dapes', line 2), and the implication of this is therefore that Domitian himself is Jupiter's equal. For the equation of Domitian with Jupiter and for M's flattery of Domitian generally, see at 13.4.1 *serus* and *imperet* above.

1 ad Palatinas ... mensas: the Palatine was a favoured residential area from early on and, especially after the fire of AD 64, became increasingly dominated by imperial residences. Domitian's building activity on the Palatine eventually covered much of the hill: see R.H. Darwell-Smith, *Emperors and Architecture*, Brussels 1996, 182; cf. Jones 23-4, 95-6. M celebrates it in effusive tones e.g. at 8.36, which is usually taken to refer to the domus Flavia-domus Augustana. Note especially lines 11-12: 'haec, Auguste, tamen quae vertice sidera pulsat,/ par domus est caelo, sed minor est domino.'

For *palatinus* meaning 'imperial', see L-S s.v. *palatinus* §IIb; cf. Juv. 6.117 'ausa Palatino tegetem praeferre cubili'. M uses it with *mensa* again in 8.39:

> qui Palatinae caperet convivia mensae
> ambrosiasque dapes non erat ante locus:
> hic haurire decet sacrum, Germanice, nectar
> et Ganymedea pocula mixta manu.

The first syllable of the word *palatinus* was originally scanned short, but a long scansion became fashionable in poets around the time of Domitian. Of the word's twenty instances in M, fifteen have long scansion. See Kay at Mart. 11.8.5, who cites *RE* XVIII(3).15 s.v. *Palatium* [Konrat Ziegler] and Citroni at Mart. 1.70.5.

mittite: the plural may have been influenced by metrical concerns, but is more likely to constitute a general injunction to all Domitian's subjects, themselves unworthy of the fish, to do their emperor appropriate honour.

2 ambrosias ... dapes: cf. Mart. 8.39.2 quoted above (noting as well the references to nectar and Ganymede: 3-4), and 49(50).8-9 'vescitur omnis eques tecum populusque patresque/ et capit ambrosias cum duce Roma dapes' (of the public celebration following Domitian's Sarmatian victory). Also 4.8.7 ff., in a poem asking Euphemus to choose his moment when commending M's work to the emperor:

> hora libellorum decima est, Eupheme, meorum,
> temperet ambrosias cum tua cura dapes
> et bonus aetherio laxatur nectare Caesar
> ingentique tenet pocula parca manu.

For the elevated associations of the word *daps*, see at 13.14.1 'cludere ... cenas' above.

munera rara: PQ's 'munera cara', which might have been influenced by 13.102.2 below, makes good sense; but *rara* is better since it has two applications: it refers partly to the (continued) scarcity of the fish (cf. Pliny *Nat.* 9.60 quoted above), and it also carries implications of cost, referring generally to *munera* which might suitably grace (*ornent*) the imperial table: cf. the cost connotations of *rara* at Catul. 69.3-4 'non si illam rarae labefactes munere vestis/ aut perluciduli deliciis lapidis'.

13.92-100: the careful arrangement of these poems, which deal with game, is outlined above: Intro. (iii). Hunting was a winter activity, and so game would have been in season at the Saturnalia; cf. Hor. *Epod.* 2.29 ff., Mart. 1.49, esp. 19 ff., which mentions deer (23; cf. 13.94), boars (24; cf. 13.93); hares (25; cf. 13.92) and stags (26; cf. 13.96).

13.92 Hares

If anything according to my judgement is certain, the thrush is the foremost delicacy amongst birds, and amongst quadrupeds the hare.

le. lepores: although keenly hunted (on horseback at Mart. 1.49.25: see Howell ad loc. for some details), hares were also bred, and from early on, for the table: Jennison 133, 135, Keller I.214-15. It was, of course, not only M who considered hare a luxury ('si quid me iudice certum est', line 1): see Blümner *Priv.* 176 and note Petr. 36.2 and Juv. 11.138. Carving hare was thought, at any rate by some, to merit special ceremony (Juv. 5.123-4) and a half-eaten hare was a desirable left-over from a gourmet's dinner: Juv. 5.167; cf. Mart. 7.20.5 (listing *apophoreta* which Santra subsequently sells). That Apicius gives fourteen hare recipes (8.384-96 Budé; also 4.171, 9.430) is further testament to its popularity.

While hare could be served as a main course, the *lepus* of this poem is not (the singular, which follows the plural *lemma*, is generalising: see 13.11.2 n. above). Instead, it is a *mattea*, that is to say a tid-bit: cf. Mart. 10.59.3-4; 'dives et ex omni posita est instructa macello/ cena tibi, sed te mattea sola iuvat' (where *mattea* is used metaphorically of short poems). Such delicacies were not laid on tables (see Smith at Petr. 65.1), but were brought around at a late stage of the meal (Smith refers to *CGL* III.14.54 'περιφορὰ mattia' and Athen. 6.245F περιφέρειν ματτύην), being intended to restore jaded appetites or to provide appetisers for late-comers: see W. Heraeus, 'Die Sprache des Petronius und die Glossen' in *Kleine Schriften*, Leipzig 1899, 16. It is therefore appropriate that this epigram should begin a new section (see also on *prima*, line 2), and editors rightly ignore the fact that β positions it after 96. The tastiest part of the hare was thought to be the fore-quarters (Hor. *Serm.* 2.4.44, 2.8.89), which is doubtless what M has in mind here.

Hare is a luxury gift at Mart. 7.78.3. See too 13.94.*le.* n. below (hare as a lover's gift), and cf. the satirical 6.75.2, which spurns the hare sent as a gift by a notorious poisoner. (Caligula allegedly sent poisoned *matteae* as presents so that he could benefit from the recipients' wills: Suet. *Calig.* 38.2.)

1: on the *turdus* see at 13.51.*le.* above. There it is a *gustatio*. That it was also common as a *mattea* is confirmed by Petr. 65.2 (where Trimalchio serves *gallinae* instead of *turdi*) and Sen. *Con.* 9.4.20.

2 quadri(u)pes is used of a hare also at Cels. 2.18.3 'ex quadrupedibus leporem' where the animal is classed as a food of middling strength.

prima: *primus* means 'foremost' in terms of both quality and position: *OLD* s.v. §§13 and 9. Cf. Mart. 13.61.1 *primus* in a poem describing Ionian francolins which, as having the best flavour, begin the group on fowl.

lepus, last word, gives balance to the opening 'inter aves turdus', to which 'inter quadripedes', at the beginning of the line, gives contrast.

13.93 Boar

The bristly one, terror of Diomedes' land, who fell by an Aetolian spear, such was this.

le. aper clarifies *saetiger*, line 1. This epigram is a 'riddle' to which the *lemma* supplies the 'answer'. For other such 'riddles', see generally at 13.11 above (introductory note); but see also on 'metuendus saetiger' below.

Regarding wild boar, see generally André *Alimentation* 115-16. It was first served whole, as is probably the case here, by P. Servilius Rullus, who lived in the generation before Cicero (Pliny *Nat.* 8.210), and it endured as a luxury banquet dish: cf. Juv. 1.140-1 'totos/ ponit apros, animal propter convivia natum'; see Keller I.397.

The boar of this poem is compared with that of Calydon, regarding which and the Meleager legend, see conveniently Hollis, Ovid *Met.* Book VIII, 66-8. See too Homer *Il.* 9.529 ff.: Oeneus, king of Aetolia (of which Calydon was a city) failed to honour Artemis when offering sacrifices to the gods. In her anger at his oversight, she sent a monstrous boar to ravage the land, and it was only stopped when Oeneus' son Meleager killed it, helped by a band of chosen heroes. Phoenix, who tells the story in the *Iliad*, goes on to liken Achilles to Meleager since, in the dispute which followed the boar's death as to who should have its head and hide, Meleager withdrew in a sulk. It seems likely that Homer's version of the story develops an earlier Meleager poem (the *Meleagris*: see J.Th. Kakridis, *Homeric Researches*, Lund 1949, 24-5), and that the tale's epic status was long-standing. (For the heroic tone of M's epigram, see below.)

Fine boars are compared with the Calydonian boar elsewhere e.g. at Juv. 5.115-16 (a boar served to Virro): 'et flavi dignus ferro Meleagri/ spumat aper'; cf. Mart. 7.27.1-2 'aper ... Aetolae fama secunda ferae' and the (debunking) 13.41.2 above. Pork was, of course, a traditional Saturnalian dish (see Intro. (ii) section B above), of which boar was the rich man's version (cf. 13.41.*le.* n. above).

Mart. 9.48 describes, once more by reference to the Calydonian boar ('Aetola de Calydone putes', line 6), the poet's gift of a huge specimen to Garricus, and his indignation at not having been invited to help eat it. Boar is again an expensive gift at Mart. 7.78.3; cf. 12.48 (served by a legacy hunter).

For boar recipes, see Apic. 8.330-9 Budé.

1-2: M makes considered use of word order in this poem: by separating *qui* and the delayed *cecidit*, he emphasises 'Diomedeis metuendus saetiger agris' and the time and effort needed to kill the animal. The alliteration of *cecidit* and *cuspide* punctuates strongly the end of the relative clause, and this, plus the fact that the relative clause is so long and comes first, gives force to the main clause: 'talis erat'.

1 Diomedeis ... agris: Diomedes was son of Tydeus, king of Aetolia, grandson of Oeneus (hence he is *Oenides* at Ovid *Met.* 14.512) and step-nephew of Meleager. His name is used here principally to mean 'Aetolian', but memories of his heroic feats at Troy contribute to the epic stance of M's epigram.

metuendus saetiger: *metuendus* is used attributively from the time of Cicero: L-H-Sz II.371. That it is positioned here before *saetiger* helps stress the terrible nature of the boar.

On *saetiger*, see Bömer and Hollis at Ovid *Met.* 8.376, where the adjective is again used substantivally of the Calydonian boar; cf. Sen. *Med.* 643-4 'stravit Ancaeum violentus ictu/ saetiger'. The word is a kenning, which in Latin usage recalls the style of archaic high-flown poetry (cf. Hollis loc. cit.), and which can be classed as 'colloquial' and 'denominative' in type since its starting point in describing the boar is a characteristic detail: see Ingrid Waern, *ΓΗΣ ΟΣΤΕΑ: the Kenning in Pre-Christian*

Poetry, Uppsala 1951, 38 ff. and cf. e.g. the use of φερέοικος or 'house-carrier' of a snail at Hsd *Works* 571. Waern adds (50): 'The denominative type ... can advantageously be accompanied by the normal word, which is closely allied with its epithetic function'. Here, of course, the normal word is contained by the *lemma*.

2 Aetola ... cuspide: cf. Mart. 7.2.3 'ad Aetolae ... cuspidis ictus'. This noun-adjective combination sustains the heroic effect of 'Diomedeis ... agris' in the previous line.

cado: for the use of *cadere* of animal deaths, see *ThLL* III.25.1 ff. s.v. *cado* [Hoppe]. Given the epic associations of this boar, however, it is noteworthy that the word is often used also of people falling in battle: *OLD* s.v. *cado* §9a; cf. e.g. Verg. *A.* 10.830 'Aeneae magni dextra cadis'.

13.94 Deer

The boar is feared for his tusk, its horns defend the stag: what are we unwarlike deer but prey?

1e. dammae: according to the *OLD* s.v., the word *damma* (m/f) is a general term for a member of the deer family, albeit usually applied to the smaller species. That M had a particular type of deer in mind here seems, however, likely. Given 13.98 *caprea* and 99 *dorcas* below, it is unlikely to have been the gazelle or roe deer. André argues for the fallow deer (*Alimentation* 117 n. 53), to which he takes *platyceros* at Pliny *Nat.* 11.23 also to refer. While M's 'imbelles dammae' here are possibly female, this term would certainly accord with the flattened antlers of the male.

The *damma* is a luxury foodstuff (rendered tasteless to the rich man if not served on a luxury table) at Juv. 11.121-2: 'nunc divitibus cenandi nulla voluptas, nil rhombus, nil damma sapit'. It was caught in nets (cf. Mart. 1.49.23, 3.58.28), and was classed as safe prey, in contrast to boars (cf. 13.93 above), bears and wolves: Ovid *Met.* 10.537 ff.; cf. *imbelles*, line 2, although see ad loc. No recipes containing the word *damma* survive, but André, loc. cit., still arguing that *damma* = fallow deer = *platyceros*, refers to Apic. 8.2.2 (= 340 Budé): 'in platone similiter'. The recipe André cites begins a series of recipes for sauces to go with stag and even if he is wrong in all his associations, the words cited continue 'et in omne genus venationis eadem conditura uteris'.

Dammae are cited, along with hares and goats, as (lovers') gifts at Ovid *Met.* 13.831-2.

1-2: the epigram shows careful tripartite arrangement: the caesura in the hexameter divides the verse between the boar and the stag while the *dammae* have the pentameter to themselves. This division marks a progression of decreasing ferocity: the boar is feared, the stag, while not feared and most likely to run, can at least defend itself if necessary, but the *damma*, when hunted, can do nothing but flee; cf. Mart. *Sp*. 33.1 ShB 'concita veloces fugeret cum damma Molossos'. In arranging his poem, M employs careful variation, using passive and active verbs respectively in the first two sections and admitting a personifying question in the third.

1 dente timetur aper: cf. Ovid *Ep*. 4.104 'obliquo dente timendus aper'.

defendunt cornua cervum: stags were traditionally timid (Ovid *Fast*. 5.173, Hor. *Carm*. 4.6.33-4) and Lucr. 3.750-1 suggests that it was in fact rare for them to turn and fight. Surprisingly, it would appear, e.g. from artwork, that after Augustus stags were not much hunted by the Romans: cf. Howell at Mart. 1.49.26. For eating tame stags, see 13.96 below.

2 imbelles: although defenceless prey in this poem, the opposed 'imbelles ... dammae' of Mart. 4.74.1 are hostile and aggressive in the extreme; cf. 4.35. These poems, however, owe their very inspiration to the fact that such behaviour is unusual.

13.95 Oryx

Not the meanest quarry of the beasts of the morning shows, the savage oryx costs me the death of how many hounds!

le. oryx: there are three types of *oryx*, one from India, one from southern Africa (the gemsbok), and this one, the scimitar-horned oryx (*Oryx dammah*), originally from North Africa but later to be found in Roman game parks (Columella 9.1.1). It was an expensive and therefore luxury dish: note, in addition to line 2 below, the 'Gaetulus oryx' at Juv. 11.140. The animal's ferocity (*saevus*, line 2) is elsewhere attested by Oppian: *Cyn*. 2.446, and can be confirmed by the author – whose motor car was once threatened by an alarmed gemsbok. See further Keller I.292, Toynbee 146, Jennison 77.

1 matutinarum ... ferarum: *venationes* in the arena were generally held in the morning: Balsdon *LL* 298, 304 (304-8 give general information regarding animal shows), Friedländer *Roman Life* II.63 n.16, D-S V.702 s.v. *venatio* [Georges Lafaye]; cf. Ovid *Met*. 11.26 'matutina cervus periturus harena', Mart. 5.65.8, 8.67.1-4: the *venationes* have not ended by the fifth hour.

non ultima praeda: i.e. prey well worth pursuing. Cf. Luc. 4.14 'non ultimus amnis' (of a sizeable river), Hor. *Ep*. 1.17.35 'principibus placuisse viris non ultima laus est' and Pliny *Nat*. 17.91 'haec ... scientia ... non in ultimis ponenda'. *Praeda* provides both connection and contrast between this poem and the last: there the *dammae* were *praeda* because they cannot defend themselves; here the *oryx* is also *praeda*, but of a different kind because it can.

2 saevus: editors are equally divided as to whether to spell *saevus/-os*. The MSS favour *saevus* both here (Rβ: *saevos* A) and at 2.57.7 (Ⱪγ: *saevos* P): see Gilbert in Friedländer, 110. Nevertheless, the change from the Republican o to u after the consonantal u was very slow (see L-H-Sz I.49), and Quintilian remarks (*Inst.* 1.7.26) that his own teachers wrote *servos/cervos* for *servus/cervus*. It is therefore not impossible that M wrote *saevos* here. (Lindsay suspects that some scriptorium 'corrector' might have 'corrected' genuine Republican spellings as well as the Merovingian corruptions of u to o in such words as *domus*: *Orth.* 49.) It is, however, unlikely, given also the evidence of 13.96.*le. cervus* below (αβ: *cervos* γ): as Heraeus notes ad loc., γ changes u to o also at 13.39.*le. haedus* and 14.218.*le. notarius*.

constat quot mihi morte canum: i.e. the oryx does not come cheaply. The dogs it killed would have cornered it, perhaps in a net, and would have died when it turned to defend itself. For *consto* used with the ablative of price, see *OLD* s.v. *consto* §11a. The rhetorical *quot* (edd.: *quod* codd.), emphasised to some extent by the preceding caesura, gives the impression of greater cost than could have been achieved by stating a specific number.

On hunting with dogs see generally D.B. Hull, *Hounds and Hunting in Ancient Greece*, Chicago 1964. Different breeds were valued for different activities, e.g. tracking, the chase etc.: see D-S V.686 s.v. *venatio* [George Lafaye], Toynbee 102 ff. Imported dogs in particular would have been valuable and their value would have increased further when they were fully trained (cf. Toynbee 106).

13.96 Stag

This was the one tamed by your halter, Cyparissus, or was he rather your stag, Silvia?

le. cervus: on stags and for stag recipes, see at 13.94. *le.*, 1 above. Unlike that at 13.94.1, this stag is tame, contrasting therefore also with the fierce oryx of 13.95. The poem, meanwhile, ends the section beginning at 93, which alternates fierce and docile animals, and, like 93, makes reference to mythological wild life. The hexameter refers to the story of Cyparissus, who shot his favourite stag by accident and prayed afterwards to the gods to grant him perpetual grief. They turned him into a cypress, symbol of mourning: see Ovid *Met.* 10.106 ff. and Bömer 48 ff. The pentameter makes reference to the tame stag of Silvia, daughter of Tyrrheus, the huntsman of King Latinus. Ascanius shot this stag, thus starting the war between the Trojans and the Latins. See Verg. *A.* 7.483 ff. Both of these stags were fine specimens: note Ovid *Met.* 10.110 'ingens cervus erat' etc.; cf. Verg. *A.* 7.483 'cervus erat forma praestanti et cornibus ingens', and this underlies the point of M's epigram here: the stag it describes is also a very fine specimen and it is a measure of its quality that M cannot decide with which mythological story to identify it. M emphasises in similar fashion the quality of a bowl at 8.50(51).1-2 by asking which of several master craftsmen made it. He makes similar use of alternatives in 13.37 above.

1-2: Schneidewin punctuates with a question mark after *capistro* while editors after Gilbert employ a full stop. Since M had no reason to assert that the stag *was* Cyparissus', a full stop is less attractive than a question mark; but better still would be to punctuate with a comma, treating the lines of the poem as alternatives in the same question and thereby making it easier to understand *cervus*, line 2, with 'hic ... ille' in line 1.

1 tuo ... capistro: cf. Ovid *Met.* 10.124-5 (of Cyparissus): 'nunc eques in tergo residens huc laetus et illuc/ mollia purpureis frenabas ora capistris'. As it happens, training stags was very difficult (Jennison 25, 78), and the stags trained to the harness which M describes at 1.104.4 were therefore very remarkable, even though they were not unique: for further examples, see Howell's note ad loc. and Toynbee 144-5.

domitus: for the tameness of Cyparissus' stag, see Ovid *Met.* 10.117 ff.: 'isque metu vacuus naturalique pavore/ deposito celebrare domos mulcendaque colla/ quamlibet ignotis manibus praebere solebat'.

13.97 Lalisio

While the wild ass is young and is fed by its mother alone, the infant *lalisio* has this name, but not for long.

le. lalisio: reference is made specifically to the *lalisio* or young *onager* (ὄνος ἄγριος) elsewhere only at Pliny *Nat.* 8.174: 'pullis eorum [onagrorum] seu praestantibus sapore Africa gloriatur quos lalisiones appellant' (the word *lalisio* is possibly of African origin). Such rare testimony is perhaps confirmation of the speed with which the animal grew up (note line 2 'hoc ... sed breve nomen habet'), thus becoming an *onager* instead. In contrast to the *lalisio*, the *onager* (cf. 13.100 below) is regularly mentioned and was clearly well known. Mynors notes at Verg. *G.* 3.409 'saepe etiam cursu timidos agitabis onagros' that the animal was very fast and popularly hunted; cf. Pollux 5.84 and Oppian *Cyn.* 3.186; also Xen. *Anab.* 1.5.2. Although relying primarily on flight when challenged, once cornered the animal was by no means resourceless, having a vicious, reportedly stone-flinging kick: the word *onager* came therefore to be applied to a type of catapult: Amm. 23.4.7; cf. Veg. *Mil.* 4.22 and see the model depicted in Ciarallo and De Carolis, 332. (The temperament of Trimalchio's 'super mules', which have *onager* parentage (Petr. 38.4), can easily be imagined; cf. Columella 6.37.4.) Given its speed and potential for dangerous retaliation, that the *onager* could follow an elephant hunt in 13.100 becomes understandable. Good sport aside, however, it was also good to eat. Xenophon (ibid.) notes: τά δὲ κρέα τῶν ἁλισκομένων ἦν παραπλήσια τοῖς ἐλεφείοις, ἁπαλώτερα δέ. The concern of M's epigram in focussing on the *lalisio* here is not to disparage the *onager*, but to establish the especial luxury of its rarer nursling.

1-2 tener refers principally to the *lalisio*'s youth (see *OLD* s.v. *tener* §2a) but hints perhaps also at its tenderness as food (see *OLD* s.v. *tener* §3a).

solaque ... matre/ pascitur: the desirability of unweaned animals is elsewhere apparent from 13.41.1 above and Juv. 11.66 ff. (quoted at 13.39.*le.* above).

2 hoc βγ: **hic** T. T's reading was presumably influenced by the proximity of *infans*. The majority reading *hoc*, which with *nomen* elaborates on *lalisio* in line 1 and the *lemma*, makes much better sense and is plainly right.

infans, survives of animals elsewhere only at Pliny *Nat.* 10.92 (*pullus*) and 29.100 (*catulus*). At 22.93 it is used of a small *boletus*.

sed breve picks up *dum*, line 1.

13.98-9: for Lindsay's transposition of these two epigrams, see Intro. (iii) above.

13.98 Roe deer

Should you see the roe deer perched on the rock summit, you would think it about to fall. It's duping the hounds.

le. caprea: the roe deer (*Capreolus capreolus*) is mentioned as a luxury dish at Juv. 11.142. Its taste was said to vary according to its diet, however, and possibly according to the time of year: see Muecke at Hor. *Serm.* 2.4.43 'vinea summittit capreas non semper edulis' (the roe deer's fondness for vine shoots is alluded to at Verg. *G.* 2.374). Apicius gives recipes for sauces to go with *capreae* at 8.347-9 Budé. For further details, see André *Alimentation* 116-7.

Wild roe deer favour forest land and their association with mountainous terrain (note 'summa ... de rupe', line 2) is further marked by Larg. 127

160

'capreae montanae' and 'the many horns discovered in the mountainous region of Vesuvius': see Ciarallo and De Carolis 63; but they were also kept and hunted in parks: Columella 9 *praef.* 1.

1-2 pendentem ... videbis,/ casurum speres.: the punctuation adopted is that of Shackleton Bailey. With the exception of Heraeus, who has a semicolon after *speres* but nothing after *videbis*, earlier editors punctuate with a colon after *videbis* and a semicolon after *speres*. These editors (including Heraeus) also read *despicit* with αβ in line 2 (*decipit* γ Schryver, Shackleton Bailey), and Ker's Loeb translation presumably reflects their corporate understanding: 'You will see the roe poised on the summit of the rock; one can only hope she will fall; she is showing contempt of the dogs.' This understanding is, however, highly questionable: while it is possible that an anthropomorphised *caprea* might despise the hounds it has successfully eluded (for *despicio* thus, see *OLD* s.v. §2), it seems improbably extreme that someone should hope that it will fall to its death as a punishment for doing so. In contrast, Shackleton Bailey's understanding is far more satisfactory: cf. *AJPh* 110 (1989) 149-50. He has the *caprea* so perilously situated that, should you see it thus, you expect it to fall (for *spero* of expectation/anticipation, see *OLD* s.v. *spero* §5); but it does not. (The situation is easily appreciated by anyone who has ever encountered thars or wild goats on a rock face.) Shackleton Bailey's reading *decipit* then provides the reason for it to adopt such a precarious position in the first place: it is fooling the dogs (see *OLD* s.v. *decipio* §1a), who would have congregated at the bottom of the rock, also expecting it to fall.

For M's use here of the future indicative in the protasis of a paratactic conditional construction, see L-H-Sz II.657. Heinsius' conjecture 'pendentem ut' is unnecessary.

1 pendentem summa capream de rupe videbis: for *pendere* meaning 'perch', see *ThLL* X(1).1036.5 ff. s.v. *pendeo* [Reineke], *OLD* §7a. The line's spondaic opening possibly helps illustrate the *caprea*'s precarious situation. The line recalls Verg. *Ecl.* 1.76 'capellas pendere procul de rupe videbo'; cf. Ovid *Pont.* 1.8.51-2 'ipse ego pendentis, liceat modo, rupe capellas,/ ipse velim ... pascere', *Ilias* 888 'pendent in rupe capellae'.

2 decipit: the contempt denoted explicitly by *despicit* (see above) is not wholly excluded by *decipit*; but besides making better sense of the epigram, *decipio* also allows a measure of role reversal through word play: *decipio* has often the sense of *capio* and consequently appears in hunting contexts (see at 13.68.1 above). The dogs of this epigram would have tried to drive the *caprea* into a net; but instead it has eluded them and is now able to bring them to bay on its own terms.

13.99 Gazelle

You will give the gazelle as a pet to your small son: the crowd is accustomed to let it go by waving its togas.

le. dorcas α: **dorcae** βγ. Since the acc. pl. form *dorcas* survives in Grattius, quoted below, βγ's nom. pl. is not in itself impossible; but the usual form is *dorcas -adis* (cf. line 1) and, while an unusual form might be understandable *metri causa* in the poem (cf. 13.91.2 *acipensis*), it is harder to justify unusual forms in the *lemma*; cf. Heraeus' approval of the humanists' *acipenser* at 13.91.*le*. One might observe too that a plural *lemma* for this poem would conflict with the singular *lemmata* of the immediately surrounding epigrams (although note 13.92 *lepores* and 94 *dammae*). It is therefore probable that both β and γ preserve, whether independently or as a result of contamination, a simple palaeographical corruption of the original.

The gazelle was notoriously timid: cf. Grat. 199 f.: 'at te leve si qua/ tangit opus pavidosque iuvat compellere dorcas …', and it is because of this that the crowd is accustomed to take pity on it in the arena (see further below) and that it is a suitable gift for the 'parvo … nato' of line 1. Despite the food context of Mart. 13 and the fact that the *dorcas* was certainly eaten (Courtney notes at Juv. 11.121 that a gazelle appears in a Pompeian representation of a butcher's shop; cf. Keller I.287), the focus of this epigram is less on food perhaps than on the Saturnalia in general: during the festival great attention was paid to children (see my edition of Mart. 14, 5 and n. 9, which cites D-S IV(1).108 s.v. *Saturnalia* [J.-A. Hild]), for whom pets were suitable presents: see S.L. Mohler, 'Apophoreta', *CJ* 23 (1927-8), 257 n. 58; cf. *RE* IIIA.1777.56 ff. s.v. *Spielzeug* [Hug]; cf. Mart. 14.197. The *dorcas* of this poem will presumably have fallen by lot first to an adult dinner guest (for dinner-table lotteries, see Intro. (ii) section D), who will then have passed it on; hence the future tense of *donabis* in line 1. For the practice by adult recipients of passing on Saturnalian gifts to children, see my note at Mart. 14.19.2.

1 delicium: for the meaning 'pet', cf. *Copa* 26 'Vestae delicium est asinus', Phaedr. 4.1.8 and Mart 1.7.1; see *ThLL* V(1).450.22 ff. s.v. *delicium* [Simbeck].

The d alliteration of this line is probably coincidental.

2 iactatis solet hanc mittere turba togis: *missio* could be granted to defeated gladiators at their request and if the crowd approved: cf. Mart. 12.28(29).6-7 'nuper cum Myrino peteretur missio laeso,/ subduxit mappas quattuor Hermogenes', where the spectators signal their wishes by waving napkins, as opposed to the togas here. (An explanation as to what actions exactly 'togas … iactare' entailed is given at 13.100.2 'removete … sinus' below.) Alternatively, the crowd could demand *missio* by shouting, as happens at *Sp.* 31(27, prius 24).3, where the two combatants are equally matched. In the latter case, however, and one imagines in the former, the crowd has witnessed a good fight and so is inclined to be merciful; but the timid nature of the *dorcas* was unlikely to qualify it for *missio* on similar grounds. It seems therefore that the crowd customarily lets it off through sentimentality and compassion; cf. *Sp.* 33 where the *damma* is let off after it appears to supplicate the Emperor. Note too the compassion felt for Pompey's elephants in 55 BC: Cic. *Fam.* 7.1.3.

iactatis ... togis: cf. Ov. *Am*. 3.2.3-4 'sed enim revocate, Quirites,/ et date iactatis undique signa togis'. There, however, the crowd is asked to signal with its togas not compassion but disapproval (at an unfair start at the races). The meaning of the signal could evidently change according to the context in which it was made.

13.100 Wild ass

The handsome wild ass is in prospect. The hunt of the Erythraean tusk should be concluded; now draw back your folds.

le. onager: regarding this exciting animal, see 13.97.*le*. n. above. The elephant it is to replace has evidently done enough in the hunt to earn a reprieve, and the crowd is now ready for a new and contrasting spectacle.

1 adest: the *onager* cannot actually be present while the elephant hunt is still in progress. For *adsum* used of something available or forthcoming, see *OLD* s.v. *adsum* §20.

mitti: although the eventual effect is the same, M's use of *mitto* here differs from that in the previous poem, line 2. The verb now refers to the stopping of the elephant *venatio* rather than to letting go the animal on show; cf. Verg. *A.* 5.286 'misso certamine', 545; see *OLD* s.v. *mitto* § 4a.

2 dentis Erythraei: i.e. the Indian elephant. The Erythraean Sea owed its name to the coral beds of the Persian Gulf and to the reddish appearance of the neighbouring Arabian coastline: *Kl.P.* 2.367.8 ff. s.v. *Erythraei* [H. Treidler]. In M the adjective 'Erythraean' is therefore mostly used of the Gulf, and the famous pearls which were there obtained: cf. e.g. 5.37.4, 9.2.9 and 12.5; also 8.28.14; but its application could be extended as far as Sri Lanka and even beyond, and it means 'Indian' elsewhere at Stat. *Theb.* 7.566 and Mart. 8.26.5 (with reference in both instances to Bacchus in triumph).

    For elephants at the spectacles, whether to be paraded, do tricks or fight men, other animals or one another, see Toynbee 22-3, 47-9 and my note at

Mart. 14.91.1. They were by no means new to Rome: Pliny describes elephants matched with bulls at the show of 79 BC given by the aediles Lucius and Marcus Lucullus: *Nat.* 8.19. Nonetheless, they would have been a definite attraction, and M's use of synecdoche here takes account of this: the words have an exotic ring and draw attention to the part of the elephant likely to provide the greatest danger and excitement, viz. the tusks.

removete sinus: Shackleton Bailey explains (Loeb note) that this means 'Not "shake" but "pluck back (in order to shake)" '. A more detailed explanation is necessary here, however: the toga was semi-circular in shape. It was worn so that one of the corners hung a little above the left foot. The straight edge then ran up the left side of the body, over the left shoulder, under the right arm, across the chest and over the left shoulder again. The curved edge acted as the garment's hem, and everything was kept in place by the wearer's crooked left arm. Because the garment became over time very voluminous (in the first century AD, it measured 5.4 x 2.75 m = $19\frac{1}{2}$ x 10 ft), the straight edge was folded down where it passed under the right arm, and this resulted in the *sinus*, in effect a pouch which, depending on the current fashion, hung across the wearer's legs, waist or chest: see *OCD*[3] s.v. *toga* [Hero Granger-Taylor], Sebesta 16, 18-19 figs 1.4a-d, 231 fig. 13.9; cf. e.g. Gel. 4.18.9 'prolato e sinu togae libro'. By unhitching his toga where it passed over the left shoulder for the second time, the wearer would do away with the *sinus* and would then have in front of him a large body of material which he could wave about (*iactare*; cf. 13.99.2 above) as a highly visible signal to those in charge of events. To illustrate *removere*, Shackleton Bailey, *CPh* 73 (1978), 295, compares Quint. *Inst.* 11.3.124 'illud quoque raro decebit cava manu summis digitis pectus appetere ... quod si quando fiet, togam quoque inde removeri non dedecebit'.

13.101-5: on the transitional nature of this section and the ordering of its epigrams, dealing with oil, fish sauce and honey, see generally Intro. (iii) above. Some further detail is supplied below. Note that the poems all refer to or at least show an awareness of the regional origins of the gifts they describe, or those of their components, and that this ties in well with the importance of provenance in the following section, on wines: 106-25.

13.101 Oil of Venafrum

The olive of Campanian Venafrum has distilled this for you. Whenever you use the unguent, you will smell of it too.

1e. oleum Venafrum: Venafrum was a *colonia* in the Volturnus valley (cf. Pliny *Nat.* 3.63) and this accounts for line 1 'Campani ... Venafri'. It was famed for its olives: cf. Pliny *Nat.* 15.8 'principatum in hoc ... bono obtinuit

Italia e toto orbe. maxime agro Venafrano ...', Varro *R.* 1.2.6 (cited below), Mart. 12.63.1, and see N-H at Hor. *Carm.* 2.6.16.

The β reading *Venafri* derives from line 1. T preserves the epigram twice, offering the forms *Venafrum* (with γ) and *Venafranum*. The latter, more common form (cf. Pliny *Nat.* 15.8 above) appears also e.g. at Hor. *Serm.* 2.4.69 'Venafranae ... baca ... olivae' and, used substantivally, Juv. 5.86 'ipse Venafrano piscem perfundit'; but it is clearly not authorial here: for the form *Venafrum*, cf. Larg. 268 'olei Venafri', Varro *R.* 1.2.6 'quod oleum [sc. conferam] Venafro' and see Heraeus at Mart. 9.42.1 'campis ... Myrinis' (instead of *Myrinaeis*). Heraeus compares such phrases as 'Thespia moenia' [cf. V.Fl. 1.477-8] and 'Camerina unda' (for which see *ThLL Onomasticon* 118.65 s.v. *Camerinus* [Jacobsohn]).

As is illustrated by Juv. 5.86 above, olive oil was used as a fish dressing; cf. Hor. *Serm.* 2.4.50 'perfundat piscis ... olivo', 2.8.45: oil is used on 'squillas inter murena natantis'. This use of oil for fish affords a connection between the present poem and the two (on fish sauce) which follow; but *unguentum*, line 2, reveals that the oil here was in fact intended for anointing, not eating. (For the use of unguents at parties and celebrations, see N-H at Hor. *Carm.* 1.4.9 and at 13.126.*le.* below, where see also for unguents used as gifts.) The poem is therefore preparatory to the drinking of the *comissatio*.

1 tibi ... sudavit baca: given *unguentum*, cf. e.g. Stat. *Silv.* 3.2.141 'candida felices sudent opobalsama virgae', Tac. *Germ.* 45.5 'nemora, ubi tura balsamaque sudantur'. Note, however, that where *sudo* is applied to the natural exudation of oil by olives (Pliny *Nat.* 15.14), it refers negatively to those left too long between harvest and pressing, and pressing is certainly in question here. The personal pronoun suggests flatteringly that this Venafran oil was produced with the recipient specially in mind. For the value placed on good quality olive oil unguent, cf. Hor. *Serm.* 1.6.123-4 'unguor olivo,/ non quo fraudatis immundus Natta lucernis'.

2 sumis: cf. Cic. *Cael.* 27 'qui unguenta sumpserat'.

oles G Friedländer Shackleton Bailey: **olet** codd. Almost all editors follow the MSS, presumably understanding something like Ker's Loeb translation 'your unguent, as often as you use it, smells too of that oil'; but it would hardly smell of something else before use. *Oles* accords well with *sumis* (as do both with *tibi*, line 1), the unguent *is* the oil, and it is the *wearer* who smells of it whenever he uses it.

For *oleo* plus internal accusative meaning 'to smell of', see *OLD* s.v. *oleo* §2; cf. Mart. 2.12.1 'olent tua basia murram'. For *et* instead of *etiam* or *quoque*, see *ThLL* V(2).908.11 ff. s.v. *et* [Hofmann].

13.102 Company garum

Accept haughty *garum*, an expensive gift, from the first blood of a mackerel still breathing its last.

1e. garum sociorum: while γάρος is mentioned as early as Aeschylus (fr. 211), the word *garum* does not survive in Latin before Varro, and Pliny implies (*Nat.* 19.57) that fish sauce had in his day not been very long used as a relish; although once established as such it became very famous, and it was employed in a wide variety of dishes: André *Alimentation* 198.

For the manufacture of *garum*, see T.H. Corcoran, *CJ* 58 (1963), 205-6, Pliny *Nat.* 31.93, quoted at 13.40.2 above, and the *Geoponica*, 46.1 ff. According to the *Geoponica*, 46.6, it was from the blood and entrails of the tunny that the best variety was made. These were heavily salted and stored in a vessel for some two months, after which the liquid was drained off. The method described by Pliny is very similar, although he says (*Nat.* 31.94) that the best *garum*, from New Carthage in Spain, was made not from tunny but mackerel (cf. *scombri*, line 1), which was caught nearby (and apparently nowhere else in the Mediterranean). It is to this superior Spanish *garum* that reference is made at 13.40.2 above; cf. Hor. *Serm.* 2.8.46 'garo de sucis piscis Hiberi', and which is described here; for as Pliny notes in an aside (loc. cit.), 'sociorum id appellatur'; cf. Aus. *Epist.* 19.6. He adds that two *congii* (about 12 pints = 6.8 litres) cost 1,000 HS; cf. 'munera cara', line 2, and Sen. *Ep.* 95.25 'illud sociorum garum, pretiosam ... piscium saniem'.

That 'garum sociorum' was a recognised brand or trade name is confirmed by the name's appearance on both an *amphora* and jug from Pompeii (see at *CIL* IV.5659); but as to how it arose is debated. Rome had many *socii*, of whom the Spanish were not the first, and the Loeb translation ' ... of the allies' (both editions) is too imprecise to be left unquestioned. Pliny explains simply (*Nat.* 9.66) that mackerel *garum* was used to flavour other mackerel (i.e. their *socii*). R. Estienne, 'A propos du "garum sociorum" ', *Latomus* 29 (1970), 297 ff., suggests more plausibly, however, that the *socii* were in fact members of a Spanish *societas* with interests in mackerel *garum*, and draws particular attention to the complementary importance of salt production at New Carthage (cf. Strabo 3.4.6) noting also that a salt industry continues in the south of Spain today. The translation above follows a suggestion of Peter Howell, comparing the way goods of the Dutch East India Company are commonly designated; cf. e.g. 'consignments of Company goods' in T.R.H. Davenport's *South Africa: a Modern History*,[3] Cambridge 1987, 25.

1 de sanguine primo: albeit regular of non human blood, *sanguis* apparently survives nowhere else of fish blood. *Primus* also lacks precise parallels, but is apparently here a reference to the fish's (evidently desirable) freshness, picking up 'expirantis adhuc'. M's positioning of the adjectives at the beginning and end of the line, thus framing the alliterative nouns, was therefore for emphasis as well as artistic effect.

2 accipe: on the use of this word here, see Intro. (v) and n. 6 above.

fastosus is here humorously transferred to the *garum* from the sort of dainty eater who would turn down all but the best. For the tastes of such, cf. Sen. *Nat*. 3.18.3 'ad hunc fastum pervenit venter delicatorum ut gustare non possint [piscem], nisi quem … natantem viderunt'.

munera cara: the plural forms here, in apposition to the singular 'fastosum … garum', are metrically convenient; cf. the apposition of *calicem* and *monimenta* at Mart. 14.96.1. But their numerical disparity serves also to attract added attention to the gift's value.

13.103 Jar of muria

I am, I confess, the daughter of Antipolitan tunny: had I been of mackerel, I should not have been sent to you.

le. amphora muriae: the term *muria* was a loose one, but applied usually to a sort of brine: see Blümner *Priv*. 187. This could be used for cooking (cf. Apic. 7.257 and 258 Budé: recipes for *vulva* and *venter*), in preserving food, e.g. fish during transport (see Muecke at Hor. *Serm*. 2.4.65), and as a sort of relish – as here, where it appears as a cheap version of the 'garum sociorum' of 13.102: note 'essem si scombri', line 2, which recalls *scombri* at 13.102.1. As it happens, *muria* from Antipolis (Antibes) was not ill thought of by all (note Pliny *Nat*. 31.94), but it is categorised as a cheap Saturnalian gift again at Mart. 4.88.5-6 'Antipolitani … quae de sanguine thynni/ testa rubet'. *Muria* is a relish or dressing elsewhere at Mart. 10.48.12 'et madidum thynni de sale sumen erit' (in a modest dinner) and Pers. 6.20 (of a parsimonious man who uses it to flavour his 'olus siccum'), and it is mixed with oil at Hor. *Serm*. 2.4.63 ff. to make the mysterious 'ius simplex'; cf. also Petr. 70.12 'notavi … cocum … muria condimentisque fetentem'.

 For other epigram pairs describing cheap and expensive versions of the same gift, see 13.39.*le*. n. above. The gift of this poem is not necessarily that of a poor man, as are those from the *Apophoreta* quoted at 13.6.1 n. above; but it might be. Whereas those poems are apologetic in tone, however (cf. also 13.45 above), this poem, like 13.6, is not, achieving its humour by plainly suggesting that the recipient is worth no more than he gets.

1 Antipolitani, fateor, sum filia thynni: besides varying the second person address of the previous poem, this personifying line contributes to the epigram's 'riddling' status: for other such epigrams, which are made clearer by the *lemma*, see the introductory n. to 13.11 above. Its grandiloquence is ironic (for *filia* + geographical adjective, cf. 13.35.1 above and see ad loc.), being deflated by the concluding and inferior *thynni* and the blunt pentameter.

2 essem si scombri: similar expression at Mart. 14.153.2 'essem si locuples'. By placing *scombri* before the caesura, M heightens its contrast with *thynni*, similarly prominently placed at the hexameter end.

non ... missa forem: *forem* at the end of the line balances *essem* at the beginning. Regarding *missa*, see 13.3.5 'hospitibus ... mittas' n. above.

13.104 Attic honey

This noble nectar a bee, ravager of Thesean Hymettus, has sent you from the woods of Pallas.

le. mel Atticum: honey was the chief sweetener of the ancients, and apiculture played an important part in rural life. For general comment, see *OCD*³ s.v. *honey* [J.E. Sallares], André *Alimentation* 186-9. Attic honey was considered amongst, if not the best available; cf. N-H at Hor. *Carm.* 2.6.14 and note 'nobile nectar', line 2. (For *nectar* here, see *OLD* s.v. *nectar* §2b). Particularly renowned was that produced on Hymettus (cf. line 1), the mountain to the south east of Athens which was otherwise known for its marble. Honey from Hymettus remains famous to this day: *Kl.P.* 2.1268.18-20 s.v. *Hymettus* [W. Zschietzschmann].

Also very highly regarded, however (cf. Pliny *Nat.* 11.32), was honey from Hybla, a Sicilian city on the south slopes of Mt Aetna (cf. 'de collibus', 13.105.1 below). Hyblan and Hymettan honey are often mentioned in conjunction (note e.g. Mart. 7.88.8, 9.11.3, 11.42.3), and although Hyblan was generally deemed inferior, it was not by very much. Thus the Hyblan honey of Mart. 13.105 can be passed off as Attic, and a contest between the two was often envisaged: cf. Sil. 14.199-200 'quae nectareis vocant ad certamen Hymetton,/ audax Hybla, favis'.

Although it is not difficult to work out what the epigram is about, its word order (note e.g. the delayed *apis*, line 2) and elevated form of expression nonetheless mean that the *lemma* serves a clarifying function. For other such *lemmata*, see the introductory n. to 13.11 above. M refers to Attic honey again in Book 13 at 24.1 'Cecropio ... melle' and 108.1.

1 tibi ... misit: *mittere* provides a link between the honey of 13.104-5 and the sauces of the earlier poems: note *missa*, 103.2. Here, however, since the bee is so clearly connected with Attica ('Thesei ... Hymetti', *Pallados*), the use of *mitto* possibly suggests also regional exports: see on 13.23.1

'quem Setia misit' above; cf. Ovid *Am*. 1.12.9-10 'quam [ceram] … Corsica misit apis'. Meanwhile *tibi* is perhaps flattering (as at 13.101.1 above), suggesting that the recipient has been shown especial favour in taking personal delivery of so valuable a commodity.

Thesei … **Hymetti**: regarding Theseus, see *OCD*³ s.v. *Theseus* [E. Kearns]. As king of Athens his greatest achievement was the *synoecism* of Attica, the region for which Hymettus here stands. For the adjectival use of his name, see *OLD* s.v. *Theseus*²; cf. Mart. 4.13.4 '[miscentur] Massica Theseis tam bene vina favis'.

populatrix is here amusingly hyperbolic of the bee as it 'plunders' nectar for its honey: ravagers usually cause wide-scale destruction and certainly do not contribute to the production of local exports. The noun *populatrix*, elsewhere used of Scylla (Stat. *Silv*. 3.2.86), survives of the bee nowhere else. Note, however, Mart. 2.46.2 'cum breve Siconiae ver populantur apes', 9.12(13).2 'cum breve Cecropiae ver populantur apes' and, in prose, Pliny *Nat*. 11.61 'eas [apes] populantur harundines'. *Populator* is applied, again with some hyperbole, to a boar at Mart. 7.27.1 'Tuscae glandis aper populator'.

2 Pallados a silvis: Attic honey was made from the nectar of thyme (cf. Quint. *Inst*. 12.10.25; see *OCD*³ loc. cit.). M does not here have in mind Athene's gift to Attica of the olive, but is merely referring generally to the wood and scrubland where Attic bees worked (for *silva* thus used, see *OLD* s.v. *silva* §§1a, 2a).

13.105 Sicilian honeycombs

When you give Sicilian honeycombs from the heart of Hybla's hills, you may say they are Cecropian.

le. favi Siculi: for Sicilian honey from Hybla, see 13.104.*le*. n. above. While this epigram acknowledges that Sicilian honey was customarily regarded as inferior to the Attic of the previous poem (for epigrams pairing superior and inferior versions of the same gift, see 13.39.*le*. n. above), it is nonetheless confident of its gift's high and indeed equivalent quality (illustrated perhaps by the fact that *favos*, line 2, has to be understood with *Siculos*, line 1, as well as going with *Cecropios*), and is not in the least apologetic. (Contrast the defensive tone adopted by the *lanterna de vesica* of Mart. 14.62.) Indeed the matter-of-fact tone might possibly convey some cynicism in commenting on those who value something not for its taste (which they have not the discernment to appreciate), but its label or price; cf. 13.76.*le*. n. above.

1 siculos β: **siculis** γL, ante corr.: **figulos** T. Homoeoteleuton accounts for γL's reading (note *dederis*), while T mistook the letter s for f.

13.106-25: this section, dealing with wine, reflects the *comissatio*: see Intro. (iii) above. Given that drunkenness featured prominently at the Saturnalia (see Intro. (ii) section C above), it is not surprising that M includes so many poems. (The section is the longest but for the *gustatio*.) That the first poem mentions *mulsum* (line 2) serves perhaps to ease the transition from the honey of the previous section (poems 104-5). Regarding gifts of wine, see at 13.106.*le.* below and *passim*.

13.106 Muscat

The Gnosian vintage of Minoan Crete produced this for you. It is wont to be the poor man's *mulsum*.

le. passum (cf. Italian *passito*) was a dessert wine made from the muscatel/*a(p)piana* grape (cf. Pliny *Nat.* 14.81). These grapes were dried in the sun before pressing, whether being left on the vine (Pliny *Nat.* 14.81) or spread out (*pandere*) after harvest (Columella 12.27.1, 39.1) or both (Varro ap. Non. 551M). After the grapes had been pressed once, they could be soaked either in well water (Pliny *Nat.* 14.82) or the wine or must of a different grape (Columella 12.39.2) before being pressed again to yield the 'passum secundarium' to which Statius refers at *Silv.* 4.9.38 when listing 'passum psithiis suis recoctum' as a cheap Saturnalian gift: see Coleman ad loc. This cheapness may be of some relevance here (cf. 'mulsum pauperis', line 2), although M's wine was pressed only once. As line 1 suggests, *passum* was particularly associated with Crete; cf. also Juv. 14.270-1 'qui gaudes pingue antiquae de litore Cretae/passum ... advexisse' and Pliny *Nat.* 14.81 (where the emendation *Cretico* for the transmitted *Gr(a)eco* is assuredly correct). Cretan wine production is well attested from earliest times (the Linear B ideogram for wine shows a vine growing on a trellis: John Chadwick, *Linear B and Related Scripts*, London 1987, 29) and it was probably an early export: cf. Chadwick ibid. 10.

For wine as a gift, cf. in addition to Stat. *Silv.* 4.9.38 e.g. Apul. 2.11.3 (quoted above: Intro. (i)), Xen. *An.* 1.9.25 (Cyrus sends casks of good (literally 'sweet') wine as presents), Mart. 10.36, and note the *defrutum* (another dessert wine) and Laletanian must listed as cheap Saturnalian gifts at Mart. 4.46.9 and 7.53.6. (*Defrutum* is found also in Statius: line 39.)

1-2 Gnosia Minoae genuit vindemia Cretae/ hoc tibi: with this interlocking and rather grand opening cf. perhaps the hint of legendary fame at Juv. 14.270 'antiquae de litore Cretae': see Courtney ad loc. It contrives to elevate the *passum* (deliberately not identified specifically in the poem) and suggests perhaps that it was specially produced (*OLD* s.v. *gigno* §5) for the recipient (cf. on 13.101.1 'tibi ... sudavit' and 104.1 above); but it is then deflated by the pentameter: 'quod mulsum pauperis esse solet'; cf. the opening grandeur and deflation of 13.103 above.

For the explanatory function of the *lemma*, see the introductory note to 13.11 above.

1 Gnosia here means no more than 'Cretan' (on its orthography, see at 13.66.2 'si Cnidiae' above). It is balanced and reinforced by *Cretae* at the end of the line. With 'Minoae ... Cretae', cf. Ovid *Fast.* 3.81 'Minoia Creta'.

2 quod mulsum pauperis esse solet: similar expression at Mart. 13.27.2 above 'munus pauperis esse solet'. On real *mulsum* (and its cost), see at 13.108. *le.* below.

13.107 Retsina

In case you doubt that this retsina came from wine-bearing Vienne, Romulus himself sent it to me.

le. picatum: pitch or resin was sometimes deliberately added to wine, perhaps in an attempt to disguise the effects of oxidation. The 'resinata ... vina' at Mart. 3.77.8 is not held in high regard, possibly for this reason; but in any case the amphorae in which wine was transported or stored, being to some extent porous, were coated with pitch: see Kay at Mart. 11.18.24 'et mustum nuce condimus picata', and pitch was also used to seal their stoppers: Hor. *Carm.* 3.8.10. Naturally this use of pitch flavoured or tainted the amphorae's contents (cf. Younger 192). According to Pliny *Nat.* 23.47, however, the wine called *picatum* in Gallia Narbonensis (reading 'Helvico in pago' with Mayhoff) had a *natural* pitch flavour: 'id [vinum] quod sponte naturae suae picem resipit picatum ... appellatur'; cf. Younger 192, and it is this natural flavour which is central to the understanding of the present poem. Whereas Mart. 13.105 and 117 concern themselves with gifts which can be passed off as something else, this epigram seeks to establish the authenticity of its gift: it is not 'vinum resinatum' but genuine *picatum* from Vienne (line 1).

Regarding Vienne, capital of the Allobroges in Gallia Narbonensis, see generally *OCD*³ s.v. *Vienna* [J.F. Drinkwater], *Kl.P.* 5.1268.11 ff. s.v. *Vienna* [M. le Glay]. M's work was well known there (7.88), and the great pleasure he expresses at this might indicate personal knowledge of the place. Of particular interest here are the words in the pentameter whereby he seeks to guarantee the wine's provenance: 'misit Romulus ipse mihi', since evidence survives (*CIL* XII.5686.752) of a vintner in the area called Romulus, and although the name is not uncommon (P. de Rohden and H. Dessau, *Prosopographia Imperii Romani* III, 1st edn, Berlin 1898 s.v.), it

171

is nonetheless possible that it is to this very man that M refers. Not just anyone, but Romulus the vintner from Vienne himself has sent M this wine as a personal gift. (For *misit*, line 2, see at 13.3.5 'hospitibus ... mittas' above.)

1 haec de vitifera venisse picata Vienna: verbal interlocking and alliteration combine in holding this line together.

haec ... picata: as is plain from the *lemmata* of Mart. 13.106-25, the identification of wine by means of a substantive formed from a neuter participle or adjective was standard. This participle or adjective could reflect the way in which the wine tasted (as here and at 13.122 *acetum*), the way in which it was made (as does *passum*; cf. 13.106.*le.* above), or the place it came from: see below *passim*. The *lemmata* are all neuter singulars (originally one would have understood *vinum* with such words), but it is very common to find plural forms in the poems – as here. (For such numerical differences between *lemma* and poem, see at 13.11.2 above.) These neuter plurals are metrically convenient (cf. Austin at Verg. *A.* 7.91), and correspond with the common use of *vina* for *vinum*; see N-H at Hor. *Carm.* 1.18.5; cf. 13.110.2, 118.2, 120.1 (where *vina* must be understood), 123.2, 125.2 below.

vitifera does not survive before the 1st century AD, appearing in Classical Latin elsewhere at Pliny *Nat.* 3.60 'vitiferi colles'; cf. *Nat.* 6.46 and Sil. 4.347 'vitiferi ... montis'.

2 misit ... mihi: for the practice of passing Saturnalian gifts on to others, as M does here, see 13.26.*le.* n. above. As this poem makes clear, these gifts were not necessarily of poor quality.

13.108 Mulsum

Honey from Attica, you cloud nectarous Falernian. It is fitting for this wine to be mixed by Ganymede.

le. mulsum was honeyed wine. The best was made with Attic honey (on which see 13.104.*le.* n. above) and Massic (cf. Mart. 4.13.4) or more commonly, as here, Falernian wine (for which see at 13.111.*le.* below): cf. e.g. the proverb cited at Macr. 7.12.9 'mulsum quod probe temperes miscendum esse novo Hymettio et vetulo Falerno', Hor. *Serm.* 2.2.15-16 'nisi Hymettia mella Falerno/ ne biberis diluta', 2.4.24, Pliny *Nat.* 22.113. See André *Alimentation* 166, Blümner *Priv.* 202-3. As might be expected from the quality of such ingredients, it was not cheap; cf. 13.6.1 above: 'poterit mulsum tibi mittere dives', 13.106.2, where *passum* is a cheap substitute. That the *mulsum* of this poem is suitable to be mixed by

Commentary

Jupiter's cup-bearer, Ganymede (line 2), is also indicative of its value. This mixing would have to take place before each serving: dissolving honey in wine is impossible, even achieving a mixture is difficult, especially if the wine is sweet (see on *nectareum* below), and the honey in *mulsum* which has been allowed to stand will form a sediment. Hence the point of Mart. 14.127.1-2: 'haec tibi turbato Canusina simillima mulso/ munus erit': the cloak is the colour specifically of recently mixed *mulsum*, rather than *mulsum* which has been allowed to separate.

In addition to being drunk, *mulsum* was used as an ingredient in a number of recipes: see Apicius *passim*. As a drink, it was served also with the *gustatio*: see 13.6.*le*. n. above.

1 Attica nectareum turbatis mella Falernum: the hexameter is carefully constructed so that word order reflects the effect of *turbatis* while *nectareum* balances *mella* (substances) and *Attica Falernum* (places).

nectareum ... Falernum: Pliny, *Nat*. 14.63, identifies three types of Falernian: 'austerum, dulce, tenue'. (In contrast, Athen. 1.26C identifies two, ὁ αὐστηρὸς καὶ ὁ γλυκάζων.) *Nectareus*, used of wine also at Apul. *Met*. 5.3, suggests that the sweet variety is employed here. Given that this *mulsum* is suitable for a god and in particular Jupiter, it is an appropriate adjective.

turbatis: cf. Mart. 14.127.1 *turbato*, quoted above; see *OLD* s.v. *turbo* §3a. By personifying the honey and employing an impersonal verb + passive infinitive in line 2, M achieves variety; but he also admits some scope for confusion: the apostrophised 'Attica ... mella' might suggest, at any rate initially, that it is Attic honey with which the poem is principally concerned, while 'hoc ... merum' in the pentameter might be taken to indicate the Falernian. The *lemma* helps therefore to clarify matters. For other such *lemmata*, see the introductory n. to 13.11 above.

13.109 Alban

The sweet vintage, which takes pride in itself on the Julian mountain, sent this from Caesar's wine cellars.

le. Albanum: Alban wine was of high quality (Columella 3.8.5), and although the ranking of wine was a subjective business (see 13.114.*le*. n. below) it is not for nothing that some put it second only to Falernian and Setine: Pliny *Nat*. 14.61 ff. (On Falernian and Setine, see 13.111 and 112 *lee*. nn. below.) While dry varieties were known (Younger 203; cf. Seltman 154), Alban was usually a sweet wine: Pliny *Nat*. 14.64; cf. *mitis*, line 1. It aged well (Juv. 13.214), and it was apparently appropriate for celebrations (Hor. *Carm*. 4.11.2, a poem dealing with Maecenas' birthday).

173

Its natural qualities aside, however, the Alban wine of this epigram is given further recommendation by being associated both with the legendary founder of the Roman race and forebear of the Caesars, and with the emperor of the day, Domitian. The Alban Mount (cf. 'Iuleo ... monte', line 2 below) was traditionally where Iulus, son of Aeneas, established Alba Longa prior to the foundation of Rome proper: cf. Juv. 12.70 ff. 'gratus Iulo/ atque novercali sedes praelata Lavino/ ... sublimis apex'; and it was on the site of Alba Longa, off the Via Appia and overlooking the Alban lake (the site of modern Albano), that Domitian later built the spectacular villa which is recalled here by 'de Caesariis ... cellis' and which is now the modern Castel Gandolfo: see Howell at Mart. 5.1.1, Kay at 11.7.3, Jones at Suet. *Dom.* 4.4. Of his several residences, the Alban villa was perhaps Domitian's favourite, and it was here that he celebrated the Quinquatria of his admired Minerva: see Jones 100.

While praising the wine, M is of course also flattering to the emperor himself, suggesting a parallel between him and Iulus. M's flattery of Domitian (often much less subtle than this) receives general comment at 13.4.1 *serus* n. above. (For unfavourable references to Domitian's villa, see Courtney at Juv. 4.145 'Albanam arcem').

It is worth observing that without the *lemma* the subject of the epigram might not have been immediately clear. For other such explanatory *lemmata*, see the introductory n. to 13.11 above.

1 mitis vindemia: cf. Verg. *G.* 2.522 'mitis in apricis coquitur vindemia saxis'.

2 misit is probably not here the effective equivalent of *dedit* (cf. Mart. 13.3.5 'hospitibus mittas'), it being in any case rather early in M's career for him to be receiving imperial gifts. The word's usage should be compared rather with that of *mittere* for regional exports: see on 13.23.1 'quem Setia misit' above.

Iuleo ... monte: given the connection between Alba Longa and Iulus, the humanist proposal *Iuleo* is indisputable (*Iuleto* T: *Iul(a)e* γ: *Hybleo* vel *Hib-* β). Tγ's readings may be by-forms of a corrupt exemplar, while β's geographical impossibility (= *Hyblaeo*?) may reflect an attempt at emendation. M uses the adjective again at 9.35.9, referring to the 'Iuleae ... olivae' awarded to victors at Domitian's Alban games, and 9.101.15 'Iuleas ... habenas', where it means something like 'imperial'. It is otherwise confined to Augustan poets (Propertius and Ovid): *OLD* s.v. *Iuleus*.

sibi ... placet: the expression is often used with pejorative sense (*OLD* s.v. *placeo* §1c), but this can clearly not be the case here.

13.110 Surrentine

Do you drink Surrentine? Take up neither coloured murrine nor gold. This wine will give you its own cups.

le. Surrentinum: Surrentum (modern Sorrento) produced a thin sweet wine which was highly regarded by some (Columella 3.8.5), being compared by Pliny to Massic (*Nat.* 14.64) and ranked by Statius with Falernian: *Silv.* 2.2.5 'et prelis non invidet uva Falernis'; cf. Pliny *Nat.* 23.33 'Surrentinum veteres maxime probavere, sequens aetas Falernum'. (On Massic and Falernian, see at 13.111.*le.* n. below.) Others, however, were condescending: Tiberius called it 'generosum acetum' while Claudius considered it 'nobilem vappam': Pliny *Nat.* 14.64. Younger suggests, 203, that they may have drunk it too young, but the vessels they used (see below) or personal taste might otherwise have had influence: see 13.114.*le.* n. below.

For Surrentine cups ('calices ... suos', line 2), cf. Pliny *Nat.* 35.160 and Mart. 14.101 *Calices Surrentini*: 'accipe non vili calices de pulvere natos/ sed Surrentinae leve toreumata rotae'. Although not worthless ('non vili ... de pulvere'), being carved and decorated in imitation of metal (cf. *toreumata*), they could not compare in value with the murrine and gold of line 1. It may, however, generally have been fashionable to serve regional wine in locally manufactured vessels: cf. Mart. 14.100 *panaca*: 'si non ignota est docti tibi terra Catulli/ potasti testa Raetica vina mea' (to my notes ad loc. add *CQ* 47 (1997), 322-3); and, of reference more specifically to this poem, local vessels may not have tainted Surrentine wine whereas gold might (cf. Petr. 50.7) and murrine would have (see my note at Mart. 14.113.*le.*)

In commenting on the didactic features of the *Xenia* and *Apophoreta*, Citroni alludes (208) to Ovid *Trist.* 2.489-90 'alter humum, de qua fingantur pocula, monstrat,/ quaeque, docet, liquido testa sit apta mero', and cites this poem and the already mentioned Mart. 14.113 *murrina*: 'si caldum potas, ardenti murra Falerno/ convenit et melior fit sapor inde mero'. For fuller discussion of M's didactism, see Intro. (v) above.

1 Surrentina bibis?: on the plural form of *Surrentina*, see at 13.107.1 'haec ... picata' above. As to M's use of a question here to correspond to the protasis of a condition, cf. on 13.116.1 below.

murrina picta: there has been lengthy debate as to what murrine was, but learned opinion now seems agreed that it was a type of fluorspar like Derbyshire Blue John: see e.g. A. Loewenthal and D.B. Harden, 'Vasa Murrina', *JRS* 39 (1949), 31-7. (More references are given in my notes on Mart. 14.113 *Murrina*.) Murrine was first introduced to Rome in 63 BC, amongst booty taken from Mithridates, and it was very costly indeed. *Picta*, here, recalls the contrasting purples, reds and whites mentioned by

Pliny, *Nat.* 37.21-2, when describing the substance. (For the adjective *pictus*, 'coloured', used by the poets of natural objects, see *OLD* s.v. *pictus* §1b.)

aurum: cf. Ovid *Met.* 6.488 'Bacchus in auro ponitur'; see *OLD* s.v. *aurum* §4b, L-S s.v. *aurum* §IIA1. The singular, metonymical noun affords *varietas* following the plural, substantival and qualified *murrina*.

2 dabunt calices haec tibi vina suos: these words underpin the implicit command 'drink from them'. Thus they afford *varietas*, emphasised by juxtaposition, with the imperative *sume*.

Although the Greek κύλιξ is well known, there is nonetheless some uncertainty regarding the shape and appearance of the Latin *calix*. Hilgers, 45, speculates that it was hemispherical or ovoid ('oder mehr in die Höhe gestreckt (also eiformig)'), that it had a wide opening, a foot to stand on, and may have had handles. Regarding its form and uses, see also 44, 130 f., Tafel 1, Blümner *Priv.* 405, Marquardt *Prl.* 652.

13.111 Falernian

Massic has come from the presses of Sinuessa. Laid down under what consul, you ask? There was none.

On the structure of this poem, see the introductory note to 13.74 above.

le. Falernum: the *Falernus ager* was a district in the north of Campania, several miles to the east of the coastal town of Sinuessa (cf. line 2), the modern Mondragone. Falernian wine was not necessarily the best available (Younger 202-4; cf. N-H I.251), but it enjoyed an outstanding reputation (cf. Pliny *Nat.* 14.62 'nec ulli nunc vino maior auctoritas'). There were several varieties (see Younger 203 and at 13.108.1 'nectareum ... Falernum' above); but it is impossible for us to tell which M has in mind here, despite there being a possible clue in his conflation of Massic and Falernian (cf. *ILS* 8579, quoted below): the Monte Massico lies just to the east of Sinuessa and thus in the Falernian area, but Massic wine, albeit highly regarded (Columella 3.8.5, Mart. 3.26.3) and doubtless similar to Falernian, was nonetheless usually distinguished as being of a different sort: Howell at Mart. 1.26.8, Marquardt *Prl.* 451, Younger 203.

The epigram turns on the fact that, unlike most Roman wine, Falernian improved with age, not being fit for drinking in under ten years: cf. Seltman 153. Pliny, *Nat.* 23.34, regarded it as best after fifteen: 'media eius aetas a XV annis incipit'; cf. Athen. 1.26C. Thus the Falernian must of 13.120 below tastes worse even than Spoletine which has gone off, while the quality of Falernian is consistently suggested by such words as *vetus* (Hor. *Serm.* 2.3.115) or the affectionate *vetulus* (Mart. 1.18.1, 8.77.5,

11.26.3). It was, of course, not actually true to suggest that Falernian continued to improve no matter how old it became (cf. Cic. *Brut.* 287 'sed nimia vetustas nec habet eam quam quaerimus suavitatem, nec est iam sane tolerabilis'; see Seltman 154); but wine aged even to excess could nonetheless still be valued (cf. on 13.113.1 *Opimi* below) and in any case this epigram is concerned less with the actual facts regarding the ageing of wine than with humour and Saturnalian custom (see below).

1 Massica: regarding this plural usage, see at 13.107.1 'haec ... picata' above.

prelis: the *prelum* (from *premo*) or beam-press could be used for grapes or olives and might be 6-7.5 m long (20-30 ft): Cato *Agr.* 18.5; cf. also Pliny *Nat.* 18.317 'longitudo in his refert, non crassitudo' and see Drachmann 50 ff., Forbes III.140 ff. For illustrations, see *RE* VIA.1743-4 s.v. *Torcular* [Hörle]. N-H draw attention at Hor. *Carm.* 1.20.9 to the reconstructed press in the Villa of the Mysteries at Pompeii; cf. the model depicted in Ciarallo and De Carolis, 332.

2 condita quo quaeris consule?: see N-H at Hor. *Carm.* 1.20.3 'conditum levi': after the new wine had fermented in large casks, it was decanted into small *lagoenae* or *amphorae*, which were then sealed with pitch (cf. 13.107.*le*. n. above). Finally, the date was added by reference to the consuls of that year: N-H cite *ILS* 8580. Note too *ILS* 8579 'Fal. Mas./ Q. Lutatio/ C. Mario/ cos.' and see Dessau's notes on both. Cf. also e.g. Tib. 2.1.28 'fumosos veteris proferte Falernos consulis', Hor. *Carm.* 3.8.12, 21.1, *Epod.* 13.6.

The assumption in the pentameter that the recipient of this gift would immediately want to know the wine's vintage is somewhat ironic and is founded on the materialistic interest with which Saturnalian and other gifts were regarded and the close attention paid to their value: see Intro. (ii) section D above. In replying to the recipient's presumed question, M confirms with humorous exaggeration that not only is the Falernian old, but that it is so old that it was bottled before consuls even existed: 'nullus erat' (β's *erit* is nonsensical). Cf. the similar hyperbole at Mart. 3.62.2 'quod sub rege Numa condita vina bibis' (of a certain Quintus, who mistakenly believes that indulging in luxury indicates greatness of mind) and 13.113.1 *Opimi* n. below.

13.112 Setine

Setia, which perched aloft looks on the Pomptine flats, has sent from a tiny city good old jars.

le. Setinum: Setia, modern Sezze, is situated on the southern slopes of the Volscian mountains, between Norba and Privernum, and overlooks the

Pomptine marshes. A Latin town of some antiquity, it remained small (cf. *exigua*, line 2), becoming a *municipium* (*CIL* X.640, Pliny *Nat*. 3.64) but not a colony (*CIL* X.LXXXVII Setia; cf. Pliny *Nat*. 3.64). In general, see *Kl.P*. 5.151.38 ff. s.v. *Setia* [G. Radke]. The modern Sezze is perhaps best known for its annual passion play (cf. Blanchard 88). Setia, however, was known for its wine. According to Pliny, this was preferred by Augustus to all others (*Nat*. 14.61), and it is always mentioned by M in contexts of wealth, extravagance or appreciation: Kay at Mart. 11.29.6 (on the value of a Setine vineyard); cf. e.g. 4.69, 3.50(51).19, 10.14(13).5, 36.5-6, 12.17.5. Regarding its quality, see too Younger 202-4; cf. Strabo 5.3.6. That it was sharp and tangy as well as being strong can be assumed with some degree of probability from 13.23 above: see *le*. n.

1 pendula Pomptinos quae spectat Setia campos: cf. Mart. 10.74.10-11 'nec quae paludes delicata Pomptinas/ ex arce clivi spectat uva Setini.'

Diaeresis after the third and fourth feet here means that it is metrically possible to switch round *quae* and *spectat* (for such lines, see Platnauer 21-2). Heraeus approves of Marx's suggestion that 'spectat quae' was what M originally wrote (Friedrich Marx, *Molossische und bakcheische Wortformen in der Verskunst der Griechen und Römer*, Leipzig 1922, 229-30), and wonders whether this reading lies behind γ's *pompino* (rather than *-os*); but, while the Augustans had no marked preference in such cases, M's practice elsewhere in Book 13 (32.1, 38.1, 49.1, 125.1) is to favour the third foot monosyllable and fourth foot spondee. It therefore seems prudent to follow the MSS here.

All previous editors place a comma after *campos*, but there seems merit in not punctuating at all.

pendula ... Setia: cf. 4.64.33-4 'pendulam ... Setiam'. Setia is not very high above sea level (319 m = 1063 feet), but it is sufficiently elevated relative to the neighbouring lowland to 'perch aloft'. *Pendulus* is used of places on hillsides again at Mart. 10.13(20).2, Columella 2.17.2.

Pomptinos ... campos: cf. Sil. 8.379 'Pomptini ... campi'. These flats and marshes were named after the old town of Pometia and resulted from the damming up and stagnation of the rivers Ufens, Nymphaeus and Amasenus. For further details, see *OCD*[3] s.v. 'Pomptine Marshes' [E.T. Salmon, T.W. Potter], *Kl.P*. 4.1041.25 ff. s.vv. *Pomptinus ager* [G. Radke].

2 vetulos ... cados: i.e. aged wine, on the value of which see 13.111.*le*. n. above. The endearing diminutive *vetulus*, more usually applied to Falernian (see Fordyce at Catul. 27.1 and cf. 13.111.*le*. n. above), here gains emphasis from its juxtaposition with the contrasting *exigua*: the standing of Setine wine is out of proportion with the size of Setia.

misit: see at 13.23.1 'quam Setia misit' above.

13.113 Fundan

The fruitful autumn of Opimius bore this Fundan. The consul pressed out the must and drank it himself.

le. Fundanum: Fundi was a Volscian town on the coast of Latium, on the Appian Way between Formiae and Tarracina. It is now Fondi. For the remains of the ancient town, which include kilns for the firing of transport amphorae, see *OCD*[3] s.v. *Fundi* [E.T. Salmon, T.W. Potter]. See too Blanchard 94. In general, see *Kl.P.* 2.637.46 ff. s.v. *Fundi* [G. Radke]. On Fundan wine, which was full bodied and nourishing, see Seltman 154, Younger 203; cf. Athen. 1.27A, *CIL* XV.4566-9. It was well regarded (cf. Strabo 5.3.6); and Caecuban wine, which came from a small district in the area of Fundi (see 13.115.*le.* n. below, Muecke at Hor. *Serm.* 2.8.15) was very well thought of indeed.

1 haec Fundana: on the plural usage, see at 13.107.1 *haec picata* above.

tulit felix autumnus: grapes were usually harvested in autumn; cf. Ovid *Pont.* 3.1.13 'nec tibi pampineas autumnus porrigit uvas', *Fast.* 4.897 'venerat Autumnus calcatis sordidus uvis'. For *felix* of fruitful seasons, see *OLD* s.v. *felix* §1c, which refers in addition to this poem to Tib. 2.5.82 'omine quo felix et sacer annus erit'. For *fero* of seasons bearing fruit, see *OLD* s.v. *fero* §25a.

Opimi: L. Opimius was consul in 121 BC, a year whose wines were of legendary quality: see Howell at Mart. 1.26.7 'testa sed antiqui felix siccatur Opimi'. For the consular dating of wine, see 13.111.2 n. above. According to Pliny, *Nat.* 14.55, it was still possible to obtain real Opimian in the first century AD, although it was undrinkable on its own (on the ageing of Roman wine, see 13.111.*le.* n. above) and could be used only to give body to younger wines. Nevertheless, it would still have been valued for its antiquity, if not its taste.

   Given the evidence of Pliny, just cited, it is theoretically possible that the wine described by this poem is real Opimian; but the pentameter's heavy insistence on the wine's authenticity (note especially the emphatic *ipse*) overturns any credibility the hexameter might have had. M's purpose in promoting the wine is ironically humorous, and his exaggerated claims can be taken in context of the materialism with which gifts were viewed by their recipients and the fun M makes of them; cf. 13.111.2 n. above.

2 expressit mustum consul et ipse bibit: comparable to some extent is 14.93.2 'primus in his, dum facit illa, bibit', where M is concerned to establish the *pocula archetypa* described by the poem as being the genuine work of Mentor (see my notes ad loc.) M presumably has in mind the traditional style of grape-treading: cf. Tib. 1.7.36 'expressa incultis uva ... pedibus'.

13.114 Trifoline

A Trifoline vine, I am not, I confess, of prime vintage; nonetheless, among wines, I shall be seventh.

le. Trifolinum T: **Trifolium** βγ. Trifoline was an earthy wine (cf. Athen. 1.260E) from the district of Trifolium, near Naples. The substantival adjective *Trifolinum* is unparalleled, but accords with the surrounding *lemmata*. *Trifolina*, line 1, might appear at first glance also to be a substantive (cf. *picata* at 13.107.2, on which see ad loc.); but it would then conflict with the singular verbs. As Shackleton Bailey explains, referring to the index entry of Heraeus, it is to be taken with *vitis*, line 2. Shackleton Bailey accordingly dispenses with the comma placed after *Lyaeo* by earlier editors (including Heraeus). Although it would enhance the adversative *tamen*, line 2, he is possibly right to do so.

Despite the hexameter's confession (*fateor*) of subordinate quality, Trifoline wine was not despicable (Pliny *Nat.* 14.69): it was a favourite of Augustus (Pliny *Nat.* 14.61), and the Trifoline vineyard at Juv. 9.56 is clearly not worthless. Pliny himself ranked the wine in the fourth class. M's choice here specifically of seventh place requires explanation, especially as it is the ninth wine he writes about. The poem clearly involves some sort of numerical game concerning the numbers one (*primo*, line 1) and possibly three (*Trifolinum*) as well as seven. All of these numbers were accorded particular significance in the ancient world, and the number seven became a regular canonical figure. Hence there were seven sages, seven wonders of the world, seven hills of Rome, and so on. It is possible here that, while the Trifoline vine acknowledges that it is not of the first quality, in claiming seventh place the wine it produces is concerned nonetheless to assert its membership of the canon of wines. Compare Shackleton Bailey's Teubner notes on this poem, where he compares the canonical ranking of the comic poets by Volcatius Sedigitus: see Morel 46 (= Courtney fr. 1). Although Sedigitus lists ten poets, note e.g. W.H. Roscher, *Die Hebdomadenlehren der griechischen Philosopher und Änzte* (Abhandlungen der phil.-hist. klasse den königl. Sächs. Gesellschaft der Wissenschaften 24.6), Leipzig 1906, 194 ff.: 'Gruppen von siebern Lyrikern, Tragikern, Dichtern, Kunstrichtern usw. in alexandrinischer zeit'.

The ranking and classing of wine is, of course, a somewhat subjective business, and although Pliny indulges in it (see above), he candidly acknowledges nonetheless (*Nat.* 14.59) 'genera autem vini alia aliis gratiora esse quis dubitet, aut non norit ex eodem lacu aliud praestantius altero germanitatem praecedere sive testa sive fortuito eventu? quamobrem de principatu se quisque iudicem statuet'; cf. 23.33.

1 de primo ... Lyaeo: the adjective *Lyaeus* is commonly used metonymically by the poets to mean 'wine' (cf. 13.22.1 n. above) or to refer to the vine: *OLD* §1b s.v. *Lyaeus*. More unusually here, it designates a particular type or class of vine – to which the Trifoline does not belong. For the combination in *primo* of the meanings 'first' and 'best', see 13.92.2 *prima* n. above. For *de* indicating membership of a class or group, see *OLD* s.v. *de* §11.

2 inter vina ... septima vitis ero: *ero* counters *sum* (line 1) while the alliterative balance of *vina* and *vitis* is perhaps intended to emphasise the vine's assertion of its canonical status.

13.115 Caecuban

Noble Caecuban is ripened at Amyclae near Fundi, and its vine flourishes, born in the middle of a marsh.

le. Caecubum: Caecuban was produced in the poplar swamps (cf. *palude*, line 2) bordering on the Gulf of Amyclae, somewhat to the south of Fundi (for which see at 13.113.*le.*) and near the 'lacus Fundanus' (Pliny *Nat.* 14.61; cf. 3.59). Although it is now lost, the town of Amyclae (or Amynclae, as at Tac. *Ann.* 4.59) lay between Caieta and Tarracina. According to Servius at Verg. *A.* 10.566, it was destroyed 'by silence' since, after a series of false alarms, it was decreed that no one was allowed to announce an enemy's approach. Caecuban wine was strong and aged well (Athen. 1.27A). It was originally amongst the very foremost Italian wines (Columella 3.8.5; cf. Mart. 3.26.3, 12.17.6 and *generosa*, line 1), being therefore considered a suitable gift for use by legacy hunters: cf. Mart. 2.40.5, 6.27.9. Nevertheless, although its reputation endured (cf. Blümner *Priv.* 198 n. 15), its quality was compromised in the first century by poor husbandry and allegedly by Nero's canal construction between Baiae and Ostia (for which see Russell Meiggs, *Roman Ostia*, Oxford 1973, 57-8 and Ray Laurence, *Omnibus* 35 (1998), 17-19), since this deprived the vines of their accustomed soil (cf. Pliny *Nat.* 14.61; see Seltman 153). Indeed at *Nat.* 23.35 Pliny comments 'Caecuba iam non gignuntur'; cf. Younger 303.

1 Caecuba ... generosa: for the plurals, see at 13.107.1 'haec ... picata' above. For *generosa* thus ('of good stock'), see *OLD* s.v. *generosus* §3b, which cites e.g. Hor. *Ep.* 1.15.18 '[vinum] generosum et lene requiro' and [Tib.] 3.6.5.

Fundanis … Amyclis: given the existence of Spartan Amyclae, *Fundanis* is not an otiose qualification here. The nonsensical *amicis* offered by β is probably no more than a palaeographical corruption.

cocuntur βγ: coluntur T. *Colo* is not without sense in the context of vine growing (see L-S s.v. *colo* §1A, *OLD* s.v. *colo*[1] §3b); yet the subject of the hexameter is not the vine but the wine derived from it. (This is confirmed by 'vitis et' in the pentameter, where the vine *is* the subject.) T's reading can therefore safely be rejected. In the context of wine making, *coquere* is applied most accurately to the ripening of grapes (cf. *ThLL* IV.927.36 ff. s.v. *coquo* [Gudemann]), but it can also be applied as here, by transferred usage, to the wine itself: cf. Mart. 2.40.5-6 'Caecuba saccantur quaeque annus coxit Opimi,/ conduntur parco fusca Falerna vitro'.

2 vitis et in media nata palude viret: most vineyards are well drained. The purpose of the epigram seems to be to highlight the surprising fact that the vine which produced such quality Caecuban not only grew in a swamp but thrived there (*viret* carries emphasis at the end of the line); but in any case the word order is carefully arranged to illustrate the vine's situation right in the middle of the marsh: the alliterative and balancing *vitis* and *viret* frame the pentameter, while in the centre *nata* (see *OLD* s.v. *nasco* §11) nests between *media* and *palude*. For comments on the extreme conditions under which crops could grow, see Pliny *Nat.* 17.31-2.

13.116 Signine

Will you drink Signine, which stalls loose bowels? Lest you stop them too much, let your thirst be moderate.

le. Signinum: Signia (modern Segni) in Latium was founded by Tarquinius Superbus (Livy 2.21.7). Signine wine, which was said to improve after six years (cf. Athen. 1.27B), was harsh (Sil. 8.378 'spumans immiti Signia musto') and dry: Pliny *Nat.* 14.65. For its use in treating stomach complaints, cf. Pliny *Nat.* 23.36 'alvo citae Signinum maxime conducere indubitatum est'. Note also Cels. 4.5, 4.12.8, 4.26.9, Larg. 112-3. M mentions another astringent at 13.26, on which see above. As already noted (at 13.14.2, on laxatives), the Romans were fascinated by bowel functions.

Its wine aside, Signia was known for its pears (*OLD* s.v. *Signinus* §1b) and its temple of Jupiter Urius, remains of which can still be seen (Blanchard 76). In addition, it gave its name to a type of plastering: *OLD* s.v. *Signinus* §1a. For further details, see *OCD*[3] s.v. *Signia* [E.T. Salmon, T.W. Potter].

1: the question mark at the end of the line is Gilbert's, who compares 13.110.1 'Surrentina bibis?'. Without it the couplet would be considerably less engaging. The questions in both places are effectively the protases of conditions. Regarding this phenomenon, see Post at Mart. 1.70.3 'quaeris iter, dicam'. (Post punctuates with a question mark after *iter* although this is unnecessary: *quaeris* is interrogative enough.) On the similar use as protases of statements and commands, see Post's note on Mart. 1.79.2 'est, non est'.

potabis: the poem's opening word is balanced by its conclusion: 'sit tibi parca sitis'. Its juxtaposition with *liquidum* is humorous.

liquidum Signina morantia ventrem: cf. Priap. 51.10 'sorbum ... ventros lubricos moraturum', Cels. 2.8.23 'si venter liquidus [est]'; contrast Trimalchio's use of *solide* at Petr. 47.4. For *venter* cf. additionally 13.26.1 'molles ... tendentia ventres' above and see ad loc. On the plural *Signina*, see at 13.107.1 'haec ... picata' above.

morantia γ: **potentia β** (T omits the poem). Lindsay wonders whether β's reading is 'pro *tenentia*', but Shackleton Bailey's explanation that it arose under influence of *potabis* is far more credible.

2 ne nimium sistas, sit tibi parca sitis: *nimium* is balanced by *parca*. The play on similar words (*sistas*, *sit*, *sitis*) doubtless contributed to the confusion in the MSS (see below). For *sisto* used of stopping bowels, see *OLD* s.v. *sisto* §7b, L-S s.v. *sisto* §IIIB2b.

sistas sit M Lindsay Duff Shackleton Bailey: **sitias sit** β: **sis tanti** γ: **sistant, sit** ς edd. cett. Neither of βγ's offerings is acceptable: γ's is unmetrical nonsense while β's, which suggests that Signine increases one's thirst, does not follow from the hexameter and makes *sitis* repetitive. The humanist reading, derived from γ, takes as its subject *Signina*, but this change of subject weakens the force of the poem's advice. *Sistas sit* (cf. β's offering) is far more satisfactory.

13.117 Mamertine

If a Mamertine jar with the age of Nestor should be given to you, it can have any name you please.

le. Mamertinum: the Mamertini, whose name comes from the Oscan form of Mars, were a crew of Campanian mercenaries who seized and colonised Messana (modern Messina) in 289 BC: see *OCD*[3] s.v. *Mamertines* [P.S. Derow]. Mamertine wine seems to have been very highly regarded (cf. Younger 202) but it was not considered the best, being ranked fourth (behind Falernian, Chian and Lesbian) amongst those served at a banquet during Caesar's third consulship and at public banquets subsequently (Pliny *Nat.* 14.97; cf. 66). It is known from Athenaeus, 1.27D, to have been sweet, light and vigorous.

1 amphora Nestorea tibi Mamertina senecta: the arrangement of nouns and adjectives is both chiastic and symmetrical: n A a N. That both adjectives are formed from proper nouns adds to the line's balance.

amphora: i.e. wine; cf. Mart. 1.18.8 'amphora non meruit tam pretiosa mori', 8.45.4 'amphora centeno consule facta minor'.

Nestorea ... senecta: for Nestor's proverbial old age see Otto 1223; cf. e.g. Stat. *Silv.* 1.3.110 'Nestoreae ... senectae', Mart. 2.64.3, 5.58.5, 7.96.7.

2 quodvis nomen habere potest: cf. Mart. 1.105:

> in Nomentanis, Ovidi, quod nascitur agris,
> accepit quotiens tempora longa, merum
> exuit annosa mores nomenque senecta,
> et quidquid voluit, testa vocatur anus.

Although some Roman wines improved with age, they did not do so indefinitely. Nevertheless, they might be valued even when aged to excess (see 13.111.*le*. n. above). In this poem M acknowledges that Mamertine is a middle order wine, but makes the point that if it is old enough its name no longer signifies (the poem's *lemma* is consequently not without irony): wines which have deteriorated significantly all taste the same and an ordinary vintage can then either be presented for what it is or passed off (cf. the honey of 13.105 above) or even on (cf. 13.26.*le*. n. above) as something grander and more expensive without anyone being the wiser. In this poem, therefore, the materialism with which recipients would regard and compare the value of their presents (see Intro. (ii) section D above) is completely undercut.

13.118 Tarragonese

Tarraco, that will yield only to Campanian Lyaeus, bore this wine as a rival to Italian jars.

le. Tarraconense: Tarraconensis was the largest of Rome's Spanish provinces. Its capital, Tarraco (cf. line 1), is modern Tarragona, on the N.E. coast. In addition to wine (on which see below), it produced fish sauce and linen. See *OCD*[3] s.v. *Tarraconensis* [S.J. Keay], *Kl.P.* 5.528.5 ff. s.v. *Tarraco* [K. Abel].

1 Tarraco, Campano tantum cessura Lyaeo: cf. Sil. 3.369-70 'Tarraco ... vitifera et Latio tantum cessura Lyaeo' and the sentiment at Pliny *Nat.* 14.71 'elegantia vero Tarraconensia ... conferuntur Italiae primis'. (On *Lyaeus* (= wine), see at 13.22.1 above.) While it is debatable whether Campanian wines really were, as this poem suggests, the best in Italy (cf. also 13.111.*le.* n. above), they were certainly of the very highest order. (For the subjectivity of wine rankings, see at 13.114.*le.* above.) The juxtaposition of *Tarraco* and *Campano* helps emphasise the assertion that it was only to Campanian that Tarragonese yielded.

2 haec ... vina: instead of *vina* (βγ), T reads *brena*, from which Heraeus suggests *prela*; but *prela* does not elsewhere signify 'wine', which is the sense here required.

Shackleton Bailey translates *vina* as 'wines' in his Loeb, but understanding it as a singular makes for a more manageable present and yields a beᴜᴇ ..ᴄntrast with 'Latiis ... cadis'. For *vina* used for *vinum*, see at 13.107.1 'haec ... picata' above.

Latiis Gilbert: **tuscis** Tβγ. Most editors print *Tuscis* although it has long been questioned. As Friedländer points out, Tuscan wine was cheap: at Mart. 1.26.5-6 it is characterised, along with Paelignian (fit for freedmen: 13.121 below), as wine for binges – in contrast to Opimian Massic, which deserves to be savoured. That Tarragonese rivals Tuscan is therefore no recommendation, and so, since irony is impossible after line 1, *Tuscis* must here be corrupt (*pace* Howell 38). Although Shackleton Bailey prints *Tuscis* in his Teubner text, he therefore adopts Gilbert's *Latiis* in his later Loeb. In referring to Sil. 3.369-70 (quoted above) in his discussion of the question (Loeb Appendix 321-2), he notes that, since Silius refers (3.617) to Domitian's Sarmatian war in 92, the borrowing is from M rather than the other way round. He suggests that *Tuscis* possibly arose thus: *Latiis = tiistis = tuscis*.

While wines from Campania's neighbour Latium could command considerable respect (see e.g. 13.113.*le.* n. above), understanding a reference just to Latium here would detract considerably from the poem's boast. For *Latius* meaning 'Italian', see *OLD* s.v. *Latius* §2.

13.119 Nomentan

A Nomentan vintage gives you my wine. If Quintus loves you, you will drink better.

le. Nomentanum: according to Athenaeus, 1.27B, Nomentan wine ripened quickly, it was neither too sweet nor too light and it was ready for drinking after five years (cf. Mart. 10.48.20 'bis ... trima'). It was not of the very highest quality (cf. Columella 3.2.14), but it was nonetheless highly regarded. Particularly famed in Columella's day were the Nomentan vineyards of the Younger Seneca's estate (3.3.3). Many have supposed that M's estate was originally part of Seneca's, although this is by no means certain: see at Mart. 13.12.2 'suburbanus ager' above. Of course, if M did acquire his land from Seneca, his playful disparagement here of the wine he produced can be seen in interesting perspective even though humour regarding the poor productivity of suburban holdings was widespread and traditional: see Mart. 13.12.*le.* n.

By praising in contrast to his the wine of his friend and neighbour Quintus (on whom see further at line 2 below), M here combines humour with a friendly compliment. He jokingly belittles the produce of his estate also at 10.94 where, because of its indifferent quality, he sends as harvest gifts fruit bought in the Subura; cf. 2.38 which acknowledges that the estate yields nothing but respite from the troublesome Linus.

1 Nomentana meum γ: **Nomentana malum** β: **Nomentaneum** T. *Malum*, which is preserved by β and may have been a conjecture to balance *commodiora*, line 2, would rob the poem both of its self-deprecating humour and the complimentary contrast between M's produce and Quintus'. (For *Bacchus* meaning 'wine', see 13.23.1 n. above.) Lindsay's explanation of T's reading, that it came from *Nomentanāeum*, is very plausible.

2 si te Quintus amat, commodiora bibes: on Quintus Ovidius, see Sullivan 20 and Howell at 1.105 (a poem also on wine: see the quotation at 13.117.2 above). M, who is our only source of information regarding him, held him very dear: cf. 7.93.5-6 'quid Nomentani causam mihi perdis agelli,/ propter vicinum qui pretiosus erat'. He addresses several poems to him: for example, in 7.44 and 45 he praises his loyalty to the exiled Caesennius Maximus, whom he accompanied to Sicily following the Pisonian conspiracy; in 9.52 and 53 he celebrates his birthday (the latter poem, of possible relevance here, suggests that where his friends were concerned, Quintus preferred to give rather than receive presents); and at 10.44 he remonstrates with him gently for agreeing to accompany a friend to Britain. He addresses him on the subject of wine once more at 9.98.

commodiora bibes: for *commodiora*, see *ThLL* III.1922.47 ff. s.v. *commodus* [Mertel]. *Bibas*, T, doubtless derives from 13.120.2 below: Lindsay and Heraeus.

13.120 Spoletine

You would prefer fusty wine from Spoletine flagons to drinking Falernian must.

le. Spoletinum: Spoletium (now Spoleto) was a city in Umbria, for which see *OCD*³ s.v. *Spoletium* [E.T. Salmon, T.W. Potter], *Kl.P.* 5.319.57 ff. s.v. *Spoletium* [G. Radke]. Its wine, which was sweet and golden coloured (Athen. 1.27B), was poor: see Blümner *Priv.* 200 and cf., in conjunction with 13.121.*le.* n. below, Mart. 14.116, which queries the usefulness of luxury iced water to drinkers of wines like Spoletine and Marsian. The humour of this poem rests on the fact that despite the fame of mature Falernian, its must was undrinkable (see 13.111.*le.* n. above) and that it is therefore scant recommendation that the decayed Spoletine of this poem should taste better.

1 de Spoletinis ... lagonis: regarding the *lagona*, see Hilgers 203 f. and Tafel 1, Blümner *Priv.* 404, D-S III(2).907 s.vv. *lagena*, *lagynus* [Louis Couve]. It was a flask-shaped vessel, used originally for water but later mostly for wine, although other liquids were not excluded: at Mart. 6.89.1-4, as commonly (see Grewing at line 1), it is a urine flask: 'cum peteret ... matellam ... Panaretus,/ Spoletina data est quam siccaverat ipse,/ nec fuerat soli tota lagona satis'.

quae sunt cariosa: sc. *vina*. Regarding the plural, see at 13.107.2 'haec ... picata' above. *Caries* survives of flat or over-ripe wine in both Columella and Pliny (cf. Columella 3.2.17, Pliny *Nat.* 15.7 'blanda inveterati caries', 14.55), but the adjective *cariosus* survives of wine here only: *ThLL* III.459.15 f. s.v. *cariosus* [Elsperger]. The adjectival ending *-osus* is, however, often derogatory in import: see Brown at Lucr. 4.1168 and cf. Mart. 14.149.1 'mammosas metuo'.

13.121 Paelignian

Paelignian yeomen send clouded Marsic. Don't you drink it, but let your freedman do so.

le. Paelignum: although different peoples, the Paeligni and Marsi (cf. *Marsica*, line 1) were related and closely allied. Both lived in central Italy, in adjoining territories (cf. Sil. 8.509-10), spoke languages possibly derived from Oscan and played a leading part in the Marsic or Social War. See *OCD*³ s.vv. *Marsi* and *Paeligni* [E.T. Salmon and T.W. Potter]. Also *Kl.P.* 3.1049.26 ff. s.v. *Marsi* [H. Cüppers], 4.403.4 ff. s.v. *Paeligni* [G. Radke]. The two peoples were often associated in literature (cf. also e.g. Enn. *Ann.* 229 with Skutsch, 409, and Caes. *Civ.* 1.15.7), and it is no surprise that in this poem M should equate Paelignian and Marsian wine (note the juxtaposition of *Marsica* and *Paeligni* in line 1).

Most famous of the *Paeligni* was the poet Ovid, who wrote of his homeland 'terra ferax Cereris, multoque feracior uvis' (*Am.* 2.16.7; cf. Sil. 8.507 of the fruitfulness of Alba, a Marsian city); but although the area may have been productive where grapes were concerned, the Marsian/Paelignian wine made from them was not highly regarded. Hence M's recommendation (line 2) that it be reserved for freedmen; cf. 1.26.5 where Paelignian, along with Spoletine (cf. 13.120 above) is considered suitable for bingeing, but not for savouring. (Marsian wine is associated with Spoletine in Mart. 14.116, on which see 13.120.*le*. n. above.)

1 Marsica: for this plural usage after the singular *lemma*, see at 13.107.1 'haec ... picata' above. Not only is the wine in this epigram poor, but it has been shaken up (cf. the use of *turbo* at 13.108.1 above), possibly in the course of being exported (on the use of *mittunt*, line 2, see at 13.23.1 above) and so is full of sediment. This made it all the more undrinkable. (For straining wine to remove its sediment, cf. Mart. 2.60.9 'turbida transmittere Caecuba sacco', 8.45.2-3, and see Muecke at Hor. *Serm*. 2.4.54.)

Paeligni mittunt ... **coloni**: cf. Ovid *Med*. 53, quoted above at 13.12.1.

2 non tu, libertus sed bibat illa tuus: this line might refer to the practice of passing on unwanted Saturnalian gifts (see at 13.26.*le*. n. above), but it is more likely to reflect the ranking of guests at dinner parties, and the serving of inferior fare to inferior guests: see at 13.41.*le*. n. above.

On the delayed position of *sed*, found in poets from the time of Augustus, see L-H-Sz II.488. Here it allows the juxtaposition of *tu* and *libertus*. *Tu* is further balanced by *tuus* at the end of the line.

13.122 Vinegar

Don't regard as cheap a jar of Egyptian vinegar. When it held wine, it was cheaper.

le. **acetum** is vinegar, but the word is also used to refer to sour wine (cf. *acere*, 'to be sour') which is therefore cheap: cf. Hor. *Serm*. 2.3.117, Mart. 10.45.5, Juv. 3.292; see Kay at Mart. 11.56.7. This double usage lies behind some of the epigram's humour here. One initially expects the *lemma*, in keeping with those which surround it, to refer to wine; but rather than cheap wine, the poem actually deals with Egyptian vinegar (concerning *Niliaci*, line 1, see at 13.1.3 above), which was one of the best known (and highest quality) varieties available: see Mayor at Juv. 13.85 'Phario ... aceto', where he cites Cicero ap. Non. 240 (= *Hort*. fr. 89) 'alterius ingenium, sicut acetum Aegyptium, acre' and Athen. 2.67C (where Chrysippus says that the best vinegar came from Egypt and Cnidus). The humour continues, however, in that M undercuts his opening 'non sit tibi vilis' with *vilior*, line 2: it appears that, despite its reputation, Egyptian vinegar is nonetheless still cheap. It is just less so than the wine it is made from. The poem is, of course, mocking the materialism with which the value of gifts was keenly observed by their recipients: see Intro. (ii) section D above.

On the preparation and uses, culinary and otherwise (e.g. medical), of (various types of) vinegar, see André *Alimentation* 193-4, Blümner *Priv.* 192, *Kl.P.* 2.378.45 ff. s.v. *Essig* [G. Schrot].

2 esset cum vini, vilior illa fuit: the line is carefully balanced, with forms of the verb 'to be' at both ends and v alliteration in the middle. As well as 'cheap', *vilis* can mean 'contemptible' (*OLD* s.v. *vilis* §3), a sense which is surely also present here.

vini γ: **vinum** αβ. Heraeus notes, comparing 13.103.2 'essem si scombri' above, that *vini* is possibly right; but only Shackleton Bailey prints it. He is surely correct to do so, however: not only is it desirable in terms of compositional balance and economy not to have to understand a second subject in the pentameter (= *acetum*), but also *vini* (followed by *vilior*) is probably more easily corrupted to *vinum* (VINIVI-) than *vinum* to *vini*.

13.123 Massilian

When your sportula is going to cross off a hundred citizens, you can serve the smoky wine of Massilia.

le. Massilitanum Pfγ: **Massalitanum** TLQ. I.e. wine from what is now Marseille. With the exception of Lindsay and Duff, editors follow Pfγ. That they are correct to do so is suggested by Mart. 3.82.23 'vel cocta fumis musta Massilitanis', where the MSS all agree on *Massil-*, and by the fact that it is usual in the process of Latinisation for the Greek α to be reflected by the letter i: *Kl.P.* 3.1066.16-7 s.v. *Massalia* [H. Volkmann], L-H-Sz I.82. Nevertheless the best MSS preserve the Greek spelling at Pliny *Nat.* 3.33 *Massalioticus*; cf. Heraeus (Teubner 1908) at Livy 40.35.3, and so room for some hesitation remains.

Although wines could be matured quickly using a smoking process (Pliny *Nat.* 33.40, Younger 212-3), excessive exposure to smoke would taint the wine (Columella 1.6.20) and ruin its quality. M often denounces Massilian wine as over-smoked and therefore inferior (cf. line 2 below, 3.82.3 cited above, 10.36.1 'improba Massiliae quidquid fumaria cogunt', 14.118.1 'Massiliae fumos'); but the justice of this has been queried, e.g. by Shackleton Bailey, who notes at Mart. 10.36.1 that Pliny commends the wine (*Nat.* 14.68; cf. also the approving καλός and σαρκώδης of Athen. 1.27C); cf. Younger 161. Since Pliny says that other wines of Gallia Narbonensis were corrupted by smoke, Shackleton Bailey suggests, but not very satisfactorily, that M should perhaps have criticised these instead.

Commentary

1 cum tua centenos expunget sportula civis: Shackleton Bailey (Teubner) explains: 'i.e. cum clientium catervam ad cenam vocabis.'

tua ... sportula: cf. Mart. 10.27.3 'et tua tricenos largitur sportula nummos'. The *sportula* was originally a small basket of food, but in the first century was usually replaced by a sum of money (normally 100 quadrantes) which was handed out to clients at the early-morning *salutatio*. In return, these clients would be expected to perform duties for their patrons, e.g. escorting them through Rome's crowded streets, or rigging the applause at their *recitationes*. See conveniently Balsdon *LL* 22-3 and note too the information assembled by Friedländer, *Roman Life* 4.77-81. In this poem, however, *sportula* is used almost to mean *cena*; cf. perhaps Suet. *Cl.* 21.4 'extraordinarium [munus] ... appellare coepit sportulam, quia daturus edixerat, velut ad subitam condictamque cenulam invitare se populum', cited by Courtney and others at Juv. 3.249-50 'nonne vides quanto celebretur sportula fumo?/ centum convivae, sequitur sua quemque culina', lines which are reminiscent of M's poem. Juvenal's *sportula* is generally taken, however, to refer to a sort of ἔρανος or club dinner to which each guest brings a share of the meal, and this is unlikely to be the case here. Instead, it is worth remembering that often at the *salutatio* clients were also invited to dine that evening: Balsdon loc. cit. Again, this would have been in return for duties. Indeed, Domitian seems even to have tried, albeit unsuccessfully, to make these dinners or 'cenae rectae' the only permissible form of recompense for client service: see Jones at Suet. *Dom.* 7.1, citing Mart. 8.49(50).10 'promissa est nobis sportula, recta [cena] data est'. As recalled above (see 13.41.*le.* n.), lowly dinner guests were regularly treated to inferior service, and the over-exposure to smoke of M's Massilian would therefore have made it seem well suited to some for entertaining their clients, especially *en masse* (*centenos*).

expunget γ: **expugnet** Tβ. *Expugno* is totally out of place here. *Expungere* is often used of marking or crossing off a list, especially to indicate the settlement of a debt: *OLD* s.v. *expungo* §2a, which glosses M's usage here as 'to discharge your obligation to'; cf. *ThLL* V(2).1813.59-61 s.v. *expungo* [Bulhart].

civis: all clients were, of course, citizens; but some in the 1st century were only nominally so, being e.g. so desperate for the morning *sportula* that they would endure the insults and arrogance even of servile doormen whom they would often, it seems, have to bribe to gain access: Balsdon *LL* 22; cf. Juv. 3.184 ff. with Mayor ad loc. By using *civis* here, emphasised by position and alliteration, M cynically highlights their demeaned position; cf. Juvenal's references to the worthless citizen status of Virro's guests: 5.112, 125 ff., 161 ff.

2 fumea, first word in the line, emphasises the wine's failings. On the plural form *vina*, see at 13.107.1 'haec ... picata' above.

13.124 Caeretan

Let Nepos serve Caeretan, you will think it is Setine. He does not serve it to a crowd but drinks it with three guests.

le. Caeretanum: wine from Caere (Cerveteri), an Etruscan town today famed for its unbroken sequence of tombs dating from the iron age to the early empire: see e.g. Nigel Spivey, *Etruscan Art*, London 1997, passim. In contrast to the town's fine bucchero wine vessels and despite the fertility of the area (cf. Mart. 6.73.3-4), one infers that its wine, mentioned here only in extant Latin, was nonetheless not of the highest quality: see below, and cf. at 13.118.2 above.

Nepos, line 1, appears again at Mart. 10.48.5 and in 6.27, where, addressed as an old friend and neighbour (see Grewing at Mart. 6.27: 202), he is advised to drink and enjoy his aged Falernian and Caecuban rather than store them up to leave to his daughter, (legitimate and therefore) beloved though she is. (Contrast the commonly expressed hostility towards heirs documented at 13.126.1 *heredi* below.) Such advice is admittedly a literary commonplace (cf. Grewing, op. cit., 202-3), but it seems nonetheless possible that Nepos really did have a reputation for hoarding his fine wine, and that M is therefore pulling his leg in the present poem by saying that when he served Caeretan, which was evidently suitable for a crowd (*turbae*, line 2; cf. 'centenos ... civis' of the previous epigram), he did so just to a few intimate friends ('cum ... tribus bibit', line 2) as if it were Setine, a quality wine for which see at 13.112.*le.* above.

1: on the conditional construction in this line (common in the poets), see L-H-Sz II.657, citing e.g. Hor. *Ep.* 1.16.54 'sit spes fallendi, miscebis sacra profanis' and Ovid *Rem.* 743 'perdat opes Phaedra, parces, Neptune, nepoti'. *Putabis* may have influenced β's *bibet* in line 2.

Caeretana: on the plural, see at 13.107.1 'haec ... picata' above.

2 cum tribus: the number three is here used loosely to represent a small number: see L-S s.v. *tres* §II, *OLD* s.v. *tres* §1b; cf. Ter. *Ph.* 638, Sen. *Apoc.* 11.3 with Eden, Catul. 79.3-4.

13.125 Tarentine

Let Aulon, both renowned for its wools and blessed with its vines, give costly fleeces to you, to me wine.

191

le. Tarentinum: on Tarentum, now Táranto, see *OCD*³ s.v. *Tarentum* [K. Lomas], *Kl.P.* 5.518.55 ff. s.v. *Tarentum* [K.D. Fabian]. Today known for the collection of antiquities (largest in southern Italy) housed in its Museo Nazionale, it was famous in Roman times for its purple dye (cf. Mart. 2.43.3) and, as this epigram attests, for its wool and sheep (cf. Pl. *Truc.* 645 ff., Columella 7.2.3) and its wine and wine consumption: cf. Hor. *Carm.* 2.6.18 ff. (with N-H on 19 *Baccho*), Pliny *Nat.* 4.69 and Athen. 1.27C, paraphrased ad loc. by Shackleton Bailey (Loeb): the wine was sweet, mild, good for the stomach but lacking in 'punch'.

Numerous attempts have been made to identify Aulon (line 1), the valley (cf. αὐλών) in which the wine was grown. N-H observe at Hor. *Carm.* 2.6.18 that the name has been thought to lie behind that of Monte Melone, which rises some ten miles to the east of Táranto (cf. *RE* 4A.2303.55 s.v. *Tarentum* [St. Weinstock]); but this is not conclusive.

1: on the scansion of this line, see at 13.112.1 above.

2 det pretiosa tibi vellera, vina mihi: the concern of this poem is perhaps to stress to the recipient of the wine its value by making it plain that the donor would far rather have kept it for himself, giving an expensive alternative instead; cf. 13.48 above. The juxtaposition of the alliterative *vellera* and *vina* gives emphatic contrast, as do the encircling *tibi* and *mihi*. On the plural *vina*, see at 13.107.1 'haec ... picata' above.

det codd.: **des** Heinsius. Heinsius' conjecture would envisage a poem in which M addresses to the personified Aulon his rejection of its precious wool for its wine; but 'des ... tibi' would not normally mean 'keep your ...' (contrast 'tibi habe' at 13.53.2 above). The use of *dare* at 13.126.2 'haec tibi tota dato' is a special case since it takes up 'nec ... relinquas', line 1, and focusses not so much on the retention as the sole enjoyment of one's possessions.

13.126 Unguent

Never leave unguent or wine to your heir. Let him have the money. These give all to yourself.

le. unguentum: unguent and garlands (13.127 below) were standard adornments at the *comissatio*; cf. e.g. the drinking party arrangements at Hor. *Carm.* 3.29.1-4 and Mart. 5.64:

> sextantes, Calliste, duos infunde Falerni,
>   tu super aestivas, Alcime, solve nives,
> pinguescat nimio madidus mihi crinis amomo
>   lassenturque rosis tempora sutilibus.

tam vicina iubent nos vivere Mausolea,
cum doceant ipsos posse perire deos.

It was, however, common for guests to be presented with them when the
comissatio began: see Smith at Petr. 60.3, who refers to Marquardt *Prl.*
331. That M rounds off rather than begins the *Xenia*'s wine section with
this poem (note *vina*, line 1) and the next might appear surprising but for
two things: he has another, preparatory poem which deals with unguent
(see 13.101.*le.* n. above) and 127 has special significance for the ordering
and conclusion of Book 13 as a whole (see Intro. (iii) above, 13.127.*le.* n.
below).

The unguent *apophoreta* of Petr. 60.3-4 aside, one might note that when
Habinnas comes in late, having already been to another dinner, he arrives
'oneratus aliquot coronis et unguento per frontem in oculos fluente' (Petr.
65.7). Unguents are *apophoreta* also at Mart. 14.57 and 59.

1 heredi: although the pentameter's advice 'haec tibi tota dato' is indebted
to popular philosophy (see below), distaste at the thought of leaving one's
hard-earned property to someone else to enjoy was nonetheless commonly
expressed in antiquity and supplies the wider context of this poem. In
treating the matter at Hor. *Carm.* 2.14.25 *heres*, N-H cite examples from
the Bible (e.g. Eccles. 2.18 'Yea I hated all my labour which I had taken
under the sun: because I should leave it unto the man that shall be after
me ...'), Egypt and Greece. They note with others, however, that in Roman
authors criticism of heirs is particularly common since those named were
guaranteed by law a quarter of the estates in question (*lex Falcidia*, 40 BC)
and those with fortunes exceeding 100,000 sesterces were prohibited from
leaving estates to women (*lex Voconia*, 169 BC). This legislation, combined
with the declining aristocratic birth rate, meant that heirs were often quite
distant relations and there was thus considerable incentive for property
owners to derive full enjoyment from their possessions before they died.

nec vina relinquas: *nec* sustains the force of *numquam*. *Vina* could here
be a 'real' or poetic plural. For *relinquo* of leaving an inheritance, see *OLD*
s.v. *relinquo* §8b; cf. Mart. 6.27.6, cited below, and 9.82.3.

2 ille habeat nummos: cf. Mart. 6.27.5-6 'tu tamen annoso nimium ne
parce Falerno,/ et potius plenos aere relinque cados'. Although he would
have liked more money than he had (cf. at 13.3.6 above), M also maintains
regularly, in keeping with popular Epicureanism, that people should eat,
drink and be merry while they could; cf. Mart. 5.64, quoted above, and see
Grewing at Mart 6.27 (203). Hence his priorities here. (He values food
above unguent and garlands at 13.51.)

Ille finds contrast in *tibi*, which begins an alliterative sequence of
dentals, while *nummos* contrasts with the juxtaposed *haec*.

13.127 Rose garlands

Winter gives you forced garlands, Caesar. Once the rose was Spring's, now it has become yours.

le. coronae roseae βγ: **corona rosea** α. On α's tendency to favour singular *lemmata* where βγ have plurals, see 13.49.*le.* n. above. It was doubtless influenced here by the generalising *rosa* in line 2.

Regarding garlands at banquets, see at 13.126.*le.* above. Rose garlands are mentioned also at 13.51.1 above: '[corona] texta rosis'. It is only in comparatively recent years that hardy roses have been developed, and the Romans therefore knew them as spring flowers (cf. 'veris erat', line 2) which did not last long: cf. Hor. *Carm.* 2.3.13 ff. 'nimium breve/ flores amoenae ... rosae'. Winter roses were therefore a great luxury (see N-H at Hor. *Carm.* 1.38.4), being specially grown in green houses (cf. Mart. 4.22.5-6 'condita ... puro numerantur lilia vitro, ... prohibuit tenuis gemma latere rosas') and valued for their rarity: Mart. 4.29.3 f. 'rara iuvant: ... hibernae pretium sic meruere rosae'. Predictably, they were deplored in consequence by the moralists as being contrary to nature; cf. Sen. *Ep.* 122.8 'non vivunt contra naturam qui hieme concupiscunt rosam ...?' In this epigram, M flatteringly suggests that their unseasonal existence is due to nature's acknowledgement of the emperor's super-human greatness; cf. his panegyric use of winter roses at 6.80, on which see Grewing's very comprehensive notes. For Domitian's alleged power over nature, cf. Stat. *Silv.* 4.3.135 'natura melior potentiorque'. Compare the acknowledgement allegedly accorded his *numen* even by animals: cf. *Sp.* 20(17).1-4 and see Otto Weinreich, *Studien zu Martial: literarhistorische und religionsgeschichtliche Untersuchungen*, Stuttgart 1928, 74 ff. Regarding M's flattery of the emperor, see generally at 13.4.1 *serus* above.

Although referring to festive garlands, however, this poem has, as noted above (see Intro. (iii)), a further dimension: it recalls the artistically arranged ἀνθολογίαι or garlands of poetry assembled by e.g. Meleager and Philip (cf. Lord Wavell's *Other Men's Flowers*) and therefore, while acting as a *sphragis* of sorts, contains also further flattery in the form of a concluding dedication to Domitian; cf. the concluding poem (82) of Book 8, esp. line 4: 'scimus et haec etiam serta placere tibi'. Just as Domitian's power over nature claims for him springtime roses in winter, so he receives as of right the outcome of M's poetic endeavours.

1 festinatas ... coronas: *festino* is possibly a technical term for the early budding or maturing of plants: cf. Pliny *Nat.* 16.97 'primo favonio cornus [germinat] ... festinat et platanus'; but used here of roses which have been made to bloom before their time, it must carry the basic (and neutral or favourable) sense 'hastened' or 'accelerated'. The word has, nonetheless, also to refer negatively to M's book, allegedly rushed to be in time for the

194

Saturnalia (see 13.1.4 n. above on *bruma*); cf. Mart. 2.91.3 'festinatis ...
libellis', 10.2.1 'festinata prius decimi ... cura libelli'; cf. D.P. Fowler,
'Martial and the Book', *Ramus* 24 (1995), 55. For the nature of M's
self-effacement, see, however, Intro. (v) above.

2 quondam veris erat, nunc tua facta rosa est: cf. *AP* 6.345-6 εἴαρος
ἤνθει μὲν τὸ πρὶν ῥόδα, νῦν δ'ἐνὶ μέσσῳ/ χείματι πορφυρέας ἐσχάσαμεν
κάλυκας. The contrast between then and now, common in epigram (see
further Siedschlag 29), is here reinforced by the contrasting *erat* and *est*.
The possessive adjective *tua* affords *varietas* with the genitive *veris*.

Index

197